Sugar Rush

Also by bestselling author Donna Kauffman

SWEET STUFF

OFF KILTER

SOME LIKE IT SCOT

A GREAT KISSER

LET ME IN

THE GREAT SCOT

THE BLACK SHEEP AND THE ENGLISH ROSE

THE BLACK SHEEP AND THE HIDDEN BEAUTY

THE BLACK SHEEP AND THE PRINCESS

BAD BOYS IN KILTS

CATCH ME IF YOU CAN

BAD BOYS NEXT EXIT

JINGLE BELL ROCK

BAD BOYS ON BOARD

I LOVE BAD BOYS

Sugar Rush

DONNA KAUFFMAN

KENSINGTON BOOKS
http://www.kensingtonbooks.com

ISBN-13: 978-0-7582-6635-4
ISBN-10: 0-7582-6635-9

First Kensington Books Mass-Market Paperback Printing: August 2013
First Brava Books Trade Paperback Printing: January 2012

eISBN-13: 978-0-7582-9328-2
eISBN-10: 0-7582-9328-3

First Kensington Books Electronic Edition: August 2013

10 9 8 7 6 5 4 3 2 1

Printed in the United States of America

This book is dedicated to
all of you who understand the simple joy to be found in
peeling the paper off of a little cup of frosted goodness,
and savoring the wondrous deliciousness there is to be found
in a single cupcake.

You're all in my Cupcake Club.

ACKNOWLEDGMENTS

So many people to thank, not the least of which is the Zumba instructor at my gym, who is helping me shed the inches of "research" I've gained since beginning this book. I will say, they were a lot more fun to put on!

My heartfelt appreciation to all the cupcakery and bakery owners and workers who have answered endless questions, given multiple kitchen tours, explained numerous and detailed business and baking processes, and, most of all, allowed me to sample the product! (All in the name of research, of course. See: first paragraph.) Crumbs on Broadway, Magnolia in midtown, Edibles Incredible in Reston Town Centre, The Cupcakery in St. Louis (Crave the Cup!), Nostalgia in Annapolis, and Hello, Cupcake! in Dupont Circle . . . just to name a few.

Thank you also to my web gurus who helped me figure out how to put my cupcake blog together (Cakes bytheCupBlog.com) and get it up and running, so I could chronicle and share my own (mis)adventures in discovering, firsthand, what it takes to be a pastry chef and master cupcake baker. I'd warn you not to try this at home, except I totally did. And I still am.

Thank you Frank, James, Martha, and Mom for being my instructors in person, in print, and over the phone. I swear, I will get better at this. And I promise that whole burning-butter-in-the-stove incident? Will never happen again.

Thank you to everyone at Food Network and Cooking Channel for helping me with all the behind the scenes peeks into how your shows make it on air, and for patiently answering my questions and providing me with access to so much information. And to Giada, Bobby, Tyler, Ina, Alton, and the Chairman, thank you for keeping me company in the wee hours. You guys are the best television bff chefs a girl could ever have.

To all of those who have given so graciously of your time and so generously shared with me your considerable talents, please accept my apologies up-front for those instances where I've taken literary license for story purposes. You all helped so much, enabling me to ground this story in as realistic a world and setting as possible. Any mistakes made or liberties taken are purely my own.

And lastly, thank you to the wonderful Alicia Condon, whose enthusiasm for this book, both as my editor and as a fellow baker, has been everything this writer could have hoped for, and more!

Bon appétit, cupcake!

Chapter 1

It was the cupcakes that saved her.

Leilani Trusdale thought about that as she carefully extracted the center from the final black forest cupcake, then set the corer aside and picked up the pastry bag of raspberry truffle filling. She breathed in the mingled scents of dark chocolate and sweet berries. It was inspiring, really, how much power a single, sweet cup of baked deliciousness could wield. Cupcake salvation.

Lani shifted the tip into position. "So, it's all on you, my tasty little friends. Work your magic. Heal me now." She focused intently—fiercely, even—on her way to piping the precise amount of filling into each and every one of the one hundred and fifty-six cupcakes that lined the racks on the stainless steel worktable in front of her—which was totally unnecessary. The fierce focusing, not the filling. She could fill a table of cupcakes blindfolded. In her sleep. With one hand tied behind her back. Possibly on one foot. She'd never done it, but she'd take the bet.

Of course, there were other things she'd never

done before—big things, important things—that she'd also taken the bet on. And those bets had all paid off. Every last one. So, she should feel confident, right? About this most recent bet. This huge, ridiculous gamble that kept her awake every night, wondering what in the hell she'd been thinking.

Had she been completely insane, walking away from the career she'd slaved actual blood, sweat, and many, many tears to construct in New York City, to start over on little Sugarberry Island and open her own shop?

Who did that?

"I did," she said out loud, rather defiantly, hoping the statement alone would inspire confidence. It wasn't like she couldn't go back to New York if all else failed. She hadn't hated her life there. Exactly. So, she had a backup plan . . . if absolutely necessary.

Her cell phone buzzed in her chef's jacket pocket. Frowning, she set the pastry bag down and wiped her hands before digging it out. Only one person would be calling her at the crack of dawn. She hit the mute button on the stereo remote, silencing the cantina band from the Star Wars soundtrack—everyone had their own mix tape, hers just happened to be made up of her favorite movie theme song hits—then touched SPEAKERPHONE before propping it on the worktable. "Hey, Charlotte," Lani said in greeting. "What's up, besides us pastry chefs?" She picked up the bag again and went back to work, too antsy to stand still and chat.

Antsy, and angry.

"You sound awake," Charlotte said, "which means you're in the kitchen."

"Where else would I be?"

"You live in Georgia now—where even pastry chefs probably sleep past five AM."

"Not if they want to get their product baked and frosted before opening, they don't."

"You're not in Atlanta. How many cupcakes could the entire island of Sugarberry consume in a day?"

"Char—"

"Answer me this. How many racks of cupcakes are in front of you right now?"

Lani didn't answer. On the grounds that the truth would totally incriminate her. Friends could, occasionally, be a pain in the butt. Especially best friends. They knew too much.

"Chocolate?" Charlotte prodded.

Lani sighed. "One hundred fifty-six. Black forest." At Charlotte's continued silence, she sighed again. "Okay, okay. With raspberry truffle filling. And Dutched chocolate ganache frosting."

"Oh no, I'm too late! You already heard."

"I have to make these." Lani tried not to sound defensive, knowing she failed even as she said the words. "They're for the Kiwanis Club."

"What on earth is a Kiwanis?" Charlotte asked. "Never mind. I don't think I want to know. Much less why they're congregating in clubs."

"It's all part of the annual fall festival here," Lani explained. "It starts with a huge community dinner tonight. The Kiwanis raises money for local civic improvements, so I'm contributing cupcakes to help the cause."

"Good heavens, Lan, you're working . . . what, bake sales now? Is it going so badly as all that?" The lilt of Charlotte's Indian accent came through a little stronger than usual. It always did whenever she was upset.

"Your confidence is inspiring. It's not like I'm helping the high school glee club earn money at a table in
front of the local grocery store. I'm doing signature
cupcakes in boxed sets as part of a huge auction
they'll hold as a kickoff event after the dinner. The
people here support me. I'm happy to do it. Plus, it's
good marketing. And the Kiwanis Club I'm sponsoring is going to donate all the money they earn from
their auction entries to expand and improve the
youth and senior centers."

"See, the fact that you need to keep your youths
and seniors in centers is a big part of what concerns
me about this sudden life shift," Charlotte replied.
"But we've had that little talk. As long as you think you
need to be on your little island in the middle of
nowhere, you know I am your biggest cupcake cheer-
leader."

Lani did know that. Charlotte might not understand, but she did her best to support. "You really
need to come down here, Char. You'll see. This town
is like living inside a sustained, continual group hug.
You can't believe what it's like to have such loyal support. I mean, I know it's mostly because I'm a Harper,
and my great-grandmother was revered here, but
they're very sincere about it. And it just feels . . . well,
great, actually. Come down. Feel the Sugarberry love.
You'll understand then, I know you will. You never
know, you might even stay." Lani smiled. If you could
hear a person shudder, she was pretty sure she'd
heard Charlotte do just that. "I miss you."

"I miss you, too. At the moment, however, we have
more important things to discuss. I didn't think you'd
already know. That's why I called so early. I wanted to
get to you first. Are you okay?"

Lani squeezed a bit harder on the pastry bag than

necessary, but managed to keep from making a raspberry truffle volcano out of the next cupcake. She didn't pretend to not know what Char was talking about. "I'm fine." Total lie, and one Charlotte wouldn't buy for a second. Especially given the black forest and Dutched ganache. Dead giveaway, really. "How in the world do *you* know? I just read about it in our little local daily less than an hour ago." Which was why, less than an hour later, she was filling cupcakes as if her life depended on it.

"I'm still in New York, remember? We know everything first. Franco told me this morning when he came in. He's here helping me with setups. We're catering a champagne gala at the Lincoln tonight. It's crazed."

"Bon matin, ma chère!" came Franco's shout from somewhere in the distance, via the speakerphone.

The accent affectation never ceased to amuse Lani. Franco was definitely tall, dark, and swarthy. He was the youngest from a family of seven with six older sisters, and just about the best gay boyfriend a girl could hope to have. But he'd been born Franklin Ricci and raised in the Bronx. He was about as French as baseball and Mom's apple pie. Still, he somehow made it work.

"Bonjour, mon ami," Lani said, warmed by his always cheerful voice, feeling anything but, herself.

"Before you ask," Char said, "Franco got the news last night from a production assistant on Baxter's show he's been hot after for a month now. I had to tell you the second I heard. It's not out for public consumption—yet—so it's not national news."

"It will be international news when we finally get together, *ma chère*," Franco crooned. "And we will. Like the finest Belgian chocolate with French vanilla filling. Mmm mmm. For private consumption only." His rich laughter echoed into Lani's kitchen.

"Seriously, Franco," Char scolded him. "No one cares about your latest conquest. We're in a state of emergency here."

"Almost conquest. And it's true love, this time, *chérie*," Franco said with a wistful, dramatic sigh. "Or could be."

"What else do you know about this?" Lani asked, feeling a bit sick, along with antsy and angry. "What exactly did you find out, Franco?"

"Not much," he said, dropping the accent momentarily. "Just that production is gearing up to start filming the next season on location in Sugarberry. I made the connection immediately, of course, but no one else is saying anything about it. Or you. At least not that I've heard. At the moment, Baxter's website and the show website are touting the third season, which launches this week. Baxter is going around doing all the standard promo for the season premiere, but it's only a matter of time before he mentions the next season, since it's going into production this week, too. His ratings are so high there's a lot of buzz about the major networks trying to steal him away for his own daytime show. Apparently, his network execs are pushing like mad to get him going, filming this next season. They want to get all the sponsors inked early on, before the rumors get out of hand." Franco came closer to Charlotte's phone. "Brenton told me they're going to make a big splash about the season premiere on the morning talks all this week. Someone will get him to spill."

"Brenton?" Lani asked. "Really, Franco?"

"It's adorable on him, trust me," he said, all Bronx

now. "Listen, Baxter is supposedly doing a surprise spot on *Today* tomorrow. And honey, you know Hoda and Kathy Lee will be all over him, because—straight or gay—who wouldn't be? They'll bring up the network rumors, and I wouldn't be surprised if he mentions that he's already begun the next season of filming, just to squash the buzz. Word is going to get out, *ma chère.* Of course they'll make the connection as it's the only one to make. It's only a matter of time."

Charlotte came back on the line. "We just wanted to give you a heads-up, Lan. I didn't want you hearing about it from anyone else. How did it make your little local paper before making the entertainment news here?"

"Ask Baxter." Lani was certain he was behind the personal little news bulletin. He was nothing if not a master at controlling the whims of his own fate. The question she still had no answer for was *why?* Why was he doing this? Any of it? She said as much out loud.

"I don't know," Charlotte responded. "But, like Franco said, your name hasn't come up in conversation amongst the crew or production, so I don't think anyone else has made the connection yet."

"Well, I'm not news, entertainment or otherwise, so why would anyone on the set care? The only one who will be bothered by this whole thing is me. I just don't understand what possible explanation he used for wanting to set his show here on Sugarberry, of all places."

"Lani," Franco said, butting back in, "you know it's not coincidence. I don't know what he told his bosses, but they obviously went for it. There has to be a hook, don't you think? And the hook has to be you."

"But, why? Just because I worked for him?"

"You know better than that. The world might not

care now, but you know it's only a matter of time before it's all out there. Any news that includes Chef Hot Cakes being interested in a woman—particularly one he worked with, mentored, and handed over the running of his beloved shop to . . . and about whom there was some pretty juicy gossip back in the day—is not just going to be any news. It's going to be *the* news."

The very suggestion made Lani's stomach sink further. Just like it had, regularly, "back in the day." Those days had mercifully ended ten months ago. She wanted to keep it that way. "There's nothing *to* get out. Come on, you and Char know that better than anyone. There was never any substance to those rumors. Most definitely not from Baxter's perspective. You two are the only ones who ever knew how *I* felt, and you both know I'd kill you in your sleep if you ever breathed a word."

Charlotte gasped. "You don't think we—"

"No, of course I don't." Charlotte and Franco were the two people Lani trusted most in the world. They were "her people," and she was theirs. "It wouldn't have mattered anyway, even if you had," she went on. "I mean, the world won't care what I might have felt for him, because Baxter doesn't care. It's certainly not newsworthy now. Yes, he made my professional life utter hell for the better part of three years—which I signed on for—and yes, he never once stepped up to defend me when the personal gossip started. Not once. But, though I hated it, and it hurt, it wasn't exactly a surprise that he didn't. Baxter is notoriously, completely oblivious to anything not in his own personal line of interest. So, I'm equally sure he had no idea what kind of hell my life was then, and I'd certainly like to believe he doesn't have a single clue about the hornet's nest he's stirring up coming down here now. I can't imagine he'd intentionally do something so—"

"Heartless?" Franco said.

"Sadistic?" Charlotte added.

"Thoughtless," Lani finished.

Charlotte sighed. "Like I said, he had to sell this idea somehow."

"You think he purposely used me as, what, some kind of bait? Even if he had, why would they go for it? There's nothing to mine here. We never were anything but business associates."

"You're right, it doesn't seem like something he'd do. Yet, he's heading your way, with a production crew in tow. Clearly he had to tell the network something, and I don't know how else he'd have sold Sugarberry as a location if not for you."

"Maybe he does realize how hard he made it for you to be taken seriously," Franco offered. "Maybe, from his perspective, he's bringing his show to Sugarberry Island as a way to help make amends. That sounds more like something he'd try to do."

Lani almost choked on her own tongue. "*Help?* How? By invading my sanctuary? My home? And turning it into some kind of media circus? How on earth would that do anything other than turn my new life into the same crazed hell I just left behind? Even he's not that obtuse." *Was he?*

"Maybe the gossip and behind-the-scenes kitchen controversy wasn't the hook he pitched. Maybe he just simply pitched you, going from fast climbing, award-winning pastry chef to running your own little island cupcakery. How you're blending the two worlds? I don't know, but that is unique, and something of a hook," Charlotte said, though she didn't sound completely sold on the idea.

"Besides," Franco added, "by the time you took off, what you actually left behind was a whole bunch of people who were in awe of your talent."

When Lani snorted, Charlotte added, "All right, so maybe they were in awe while their mouths hung open in stunned disbelief, after you proved they were all narrow-minded, gossip-mongering, donkey's asses. But, the point is, no one doubts you or your talent now." Charlotte's lovely, proper accent was always an odd contrast when she was angry. It was like being bitched out by royalty. "Baxter's favoring you and singling you out because your talent warranted that kind of support and mentoring. He left you in charge of his shop because you were accomplished enough to handle it. He treats Gateau like his firstborn child. He'd have never trusted it to just anyone. When you left, everyone knew you'd earned your place the right way."

"Those were still the same people who had nothing better to do than dish vicious, snide dirt about exactly how they thought I'd 'earned' my position, and just how many positions I had to get into, and how often, to do it," Lani said. "I know what they were saying, Char. We all know what they were saying. It was ugly and gross, and I won't pretend it didn't hurt. A lot. I'd never come up against anything like that in my entire life."

"Because you're the good girl," Franco said. "The nice one, the kind-hearted BFF everyone wants on their side. Of course they chewed you up and spit you out. But you showed them what you were made of."

"Franco, I didn't stay and run Gateau when Baxter left to do his television show to prove to them, or even Baxter, that I was worthy. I stayed because I thought it was what I wanted, what I'd worked so hard for. It was the pinnacle, the dream. *I* knew I'd earned my way to that success, because I'm the one who busted my backside to achieve it. And that was all that mattered."

Back then, anyway. Now she knew what was truly important. And the icing on that cake was the fulfillment she'd found here. Yes, she was scared to death, because Cakes By The Cup mattered so much to her. More than anything ever had. But she knew her path had ultimately led her to this place. So, she was thankful for what she'd been through because of what she'd ultimately learned about her craft . . . and what life would always be like in five-star kitchens. If there was a way to apply that knowledge and make her bakery a sustainable success, she'd find it. In Sugarberry, she'd found happiness and contentment. With no outside pressure or unwanted ugliness, her goals were her own to achieve, and the rewards her own to reap.

Only now, all the stuff she'd left behind—specifically the not-so-great parts—were about to stroll right back into her life again. It wasn't even the potential return of the gossipmongers and haters that she dreaded most. She'd expect nothing different from them. What did it matter now, anyway? She was safe and sound and living happily in Sugarberry, far away from that world. And from Baxter.

How could he?

Lani shot raspberry truffle filling in rapid-fire succession as her own steam built. "I'm all settled in here now, Charlotte, doing my own thing. Baxter—who I've never heard from, by the way—is happy in television land. And Gateau is doing just fine without either of us on-site. So why can't he leave well enough alone? What does he possibly hope to gain by coming down here? It's not a coincidence, right? I mean, sure, if

Baxter or his producers or whoever just wanted an unusual, quirky remote location, I get that. Most people
don't even know there are islands off the coast of
Georgia. We have a whole string of them south of here
loaded with fancy resorts and posh country clubs that
sport the kind of four-star establishments that would
be the perfect venue for Baxter's crazy elaborate desserts. We're this little rural burg of an island in the
midst of wilderness sanctuaries and fishing boats.
Close in miles, maybe, but a world apart from the
Golden Isles. If St. Simon is the Palm Beach of barrier
islands, then we're . . . we're Mayberry. Who comes to
Mayberry to put on a television show when you can go
to Palm Beach? I'll tell you who, nobody."

"Unless Mayberry has a pastry chef who happened
to work for the hot host, the same chef everyone assumed was sleeping her way to the top with said hot
host, who went on to prove them all wrong, rose to the
top, got a James Beard nomination for her work, then
took off and opened a tiny bakery off the coast of
Georgia."

Lani was silent for a moment, while her stomach
went full lead balloon. "I was executive chef for
Gateau for just over a year, and sure, maybe I'm
known in culinary circles. Or I was. I was a blip on the
screen, at best, and now I'm gone. Even if that's true,
why would he drag me back into all of it? Why? He's
quite successful enough and will continue to be, without using me, I'm sure."

Charlotte sighed. "I don't know. All I can figure is
that he thinks he's helping you in some way."

"Which is kind of condescending and insulting,
don't you think? I didn't ask for help, definitely not
his help. I don't even need help. I'm doing okay."

So far.

The truth was, she knew nothing about running her own place.

When she'd made the decision to stay, she'd signed the lease, ordered the equipment, and forged a rudimentary business plan, all with only her father's health and well-being in mind. Well, that and trying not to feel guilty for abruptly abandoning Gateau or worrying about walking away from the success she'd worked so hard for in New York. It only got more confusing when she realized the main thing she felt about leaving her hard-won career behind . . . was relief.

Even so . . . no one had been more surprised than Lani when she discovered that, at some point during the crazy intense time it took her to choose the name of the shop, install the kitchen equipment, line the shelves and cabinets with the tools of her trade, and set up her pastry displays . . . she'd fallen in love. Head over heels, hopelessly, completely, stupidly in love. With her own little shop.

She felt as possessive, as proprietary, and as downright proud of it as a new parent. She wanted to show it off, see it grow, and thrive . . . and she wanted to keep it all to herself. Like her own personal, adult-sized Barbie Bakery, where she could play and indulge her every creative whim . . . without any risk of failure. Or commentary.

Only six and a half months from initial conception to opening day. It was a minor miracle to pull off anything like that so quickly. Even in a place as rural as Sugarberry, and leaning heavily on her dad's influence to get all the permits, it had taken every second of every day to pull it off before the fall festival, which

was when she'd determined she'd have the best opportunity to make the biggest splash. But pull it off
she had. Cakes By The Cup had officially opened for
business four weeks ago.

And she'd been having mini heart attacks ever
since.

She would happily do whatever it took to keep it up
and running. Everything except turn to Baxter for
help. He'd done his part. And she was grateful. More
than. If all it took to run a successful cupcake shop
was being a good baker, then it was a slam dunk. Even
blindfolded and on one foot. Baxter had seen to that.
But he hadn't mentored her in the business end of
things. That hadn't been the point of their collaboration. As his assistant, her focus had been on learning
the craft and gaining confidence in her natural talent.
Later, as executive chef of Gateau, she'd been responsible for the menu, the output, the quality and creativ-
ity. Baxter and his financial partners had been the
ones responsible for the business end, for signing the
paychecks.

"You know, there is one way to find out what's
going on," Charlotte said, snapping Lani from her
reverie. "Call him."

"What? No. I am not going to give him the satisfa—"

"Think about it, Lani. This way you control the
meeting, you take charge of the situation."

"Take charge," she said flatly. "With Baxter. How
often has anyone been successful doing that? Oh,
right. Never."

"I'm simply saying—"

"Charlotte has a point," Franco chimed in. "At least
you can let him know that you know what's going on,
and set the tone for how you're going to handle it

with him. You don't work for him anymore, you don't run his place anymore, you aren't beholden to him for anything, Leilani. Think about it. He has no hold on you."

Oh, if only that were true, Lani thought, then paused, hands ready at the squeeze. Franco did have a point, though. She really hadn't thought about the situation like that. Not in a purely professional sense. She'd been confronting the news like the woman she'd been before leaving New York, the one still pathetically half in love with a clueless man who'd have never even noticed her if it weren't for her crazy mad baking skills.

But she wasn't that woman any longer. Not entirely, anyway. It hadn't been all that long since she'd left New York for good, but so much had happened since she'd come to Sugarberry. Her entire life had changed. She had changed. "You know, maybe you're right."

A short cheer went up on the other end of the line.

"I want to hear every detail," Charlotte said.

"You go, *ma chérie amour!*" Franco sang out.

A series of buzzers going off came through the speaker. "I've got to go, the cakes are coming out," Charlotte said hurriedly.

"We've been making solidarity cakes this morning in support of you, *ma chère,*" Franco said. "We're featuring your to-die-for black walnut spice cakes with cream cheese and cardamom frosting as today's special."

"Thanks, you guys," Lani said sincerely.

"Every detail! Call me!" Charlotte ordered before clicking off.

Lani stood there, pastry bag still at the ready, and looked at the racks in front of her. And thought about her friends in New York. Solidarity cakes. Salvation cakes. "Healing the disgruntled, displaced, and just plain dissed," she said, smiling briefly. "One cake at a time."

She and Charlotte knew a lot about that. They'd been friends since culinary school. Charlotte had more actual business experience than Lani, as she'd gone straight to work post-graduation as a pastry chef for a small boutique hotel in midtown, while Lani had gone overseas to continue her studies in Belgium and France. Lani's mom and dad had moved from D.C. to Sugarberry shortly after that.

It had been a time full of transition and change, but also one of promise and excitement. Lani's best friend had been launching her career in earnest while Lani was grabbing the chance to learn at the hands of Europe's best. For her dad, it had been retirement from the D.C. police force and taking on a very different challenge in Georgia . . . and for her mom, who'd grown up in Savannah, it had been a chance to go back home again, to a place she'd always missed dearly.

Lani and Char had kept in touch throughout that time, their friendship only deepening as their separate experiences widened their respective paths and boosted their dreams. When Lani had come back, Char was still in New York, having already worked her way up to executive pastry chef at the same hotel. Franco was on board by then as her right hand and had quickly become Lani's other best friend. Lani had gotten an offer in the city, as a staff baker for a well-known restaurant in a five-star, Upper East Side hotel. The same hotel that had just brought on board the hottest import from the U.K. America was the new playground for the young and impetuous, and ridiculously charismatic Baxter Dunne.

He'd risen quickly, and had taken Lani with him, plucking her from the ranks to make her his personal assistant and protégé when he'd opened Gateau a miraculous eighteen months later. His had been a rare, meteoric rise in a very challenging and competitive industry. By the time he'd made his move to the television cooking world three years later, his immediate dominance hadn't surprised anyone.

Lani blinked away mental images of him, how he'd been then, how totally infatuated she'd been with his charisma and his talent almost from the moment she'd first set foot in that Upper East Side kitchen. Okay, the lust had started before then. She'd known a lot about him, more than most, having heard quite a bit during her time in Europe. He was three years younger than her, and light years ahead in every way measurable in their field. The baker in her wanted to be him when she grew up. And, the woman in her wanted to be with him *as* a grown-up. It had been harmless idolatry and fantasy.

Then she'd gotten the opportunity of a lifetime.

She'd been convinced the heavens and fates were sending her a direct message when she'd tried for, and gotten the job working under him.

Under him.

Lani made a face at that unfortunate double entendre and moved to a fresh rack of cupcakes, forcing her thoughts back to the job at hand.

The pathetic irony was that she'd wished she had been under him. In every possible sense. Then everyone else had speculated, quite nastily, that the very same thing was actually happening. When it wasn't. Lose-lose.

The competition in any kitchen was fierce, but with a rising star like Baxter running the show, the battle to dominate his kitchen was downright apocalyptic, the chance to make a name and launch huge careers the spoils of winning the war. He was the epitome of the golden boy, from his looks to his demeanor, to his unparalleled talent. The speculation regarding their relationship was the hot topic of the day, every day. Fueled by jealousy, fear, and paranoia, the chatter was nasty and vicious. And not particularly quiet.

In order to keep up with the chaotic pace and the insane demands, every kitchen had to work like a well-oiled machine, which meant teamwork in the most basic sense. It was a close, if not close-knit, environment, where you worked all but on top of each other. There was no place to go, no place to hide. And certainly no place to speak privately. Not that the gossips would have bothered to, anyway.

Every chance they got, at least when Baxter didn't have her working right by his side, they'd done everything they could to undermine her.

As her esteem had risen in his eyes, and he'd given her more and more preferential treatment, the gossip had just gotten uglier and uglier. What could he possibly see in the mousy girl from D.C. who was too nice to know better? What made her so special? That Lani was certain she'd looked at Baxter like the pathetic little smitten kitten she'd been only made the whole ordeal even more painful to recall. She'd tried to rein that part in when she'd realized what was happening, heard what was being said. She knew she was only hurting herself further with her stupid crush, personally and professionally.

Of course, at some point, as it all escalated, she'd privately thought—hoped—that Baxter would ride to her rescue. He was the white knight, after all, wasn't he?

So many illusions had been shattered, so rapidly.

She was tougher than any of them had thought, her time overseas preparing her in ways many of them couldn't have imagined. She was calm and well mannered because she chose to be, not because she was some silly ninny who couldn't defend herself. She simply chose not to, as any attempt would be drowned out by the chorus against her, anyway. She'd rather hoped her hard work and Baxter's faith in her would speak for her, but that hadn't been the case. So, ultimately, she'd figured out that if she wanted to survive there, the easiest path was simply to stay in her own world, build a certain kind of calm around her, where she could focus on learning. And on Baxter. Preferably doing both at the same time. But . . . not always.

She'd endured almost five years of that constant bedlam. And, in doing so, had learned more, professionally, from Baxter, than she'd ever hoped. She had no regrets. So what if Baxter never had come to her rescue? So what if he had, in fact, thrown her directly to those very same wolves when he'd left for the bright lights of his own brand-new television show, and put Gateau, his baby, essentially in her hands? She'd done it, hadn't she? She'd shown them all.

Though it had come at a cost. No matter how calm and centered she remained, that kind of life took a toll. She thought about all the baking therapy she and Char had done together during that time. Usually in the wee, wee hours. Those sessions never had anything to do with their respective jobs.

And everything to do with salvation.

Their worlds might be uncontrolled chaos, but baking always made sense. Flour, butter, and sugar were as integral a part of her as breathing.

Lani had long since lost count of the number of

nights she and Charlotte had crammed themselves
into her tiny kitchen, or Charlotte's even tinier one,
whipping up this creation or that, all the while hash-
ing and rehashing whatever the problems du jour
happened to be. It was the one thing she truly missed
about being in New York.

No one on Sugarberry understood how baking
helped take the edge off. Some folks liked a dry martini. Lani and Char, on the other hand, had routinely
talked themselves down from the emotional ledge
with rich vanilla queen cake and some black velvet
frosting. It might take a little longer to assemble than
the perfect adult beverage . . . but it was the very so-
lace found in the dependable process of measuring
and leavening that had made it their own personal
martini. Not to mention the payoff was way, way better.

Those nights hadn't been about culinary excel-
lence, either. The more basic, the more elemental the
recipe, the better. Maybe Lani should have seen it all
along. Her destiny wasn't to be found in New York, or
even Paris, or Prague, making the richest, most intricate cakes, or the most delicate French pastries. No,
culinary fulfillment—for her, the same as life fulfillment—was going to be experienced on a tiny spit of
land off the coast of Georgia, where she would happily populate the world with gloriously unpretentious,
rustic, and rudimentary little cupcakes.

"That's me." She lifted her pastry bag in salute.
"Cupcake Baker Barbie!" She aimed the silver tip, and
bulleted a row of raspberry shots with rapid-fire precision, then another, and another, before finally
straightening, spent pastry bag cocked on her shoulder like a weapon. She was a take-no-prisoner's Baker
Barbie, that's what she was. "Yeah. Welcome to Cup-

cake Club," she said, giving it her best Brad Pitt impersonation. She grinned at that, and tried to convince herself she was ready to take on the true test of her newfound toughness, the real proof of her independence.

The phone call.

She could do it. She would do it. She didn't need to bow down to the whims of Baxter Dunne any longer. Wasn't she standing right there, in her own kitchen, working for her very own self?

"Damn straight I am." She moved to the next tray, discarding the spent bag for a freshly filled one, then positioning it like an expert sniper lining up his next kill shot. "Hear that, Chef Hot Cakes?" She completed the next three rows with deadly precision. "I . . . don't . . . need . . . you." She punctuated each word with another squeeze.

She straightened. And swore. "Yeah, that's why I'm standing here at the crack of dawn, shooting raspberry truffle filling like a woman armed with an AK-47." But, she had to admit, it felt good. Powerful, even.

Salvation cakes, indeed.

So, she went with it. Moving to the last tray, she shot another squirt of raspberry, picturing his smiling, handsome face as she did so. "*Why* are you doing this to me, Bax?" *Pow, pow, pow.* "Why are you invading my world?" *Bap, bap, bap.* "*My* world, *my* kitchen, *my* home." So many questions scrambling her brain. Making it impossible to think straight, impossible to concentrate on anything except—

"Dammit!" Lani glared at the oozing, overly truffled cupcake like it had committed an unspeakable cupcake crime.

She blamed Baxter for that, too.

She might have growled, just a little. It was stupid to be so upset about this. Like Franco said, she was operating from a position of strength here. Who cared why he was coming to town?

Or what laying eyes on him again might make her feel?

She'd handled worse things, she reminded herself. Far, far worse things. Losing her mother two years ago. Almost losing her father ten months ago. "I can handle Baxter Dunne," she muttered.

But as she stood there with flour powdering her hair, a smear of raspberry truffle across her chin, a spent pastry bag in her hand—happily content in her own element—she thought about it all, and tried to harness her inner Smackdown Baker Barbie . . . she really did. But she kept picturing his face, hearing his voice, seeing his hands move so precisely perfect, so beautifully efficient as he worked, making every step look so effortless, so simple . . . and wishing he'd put those smart and clever hands on her . . . and found herself failing. Miserably.

The sound of the delivery door slapping shut behind her made her spin abruptly around, the flailing pastry bag sending at least a half dozen freshly filled cupcakes skittering to the floor.

The sight that met her eyes sent her heart skittering as well. As only Baxter could.

He was very tall, with long arms and legs that would be gawky and awkward on anyone else, but were graceful and elegant on his lean, muscular frame. He had a wild thatch of wheat blond hair that was forever sticking out in all directions, brown eyes so rich and warm they rivaled even the most decadent melted chocolate, and a ridiculously charming, crooked grin that always made her secretly wonder what trouble he was about to get into . . . and wish, desperately, that she could join him.

"Hello, luv. Happy to see me? My God, you look a fright."

And, always—always—too late, she remembered the trouble she was forever getting into . . . was him.

Chapter 2

Indeed, she did look quite the fright. Her dark brown hair, always neatly tucked into a shiny, sleek twist at her nape, was lighter now, streaked by the sun, he supposed, and hung in loose wisps and straggles about her face, the knotted bun at the back of her crown escaping whatever she'd used to secure it. At Gateau, she'd employed some kind of slim, clever chopstick-like affair, holding it strategically, perfectly in place. All he could see now was something puffy . . . and pink. A very bright pink—which seemed even brighter against her skin.

Gone was the cream and rose complexion he'd remembered. She was tan, which changed everything. What with the loose, wild hair, it lent an almost . . . heathenish edge, giving her normally pretty blue gaze a somewhat piercing, laser-like quality. Conversely, though she'd always been a sturdy thing, lithe, but strong and solid, at the moment, she looked . . . enveloped by the chef coat she wore, as if it were a size too big, or she'd suddenly grown smaller.

None of that mattered. Just stepping into the same

room with her again settled something inside him. Something vital. Necessary. As he'd hoped it would. In fact, prayed it would. Nothing short of believing that would have driven him to come to this god-forsaken, beastly hot, bug-infested place. It was October. Humidity of that sort shouldn't be possible.

Standing there now, he couldn't believe he'd ever been foolish enough to let her go.

"Why?" she asked, ignoring the cupcake carnage at her feet.

It was only then he noted the uncharacteristic mutinous set to her raspberry-smeared chin . . . and realized she wasn't so happy to see him. Or at all happy to see him, it appeared. "You might want to mind your step there," he began, nodding to the floor, but was cut off from offering further assistance when she repeated herself.

"Why, Baxter?" And, in case he hadn't understood what she meant, she clarified—through tightly gritted teeth. "Why are you here?"

Confused, and thinking he was obviously just missing something, he grinned and held out his hands. "Is that any way to greet an old chum?"

"Chum?" It hadn't come out as a screech. Exactly.

He winced all the same, and the confusion grew. "Compatriot, then?"

"There are a number of terms that come to mind when I think of you—which I don't—but, if I did . . . that one wouldn't make the list, either."

"Oh." His smile faded. "I see." Except he didn't. Not at all. He hadn't really known what to expect seeing her again, but it hadn't been this. Her parting from Gateau had been rather abrupt, and though he'd wished her well, and Godspeed to her family, he hadn't been able to see her off personally before she'd left New York. Was that it? Then she'd made the decision to stay in Georgia with her father, and he'd never seen her, or worked with her, again. He couldn't help that, could he? Just as he couldn't have known how that sudden shift in his world would make him feel. He did now.

"Did you get the flowers?" he asked, treading more carefully. "For your shop opening?"

"I did. You didn't have to do that."

He lifted his shoulders, tried a bit of a smile. "I wanted to. I know it hasn't been long, but I hope it's been a successful launch thus far." He was nervous, he realized. It wasn't a state he regularly found himself in. Rarely, if ever, in fact. Her reaction had thrown him badly. "You're wearing your Gateau jacket, I see." Striving for some common ground, he was hoping to quickly whisk out the lumps and smooth things between them. "Haven't gotten your own shop jackets as yet?"

She looked down, then back at him, and he could have sworn a bit of pink that wasn't raspberry filling colored her cheeks. Though what on earth she had to be embarrassed about, he hadn't a clue.

"I—uh, no, I don't have—I wear aprons. Out front. With the customers. I've always had—I collect them. I have since—" She broke off. "I only wear this back here, when I'm baking, because—" She stopped again, frowned, at herself or him, he wasn't sure. "It doesn't matter why. What does matter is why you're standing in my kitchen, unannounced, at"—she glanced at the wall clock—"six-fifteen in the morning."

He was truly flummoxed. She'd never been anything other than absolutely professional with him. Always in a good mood, the calm in the center of every storm. And there had been many. He could depend on her to be consistently cool, competent, and focused. Aside from her rather amazing talent, the way she handled the day-to-day chaos of the kitchen with such smooth aplomb was the thing he'd admired most about her. He'd been convinced that bombs could be going off, and she'd be steadily working away with that quiet smile of hers, truly content, as if she existed inside her own personal sunbeam.

To him, she'd been the perennial Snow White, kind to one and all, always making life easier for those around her. It was why he hadn't immediately noticed, hadn't realized . . . well, so many things, actually.

The difference was she no longer worked for him, and was therefore, he supposed, no longer required to maintain a professional demeanor in dealing with him.

Perhaps he should have taken that into consideration.

"Why are you here, Baxter?" she asked again, her tolerance clearly being tested.

"You know, I don't ever recall you being—"

"Bitchy?"

His eyebrows climbed slightly. "I was going to say impatient. Or irritated. I've never seen you be either of those things."

"That's because you've never seen me."

He frowned then. He had not a single clue as to what she could mean by that. They'd worked side by side for years. Of course he'd seen her. "You seem put out with me. Quite . . . annoyed, actually. I thought we parted on rather good terms, all things considered. I mean, of course I hated to lose you, and so suddenly. Gateau will never be the same without your vision and talent. But I'm not heartless. I understand the importance of family obligations." He tried not to look around and actually take stock of her fledgling effort, for fear she'd see his utter bewilderment regarding her new direction. She was meant for far, far better than this. "Of course, I was deeply disappointed that you chose not to return, but please understand, Leilani, I'm not angry with you for leaving."

"You? Angry with m—" She broke off once again, clearly fighting to hold on to what was left of her swiftly dwindling control if the grip she had on that poor pastry bag was any indication.

Snow White with a temper? He couldn't get that to measure up.

"This isn't getting us anywhere," he said, hoping they could begin again.

"Because, as usual, you're not listening to me. Or to anything but the voices inside your head, dictating that you stay stubbornly focused on whatever it is that *you* want."

"What are you talking about? Voices in my head? Are you saying I'm mad?"

"You don't listen, Baxter. You never listened. If you had, you'd know why I am not happy to have you come onto my island, or invade my town, much less set foot inside my shop. *My* shop, Baxter. You don't have any say here."

"Of course I don't." He wondered how and when he'd fallen down the rabbit hole without noticing the drop. "I don't want a say."

"Good, finally! Now we're getting somewhere. What *do* you want?" She'd enunciated that last part as if he was hard of hearing.

"I honestly don't understand at all why we're even arguing. We never had problems communicating before. I could always depend on you to be straight-forward, the voice of reason—"

She barked a laugh, making the loose tendrils of hair dance around her face, and looked a bit mad herself. "Because there was no point in being any other way. It was energy I couldn't afford to waste. And it would always have been a waste. The reason we communicated well was because you did all the communicating. But not anymore, Baxter. You can be as single-mindedly charismatic and inadvertently obtuse as you want, but it's not going to do you a bit of good in getting whatever it is you came here to get from me. And don't bother telling me you just chose some dinky island off the coast of Georgia as a remote set for your show and, lo and behold, what a coincidence I happen to now live on that same island. Obviously you came here on purpose. I just can't figure out why. You know why I left, why I'm here. Nothing about that has changed. I'm not coming back."

"Is that why you think I'm here? To get you to come back to work for me?"

"What other reason could you possibly have? I can't even figure that out. Your show is a smash hit, consistently the highest rated food show ever on television, I think I read somewhere. I keep in touch with some of the staff at Gateau, so I know Adjani is doing an amazing job running the kitchen and menu, and you're doing just fine without me there."

"You're right, I don't need you on my television show. And Gateau is surviving, yes, and doing as fine as can be expected without you."

"Then why—"

"Because, Leilani." He walked fully into her kitchen, meaning to stop a few feet from her, simply wanting her to understand how earnest he was, how sincere. Somehow, though, he ended up not stopping until he was right inside her most personal space. It was a place they'd been many times with each other, elbow to elbow. But never face to face. And never for personal reasons.

"Because?" she repeated, her tone not nearly so strident.

And her jaw, when he placed his finger beneath it, wasn't nearly so tightly clenched. In fact, he was certain he felt a slight quiver. Or was that him?

Her skin was remarkably soft . . . how had he refrained from touching it for so long? Up close he could see the light scatter of freckles against her newly golden cheeks, and found himself surprisingly enchanted by them. He wanted to lean in, breathe in her scent, taste her, touch . . . fully engage every one of his senses. Wallow, revel, drown. "It's quite simple, actually, my irrationally irritated former compatriot." He was forced to employ a rather remarkable level of restraint just to speak at all and not simply take what was, finally, right in his hands. He drew a thumb lightly across those cheeky freckles and smiled into the dearly missed, familiar blue of her eyes. "I'm here because *I'm* not doing fine without you."

He'd sworn he would take it slowly, so she would understand what he was thinking, feeling . . . and hopefully find something of the same inside herself. It was critical, crucial, that he give her the time and space to be certain of him, of herself. That plan swiftly deserted him. He did manage to lower his mouth slowly . . . but even that was a close call.

She didn't stop him. Nor, he realized, when he finally touched his lips to hers . . . did she respond to him. At all.

He lifted his head.

Her gaze was fixed on his. Her mouth, still tightly shut.

Bloody hell.

What a blooming idiot he was, risking what might have been his one best chance. What he regretted even more was that the seconds were stretching out like their own little individual chasms of time . . . and every one of them was awkward. They'd never once been awkward with one another.

"I don't know what this new game is," she said finally, her words slow and as precisely measured as a knife across starch. "But please, don't . . . ever . . . do that again."

"Leilani—"

"I have work to do."

He spent another second or two weighing the relative merits of trying to stand his ground and make her understand everything that was going through his mind, but one look in her eyes had him deciding retreat might be the better part of valor. For today.

Her continued anger he could have accepted, even if he didn't understand it, which he didn't. Hell, even indignant fury, though he'd never had it from her, he could have handled, certain he'd get to the root of it eventually. But the look in her lovely blue eyes wasn't either of those things. She looked bewildered. And rather . . . lost.

He understood both feelings. Intimately. Specifically as they pertained to her.

But they were emotions he'd never thought to see on her sweet, enchanting face. Made worse, by the fact that he'd been the cause of them.

"All right," he said, and stepped back. It was then he noticed she had a white knuckled grip on the worktable behind her. And he felt like even more of a sodding bastard. What the hell had gotten into him?

But even more worrisome to him was . . . what the

hell had happened to her? She was the good one, the sweet one, yes? There was a certain kind of tempered steel inside her that he'd recognized from the start. She wouldn't have lasted a minute in his professional world if she didn't have backbone. He'd never witnessed her in any compromising personal situation, or even heard of her being in one. If there had ever been a man—or men—in her life during the time they'd spent working together, she had been very discreet about it. Had she ever been subjected to unwanted personal advances, he wouldn't have anticipated this as being her response. More likely she'd have fended the perpetrator off with a rolling pin thrust to his chest, like a lance.

The very idea of that happening to her was enough to snap him out of his uncustomary daze. The only one to be mad at was himself. The only one to put her in a compromising personal situation . . . had been him. *Goddammit.*

He made his way back to the rear delivery door, knowing he should just keep walking straight through and out. Removing himself was the very least he could do for her at that moment. But no. He turned back, stupidly thinking he could still, somehow, fix the damage.

She hadn't moved so much as a hair.

"I'll apologize," he said, "for the poor timing. And the sorry lack of forethought in not making my interest known. But no' for kissin' you, Leilani. Or, more t' the point, for wantin' to." He stopped, hearing the accent of his childhood creeping back into his words.

He smiled broadly then, to cover how much that little backslide had shaken him, knowing full well he was relying on his infamous rapscallion grin that had, from a very young age, gotten him out of countless scrapes and sticky situations. For a very long time, it had been the only thing he'd had going for him. Leilani would not likely be swayed . . . but it was a defense mechanism he couldn't override at the moment. "It wasn't exactly how I'd imagined it, but I promise you, I'm nothing if not diligent when trying to perfect something new."

She said nothing to that.

Keeping the smile in place suddenly took quite a bit of work, so he turned and opened the door.

"You imagined kissing me?"

He jerked his gaze back to hers, his grin broadening further, without the least bit of calculation this time. "It's been the centerpiece of some of my very best daydreams." He wisely left unspoken the far more vivid ones he'd had at night.

She opened her mouth, then apparently thought better of responding, and shut it again. Her free hand still tightly gripped the table behind her. But, from where he was standing, he didn't think she looked quite so lost or bewildered any longer.

It was a start.

Chapter 3

L ani watched Baxter close the door behind him. Then stood exactly where she was for several more full minutes.

So. Apparently she'd embraced her inner Smackdown Barbie a bit more fiercely than she'd realized. "Welcome to Cupcake Club, indeed," she murmured, then slumped back against the worktable.

Holy crap.

But even as she went over the entire interaction, moment by moment, it still seemed more surreal hallucination than actual occurrence.

Had she really chewed out Baxter Dunne?

The man responsible for her being the pastry chef who had been nominated for the James Beard? The man who had given her the foundation of knowledge and confidence to go anywhere in her field?

And . . . had that same man, the man she'd fantasized about having wild, crazed, right-on-the-worktable, sugar-fueled sex with for more than four years, actually just walked right up and kissed her? *Her?*

Really?

"Why?" she whispered, plagued with even more questions than she'd had before he'd strolled back into her life.

Another thought snuck in, and made her stomach clutch all over again. She and Charlotte had been speculating that he'd come to Sugarberry to do something to help her. But it seemed clear to Lani that perhaps he'd come there to help himself . . . and needed her to complete the task.

I'm not doing fine without you.

His words echoed through her mind. That, along with the kiss, would lead any normal, sane woman to think that he wanted her. Personally. Romantically. Sexually.

But she was far from normal at that moment, much less feeling remotely sane. She'd been quite uncharacteristically mad at him. In fact, during their entire time working together, she'd never been angry at him, not once. To his face. So . . . upon seeing her irritation, had he just taken things up a notch, hoping to nudge her back into being sweet and helpful and compliant, the way she'd always been with him? Would he—could he—really be so manipulative?

Charlotte and Franco had agreed with her that he wasn't like that. He usually just charmed what he wanted out of people. Which, she supposed, was a form of manipulation, though it came so naturally to him, she'd thought it pretty harmless. Other than what it did to her libido, anyway.

Was it possible he'd known all along about her feelings for him, and was just now opting to use them to his advantage? What situation could he possibly be in that would cause him to make that kind of choice? It seemed to her it would have to be pretty dire and desperate, and his current successes didn't seem to point to that. But what did she really know?

The beginnings of a headache started to throb in her temples.

Fall festival started tomorrow. It was her first and best opportunity since opening her shop to really establish Cakes By The Cup and herself in the community. It was an important event to everyone who lived on the island, and everyone was part of it in some way. She'd spent a lot of time, and not a little of her budget, thinking about the best way to make a splash during the festivities, hoping to boost her professional standing in the business part of the community, and establish an even stronger personal identity with the townsfolk, who were her new neighbors and, hopefully, soon-to-be-friends.

She'd been excited about the possibilities, nervous, too, but in a good way. The Kiwanis connection had really helped to solidify her plan.

"And he chooses *now* to come back into my life? *Now?*" She looked upward, talking to her mom or a higher power, or both, she wasn't quite sure. "Really?"

And kiss me?

She sank her weight further onto the edge of the worktable as she lifted her raspberry truffle-covered fingers to her lips. "He did. He really kissed me."

"You back there, babycakes? I saw the light on, used my key."

Lani startled guiltily—which was ridiculous. She hadn't done anything to feel guilty about. She had bells on the front door, but hadn't heard them. Something else she happily blamed on Baxter. "Hey, Dad," she called out, snapping immediately back into work mode, moving swiftly to clean up the mess on the floor, tossing the ruined cupcakes into the trash can behind her, washing her hands. "Come on back." He'd do it anyway, but always called out first to let her know he was there, even if she was open for regular business. It was the cop in him.

She smiled. That was another thing about her life that had changed. These days she found herself perfectly happy to be overprotected. Happy to hear that gravelly, grumbly voice, knowing how close she'd come to never hearing it again.

Using a wet wipe, she cleaned up the filling that had oozed out of the cakes onto the floor, then tossed that in the trash, too, straightening just in time to spy the newspaper she'd slapped on the empty worktable early this morning. She slid that into the trash can on top of everything else. If only she could rid herself as easily of the problem that had landed in her kitchen this morning along with it.

Sheriff Leyland Trusdale ambled into the kitchen as she finished washing her hands a second time, and took a seat, as he always did, at the end of the table closest to the door. He could see the swinging door connected to the shop front, the delivery door at the back, the window at the far end next to the door to her office, and her, all without having to shift so much as an inch in any direction. It also put him right at the table where she was working.

Still feeling more than a little discombobulated, Lani grabbed the volcano cupcake she'd last filled and started cleaning up the truffle explosion.

Her father nodded toward the messy cupcake. "Here, let me make that go away."

"The doctor said—"

"I'm not going to have another coronary because I eat a damn chocolate cupcake."

"If it was just one damn chocolate cupcake, I wouldn't say anything. Besides, these are for an order. I'm a sponsor for the Kiwanis Club. These are for the auction tonight."

"You made extra, right?"

"Of course, but that doesn't mean—" She sighed as he reached over and plucked it out of her hand. She didn't attempt to snatch it back, nor did she bother continuing with the lecture. This time. She'd learned to pick her battles. Privately, she was beyond relieved that her father had implemented as many of Dr. Anderson's orders as he had. That he'd even allowed a woman doctor to tell him anything had been a miracle in and of itself.

Not that Lani had said as much. But someone had to stay after him, make sure he didn't revert back to a diet filled with fried foods and extra salted everything. She was the only family left to do it. She was the only family left, period.

She picked up the pastry bag and decided it was best to pretend nothing had happened, just go back to work, fill the cupcakes, and everything would work itself out. Salvation cakes, indeed. "Things going okay with the council regarding the festivities?" she asked, making small talk. Making anything-but-think-about-Baxter talk. "Arnold isn't still giving you grief over having to file for the right permits, is he? Even the mayor—especially the mayor—has to follow the law."

"Arnold Granby is an old gasbag who likes the sound of his own voice. I let him rant a little and fed his already overfed ego. Barbara will eventually have had enough of listening to him and get the damn permits done anyway. The fine citizens of Sugarberry will get their fall festival, complete with tents, tables, chairs, and Porta-johns."

Barbara was Mayor Granby's executive assistant, secretary, all around problem solver, and people handler. Mostly, she handled Arnold. She also happened to be his wife, so she had unique leverage in that department. She needed it. If it wasn't for Barbara actually keeping the office running, the fine citizens of Sugarberry would have pushed Arnold out of office ages ago.

Her father polished off the cupcake in three bites, then leaned over to drop the paper cup in the trash before Lani could block the move.

He paused, glanced in the trash, then back to her. Why she'd ever thought she could get anything past one of the best detectives the nation's capital had ever seen, she had no idea. Retiring to become sheriff of a sleepy little southern island, where the biggest crime wave was perpetrated by whatever critter had gotten into Conway Hooper's "Utopian peace garden" that week, hadn't dulled his instincts in the least.

Leyland fingered the cupcake liner, cleared his throat, but didn't say anything. He finally crumpled it, and tossed it in the can. Right on top of Baxter's handsome, smiling face. "Want to talk about it?"

"Not especially." Lani's mother had been the go-to parent for all things emotional and personal. Lani knew her father loved her with all his heart, but he had his own way of showing it. If she wanted to know what kind of tires to get for her car, or debate whether the Redskins had a chance at the playoffs, he was right there. Beyond that, his advice leaned more toward how a woman was supposed to protect her body. Lani was loaded with enough mace and pepper spray to bring down an angry mob, and was probably the only person ever to get a taser in her Christmas stocking. However, when it came to helping her protect her heart, he was completely out to sea, hopelessly rudderless.

She had no idea what her mother had shared with him during the time Lani had worked for Baxter. She did know her father was aware that his daughter's former boss and mentor hadn't made her life easy, and, in many cases, very hard. Professionally, anyway. But that had been Baxter's job.

Looking at her father now, and the awkward, uncomfortable way he was shifting on his stool, Lani suspected her mother had shared a lot more with him than her daughter's professional frustrations.

In earlier years, he never would have offered to talk. Even since her mother had passed away, he hadn't stepped in to try to fill that particular void. Nor had Lani asked him to. But, with his heart attack just after the first of the year, and her permanent move to Sugarberry at the end of March, the dynamic between them had shifted. Not in a bad way, exactly, but their roles weren't the same anymore. And neither of them quite knew what to do about it.

She suspected it made him miss her mom even more. Lani certainly did. Marilee Harper Wyndall Trusdale would have known exactly what to do, what to say.

At the moment, however, it was her father's awkward attempt at fulfilling that role that had her eyes suddenly welling up, making her want one of his rare, big bear hugs. Because she knew he definitely wouldn't know what to do if she hugged him, she ducked her head and tried to frown the tears back as she shot rapid fire wads of raspberry into the last of the unsuspecting little cakes. "I still need to get the frosting piped on these, then get them packed in their delivery boxes. Walter is coming by to get them later today."

Normally, excusing her father from any mom-style parental duties was a relief to them both. She'd expected him to gratefully take the cue, make his excuses, and leave. Surprisingly, he lingered.

She didn't look up. But she was rapidly running out of cupcakes.

He cleared his throat. "Do you want me to . . . do something? Stop him from coming on the island?"

Lani spurted out a shocked laugh, then blinked away the tears, and looked at her father with a smile. "I appreciate the offer, Dad. But what, are you and Arnold going to pass some quickie ordinance that prohibits the country's most famous pastry chef from airing his immensely popular cooking show from anywhere on Sugarberry Island? Those same fine citizens might lynch you both. They all love Baxter." She swallowed a sigh. "Everybody loves Baxter."

She saw the corner of her father's mouth pull up a little—his version of a smile—and, worse, that spark of determination enter his clear blue eyes. She groaned silently. She should never give him ideas like that. She, of all people, knew better. "I wasn't being serious. You can't—"

"They all think we're backward hicks down here in Georgia anyway, with all kinds of bizarre laws and such. And if Arnold wants me to look the other way on those safety permits—"

"Dad," she said, in the long-suffering tone that only a long-suffering daughter could manage. "First of all, you were born and raised in D.C. and couldn't pass as a local if you wanted to, much less a good ol' boy. And secondly, you'd no more compromise the safety of anyone here on the island just to prevent me from having to deal with—"

"The man who made your life miserable? You bet your sweet ass I'd do that and more."

"No." She was stunned by his papa bear attitude. What had gotten into him? "You won't. It's because of Baxter that I'm the chef I am, that I had the career I did, one that allowed me to indulge myself in this." She gestured to the well-stocked kitchen surrounding them. She looked at him and decided to just put it out in the open. With Baxter on the island already, it was likely to come out anyway. Especially if that kiss actually meant anything. Which— She rapidly shut down that thought track. "It's true"—she took a steadying breath—"my feelings for him didn't help me any, and maybe he should have been more aware of the difficulties I had to deal with because of how differently he treated me, but I handled it, Dad. I handled myself. I handled the people who doubted me. And I handled Baxter." *Right here in this kitchen,* she added silently. "I can certainly do it again." She prayed like hell she was right. She wasn't sure how many Commando Baker Barbie performances she had in her.

"You shouldn't have to." Her father sounded a lot more like the grumbling, hardnosed cop he usually was. "Sure, he taught you what he knew, but then he dumped all the responsibility on you and took off for fame and fortune. You stayed behind, in a hostile work environment, and ran that place and made it sparkle. Then, when it was your turn, you left to start your own place. I'd say, at the very least, that makes the two of you even."

"I agree, Dad, which is why I'll handle . . . whatever it is he's coming here to do." In the odd mood her dad was in, it was definitely not the time to reveal she'd already seen Baxter. And definitely not the time to tell him about the kiss. Not that she ever planned to tell him about that part.

"Do you know why he's here?" her dad asked. "Have you spoken with him?"

"No, I don't know," she said, quite honestly, opting to dance around the other question. "I talked to Char and Franco this morning already, and though there's a chance Baxter will mention it during a series of talk show spots this coming week to promote the current season, no word has leaked out in New York, or from Baxter's production company or television network as yet. All I know is what was in our paper this morning—that he's coming here to use Sugarberry as a remote location to shoot a week's worth of episodes for his show." She lifted a shoulder. "Maybe that's all it is. Part of some sweeps or ratings stunt." She wished she believed that.

Her father's expression said he thought there was as much a chance of that being the case as she did.

Before he saw something in her face that gave anything else away, she stepped around the end of the table. "I don't want you to do anything to complicate matters further." She kissed him on the forehead, surprising them both into silence. "But I really appreciate that you want to." Tears threatened suddenly again, and she knew she had to end this little chat before it became even more awkward. "I'll deal with Baxter Dunne."

"I've no doubt that you will. You're a sweetheart, and everybody loves you for it, but I know your mom and I didn't raise you to be a pushover." He scooted the stool back and stood. "It's just . . . you shouldn't have to deal with him again, Lei-lei. Not if you don't want to. That's all I'm saying. You shouldn't have to."

He didn't call her that very often. She'd been named for him, after a fashion, anyway. He'd wanted a son, a namesake, but her mother had had such a difficult delivery, they both knew their daughter would be their only child. Her mom had honored him the best way she knew how. He'd shortened her name, calling her Lei-lei when she was little. But the more traditional Lani was the nickname for Leilani that eventually stuck. So, being stubborn, as he certainly could be, he'd called her by her full name. It was a rare occasion when his old pet name for her popped out.

It had been awhile. Since her mother's funeral, in fact. It took her a second to regroup, and speak past the lump in her throat. "I've dealt with worse, Dad." She immediately wished she'd thought that comment through a little better. She hadn't intended to invoke the memory of her mother's death, which had been by far the most difficult thing either one of them had ever dealt with, far worse than any nightmare work scenario Baxter could have inadvertently gotten her into. Her dad spoke of her mother often, in that way some people did, as if she was still there. It was just . . . easier. Talking about her death, the impact of it, the gaping hole it had left in their lives, was still a hard thing for him. A very hard thing.

She winced when she saw him duck his gaze, then realized there was one other thing that could hurt him. She laid a hand on his arm, a gesture that would ordinarily be a little too touchy-feely for him, but, at the moment, felt natural. "I might have come down to Georgia for you," she told him steadily, having long since figured out being direct with her father was the only way to really get through to him. "But I stayed here for me."

"Leilani—"

"Dad, I'm fine. We're fine." She squeezed his arm once, then let go. "Now go keep the citizenry safe. I need to make these cupcakes fabulous, so they can bring me business after they're auctioned off." She smiled. "Then I can become ridiculously successful, and make Baxter regret not being a little more sensitive to the people who worked for him, right?" She wanted to lighten the mood, get them back on familiar footing.

But when she glanced up at him, instead of the impenetrable look he normally wore, she saw . . . honestly, she wasn't quite sure what she saw there. It wasn't an expression she could recall ever seeing before.

"You're already ridiculously successful," he said, almost angrily. "And I haven't met the man, but I know that Baxter Dunne is an ass for letting his best business asset get away, and a blind fool idiot for not seeing you're the best thing that ever happened to him."

Lani stood there, mouth agape, then finally pulled it together and responded to the one part—the only part—she could. "Dad, I don't want to work for Baxter again. And I don't want to go back to New York. Or anywhere else. I love my shop. I love Sugarberry. I want to be here. I want to do this." She saw the stubborn set to his jaw, and her heart broke a little. "Is that what this is all about?" She swallowed hard against tears that sprang forth again, but for entirely different reasons. "Are you . . . embarrassed? By my decision to run my own place here on the island instead of running Gateau?"

She'd worried about making her father understand that she'd wanted to stay for her own reasons, not because she thought he needed her help. He was stubborn and had too much pride for his own good. It had never once occurred to her that he might not actually support her choice because he thought it was beneath her.

"I've never been anything but proud of you," he said, his tone still rough. "But you used to cater UN functions and visiting dignitaries from all over. Your desserts have been served to some of the most important people in the world. Are you really expecting me to believe you're satisfied with feeding cupcakes to a bunch of—"

"Hardworking men and women who support their community and do what they can to improve the lives of those around them?" She set the pastry bag down before she squeezed it so hard it exploded. She didn't know if she was more pissed off, or crushed. She did know she was shaking. "Yes, Dad. Yes, I am. I like working for myself. Correction, I love working for myself. And, even better, I like making people happy with my food. People I know. People I will see more than once in a lifetime. People who matter. People who care about me, too. Really care." She knew, deep down, he wasn't trying to insult her or hurt her feelings, that he wanted what was best for his only child. But it was hard—very hard—to hear that he apparently thought she'd taken a step down by moving here, by opening her own place.

Impulsively, she scooted around the end of the table again, and hugged him—hard—then bussed him on the cheek. "I'm happy here, Dad. More fulfilled than I've ever been, personally and professionally. And that's the God's honest truth. I know you may not understand that, and of course, I want you to be proud of me, but I mostly want you to stop worrying about me."

"I am proud of you, babycakes." He shocked her

again by hugging her back. Hard. That bear hug she'd wanted so badly. It was as good as she remembered it to be. Better. "As for not worrying . . . I'll do that," he said, gruffly, "just as soon as you stop worrying about me." He let her go, then leaned past her and snagged another cupcake before she could gather her wits. He saluted her with it, then walked out through the front. "I'll lock it," he called, not sounding particularly angry anymore. Or particularly settled, either. She didn't know how he was feeling, actually.

"Join the club," she muttered.

She'd been worrying about telling him about Baxter, and what that conversation would lead to. Now she had a whole new slate of things to think about, worry about.

She turned and looked at the worktables filled with silver cooling racks, relieved beyond measure that she had over a hundred cupcakes to pipe frosting onto.

That, at least, she understood.

A whole seven hours went by before she had to deal with the matter of Baxter Dunne again. She wasn't any clearer on how she intended to deal with the matter, much less him personally, than she'd been at six-thirty that morning. She hadn't seen him since he'd walked out her delivery door, had no idea where he was staying, or what he was doing, or who else might be on the island with him, in terms of a production team.

She'd opened her shop on time at nine. Her special blend coffee was percolating and ready for serving, along with her warm-from-the-oven streusel-topped cupcakes—both popular items with her growing group of steady morning customers—and proceeded to jump every time the chimes on the door jingled. She'd been half expecting to look up into Baxter's smiling eyes again. When it wasn't him—which it hadn't been, yet—she'd waited for the inevitable gushing, excited, eyewitness story from each and every customer, telling her all about how they'd spotted him somewhere in town, or on the island.

There had been plenty of buzz about the television show coming to town based on the story in the morning paper, which had worked some of her customers into a veritable fever pitch of anticipation over the arrival of the show's star host. She was pretty sure she'd sold several dozen cupcakes, all before noon, just because her customers had been hoping to pump Baxter's former employee for what she might know about his possible whereabouts and details about the show. To their great dismay, she'd been an utter disappointment in both departments. She hoped the cupcakes made up for it a little bit.

It was after two in the afternoon, and there had been nary a single Chef Hot Cakes sighting. On an island the size of Sugarberry, if he'd been seen by anyone, anywhere, every last man, woman, and pelican would know about it within five minutes. She'd even shamelessly debated on the relative merits of leaving the shop in the hands of her part-time helper, Dre, and going home to hide out until he surfaced—somewhere, anywhere—but had decided she was a better woman than that. Well, that, and Dre hadn't been in her employ for a full week as yet. Still, she'd like to think she'd stuck it out because she was strong, independent, and didn't really give a good ganache where Baxter was or what he was doing.

So . . . where is he? What is he doing?

And how was it no one knew he was already here but her?

She'd almost talked herself into believing the entire episode had been some sort of stress-fueled hallucination, or a waking dream of some kind. Considering the way she'd all but yelled at him . . . after which he'd kissed her—kissed her!—that was almost the more sensible, rational explanation.

Then Alva Liles rushed into Cakes By The Cup just as Patty Finch, the local librarian, and her nine-year-old daughter, Daisy, were leaving . . . and Lani's tidy little it-was-all-a-dream rationale went straight in the Dumpster.

"Afternoon, Patricia, Miss Daisy." Alva smiled as they held the door for her. "Why, Lani May, there you are!" The petite senior bustled—which was the perfect description for how Alva Liles moved—straight up to the counter. She was also the very definition of *all aflutter.*

It made Lani's heart sink. And her gut clutch. *Here it comes,* she thought, and braced herself. Of course, it was going to be Alva. She should have guessed. "Yes, Miss Alva, here I am." Lani refrained from pointing out it was unlikely, during business hours, that she'd be anywhere else. Or that her middle name was Marie, not May. She'd learned it was apparently an affectionate Southern thing, then remembered Charlotte's Indian-inflected version of a Southern twang as she'd repeated the name several times after Lani had shared it with her. Lani's smile came more naturally, then.

"I'm sure you read this morning's paper," Alva said, her perfectly coiffed white-blond curls all but vibrating around her head like a miniature beehive. Everything about Alva Liles was in miniature, from her

height, to her frame, to the itty bitty silver rimmed bi-
focals perched on the end of her perfect, tiny nose.
She was, in a word, adorable. Sugarberry's answer to
Betty White.

Normally, Alva was one of Lani's favorite customers
and Lani always enjoyed seeing her come through the
door. Normally. Alva had the best stories, yet somehow managed to sound like she truly cared, and cared
deeply, about each and every person on the island . . .
as she threw them directly under the gossip bus. Lani
loved her.

Normally.

She had a feeling, however, that the gossip bus was
going to be aimed straight at her.

"I got a glimpse of it," Lani replied. "I was up early
working on a few special flavors I'm featuring during
the fall festival tomorrow." Hoping to distract and
redirect, she leaned on the counter, inviting Alva to
step in closer. "I have one available for limited taste
testing. A new take on Boston Creme. The filling has a
bit more of a kick and I think the new chocolate glaze
is something special."

"I'm certain you outdid yourself," Alva said sincerely, "but then I'd expect nothing less. You're an absolute marvel. My waistline might never forgive you,
but I can't seem to walk by without stepping inside."

Lani smiled. "Then my work here is done."

The twinkle in Alva's eyes turned to more of a speculative gleam as she leaned across the counter and
dropped her voice to a whisper. "What decadent treat
are you tempting us with for the auction tonight,
dear?"

Lani raised her eyebrows in surprise, as she was certain Alva was anticipating she would, given the satisfied smile on her powdered face. "Now that sponsor

list is supposed to be secret," Lani said mildly, but she wasn't really shocked.

"You know nothing stays secret on this island for long."

Lani wanted to point out the reason for that was standing right in front of her, but just smiled instead. "What did you hear?"

"That you've whipped up boxes full of something deliciously decadent to tempt us all." Alva pouted a bit. "Walter, the old bear, wouldn't budge when I asked him for more details this morning over my morning biscuits and jelly at Laura Jo's place. By the way, have you seen Laura Jo since she talked Cynthia over at the salon into dyeing her hair? My land, she's a sight, but she dearly loves being a redhead, let me tell you. Claims it makes her feel bold, willing to take risks." Alva lowered her voice, but just slightly. "Ask me, I think if she wants to be bold, she should reconsider those floral blouses she favors for solid colors and something a little more form fitting. Show a little cleavage. I keep telling her she's got a figure under all that foliage. Assuming, of course, that this entire makeover business is really all about snagging the attentions of that new fellow who took over Biggers' Bait and Tackle after Donny Biggers up and took off with Delia Stinson. Delia Stinson. Twenty years younger and she could do much better if you ask me. I didn't see that coming. Felipe Montanegro is the new fellow's name. Have you met him?"

Lani shook her head, trying to keep up. Twitter had nothing on Alva Liles. For that matter, neither did all of Facebook. She was a superhighway of information, all by herself. "Not yet."

"Well, he's dashing enough, I suppose. If you like the swarthy Ricardo Montalbán type."

Lani had no idea who Ricardo Montalbán was, but didn't ask for further illumination.

"Although, I suppose being a redhead certainly didn't hurt Lucy when she went after Desi."

Okay, Ricky Ricardo she did know, but Lani didn't know whether to nod or shake her head. She'd lost track, so she changed the subject. "I'm sure she'll figure something out. Did you want to look at today's special flavors? Maybe try a taste bite of the Boston Creme?"

Alva bent slightly so she could peer down her nose through her bifocals as she investigated the various trays and stands filled with cupcakes lining the inside of the pastry case. "I'm tempted, but your red velvet there is simply sinful. Like heaven in a cup." She glanced up at Lani, with a speculative twinkle in her eyes. "It's by far your best, if you ask me. Is that, perhaps, what you made for the auction?"

Lani shook her head.

"Oh, come now, don't be coy. You know you can tell me. I won't breathe a word to a soul."

Lani struggled not to roll her eyes, but her smile was genuine. "You'll have to wait until they put the official auction list up before the dinner tonight."

"You know, I tried to explain to Walter and Arnold that they're being very shortsighted about this whole secret silent auction thing. If they'd let us know more in advance about the sponsors and the specifics of the auction items, we could start talking them up, get a bidding war going before the auction even begins."

Lani knew exactly why the silent auction was a secret silent auction, but there was no point in belaboring it directly with the very person responsible for the rule change.

"I will tell you this much," Lani said, and Alva

moved closer, her expression sparked with conspiratorial glee. "If you do score a dessert box? Your poker group will think they've died and gone to heaven. I promise. These are the most decadent cupcakes I've created yet."

Most women Alva's age played bridge. Lani's mother, her grandma Winnie, and her great-grandmother Harper—Nanny, as Lani had called her—had all loved the game, and Sugarberry had always boasted quite a lively and active women's bridge club. Lani had learned, however, that the Sugarberry senior center sponsoring the card club had politely asked Alva to quit their bridge group when they found out she was taking side bets on the North and South partnerships versus East and West teams. Betty White the neighborhood bookie.

Alva had responded by starting her own ladies poker club, which had all but decimated the ranks of the original bridge club. They played once a week in the back room at Laura Jo Starkey's diner and had the reputation for being quite the competitive poker sharks. Average age: seventy-six.

In fact, it was Alva's penchant for setting up betting pools for everything from how many hurricanes would threaten their shores in a season (Category 3 or higher, no wimpy hurricanes for Alva) to, oh, what item would take the highest bid at the fall festival silent auction. That had been the cause of the silent auction rule change. Last Lani heard, Alva wasn't allowed in the senior center on bingo night anymore, either.

"My dear Lani May, I have had *that* little talk with Walter," Alva said, the twinkle a bit smug. "I don't know what's in them, but I've got dibs on two boxes, sight unseen. We're having our monthly all-nighter tournament this Monday." She leaned closer. "Can't you just give me a tiny little hint?"

"How exactly did you find out I was a sponsor?"

"You know Walter's wife, Beryl? Well, she currently holds the number two ranking in the club." Alva lowered her voice again, despite being the only one in the shop at the moment. "It's no secret she wants her title back. Dee Dee Banneker—she took the points lead after the last tournament. Well, she's a wiley one, Dee Dee is. So, Beryl will take any advantage she can get. And don't you know she's not above hoping a little sugar rush will put the other girls off their game. Namely Dee Dee and her two closest friends, Suzette and Louise. Those three make a formidable little clutch, let me tell you. But your cupcakes are simply to die for, and Beryl knows the girls won't stop with just one. Plus Beryl's got Laura Jo on her side." She dropped her voice to a whisper. "Laura Jo is going to serve that sangria she learned to make on her cruise last year. Between that and all the chocolate—I know you had to do something chocolate, am I right? Well, between the cupcakes and sangria, if Beryl can just resist temptation, I think she's got this one in the bag."

Only because all the other women will be half in the bag, Lani thought, thinking that mixing black forest ganache cupcakes, sangria, and senior citizens up past their bedtime was trouble just waiting to happen, but she kept a smile on her face all the same. Picturing Alva's peers getting looped on sweet wine and chocolate pretty much did the trick.

"What happens if you don't win the bid?" Lani asked.

Alva's smile curved more deeply. "Mark my words, Beryl will make Walter's life taste like a bitter, bitter pill if we don't serve your delicious cupcakes Monday night. She can't bid herself, conflict of interest and all, so she came to me. I've already got odds on Beryl, but the line, of course, still favors Dee." Alva winked, then primly tucked her itty bitty clutch under her arm and stepped back from the counter, looking as innocent as a nun in church. "They don't know we'll have the secret weapon."

Lani couldn't help grinning. Betty the Bookie, indeed. With her secret weapon cakes. "Speaking of weapons, how's the campaign for your column coming? Have you convinced Dwight yet?" Lani leaned her hip against the counter and smiled. "You know, I hear he's a sucker for cupcakes. Just saying."

Dwight Bennett was the editor of the local *Daily Islander,* for which Alva had been quite vocally lobbying to write an advice column. Dwight wanted a gardening column, or what he termed "ladies club" news. But since Alva's idea of a ladies club included no-limits Texas hold 'em tournaments and bourbon tastings, he somehow didn't think she was the right woman for the job.

Too late Lani realized she'd led Alva straight back to the topic she'd come into the shop to gab about in the first place. *Dammit.*

"The dear man can't see beyond his stodgy, narrow-minded view of how the world should be, bless his heart," Alva said, and Lani couldn't really tell if she was sincerely worried about the man . . . or wanted him dead. "I tried to explain that it was hardly an unbiased, balanced, and fair approach to reporting the news when he only printed the parts he personally approved of. We might as well just call it the *Dwight Bennett Herald* then. But actually, dear, it was an article in this morning's paper that brought me in here to see you. Of course we've all read the little write up about your boss coming right here to our island! And bringing his television show along with him!" She clasped her hands together, purse still tightly tucked under one arm. "Isn't that just the most exciting news we've had in ages?"

"Former boss," Lani clarified, not that it would matter.

"Why, you've been holding out on us, Miss Lani May," Alva said, her tone scolding, even as she smiled. "Surely you've known all along about this little surprise visit. Were you the one to coordinate the show coming here? Certainly that's the way to guarantee a big debut at your first fall festival." She leaned closer, clutching her tiny bag to her thin chest. "Naturally, I wanted to be the first to talk to you about getting him to stop by the club tournament Monday night. Talk about distractions! And, just between us, if I scoop that story, Dwight will simply have to let me have my column."

"Well, I don't have anything to do with—wait, I thought you wanted to write an advice column? A Dear Alva sort of thing. What would Baxter dropping by the poker tournament have to do with that?"

Alva straightened, squaring her narrow shoulders. "I want to write what the women on Sugarberry want to read. A little advice here, a little gossip there. The kind of thing everyone goes to Cynthia's salon to find out. Or Laura Jo's. But then it has to make the rounds, and surely you know how it gets turned entirely upside down and backwards from how it actually happened. Not that anyone intentionally twists the truth, of course."

"Of course."

"I just want to put the news all in one convenient place and tell it like it really is, as it actually happened.

Along with that, of course I'll offer advice as I think it would benefit everyone. A true public service." She smiled so sweetly, Lani thought she actually believed that. "Trust me, it'll be the first thing they turn to when they pick up the paper. Mark my words."

Lani didn't doubt it. "Sounds like you have it all figured out, Alva, and I wish I could help you with your scoop, I truly do." The bells jingled on the door, so Lani leaned closer and hurried to say what she had to say, wanting to close that particular conversational thread—the thread being Baxter—before it got picked up by the next customer. Alva had a point—a big one—about how the actual details of this story or that one were forever getting spun all out of proportion to the original happening. "Unfortunately, I don't have anything to do with Baxter's itinerary while he's here. I found out about the show the same time you did. So, I can't do anything about getting him to come to your club—"

"What club would this be?"

At the sound of the new voice, Lani looked up . . . and there he was. How was it he always seemed bigger than life, no matter the size of the room he was in? *It's that smile,* she thought, as Alva spun around and beamed up at him with enough wattage to light the Vegas strip.

"Why, my goodness gracious," she said, fluttering a hand over her hair, then tucking her purse smartly back under her other arm. "I can hardly believe my own eyes. If it isn't Baxter Dunne, Chef Hot Cakes himself. Right here in our little town. My, my, and look at you." She glanced at Lani, then beamed right back at Baxter. "Quite the tall drink of water, aren't you? I had no idea. The television doesn't nearly do you justice, and of course, we all think you're just the handsomest thing to ever put on an apron."

"Chef's jacket," he said, but his responding smile was wide and sincere.

Lani watched the scene unfold, thinking it was sort of like having an out-of-body experience. Only she wished she really could leave her body at that moment, and be just about anywhere else.

"And please, you can call me Baxter." He glanced at Lani. "I only make my employees call me Chef." He leaned down—way down—so he could put his mouth near Alva's ear. "I'll leave it your call on the Hot Cakes part, however."

Lani thought Alva might simply expire right there on the spot. She'd never seen the woman blush before—ever—that she could recall. Alva might look tiny and fragile, but she was pretty much bulletproof, in that steel magnolia kind of way most women on Sugarberry were. At the moment, however, Alva was as bright pink as the plump, perfect raspberries Lani had placed on top of each and every one of the twelve dozen surviving Kiwanis cakes that morning.

"Why, listen to you!" Alva exclaimed, trying to look properly shocked at his cheeky forwardness, but clearly enamored straight down to her sensible senior pumps. "Aren't you just the charming devil." Alva's hands still fluttered about. "I was just telling Miss Lani May how excited we all are to have you here."

Baxter glanced at Lani with a lifted brow and a delighted twinkle in his dark brown eyes. She scowled back at him, then quickly shifted to a sunny smile when Alva glanced from one to the other.

Alva turned right back to Baxter, and continued gushing. "And to think you're going to film your television show right here on our little island. Why, I can't even believe our good fortune. Perhaps I could interest you in a cup of coffee? You see, I write this little column for the local paper, and I'd love to get a one-on-one interview."

Alva glanced back at Lani then, with an overly bright smile and an eyebrow wiggle that only Lani could see—apparently a plea not to out her little white lie to Baxter—then she was all beaming smiles again as she turned back to him and put her small, blue-veined hand on his arm, as if she was fragile and needing his strength for support. "What do you say, Mr. Dunne?"

Fragile, Lani thought, *if pit bulls were fragile.* It had been more of a Betty White lie.

"Baxter," he corrected, still all smiles. "And I'm honored—flattered—but I'm afraid I don't have time to spare at the moment."

Alva looked instantly deflated, but Lani saw the steel still in her spine. Deflated, maybe, but if she knew Alva, far from defeated.

Baxter looked up at Lani, and his smile grew. He covered Alva's hand with his own and patted it. "You see, Miss—?"

"Liles," Alva said, not missing a beat, though her cheeks pinked right back up when he patted her hand. "Alva Liles. Alva to you."

"Miss Alva." The wattage of his smile almost made Lani blush, and she'd thought herself at least somewhat immune given her lengthy exposure to it. "I would love a chat," Baxter went on to say, "but I need to confer with Miss Trusdale about the details of the show."

"With Lani May?" Alva looked back at her. "But, I thought you said you didn't know—?"

"It's rather a surprise," Baxter cut in, then looked up and locked his chocolate-eyed gaze directly on Lani's.

Which was the moment Lani realized things were about to get a whole lot more challenging for her in the "I can deal with Baxter" situation.

"I'll need a kitchen setup, and Leilani's—um, Lani May's—little shop here is perfect." His eyes twinkled brightly as he used her island nickname, with a bit of a quirked brow thrown in, just to be utterly incorrigible about it. "I'm hoping she'll agree to let us film some of our episodes of *Hot Cakes* right here." His smile widened to his trademark grin, his gaze still only on Lani, even as Alva literally squealed in delight. He lifted his hand and did a cheeky little wave to go along with it. "Surprise."

Chapter 4

Well. That hadn't exactly gone as he'd planned.

In fact, it had gone absolutely nothing like he'd planned. He'd intended to sneak her out of the shop for a bit, and make his pitch to her in private. In fact, he'd come to her shop at the break of dawn that morning for exactly that purpose. He'd been confident she'd be in her kitchen when he'd left his hotel before dawn and crossed the causeway, winding his way through the dark, narrow island roads to the center of its only commercial district. If one could call the tiny town square that. Bakers and newsboys—the two folks a person could count on to be up before the sun. He'd relied on them both that day.

For all the good it had done him. So far, his carefully laid plans had netted him a big fat goose egg. If the way Leilani had folded her arms across her chest was any indication, he'd taken another giant step backward. As if the kiss that morning hadn't been a big enough blunder.

He wasn't used to making big mistakes. The truth of it was, more often than not, he got what he wanted.

Mostly, because his ideas were solid ones, but he was aware he was blessed in other ways when it came to convincing people to follow his lead. A bit of charm and a nice smile could give a bloke a healthy headstart down the path toward achieving his goals. As he came by it quite naturally thanks to generous genetics, what was he to do? Pretend to be dour and dry?

He'd honestly thought he and Leilani would have a quite congenial "hullo, so good to see you"; then he'd ask, one professional to another, for the use of her kitchen. Though his real reasons for wanting her workspace were of a far more personal nature, he'd been certain she'd quickly agree to the collaboration. After all, featuring her little shop on national television could only be positive for her. It had all been rather foolproof, really. The hard work would come after their agreement was sealed.

However . . . he wasn't quite so optimistic of his chances to execute even the first part of his foolproof plan. Though he could readily admit he'd handled things ever so wrongly thus far, what with foolishly revealing his personal reasons for being there before even mentioning his professional plans, he was really starting to wonder what in bloody hell her problem was with him.

"Well, dears, I must get along." Alva beamed up at Baxter, who felt like a towering oak over the tiny bird of a woman.

"It was a pleasure, Miss Alva," Baxter said, trying not to glance at Lani, hoping she took the moment while Alva departed to clear her thoughts, see the bigger picture, and realize the boon he was dropping in her lap.

Alva squeezed his hand with surprising strength, even as her eyes glittered. "I am so excited, I simply can't wait to spread the news about your show being filmed right here! In our very own cupcake shop!" She beamed at Lani. "Imagine!"

"Imagine," Lani echoed with a faint smile, and far less enthusiasm. Okay, without any enthusiasm. But she didn't exactly leap in to dissuade Alva from her excitement or her stated mission.

Baxter took that as a positive sign. Though he was already grasping at the slenderest of straws if he could interpret anything about Leilani's current demeanor as a positive sign.

"Wait until I tell Beryl! Dee Dee and Suzette will be beside themselves, now!" The bells jingled as Alva made her merry exit.

Baxter wouldn't have been surprised if the spry little thing had clicked her heels and skipped across the small town square. She'd have been quite the vision in her matronly pumps.

"How dare you."

Baxter turned back to face the heat, thinking he'd taken far, far worse in his climb up the ladder, toiling in downright volatile kitchens the likes of which Leilani couldn't possibly even imagine. He was no stranger to battle.

Yet, one look at her intractable expression, and he felt at a slight disadvantage. If they ever created *Iron Pastry Chef*, she'd win the contest hands down on glower ability alone.

"I do apologize," he said, moving a step closer. "Heartily, in fact. I'd intended to talk with you this morning, but we got rather—"

"You got," she corrected. "I was working, minding my own business. Literally."

Baxter studied her more closely and realized she wasn't angry—well, she *was* angry—so much as flustered, which probably explained at least a percentage of her annoyance. The woman he'd worked with, taught, and been consistently amazed by, had never once been flustered. Not that she'd shown outwardly at any rate. At that moment, Lani was anything but the serene Snow White, whistling, so to speak, while she worked. Rather more like the dark queen. With something to hide. Namely, the reason she was flustered.

Interesting. And so unlike her.

He walked toward the counter, determined to get to the root of it. "I was going to say sidetracked," he finished, smiling and determined to simply brazen it out. If she really was angry with him, she was going to have to back it up with an explanation. And if he was making her nervous . . . then he wanted to know more about that.

"If you'd wanted a meeting, you should have called ahead and scheduled one," she said, talking faster, with more heat, the closer he got. "You come in, unannounced, and throw off my entire morning schedule—"

"I'm sorry," he said quietly, and sincerely. He thought it was probably the latter part that abruptly ended her tirade. He had meant it. He wanted to be amused by her flustered demeanor, rattle her out of it, so they could both calm down and get on with things. Instead, he found it bothered him. More so because he was somehow the source of it.

It truly was the oddest thing, this protective feeling he had. A delightful Snow White she might normally be, but with that steel in her spine, he was equally certain she could handle all seven dwarves and the evil queen, with one hand strapped behind her back, and a smile on her lovely face. In fact, she often had, he thought, when he considered what the kitchens had been like at Gateau during a service crush.

"That's why I came early, during prep. My intent was to get a word with you, in private. To discuss all of this before it became news."

"Odd then, that you planted a story announcing your arrival in this morning's local newspaper. Dwight Bennett is a good editor, but even he's not that good. He's not exactly keeping his ear to the ground so he can break the latest news in television entertainment. Why bother being stealthy and discreet, when hitting me broadside, in front of my customer base, will guarantee you get what you want? Alva is out there right now, telling God and everyone—"

"You didn't stop her."

"The National Guard couldn't stop her."

Baxter tried to stifle the smile, but having met the tiny tornado, he thought Leilani likely had a point. "Then I'll apologize for making my intentions known to possibly the worst gossip on the island. I didn't intend for that to pop out of my mouth as it did, but her enthusiasm was contagious and I simply—"

"Got carried away? Baxter, ever since your show debuted, you have women screaming at you all the time—and not in a bad way. Entire throngs of women get more than a little excited just by being within viewing distance of you. You're surrounded by adoring fans every single day. And night, I'd imagine. You come off as this unassuming but incredibly appealing guy, who is somehow sweetly earnest and passionately alpha all at the same time. Throw in the accent, and you're like . . . the Hugh Grant of baking. I get that they can't help themselves. But surely you're used to it by now. So, it's a bit of a stretch to think one tiny senior can throw you off your game."

He got hung up for a moment on her surprising description of him. Was that how she really saw him?

Quite flattering in some respects, especially considering the scowl presently creasing her brow. But . . . *Hugh Grant?*

"As you noted, she is quite the tiny senior." Baxter stopped at the opposite side of the counter from where Lani stood, arms still folded. "But you have a point. Maybe it was instinct, just put it out there, gain the advantage."

"Well, that's hardly a—what did you just say?"

"I said, maybe you're right, and I instinctively played to the advantage that presented itself. I didn't mean to, it wasn't premeditated, but that doesn't negate that I did it. Or that I'm sorry I did. It was impulsive, and out of line."

"Well . . . okay, then." The bluster went out of her.

But not, he noted, the fluster. If anything, she seemed more jumpy than before.

"So, just tell me what the bigger picture is here," she implored. "There has to be an agenda. I'm not stupid."

"Far from."

"Thank you."

"What is it I've done to anger you? I honestly don't have a clue."

"I'm not angry, I'm just—" She stopped when he simply folded his arms in a mirror pose of hers. She took an audible breath, let it out slowly. "It's . . . complicated. And you're right. I'm not being fair to you. I'm sorry for that. I'm not usually like this."

"Again, far from." He smiled then, relieved they were finally getting back to some semblance of normalcy.

But she didn't smile in return. And the slightly lost look she'd had that morning, after he'd kissed her, was back. He thought that might be worse.

"I guess it's just . . . I don't understand why you'd come here and turn my lovely new life upside down." She lifted one hand, palm out. Her quiet intensity proved more provoking than her frustration. "And please, don't use that line you tried this morning. I worked next to you for three years, and ran Gateau's kitchen for you for another year after that. You never once showed so much as a sliver of interest in me other than purely professional that entire time. We've agreed that I'm not stupid, so don't come here, into my place—*my* place, Baxter—and expect me to believe you suddenly can't live without me. Personally, or, for that matter, professionally. It's insulting, and . . . well, also not fair. I don't deserve some silly game. I deserve a straight answer."

"It seems neither of us is getting what we want today." Baxter kept his arms folded. "Did it occur to you that your refusal to believe me is also insulting? The one who should be angry here, is me. Other than not sending advance word, which I couldn't do due to the network's paranoia over secrecy issues, I haven't done anything wrong that I know of. I am, in fact, offering you a really great opportunity."

"That I didn't ask for, or need. If I wanted to advance my cause on Sugarberry by using you or Gateau, I'd have done it already. I'm building something different here. On my own."

"Leilani—"

"You should have asked me first, Baxter, before planning anything here, with or without me or my shop. I know I'm not in charge of the island, or your show, or you, but there are literally thousands of places you could have chosen. But you chose the one tiny little piece of land where I happen to live, and make my living. You had to know it was going to upend my life to some degree, no matter how altruistic you thought your gesture might be. Considering the working relationship we had, you owed me a heads-up, at the very least, networks be damned."

"I—"

"You should have just been honest and up-front about . . . whatever it is that made you come here. And no, I don't consider a local write-up intended to generate anticipation for your show on the very morning you arrive, crew in tow, an acceptable advance notice. I'm sorry—I am—but I'm not interested in anything you have to offer. Now, if you'll excuse me, I have some work to do while it's not busy. I hope you don't mind seeing yourself out."

Of my life, she might as well have added. She'd said her piece quite sincerely, but it was equally clear she'd hardly be crying into her milk and cupcakes if she never saw him again.

"Don't you want an answer to your question?" he asked mildly enough. She, of all people, would know him well enough to understand he was on a fast simmer now, as she'd been earlier. "As you noted this morning, I didn't come here because I need you to continue making my life a professional success."

"My point exactly."

"My point as well." He leaned against the counter and watched her struggle to keep her stance and not put additional space between them. For someone who'd spent the better part of four years glued, almost literally, to his elbow, her behavior was just plain odd.

"Despite my actions this morning, I'm not going to attack you, you know. You don't have to be so jumpy."

"I'm not jumpy. I'd just like to get back to work."

He leaned closer and she instinctively took a step

back, banging up against the counter behind her, setting all the trays on the racks to jiggling.

"Jumpy. I'm just curious why. I've never known you to be nervous around me before."

"I was always nervous around you."

His eyes widened at that. "Since when?"

"Since I had the opportunity to learn from someone as brilliant in the kitchen as you."

"Ah, professional nerves then. You hid them well."

She shrugged. "I wanted the job, and I wanted your respect." She hugged her arms a bit more tightly around her, drawing his gaze to the front of her apron.

"You had both. Always." On closer notice of her apron, he said, "Is that—?"

"The Mad Hatter," she said. "I told you, I have a collection."

"You collect aprons?"

"Since I was little and my mom taught me to bake." When he smiled, she arched a brow. "Some find it charmingly quirky."

"You never wore any to Gateau."

"Shocking, I know. Because I'm certain the staff would have greatly appreciated the humor in them."

His smile twitched wider at that. "You have a point, I suppose. I must say, this dry side of you is surprisingly appealing. What does it say?" He nodded toward her apron front.

She lifted her arms away so he could read the script that accompanied the copy of an original pen and ink art rendering of the Hatter seated at a long table, holding a tea cup aloft.

"YOU'RE NEVER TOO OLD TO HAVE A TEA PARTY," he read out loud, then smiled at her. "I rather agree. You make a charming and somewhat more quirky Alice than I'd have expected. I seem to recall Alice spent the better part of her time being irritated and flustered, too. Perhaps if I'd come bearing tea and crumpets, with a bewildered, bespectacled white rabbit clutching a pocketwatch in his paw, you'd have been more willing to give me the time of day."

He saw her fight the smile, and unrepentantly grinned at her.

She lost the battle and even snickered a little, but was clearly disgusted with herself for it, and not at all happy with him, despite the smile that continued to hover around her mouth. "You're incorrigible. You know that and you use it against the defenseless. Absolutely, positively shameless." She lifted a warning finger. "Just because you made me laugh, don't get any bold ideas that I'm going to hand my shop over to you and your production team. I don't want the craziness of your world coming into mine that way. And that's not to say I'm even buying any of the story you're selling."

He edged his weight onto the counter and lifted his hands out to the side. "What other reason could I possibly have?"

"I haven't the vaguest clue," she said. "And that's what bothers me."

"It's not remotely possible to you, then, that I'm speaking the truth? About missing you? Being here for you?"

She resettled her folded arms on her chest. "If you missed me, you have an odd way of showing it. Other than the congratulatory flowers, which you sent from the entire staff at Gateau, I've not heard a single thing from you in any way since I left New York. Not that I thought I would, but given this big pronouncement of yours, that seems a bit unusual. If this is a sudden realization for you, I can think of a whole list of ways to get my attention, all discreet and personal, not to mention more intimate. Not one of those ways includes dragging your entire television crew down here so you can beam your show to the whole wide world from my little country island kitchen."

He started to speak, then realized she had, yet again, a solid point. He dug his hands in his pockets. "Some would see the gesture as quirky and charming."

Her lips twitched again. "Seriously, with that. Cut it out."

"Oh, I'm quite serious," he replied, then made her eyes go wide when he braced his palm on the flat countertop and hopped over to her side in one quick maneuver.

She immediately backed up, and kept backing up, as he straightened and moved toward her. "You know what else is quirky and charming?" he asked.

"Is that a rhetorical question? Baxter, really, what do you think you're—stop!"

"No," he said quite succinctly. "You know what I think? I think you're still nervous, only it's not professional in nature."

"Maybe because you're suddenly stalking me?" She backed around the L-shaped display cabinets, then quickly realized she'd backed herself into a corner as this path led to the wall comprising the far side of the shop.

He continued his approach. "I wouldn't have to stalk if you'd stop running away."

"I'm not running, I'm . . ."

He lifted an eyebrow. "You're . . . ?"

She ran out of the room when her back hit the small stainless steel sink mounted to the wall behind the end of the side display case. She bumped up against it, and braced her hand behind her to steady herself. "Baxter—"

"Leilani." He didn't stop until he was almost hip to hip with her.

"What do you think you're doing?"

"Testing my theory." He leaned in closer.

Her eyes went wider . . . and her pupils wider still. And . . . definitely not in fear.

"Curiouser and curiouser," he murmured.

"You—don't do it, Baxter. I—there are windows. Lots of them. Right over there." She flung a hand in the general direction of the front of the shop, taking out a silver napkin holder as she did so.

"You've never been clumsy before, to my knowledge. I seem to be wreaking a bit of havoc on your natural grace and poise."

"The windows," she repeated. "With people. On the other side. Looking in. And seeing—"

He reached up and stroked a finger down the side of her cheek. Her lips parted on a little sigh. But it was when she moistened the bottom one with the tip of her tongue that his suspicions were completely confirmed.

He slid his fingers to the side of her neck, until her skittering pulse was right beneath his fingertips. "You're not afraid of me, Leilani."

"No," she agreed, the word more of a whispered rasp. Her gaze dipped to his mouth. "I'm not afraid of you."

He lost the battle—if he'd ever been seriously waging one to begin with. He'd just needed a sign that he wasn't alone in this. He cupped the back of her neck and lowered his head, craving a taste of that moist bottom lip more than he'd craved even the rarest of Belgian chocolates.

At the last possible second her gaze flew up to his. "I am afraid of being the center of nasty rumors again. And . . . and of the ugly gossip that will make my work suffer, this time threatening my shop. And making me feel like . . . like . . . I did. Before. All over again. It was one thing in the city, Baxter. But I work where I live now, and it's a very small place. Surrounded by people I know and care about. So, don't do this to me. Not now. Not here. Please."

He couldn't have imagined anything she might have said that could have shifted the mood more swiftly, or had him pulling himself up so abruptly.

But that did it.

He lifted his head, his gaze pinning hers. "What on earth do you mean?"

"Exactly what I said." She pushed at his chest, and he lifted his hands and moved away. Anything remotely playful in the tension between them was definitely gone.

"Explain it to me." He moved further back, then leaned against the case, shoving his hands in his pockets. No defensiveness on his part, just honest concern. And complete mystification. "Please. I truly don't understand. But I want to."

She held his gaze, then sighed, looked down, and muttered something under her breath he couldn't quite make out. It sounded like "why now?"

"Because now is the first time I'm hearing about it," he said.

She met his gaze again. "It wouldn't be, if you'd ever paid attention."

"Paid attention to what, exactly?"

"Me. Your staff. And everything that was being said about our supposed inappropriate relationship."

His eyes widened. "That's what you're upset about?"

If it was possible, her eyes widened even further. "You mean you know about all that?"

"Of course I do. My kitchen, my domain. I don't miss anything that happens in my kitchen. You should know that. It was rubbish then, just as it's rubbish now. Anyone with a pair of eyes in their head knew how amazing you were. Are. Your talent speaks for itself."

"It would have helped—a lot—if you'd spoken up for me. Just once."

"And give them the benefit of lending even a shred of credence to their silly chatter?"

"Ch-chatter?" Her mouth dropped open, then snapped right back shut. "Silly to you, maybe, but it made my life—my work life, which was my whole life—absolute, utter hell." She tried to smile, and failed miserably. "That was your job, Chef. Not theirs." She lifted her shoulders in a shrug, which turned into a shoulder roll. Then she blew out a long breath and shook the tension from her arms before folding her hands in front of her. As if she could shake off the memories as easily. "I signed on to be your target, take your hell. And I appreciated every challenging second of it. More than you will ever, ever know. But I didn't sign on to be their target, for mud-slinging character assassinations and sabotage."

"It's part of life in kitchens everywhere," he said. "Not an excuse, but a simple truth. And I run mine with a far gentler hand than most. I believe humor works over screaming every time. Charm has its benefits. But, at best, it merely keeps the battle under some semblance of working control, because there is no real way to diminish the reality that it's a cutthroat, competitive business. Stabbing others to get ahead is to be expected. And your back had the biggest target. The trick is to not take it personally."

Her eyes popped wide.

"Better yet, look at it as a compliment and let it make you stronger. Which it was, and it did, when you think about it. It meant you were the one to take down. The more vicious the rumor, the more confirmation you had in your ability."

"Strangely, it didn't feel that way to me. As you said, it was your domain, and you were the king. One word from you—"

"Would have made it a hell of a lot worse for you." He straightened away from the case. "For what it's worth now, from all outward appearances, you handled it with amazing aplomb. Brilliantly played— which drove them bonkers, I might add. You never let them see you sweat, as you Yanks are fond of saying, and I was quite proud of you for it." He took one step toward her. "And you quietly shoved their ignorance back in their faces when you ended up first in succession to Gateau's throne."

"Yes, that went over really well. But then, throughout history, thrones are rarely ascended by the most deserving, but the most conniving. And often, those accompanying the king are hardly looked upon as, shall we say, decent, upstanding citizens. Quite the opposite."

"As you said, it was my kingdom. And I don't run my kingdom that way. I know that. You know that. And they knew that, too. When I left you in charge of Gateau it was because you were the best choice to run it. Anyone foolish enough to think otherwise, soon had proof of their own idiocy." He shoved his hands deeper into his pockets. It was that, or reach for her. And he'd screwed up enough for one day. He ambled back around the counter, to the customer side of the display cases. She remained where he'd left her.

He turned when he got to the door. "I handled things the best way I knew how—which was to keep my hands off you, and let you fend for yourself, as I knew you would. Or you weren't meant to be there in the first place. If you'd come to me, and told me how you felt about it, I'd have explained why I handled it as I did. Though it wouldn't have changed things in the kitchen, you'd have known without a doubt, that you've always—always—had my full and utter support. What bothers me most is that I thought you already did know that. Apparently, it wasn't enough." He put his hand on the knob, then looked back at her one last time. "It was because of everything that happened, that you're not finding out until now."

She walked back to the register, standing behind the lower counter, where they could see each other fully. "Which part?"

"How I feel about you. Personally. From the moment you stepped into my kitchen you earned my professional respect . . . and neatly snagged all of my personal attention. But because of our positions and work environment, I could hardly do anything about it. I'd have never compromised you, or me, for that matter, or Gateau. But it doesn't change the fact that I wanted to. All the time. Hours on end. Pure torture. The television show offer was timely. A great opportunity, yes, but do you know what decided me on taking that leap? It offered a reprieve."

"You love being host of your own show. You're not capable of hiding your passion for things. How you feel is always written all over you. It's part of your charm. Which is why I'm still finding it hard—"

He strode across the shop in a few short steps, was around the counter before she had time to move. His hand was on the back of her neck and his mouth was on hers before his brain had a chance to make an argument against the action. He kissed her like a dying man.

And, this time . . . she kissed him back.

When he lifted his head, they were both breathing like they'd run a marathon. "Don't call me a liar, Leilani. It's insulting." He stepped back and she leaned on the counter for support after he let her go. He walked back to the door, knowing it was past time to leave. Before he put his hands on her again. Next time it wouldn't be just a kiss. And the nosy old biddies of Sugarberry would have a hell of a lot more than speculation to gossip about.

"Setting the show here was an excuse. I readily admit that. And using your shop as the set was nothing more than a way to be near you. To give me time—us time— and a good opportunity to work together as partners, not employer-employee, to see what could be, now that we're both in a position to do whatever we want. I honestly thought it was a harmless plan, and yes, that it might even be a good thing for your new business. No insult intended." Baxter braced himself in the open doorway, and looked directly at her. "I've meant every word I've said today, Leilani. And I meant what I told you this morning. I'm not doing fine without you. So, I did the only thing left to do. I came here to find out how life could be, *with* you." He closed the door behind him as he left, wishing he could close the door on their past just as easily.

And get her to open a new one to their possible future.

Chapter 5

"He kissed you."

Lani whisked the egg whites in the copper bowl so hard she was surprised they didn't turn to instant cement.

"Baxter," Charlotte stated, just as flat as Lani's egg whites. "*Our* Baxter." There was a pause, then, "Wow. That is so much better than a phone call."

Lani scowled at the cell phone she'd propped up on an oven mitt on the worktable. It didn't have quite the same impact as it would have if Charlotte were actually standing in the kitchen with her.

"So, he just . . . kissed you?" Charlotte asked. Again. "Just like that? *Twice?*"

"Yes. Don't make me repeat it over and over. I'm having a hard enough time dealing with the whole thing as it is."

"And this was yesterday, so you waited twenty-four hours to tell me. What kind of friend are you?"

"A friend who has a business to run, which was open all day today during the festival. Throw in last night's dinner and auction, an early bake start this morning in mad prep, then a crush of out-of-towners who wandered down from the Sea Islands later in the day to check out the festivities and slum with the locals, which wiped out even my refrigerated backstock, and left poor Dre up-front by herself while I baked more cupcakes. There hasn't been a spare second. I had my best sales day times ten, then went home and face planted for two whole, uninterrupted hours of merciful sleep."

"Only now you're not sleeping. You're baking. And I'm guessing it's not product for tomorrow."

"You'd think the sheer madness and constant intensity of it all would have taken my mind off . . . things. But I went through the whole day with this sick ball of dread in my stomach, waiting for Baxter to make his big entrance."

"Did he?" Charlotte asked. "What else haven't you told me?"

"Nothing. I've told you all of it. It's already bad enough as it is. No, he never showed up."

"You sound . . . disappointed."

"No. No, that's not it. Of course I'm not. I'm just . . . I'm annoyed that I was stupid enough to let him get to me like that and detract me from a day I was really looking forward to. I honestly thought he'd use the festival to make some big announcement, make his intentions known directly to everyone on the island, about filming his show here. But there wasn't a single sighting of him. I know he's not staying on Sugarberry. Everyone would know if that were the case, so he's probably over the causeway, maybe even staying somewhere in or around Savannah. Or on one of the bigger islands, at one of the resorts. Poor Alva, when he never made an appearance, everyone was starting to think she'd finally lost her marbles, with her claims of having talked to him and setting up a dinner and all."

"Alva?"

"I've mentioned her before. Poker player, renegade octogenarian, resident Betty White?"

"Right," Charlotte said, clearly not getting the reference. But she'd spent the first twelve years of her life in New Delhi. There were some cultural gaps.

"It doesn't matter. Except I had to keep vouching for her, which meant everyone is now speculating about me and Baxter. Thank God no one knows about the kiss."

"Kisses. Plural."

Lani might have growled a little.

"I'm just stating that it's only a matter of time before it's common knowledge, as he's clearly intent on—"

"Oh, I know what he says his intentions are, and, so far, he's not shy about exhibiting them. That's my whole point. I don't know what his next move is going to be. Where, when. Or what he's planning to do. And it's making me neurotic, Char. I know I'm completely wigging about this, but I have to find a way to deal with it. With him. I swear, it's like . . . it's like . . . he looked inside my head and plucked out the worst possible thing he could do to me."

"I don't think it's what's in your head he plucked at," Charlotte said, her tone considering now.

"You might be a pro when it comes to mincing chocolate, Char, but with words, not so much."

"You don't need me choosing my words carefully or coddling your sensitivities. And I was talking about your heart, not your—"

"Okay, okay." It didn't help that that part of Lani's

anatomy had also undergone a reawakening. Every time she thought about him, in fact.

"That's not what friends are for," Char went on. "And if you were a friend, you'd use your words, many of them, to tell me exactly what happened. Every last tiny detail."

"Charlotte—"

"You know, some women, women who'd been mooning over the same man for eons, would think they'd died and gone to heaven when that very man finally noticed them. Not you. You think it's the worst possible thing. I don't understand you."

"You understand me better than anyone walking this earth. You know I don't believe him. I mean . . . come on, Char. Me? All this time, he's been pining after his all-but-invisible number two? Really?"

"Hardly invisible. He kept you pinned to his side from the moment he met you. Handed his beloved baby over to you. I'd say you're about as high profile in his eyes as you could be."

"As a baker." Lani enunciated each word. "As a chef. Not as a woman."

"Put the bowl down," Char responded. "I can hear those whites turning to meringue all the way here in New York."

"They're supposed to be." But Lani clattered the bowl onto the worktable, not sure which she was more annoyed at: the eggs for not needing to be beaten longer and thereby giving her an outlet for her frustration . . . or this extended pity party she was throwing, starring herself as the featured guest.

"This isn't like you, Lan," Charlotte said, more quietly. "You're usually the grounded, rational, calm one. It's my job to be the neurotic, cynical, self-involved one. I'm worried about you. I simply think . . ."

When she trailed off, then didn't continue, Lani pushed back. "Think what? How else could I feel? Just finding out that he knew the whole time how I was being treated . . ."

"His explanation made sense," Charlotte offered, not unkindly.

"I know. It did. And . . . he's right. All things considered, he did the right thing, but he should have talked to me about it. Or I should have with him. But right now, after all that time . . . it's still a lot to take in, to process. I know this whole attitude thing isn't like me, but I feel . . . stuck. I've thought about it, a lot." It was why she was in her kitchen after her biggest business day ever, whipping up a pavlova roulade, when she should be happily falling asleep, with the lovely sound of *ka-ching* of her antique register still echoing in her ears.

"And?" Charlotte prodded.

After a short moment, Lani just spilled it all out, hoping Charlotte could help her make sense of her feelings. "I think—no, I know—I was never wholly myself with Baxter. He even commented on being surprised that I had a dry sense of humor today."

"In a bad way?"

"No, in a good way. But that's missing the point."

"So you say."

"My apron collection, that surprised him, too. He doesn't really know me, Char, that's what I'm getting at. I was only the chef part of myself with him. That meant I had to keep the foolish swooning girl with the crush locked away in the privacy of my own head, and, along with that, I kept a lot of the rest of myself locked away as well. I was never fully me. Certainly not with the staff, and not with him, either. When I came here, I think that's why I was so relieved. Here, I *can* just be me. Totally and utterly, without having to think or worry about . . . anything. Here, I am simply cupcake baker, daughter, island denizen, shopkeeper. And you have no idea how lovely, how heavenly, that has been."

Charlotte said nothing.

So Lani continued. "Then I read that stupid article yesterday morning, and my safe little haven wasn't safe anymore. Certainly everything that has happened since then has only made it worse. Far, far, worse, than even I could have imagined."

"I don't know why you're being so stubborn about this," Charlotte finally said.

Lani might have choked a little. "Stubborn?"

"About believing he really can feel what he feels for you. I mean, yes, it's inconvenient in some ways, but it's also kind of . . . exciting."

"Like watching a train wreck is exciting, maybe. Are you not hearing me?"

"I'm hearing you say you don't believe he knows you. Maybe not all of you, but enough to know that he wants to learn more. You might have only been a chef with him, but, Lan, a chef isn't just *what* you are, it's a big part of *who* you are. Possibly the biggest part. So, I think you need to have a little more faith. In Baxter— who, as far as I know, is not a manipulator or a liar— and in yourself. You two were perfect together."

Baxter's words about her all but calling him a liar echoed through her mind. "In the kitchen, as chefs, yes, we were in sync. But did you know I honestly thought he'd have respected me more as a chef if I were a man?"

"*What?* Since when?"

"I mean, I do know he respected me, obviously, but you and I have bitched many, many times about the gender bias we face in this industry, even as pastry chefs. Not that he ever said such a thing, but there was always this kind of vibe—under the surface—that he respected me despite my gender."

"You two were like a well-oiled machine from Day One. You were Yin to his Yang. And, if you ask me, vice versa. You made each other better. It wasn't just you who benefited from the Master-Grasshopper relationship. Why do you think your co-workers were so insanely jealous?"

"It was there, Charlotte. And how is it you can make an arcane character reference from *Kung Fu*, but have no idea who Betty White is?"

"I haven't the vaguest clue. Except I used to have a thing for David Carradine. He was hot, in this inscrutable, mysterious, sensitive but entirely alpha kind of way. I used to watch reruns of the show in New Delhi and want him for my very own. But, even if we go with your gender bias theory"—her tone made it clear what kind of stock she was putting in Lani's supposition—"did you ever stop to think maybe the thread of . . . whatever it was, the hint of disquiet you detected, was because of the very reason he stated?"

The sudden loud buzz of Charlotte's Kitchen Aid mixer blasted through the phone, making Lani flinch. It also, conveniently, kept her from being able to respond.

When it abruptly shut off again, Charlotte continued without giving her a chance to speak. "Your being a woman did disquiet him . . . but, if you ask me, it had nothing to do with gender bias."

Charlotte's mixer went back on, and stayed on, forcing Lani to think about what her closest friend had just said. Grumbling, Lani bumped the sound down on the phone and picked up the copper bowl and whisked in the sugar, one scoop at a time, until it thickened. She

set it down and went to get the bowl of coffee and
corn flour she'd whisked together earlier. The scent
of the ground coffee made her crave a cup. She
glanced at the clock. Ten-thirty. Definitely past a good
little baker's bedtime. And it was going to be another
very early morning.

Even after baking that afternoon while Dre covered
the counter, she'd been left with very few cupcakes to
refrigerate overnight, as she routinely did, selling
them as day olds the next day, for a reduced price. She
still had fresh frozen extra batches of unfrosted cupcakes, her base vanilla bean cake and semi-sweet chocolate, which she'd thaw, then pipe fresh frosting on in
the morning. Even with those she'd still be behind
with her freshly baked trademark flavors, no matter
how early a start she got. She'd whipped up some of
those frostings this evening, but everything else would
have to be made fresh from scratch in the morning.

She should be in bed, sleeping. Not standing in the
shop kitchen, experimenting with a pavlova roulade
she didn't need and couldn't sell. But therapy was
therapy, and she needed that, too.

Of course, she could be baking in her own little gal-
ley kitchen, where she'd at least have a bed close
by. But her place hadn't become home yet. It didn't
feel . . . therapeutic, or haven-like. Yet. She spent all
her time in the shop, happiest in the absolute haven
of her first, very own professional kitchen . . . so she
hadn't quite gotten around to doing much more than
shoving in the stuff she'd shipped down from her tiny
apartment in New York. It had hardly made a dent in
her far more spacious, though still small, island cottage. At some point she needed to work on that, but
beyond wondering how she could make the sandy soil
into a vegetable garden the next spring, she hadn't

really given much thought to what she wanted to do. Most of her thoughts and all of her energy were spent on baking and developing her business.

Besides, this feels like home, she thought. Kitchens always had for her. Her earliest memories involved helping her mom make dinner in the little kitchen in their row house in D.C., and baking with her Grandma Winnie in her big country kitchen in Savannah. Growing up, kitchens were always warm, lively, happy environments, filled with the most heavenly scents, some of which she'd helped create with her very own hands. She'd loved everything about cooking, about baking, especially for others. The fulfillment, the innate joy of making something that brought such pleasure to those she loved had only deepened as time went on.

Lani smiled at the memories, knowing those were the kind of memories she wanted to make here, even as the thought of it made the ache in her heart bloom as she missed her mom all over again. Her mother would have loved Cakes By The Cup. Lani would have given anything to be able to bake with her right here. Grandma Winnie, too.

Char's mixer abruptly stopped buzzing, jerking Lani from her thoughts. "So," Charlotte said, "can't you see that I might be right? I think he's had feelings all along. Why not give him a chance to prove to you he means what he says? You're understandably wary, but as you have that going in, you'll be careful enough."

Lani put the copper bowl down and leaned her hip against the stainless steel worktable. "And then what, Charlotte? What am I supposed to do? Have some sort of—fling—with him? I can't do that."

"Why on earth not? Last I checked you were both single, available, and now it seems, apparently willing. What's to stop you?"

"The part of me he's plucking at that's not my head. The part that will get hurt."

There was a pause and Lani braced for the mixer sound. Only it didn't come.

"Right," Charlotte said, at length. "You might have a point there." The sound of a knife, rapidly cutting on a board came through the phone. "So . . . it's still that strong for you, is it?"

Lani didn't answer. She was feeling foolish enough.

"When you saw him," Charlotte asked, "right at the first, when you turned and saw him standing in your kitchen, your initial reaction . . . what was it? That ball of dread? Or . . . ?"

"Or," Lani answered, then sighed.

"Oh, dear."

"Why do you think I left New York? I mean, not entirely. I came here for my dad, but Char, we both know I'd be lying if I said that wasn't a big part of it."

"You didn't even see him much, once he started his television show."

"Exactly. And nothing changed for me, nothing abated. It was like I couldn't have a life because I was too busy being stupid pining girl. Just running his kitchen was being too close. If I wanted any chance at moving forward with my life, my personal life, then I knew I had to get out of there. But I didn't. Couldn't."

"But you didn't have to give up your professional life, too. Why not another kitchen in the city? You could just about name your place with Gateau on your résumé."

"Because of the other part. My dad. I know you don't understand, Charlotte, not entirely, and you know how much I appreciate you supporting me anyway." Charlotte wasn't close to her parents, both of whom still lived in India and whom Lani had never met. But she knew from being with Charlotte during times when she'd been dealing with them that their cold, austere, judgmental attitudes made any real closeness all but impossible.

Thinking about her own father, Lani let out a half laugh that wasn't much of a laugh at all. "Actually, you're not alone. I found out yesterday morning that my dad doesn't really understand, either. But it's not just about me wanting to be here for him, with him. It was discovering that what made me happy and fulfilled was family, but also a sense of community, of putting down roots in a place that matters to me, that I can care about and will care back. About me. New York doesn't care whether I'm there or not."

"I care."

Lani sighed. "I know you do. I miss you and Franco like crazy. Leaving you was the only real sacrifice I made, but that says something all by itself, doesn't it? I don't miss the city. I don't miss the grind. I don't miss anything but the two of you. Now that I'm here, I can honestly say I know I wasn't meant for the intensity, the pressure of that lifestyle, that career. I thought it was what I wanted, what I had to reach for, to be the best I could be. I got all the education I could have dreamed of. And more. But this is where I really fit in. I love it here. The pace, the people. I feel like I've come home. And yes, running my own place has its own kind of insane pressure, because I don't know what I'm doing and I don't want to screw it up, but, Charlotte, I'm absolutely certain this is what I want to do with my life."

"I know," she said, unable to keep from sounding somewhat forlorn despite being supportive.

"So, I really and truly felt like I'd finally moved on," Lani explained. "In all ways. And then . . . and then,

Baxter just strolls in and announces he wants to give me the one thing I thought I'd wanted above all else? I can't risk allowing myself even a nibble of that, Char, can you understand? I mean, then what? If it doesn't work out, then he's forever left his imprint on this island, my place, my haven. That sucks. Sugarberry was supposed to forever be a Baxter-free zone."

"But what if it did work out?" Charlotte asked, though in a far more thoughtful tone than before. "Will you be okay if you never find out what might have been? Have you thought about that?"

"That's just it. It's almost all I have thought about. Since he walked out of my shop yesterday—for the second time—I haven't been able to string two thoughts together without him popping up between them. That's why I dreaded him showing up again. I didn't—don't—have an answer for him. Or for myself. Not one that makes it all better, anyway. I mean . . . the way he looked at me, and said the things he said, the way he kissed me . . ." She trailed off, then pressed a fist against the little tug she felt on her heart. "What if I do go after him, Char, and . . . and it works for us . . . then what? I'm not going back to New York, to run his kitchen or open my own there. He's hardly going to relocate his television show to Sugarberry full time, much less open his own place down here, or even try to run Gateau from here. So, what kind of future would we have? Some kind of long distance deal?"

Charlotte said nothing. Because, Lani well knew, there was nothing to say.

"So, it's just . . . it feels cruel to me," Lani said. "You know? Him coming here, dangling this dream I'd let go of in front of me. Why couldn't he just stay in New York, and let me move on?"

There was a knock on the back door, which had

Lani whirling around, clattering the empty sugar bowl to the floor. "Jesus, what is up with people scaring the crap out of me lately?"

"Lani?" Charlotte called. "What happened?"

"Someone's at the delivery door. It's after ten-thirty at night."

"Don't open it! Grab a rolling pin! Get your taser!"

Lani smiled as she put the bowl in the sink, wiped her hands, and walked to the back door. "I'm not in New York any more, Char. I hardly think it's someone come to kill me." *Just to break my heart,* she thought, girding herself for whatever was about to happen. Or, more to the point, whoever. At least he hadn't just strolled in. Of course, the door was locked.

But when she peeked through the curtains . . . it was Alva Liles standing on the other side of the door. Not Baxter. Lani quickly flipped the dead bolt, undid the lock, and opened the door, leaving the screen door between them. It was early October, but the night air was still quite warm as Indian summer lingered. And lingered. "Is everything okay?" Lani asked, not able to fathom what would bring the older woman to her back door at such an hour.

"I saw your light on in the back. I hope you don't mind the intrusion this late at night. Would it be okay if I came in? It will only take a moment."

"Uh, sure, of course." Alva stepped back so Lani could open the screen door, then moved around and stepped inside.

Lani had to bite down on a smile when she saw what Alva was wearing. It was a teal velour track suit with white piping on the jacket and down the sides of the legs, matching the bright white of the track shoes on her feet. Her hair and makeup were still first-thing-in-the-morning perfect. Only Alva. Lani had learned early on from Grandma Winnie that Southern women never left the house without eyebrows properly penciled, lipstick applied, and cheeks rouged to rosy perfection. Since Lani had never even seen Alva in pants, she wouldn't have thought the senior owned such a casual outfit. Much less that she would be seen in it in public.

"Lan?" Charlotte called out. "Is everything okay?"

"Oh." Lani dashed back to the phone. "I'm sorry, Char, it's . . . a neighbor."

"Not—"

"It's Alva, it's fine." Lani cut her off, shooting Alva a quick smile. She scooped up the phone and flipped it off speaker. "I just—I need to let you go."

"Okay," Charlotte said. "We'll talk tomorrow?"

"Tomorrow is the town picnic and softball game."

"I thought the festival was today?"

"It was. The picnic and softball game is a thing they do every Sunday afternoon, at least until we turn the clocks forward next month. Then it's touch football and a bonfire."

"How . . . quaint."

Lani laughed. "You're such a snob."

"I know. My parents would be so proud."

Only because the topic of Charlotte's parents and her rigid upbringing had long since been beaten to death in previous baking therapy sessions was it okay for Lani to laugh—which she did. "If they could only see you now."

"Right," Charlotte said. "Baking late night red velvet therapy cakes in my no-bedroom studio walk up over Mr. Lu's carryout."

"And to think, they wanted you to be a heart surgeon."

"The mind boggles. I can't imagine why I'd rather

spend my nights elbow deep in red gel paste and shaved chocolate, instead of in red blood inside a cracked open, shaved chest."

Lani made a gagging noise. "Yuck."

"My sentiments exactly. I'm in charge of a small evening cocktail and dessert event tomorrow, so I'll be in by ten for prep. Call me." Charlotte paused. "I want to know how things are going. Don't torture me."

"I won't. I'll call. Promise."

"Love."

"Me, too." Lani hung up and turned back to Alva with a true smile. "So . . . what's up?"

"I'm so sorry. I've clearly interrupted." She looked past Lani to the worktable. "You're working on something else special for us, aren't you? I shouldn't have intruded on your work time—"

"No, no, this is just"—Lani realized she couldn't explain baking therapy, so she smiled—"experimenting. It's how I come up with new ideas." It wasn't entirely untrue, just not exactly the case that evening.

"Oh. Well, then!" The worry left Alva's face, and a bit of that gleam returned to her eyes. She stepped to the table to take a closer look. "How exciting." She sounded entirely sincere. "It must be fun to work with new ideas." She turned and beamed up at Lani. "When my Harold was alive, I used to try out new recipes on him all the time. Bless his heart, he never said an unkind word. And there were some duds in there, let me tell you."

Lani's smile deepened. "Cooking for people you love is always the best."

Alva nodded in agreement and went back to examining the table. "Don't let me keep you from your work. I can talk while you do whatever it is you're doing."

From behind Alva, Lani sighed a little, but kept her smile.

"What is it, exactly, you're making, dear?" Alva asked.

Lani stepped back over to the worktable. "It's a mango passion fruit with coffee meringue roulade. Sort of like a pavlova, in a roll."

"Well, my goodness, that sounds exotic. Like something you'd have on a cruise ship. Harold and I took a cruise once. To Bermuda. Made the poor man sick as a dog. I don't think I've ever seen skin turn that particular shade of green." She stopped and glanced up at Lani again. "Perhaps not the best story to discuss while baking."

Lani's smile warmed. Alva was just so . . . Alva. "Why don't you tell me why you stopped by?" Lani picked up the copper bowl and looked at the meringue mixture of whipped egg whites and sugar and saw that it had begun to break down, so she gave it a quick whip, then went ahead and folded in the corn flour and coffee she'd whisked together earlier.

"Well, dear, I need a word with you, and I don't want the whole town to know about it. I stopped by your place, but it was dark as a crypt, so I came by here and saw the light. I was hoping you wouldn't mind. It'll only take a few minutes of your time."

"No, that's fine." Lani began spreading the meringue in a thin, continuous layer on the baking parchment she'd layered into the prepared Swiss roll pans. It would set up okay. Besides, it wasn't like she was serving it to anyone.

"Here," Alva said, stepping around to the same side of the table. "I can do that for you. Then you can get to the next step."

"Oh, you don't have to—"

"Dear, I've been making fruit rolls since your mama was a little girl. I can spread a meringue."

Lani handed her the spatula. "It should make four. When they're spread, layer these evenly over the tops." She handed Alva a bowl of pistachios sliced lengthways.

"Oh, that's going to be almost indecently delicious."

Alva went to work as Lani nodded. What she was going to do with four fruit rolls, as Alva called them, she had no idea, but it wasn't in her to just make one of something. Bakers baked. And, tonight, she'd needed the distraction.

She glanced at Alva, intently spreading away, tongue tucked in the corner of her cheek, and smiled at herself. Okay, maybe not this much of a distraction. It definitely wasn't like having Charlotte in the kitchen for a late night bitch-and-bake session, but . . . it wasn't so bad. Not so bad at all, really. And maybe Alva would take one of the roulades with her. Or two. "Let me get you an apron."

"Oh, you can hardly do anything to this old thing I'm wearing."

"Still . . ." Lani opened the door to the small cupboard she'd had built beside her office door. She pulled out the uppermost of the three drawers that filled the bottom half and fingered through the stack of folded aprons that lay inside, trying to decide which one wouldn't entirely swamp Alva's tiny body. Her smile grew as she pulled out the bottom drawer. She'd saved her childhood aprons out of sentimentality and had stored them in the cupboard of her new kitchen for good luck and because seeing them again when she'd unpacked had filled her with the kind of memories she wanted to create for herself. Didn't mean they couldn't also be useful. She took the top one off the carefully folded stack and shook it loose. Then laughed.

"What is it, dear?" Alva said.

Lani held the apron up in front of her. "How do you feel about My Little Pony?" As she turned around, she almost dropped the apron entirely when she spied Alva standing on top of an empty, upside down five gallon bucket.

"I couldn't reach the back of the pans," Alva explained. "And maybe I will take you up on the apron. When I lean over, my jacket dangles. I don't fill it out like I used to. Things have shifted over time."

Lani somehow managed not to laugh. She helped Alva down from the bucket, then looped the apron over Alva's head and Alva made quick work of tying it in the back.

The older woman smiled and held out her arms, turning to one side, then the other. "What do you think? Is lavender my color?" Alva modeled the purple-maned and spangly white horse that decorated much of the apron front.

"It's you," Lani said, and they both laughed. "But I don't want you on that bucket. I'll do the back of the pans and get them in the oven. How are you with cutting up fruit?"

Alva's eyes gleamed, a bit too brightly, Lani thought. "Actually, dear, that might be just the thing for me this evening. What do you need chopped? I'm good with a knife."

Lani narrowed her gaze thoughtfully. Alva had done an excellent job on the meringue, so Lani shrugged and got the mangoes and passion fruits from the cooler drawer. She should have prepped them first, but the whipping required for the meringue had called more loudly to her therapy needs. Better, probably, than knives, anyway, given her mood at the time.

She got out the boards and one of her smaller paring knives. "Nothing fancy," she told Alva. "Just work around the stone, and dice the fruit into chunks, about three-quarter-inch square, give or take. Try not to handle them more than necessary, so they don't get pulpy, but make the chunks as uniform in size as possible. And—"

"I'll be careful, dear." Alva reassured her with a patient smile. "I may not be a fancy chef like you, but I've made enough jams and pies in my eighty-two years. I'm pretty sure I can get through a handful of mangoes without removing any fingers."

"I'm sure you can," Lani said with a grin as she watched Alva get started, then began prepping the passion fruit. "So, what has you wanting to chop things into little pieces?" Lani asked mildly as Alva went to town on the first mango. "Would it have anything to do with why you came by?"

"Something like that." Alva continued chopping, making surprisingly short work out of the awkwardly shaped mango with its random center stone. "Remember when I stopped by before the dinner and auction and told you about Beryl and Dee Dee?"

"Of course. I'm really sorry you didn't end up getting the cupcakes." Lani sent a sideways glance at Alva, debating on how to handle things. "But I heard they went to the volunteer fire department and the sheriff's office, so that's good." It had been quite a fierce bidding war, as it turned out. And now she'd have to keep an eye on her dad's sugar intake.

"Yes, well, they're deserving young men," Alva said. *Chop, chop, chop, chop.*

Lani kept an eye on Alva's knife work. Dee Dee's

husband was retired from the sheriff's department and still very active in training new recruits, and Suzette's son-in-law was the current fire chief, so it had made perfect sense for the women to bid on the cupcakes. Lani knew it likely had absolutely nothing to do with why they spent a small fortune to secure all twelve boxes between the two of them. They'd set a record for any previous Kiwanis Club entry.

"Well, somehow Dee Dee got wind of my little side deal with Beryl, so she and Suzette got in cahoots together to trump me. I'm sure Louise contributed, too. Laura Jo said she overheard Louise saying that I've let running the group go to my head, that I've gone power mad. Her words!"

"Alva, you started the group, so I hardly think—"

"So, I told them that rather than share—generously, I might add—as I'd planned, I'd just keep Baxter Dunne to myself. I'll invite him to my place, cook him a good country meal, maybe some of Harold's favorites, and get the scoop for my first column."

"But, you haven't set up dinner with Baxter, have you?"

"I certainly will before this is over," Alva exclaimed, then made quick, violent work of the next mango.

Lani wisely held her tongue. "What can I do to help? I don't think I can convince Baxter to—"

"I don't need your help with Baxter, dear. What I wanted to talk to you about is coming up with something else for Monday night's tournament. Just between the two of us. I know I can trust you not to go blabbing, your father being the sheriff and all. And your mother was the sweetest thing this side of heaven. You come from good stock. I know I can trust you."

"Alva—"

"I need a new secret weapon, Lani May. I know

you're busy, and probably a bit done in after the festival today. I wouldn't ask if it weren't important. But it's not just about getting Beryl her title back anymore."

Lani stopped breaking down the passion fruits. "What, exactly, did you have in mind?" she asked warily.

"Well, dear"—Alva smiled ever so sweetly at Lani—"that would be up to you."

"Me?"

Alva nodded. "It has to be something original, that they've never tried before. Something decadent, impossible to resist, preferably with a lot of chocolate. A little booze in the mix couldn't hurt, either."

"Of course." Lani shook her head, and went back to her passion fruit, wondering at the wisdom of putting herself right in the middle of the Sugarberry Island Poker Tournament wars.

"Of course, if you could top those little gems you donated to the auction, well, that would just ice the cake, wouldn't it?" Alva's eyes twinkled.

No, not power mad at all. Lani found herself wondering what kind of man Harold Liles must have been. And, come to think of it, exactly how it was the poor man had died . . . "How many would you need?"

"Would thirty-six be asking too much? Of course, I'll be happy to pay whatever special order price you think is warranted." Alva finished the last mango with a flurry of chopping. "Oh, the look in their eyes when I unveil my little cakes," she said, then turned and gave Lani the sweetest smile as she handed her the chopped fruit. "There you go, dear. Are these up to snuff?"

Lani had already decided it didn't matter what they looked like, she was taking Alva's knife away, but had to admit, they were almost culinary school perfect. "Those are, well, they're great."

Alva patted Lani on the arm. "Sometimes age has it over experience."

"Sometimes," Lani agreed. "Let me think on the cupcakes and we'll go over a few ideas tomorrow?"

"No, dear, I don't want even the wisp of a suspicion on this."

"We talk to each other all the time."

"How about tomorrow morning, then? I'll come by before going to Sunday services, before you open. I'll just come around to the back here, like tonight. One knock. No, maybe three knocks." She was clearly relishing the cloak and dagger element, as much as the trump card plan itself.

Lani was already wishing she'd skipped baking therapy and gone home to bed, like a good little baker. But no . . . "Okay. That will be fine."

Alva took off her apron. "Well, this has been quite lovely." She looked at her blocks of neatly chopped mango. "Rather calming, too, I must say." She smiled up at Lani. "Makes me want to go home and bake something."

Lani didn't point out it was after eleven o'clock. Maybe the woman didn't sleep. It wouldn't surprise her in the least.

"Perhaps I'll start mentally preparing my dinner menu for Baxter. Won't that be fun?"

"Absolutely." If Lani wasn't still so mixed up about Baxter, she'd call and warn him. Then it occurred to her that she could benefit from the distraction Alva would provide.

Alva handed the apron to Lani. "Good night now, dear. You should be getting some sleep, too, shouldn't you? Big day tomorrow! See you in the morning."

With that, she bustled out the door and into the night, like a little white-haired apparition.

"You said you wanted to be part of the community," Lani muttered as she locked up behind her. "Here's your chance."

The oven buzzers went off for the cupcakes she'd put in before Alva's arrival pulling Lani back to work.

But instead of thinking about Baxter, or the roulade, or all the cupcakes she had to replenish by tomorrow, she purposely started working up a new recipe. For Alva's New Secret Weapon Cakes.

Therapy was therapy, after all.

Chapter 6

Baxter drove the causeway over Ossabaw Sound to Sugarberry, reviewing in his mind exactly what he was going to say to Leilani that morning. Considering his production crew would begin arriving in several hours and continue throughout the day, it was rather critical that he get it right this time.

After a quick overnight back to New York to film his "surprise" guest appearances on two of the national morning talk shows and three of the evening entertainment news programs, he'd actually been happy to check back into his rooms at the hotel in Savannah late last night. Despite the surprising autumn heat and humidity, he found the historic city to be charming, welcoming, and rather more delightful than he'd anticipated. It was nothing at all like England, but there was an old world feel to it that definitely resonated with him.

He was a city boy to the core, addicted to the hustle, the bustle, the vibrant energy. It matched his drive perfectly and he thrived in the push and shove of it all. He'd anticipated the slow-as-molasses pace of the

Southern way of life would frustrate him beyond reason. Perhaps it was because he was so frustrated with himself and Leilani at the moment that he'd found the unhurried pace surprisingly soothing instead.

He'd cracked open the windows in his room before climbing into bed and found the strange sounds of the night almost . . . lulling in their repetitive cycles. Nary a horn or siren to be heard. Just chirping, croaking, and several other indigenous sounds whose origins were probably better left unknown. He'd awakened refreshed and more energized than he'd anticipated after a whirlwind thirty-six hours of flying and talking. And talking, and talking, endlessly, shamelessly plugging the show. It wasn't his favorite part of the spectacle that was television, but he was passionate about *Hot Cakes,* so, at the very least, he was sincere while pitching the third season to the masses.

It was already filmed and in editing and postproduction, meaning his main duty was done. The newly picked up fourth cycle was currently dominating all of his attention. Normally a few episodes were filmed, edited, and ready to go prior to the season launch, but new material for the current season would still be filming as the first episodes began to air. Due to his brilliant idea for the next series, his team had worked tirelessly to get the entire current season in the can prior to the season debut, giving them time to prep and work through the complicated logistics required for the next run. And complicated it would be, because, this go around, they wouldn't be working in the well-appointed network studio, on a set already precision lit, engineered for proper sound, with camera angles rigged to get every view possible of the food and the chef. All of which was built around a meticulously designed kitchen set, and teamed with its own behind-the-scenes prep kitchen that was put to full use for every single episode.

No, they wouldn't have anywhere near that luxury, because Baxter had had the brilliant idea to take his show, literally, on the road. Out of the big city, and into the heartland of America, showing his viewers how his amazing, upscale urban desserts could be adapted to fit their small town lifestyles and family favorite menus.

He hadn't the vaguest clue how he was going to pull that off.

The entire rationale behind his brainstorm— which the network bigwigs had all but drooled over, despite the increase in production costs—was simply a means to an end. The end being to spend time with Leilani . . . and hopefully convince her to leave Sugarberry at some point and continue on with him. How or doing what, he didn't care. Whatever role she wanted to take on, he'd support her choice. As long as it got them back side by side.

She had to be suffocating, trapped on a tiny island, creating such a limited menu. She'd declared it her passion, but Baxter had begun to suspect that it was really a form of hiding out. Of retreating from the field of battle. She might think it was what she wanted forever and ever, but he knew her better than that. Or surely, he knew her talent would eventually demand better than that.

She'd taken a stance, and from what he'd seen, would stand by it whether she was truly happy or not. Perhaps she'd reconsider if a better offer came along, one that would allow her to make new choices without insulting anyone or looking like she didn't know what she wanted. He hoped that he might be that new choice. Or, at least, a large part of it.

Life—his life—he'd quickly discovered, was better with Leilani in it.

And so, here he was, out in the marshy hinterlands. By choice. God help him.

A variety of bugs had already decorated his windshield by the time he bumped over the grids at the end of the causeway and eased his rental car onto the little island. *How on earth had Leilani made a home here?* He knew her father lived here, and she'd relocated as a way to be closer to him . . . but Savannah was little more than an hour west. Though hardly a thriving metropolis on the scale of New York or Chicago, its unique, historic landscape was still a far better match for Lani's remarkable skills than . . . this.

Baxter squinted at the rising sun, wishing he'd thought to buy a pair of sunglasses. He wasn't used to being outside during daylight hours. By the age of twelve, he'd been in a kitchen every morning before the sun came up, and hadn't left until well after sundown. These days if it wasn't an actual kitchen, it was a kitchen set, or a planning room, or his office. And always—always—wherever he was, when he did step outside, it was to the familiar sounds and smells of a city. Whether it be London or New York, there was always a sense of familiarity, of home, just on sight and smell alone.

Driving onto Sugarberry—hell, driving at all, he didn't even own a car—he might as well have been driving onto the moon. The marshes, dunes, and wilderness landscape were that foreign to him. There was one main paved road that looped around the entire island, which, as far as he could tell, was only a few kilometers wide, and maybe twice that in length. The township, also named Sugarberry, was located on the southern end of the island, built around a small, tidy town square. He'd thought it rather incongruous in an otherwise undeveloped, rather bohemian island setting, especially one that was more marsh than proper land. Perhaps it was the Southern influence. He wasn't sure. It was a traditional square, with shops on all four sides and a small park area built into the middle. The park featured a rather large fountain at its center, in the midst of which rose quite a large statue, no doubt someone of historic Sugarberry importance.

Farther south, the tip of the island was dotted with several piers where the local fishermen tied up their boats when they weren't plying their livelihood on the open sea. There were no pleasure boats with big sails, much less yachts of any size, harbored at Sugarberry. It was a working man's island and the boats reflected that. He'd been made aware that farther down the coast, there were other barrier islands that featured upscale country clubs and resorts, beautifully designed golf courses, with restaurants and yacht clubs to match.

That was definitely not the case for Sugarberry. If the town council was making any attempt to lure the tourist trade, Baxter would be surprised.

Several narrow streets extended out from the town square on the three sides leading away from the fishing piers, some paved, some layered with centuries of crushed shells making it feel as if he were back home in London, driving over old cobblestones. The streets in that part of town were mostly lined with clapboard houses, usually painted white or gray, featuring rustic front porches and small yards largely devoid of any kind of grass. Most were covered in pine needles or otherwise landscaped with shrubs, flowers, and an occasional stubby palmetto.

Some lots were bigger and grander, with larger houses set farther back from the road. These were framed with colorful shutters and doors and often had deeper wraparound front and side porches. Those larger lots ended just before the western stretch of the island loop that led right back to the causeway. The shoreline on the west side had no beach, but devolved into a series of lagoons and marshes leading into the channel formed by the sound between Sugarberry and the uninhabited marshlands that crowded the Georgia shoreline.

To the east of the square, the streets ended at the loop road. Some houses dotted the far side along the loop road, but mostly it was an unending stretch of dense growth, sand dunes, and sea grasses, beyond which was an unbroken narrow stretch of beach, then the Atlantic Ocean. Not that he'd checked that out personally, but it was all part of the information his staff had gathered when he'd offered Sugarberry up as a location. He wasn't sure if there were other cottages or houses tucked back amongst or past the dunes, but he rather thought that would be the place he'd want to hole up . . . if holing up was what one wanted to do. Why else come to such a remote place?

The entire northern end of the island was undeveloped wilderness, lagoon, and marsh. In that same preliminary research packet, he'd read there were a few research centers set up by several local universities to study the flora and fauna. Something about some kind of small deer and loggerhead turtles, he seemed to recall. As he'd driven the loop road on his first visit to the island, that entire area had seemed inhospitable at best, and possibly dangerous at worst. Who knew what kind of beasties made their homes in the wet, dank, and dark? If anyone lived back there other than the occasional college student researcher, they were welcome to it.

Baxter kept to the developed end of the island. He drove straight to the town square, then past it a block, before turning down a narrow alleyway running behind the row of shops on the east side of the square. Leilani's Cakes By The Cup was in the center of that row. He pulled into the gravel and crushed shell lot that formed the rear parking area for the row and pulled up to the delivery door marked CUPCAKERY.

"Cupcakes," he said, turning off the engine. He could mentally picture, in great detail, some of the grand, intricately detailed pastries and cakes Lani had constructed at Gateau. Her inspired creations had drawn raves. She hadn't been a Beard nominee during her first year of eligibility for nothing. She'd worked tirelessly to perfect even the tiniest detail, not because the client—or an awards committee—would have noticed, but because it mattered to her that each effort be her best. In fact, it was her work ethic and dedication that had first caught his attention.

She wasn't a grandstander, like most with her natural ability, behaving in whatever manner it took to stick out and be noticed. She let her work speak for her. And speak it did. It fairly shouted, in fact. Once he'd noticed, he couldn't help being further captivated by how different her demeanor was from most budding chefs. Bravado, with a healthy dose of self-confidence bordering on arrogance, was a trademark of the profession. Some would say it was a requirement. Leilani's quiet charm, and what he'd come to describe as her relentless calm and ruthless optimism had made an indelible mark on him. She wasn't like any baker he'd ever met, much less any top-notch chef.

She cared, she labored—hard—and she lived, breathed, ate, and slept food, as any great chef did. But she was never frantic, never obsessed, never . . . overwrought, as most great chefs were. That teetering-off-the-cliff verve was the atmosphere he'd lived in, thrived on, almost his entire life. Leilani had that same core passion in spades, but it resided in a special place inside her. She simply allowed it to flow outward, like a quietly rippling stream, steady and true. As even the gentlest flowing stream could wear away the sturdiest stone, so had Leilani worn down any resistance he'd tried to build up against her steady charm . . . and she'd done it without even trying.

The woman he'd encountered in that very kitchen two days before hadn't been at all like the chef he'd trained and worked with so intimately. He'd thought he knew her every nuance, her every mood—most of them positive and upbeat. The tense, brusquely dismissive woman he'd encountered had thrown him off entirely. In fact, the only familiar thing about her had been her Gateau jacket.

He remembered the apron she'd worn, with the Hatter at tea. Her hair twined up, messy and soft, but her demeanor certain, and somewhat brusque, at least where he was concerned. She'd been different when he'd first walked into the front of her bake shop, when she'd been dealing with her customer, Miss Alva, before she'd noticed his arrival. Only then had he caught a glimpse of the woman who'd so completely turned his head. Changed his world. His entire world. A world he was changing again, for her.

She'd been smiling, calmly composed and content, happily at home in her natural habitat. Then she'd spied him . . . and everything had changed.

He climbed out of the car, telling himself it was that

abrupt change in demeanor that had driven him to behave so recklessly, so ... demonstratively. He'd thought a lot about that kiss. A whole lot about that kiss.

He wished he felt more sorry about it than he did, as it could likely prove to be his downfall in his mission. But he couldn't. It had been too ... perfect. Like a soufflé that combined airiness and light, with that rich, dark, kicky finish. Yes, that kiss had lingered on his lips ... and permanently in his memory, ranking up there along with the richest, most decadent desserts he'd ever had the pleasure of sampling.

Just like those decadent desserts, he was equally driven to taste her again. As passionate as he'd ever been to create the most amazing flavor combinations, the richest and most unique desserts, Lani was like that to him. For as long as he could remember, that passion had always been everything.

He opened the screen door and gently turned the doorknob, deciding entry without knocking was the only way to be certain he'd gain entrance at all. It was the one risk he had to take, but the only one he'd take. This time.

He quietly pushed the door open and was immediately assaulted with the sound of unidentifiable music—if you could call it that—crashing and cascading about the small interior of her kitchen.

He slipped inside, thinking with the music so loud, he'd wave, or do something to get her attention, so he didn't scare her half to death like last time. When he finally spied her, he found himself pausing, the door still only half closed behind him.

She was wearing her Gateau chef coat again. Only that wasn't why he paused. And was smiling.

She was dancing.

Her hair was up in a twisted, messy knot on the back of her head, a pastry bag in her hand, and more racks of cupcakes lining every table in front of her than anyone should ever have to face. At least all at once. Had he not been so entranced by the vision of her hips shimmying while she shook her shoulders to the beat at the same time, he'd have wasted at least a second or two wondering how on earth she could find even a sliver of creative satisfaction in mass producing such unexciting little bits of cake. But every last ounce of his attention was riveted on her.

He really should let her know he was standing there. It was a train wreck, really—or a cupcake wreck at best—simply waiting to happen, the moment she swiveled around and saw him. But . . . who knew she could move like that? So sinuously, and . . . and . . . hip thrusty. And then, heaven help him, she actually started singing.

Had she been all off key and off pitch, it would have jerked him out of his momentary fascinated state. But no. No. She further slayed him by whole-heartedly belting out, in a gravelly voice worthy of the best girl rocker from any era, the refrain of whatever godforsaken tune was pulsing out of the small portable stereo perched on one of the shelves across the room.

While he thought the music quite atrocious . . . her singing was not. In fact . . . where on earth did that voice come from? Where did any of it come from? She was his quiet, calm, center-of-the-storm partner in chaos. Or she had been.

"Who are you?"

He hadn't realized he'd spoken out loud until she spun around, halfway through miming a decidedly erotic air guitar riff on her pastry bag. Her accompa-

nying growl shifted to a choked scream of surprise. Simultaneously, and—he hoped—inadvertently, her
shock caused her to squeeze her pastry bag rather indelicately, resulting in him being the dead-on target
for a steady stream of chocolate buttercream frosting,
which hit him square in the chest. A chest not covered
by a chef's jacket, but by a rather expensive tailored
linen shirt. White linen, in fact. Or it had been.

"What on earth are you—" She broke off and went
over to slap, rather indelicately if you asked him, the
button on the top of the stereo, mercifully silencing
the small kitchen.

"Oh, thank God," he murmured, before thinking
better of it.

"I beg your pardon? In fact, I beg a lot of things.
First of all, why do you keep doing that? Who do you
think you are? You don't just come into my place
unannounced, especially through my back door."

"Perhaps you should keep it locked," he said, somewhat absently. He was still holding his arms slightly
out to the side, looking at the glob of chocolate cream
presently oozing down his chest.

"Perhaps you should leave. Looks like you need to
go change shirts."

"It was a good shirt." He looked up to find her glar-
ing, pastry bag still held at the ready. "Though I suppose I deserved it for startling you"—he smiled, just a
little—"again."

"You suppose?" She arched her eyebrow. His charm
was clearly not working on her.

"You're right, I should have announced myself, and
I planned to. Just as soon as I let myself in." He lifted a
hand to stall her retort. "I own up to that, but I wasn't
certain you'd invite me in. I did take that one small

liberty, then I was going to say hullo straight off, but there was loud music—if you can call it that—and you were—well, you were dancing."

"I'm sorry, does that violate a health code I'm unaware of?"

"Of course not, it was just . . . unexpected. You never once danced in my kitchen. Not so much as a hip wiggle. Much to my dismay, now that I've seen an example of it."

She didn't so much as crack the tiniest smile.

He lowered his arms and sighed. "I've managed to muck this all up again, haven't I? I swear, that was not my intent."

"Well, gosh, I should hope not. What was your intent?"

"To talk to you. Privately. Not in front of your customers this time."

"About?"

"When did you get so—"

"Didn't we have this conversation already once?"

"Yes. But I don't understand it now any better than I did then. I—you were always calm, and kind, and . . . well, cheerful. I'm really not trying to provoke you, but I've seen you under some exceedingly dire levels of stress, and your usual response was to simply get calmer, and more cheerful, which was always to me the oddest thing, but, for you, it worked. And it worked for me. Now you're . . . impatient. And short, and abrupt. It's just . . . so not at all like you. Is there something going on with the shop? Are you struggling?"

"When you came in, if you recall, I was happy. Upset, stressed out, angry people aren't usually singing and dancing."

"Fair point." He looked down at his shirt again,

swiped a dollop of buttercream onto his finger, and looked back at her. "So, it's just me then? Who provokes this response from you?"

"Pretty much."

"Why?"

"Because you're the only thing in my world at the moment that doesn't make me feel like singing or dancing."

He'd slid his buttercream covered finger into his mouth, but paused, his expression going slack. Along with his shoulders. Because, if he didn't know any better, and he did, she was being quite sincere. He licked his finger clean, then quietly said, "I'm sorry you feel that way."

"How else am I supposed to feel, Baxter? You come here, planning to turn my life into a small circus, without warning. I came here for the quiet, for the calm I don't have to create myself. It just exists around me, naturally, all by itself. All I have to do is enjoy it, embody it, wallow in it. If I'd wanted to live with the circus, I'd have stayed in New York."

"This is quite amazing, you know," he said, taking another small lick from his shirt. "What's in it?"

"Baxter—"

"I'm sorry. No," he added, when he thought she might plaster him again. "I am. But it's just . . . I wasn't expecting to taste something with such—"

"Complex flavors? Why? Because I'm just decorating cupcakes? After all, only peasants eat cupcakes and what would they know about a good flavor profile? Wow, that's insulting on so many levels I don't know where to begin. So I won't. Get out."

"Leilani—"

"Out. Of my shop. Of my life."

He sighed again, with a little swearing under his

breath thrown in for good measure. "You're putting words in my mouth."

"Are you telling me that you looked at that table full of cupcakes and thought, 'wow, what a delightful, inventive creative use of her talent?' "

"That you're so defensive—without the slightest provocation on my part, I might add—is only proof that maybe you're feeling they aren't up to your usual brilliant standards. I didn't say anything about your choice of product."

"You didn't have to. The look on your face just now when you tasted that frosting said it all for you. Which is another reason I don't need you waltzing into my life on your whim, sniffing at my work, which is my livelihood now. I respect you, as a chef, more than anyone I've ever had the pleasure to work with, or whose work I've ever had the pleasure of tasting. I thought I'd earned some measure of respect from you as well—"

"You know you have," he said. "I wouldn't have come all the way down here if I didn't respect your work."

"As long as I'm baking what you think I should bake. Right? I thought this wasn't about my abilities. You said—"

"My respect for you as a chef and as a woman go hand in hand."

"Ah. So my baking cupcakes . . . well, I guess that would certainly have to stop then, if . . . you know, that other part of what you said . . . if that part happened. Because this woman? She bakes cupcakes now. And we can't be having any of that if your respect is to be maintained."

If he hadn't have been so worked up, so . . . well, flustered himself, he'd have seen how flustered she'd suddenly become trying to discuss his previously stated interest in her. In pursuing her. As a woman. Not as a chef. Because he saw his entire hopes and dreams sinking like a half baked soufflé right in front of his eyes, he blurted, "Are you sincerely happy baking cupcakes, Leilani? I mean, are you fulfilled here? Have you just given up on that amazing creative mind you have, and working your genius in ways that—" He broke off as he saw the shutters come down over her eyes. He thought back to what he'd just said, and her comment about disrespecting her chosen livelihood when she'd done nothing but respect his . . . and wanted to grab the pastry bag from her hands and just shoot himself with it. In the head. "I'm such an idiot."

"Don't look for an argument from me."

"I don't disrespect you. As a chef, and as a woman, I have only the highest regard. I'm just . . . I'm confused, that's all. Sincerely confused. I'm not condemning your choice, I'm really not," he assured her when she merely rolled her eyes. "I'm just trying to understand it."

"Just because it's not a choice you can fathom making for yourself, does not mean it's not the right one for me."

"I do understand that. I'm . . . I'm simply trying to understand you. Who you are. I thought . . . I guess I thought I knew. And now . . ."

"I was a chef with you. Beginning, middle, and end. That's who you knew, Baxter. Leilani Trusdale, pastry chef. You don't know all the rest of what makes me who I am. I'm more than a pastry chef. I'm a woman with diverse interests, a wide range of moods, a brand-new set of goals and dreams I'm making come true. And, you know what? I honestly don't think you'd be attracted to that woman. If you can't even fathom what it is I'm doing here, or trying to do, much less

why I'd want to do it, I can guarantee you I'm not the
woman you think I am. Or want me to be. Nor will I
ever be that woman."

He was hearing what she was saying, every last word
of it. But it wasn't computing. Not because it didn't
ring true, but because it did. There was no doubt she
was speaking the truth. Her truth.

"You're saying I'm a snob, then." He was stung by it,
because it was the very last thing he'd felt he was. But,
given his boorish behavior, and his private thoughts
proving every last thing she'd accused him of thinking, there was a ring of truth to it.

"A people snob? No, not that. A food snob? Yes.
You think in terms of educated palates, and you'd be
right to assume most folks here wouldn't know a
panna cotta from a semifreddo. But what I've discovered is that food is just another form of art. The people on Sugarberry might not know why they like it,
but they know when they do. I'm discovering that I
don't need to educate people, I just want to feed them
and make them happy. And if in doing so, I get to play
with new flavor profiles and complex combinations,
even in something as rudimentary as a cupcake? That
makes me happy. In fact, trying to maximize new flavors in a tiny cup of cake motivates me, challenges
me. Seeing my customers lick their lips when they
taste my creations is all the validation I'll ever need.
Win-win, Baxter. For me."

"Okay, then," he said, nodding.

"Okay then, what?"

"Don't look so wary. I'm hardly a snake about to
strike. If anything, I've been a bumbling moose in the
china shop since my arrival. I'm certainly not capable
of stealth, much less grace, at least where you're concerned."

She cocked that one wicked brow of hers. He shouldn't find himself entranced by that little previously unseen quirk of hers, but he was finding it rather . . . intoxicating.

"Where are you capable of it?"

"New York," he said, quite sincerely. "Which is where I was when I concocted this entire scheme."

"Scheme?"

"I told you I wanted to see you again, spend time with you, see what there might be between us. And put an end to my regrets where you've been concerned."

"How . . . tidy of you."

"Come on, I'm trying here."

She lifted her hand. "You're right. You are. I don't know why, at this point, you're bothering, but you are. I have a lot to do before opening today. It's softball Sunday, our last one of the season. I have streusel cakes along with Alva's secret weapon cakes to complete before starting on my daily stock. I open in four hours and I have at least six hours of work to do. Closer to seven now," she said, nodding toward him to note he was wearing at least a half a bag of her frosting.

"Secret weapon cakes?"

"Long story. I doubt you'd be interested."

"I found Alva to be rather . . . memorable, actually."

"Yes, I'm sure you did. Where were you yesterday?"

"New York, why?"

She frowned again. "You went back to the city? We do have hotels here, you know."

"I'm well aware, and am, in fact, staying at quite a lovely one in Savannah. I had to go back to tape some interviews promoting the new season premiere later this coming week. Why does it matter?"

She shrugged. "After your spilling-of-the-beans to

Alva, I thought for sure you'd take advantage of one of our biggest annual events to officially announce the fact that your show is coming to Sugarberry. Unless, of course, you've changed your mind."

She looked far too hopeful, and his spirits were dashed a bit further. "I had faith in Alva," he said, allowing the smallest of smiles to lift the corners of his mouth. "And, I hadn't secured the remainder of the details with you," he said more seriously. "Despite the rather brash and, some would say, ill-advised manner in which I launched this proposed endeavor, I do still plan to launch it. In fact, I have no choice but to launch it."

"Really."

"Quite. Plans have been made, things put in motion. I will be filming here. Granted, it doesn't have to be in your shop, but I've been listening to everything you're telling me, and, quite honestly, I think it's more important than ever that we do this together."

Her expression fairly boggled. "What gave you that impression?"

He shrugged, and a bit of his old determination started to pump again. He simply didn't think in terms of giving up. Much less failure. "You're saying I don't get it. And, while I wish it were otherwise, as it's not a particularly flattering self-portrait, to some degree, I must admit you're right in your judgment of me."

"Wow." She looked more surprised than he liked, but seemed to believe he was sincere. "Well, that is a step in the right direction, I suppose. Only I'd think it would be a step toward the door."

"Don't you see? Doing the show here together, is the one way—possibly the only way—I'll get to see and learn firsthand, what it is about being here, running

your own shop—a cupcake shop, no less—that is so
fulfilling to you. Not to pass judgment, Lani, but to
really, truly, and fully understand. What better way
than to jump in and do it side by side with you?"

"Except you don't want to work side by side with
me. You want to take over my shop and make it the
Chef Hot Cakes show. You want to bring your work,
your desserts, into my shop. Then you expect me to
what, go back to making my simple little cupcakes, as
you assume they are, and expect that to be enough?
Like I said, the folks here might not have the most so-
phisticated palates, but I'm delivering something I
know they'll like, and that I enjoy making. If I wanted
to do ridiculously over the top pastries, I could. But
they wouldn't get it and that wouldn't satisfy me."

"So maybe they won't get mine, either."

"You're not that obtuse. You bring your celebrity
with you, a rather hot one, at least as far as the ladies
here are concerned. I can't compete with that. And I
can't help feeling it will be a letdown after you go."
Lani put her pastry bag down and faced him, sincere
now, without any added heat to her tone. "I'm not
looking for reasons to shut you out. I just . . . I just
wish you'd never come here. I'm sorry. It's not even
personal, Baxter. I don't want anybody else here, either. In that regard, I'm being entirely and completely, one hundred percent selfish. But that's why I
came here. Or why I stayed here, anyway. This place,
these people, are mine. And I don't want to share. I
definitely don't want to compete. I'm done with that
environment. And I don't want to start over again
somewhere else. I guess we're both being selfish, just
wanting what we want, and the hell with the rest. But I
was here first, dammit."

She stared at him, and she looked . . . lost again. Or

maybe just done. But not done in. He wasn't making the mistake of thinking that.

"You think I'm not being fair to you, by not giving you a chance," she said, "but at least I am being honest."

Baxter felt a bit lost, too. He wasn't used to being in such a position, especially one of his own making. "I realize I've gone about every last step of this in as wrong a way as I possibly could have. I take responsibility for that. And the fact that I've already moved my show here, production team and all." He lifted a hand, to once again stall her. "I don't deserve even being heard out, but as it pertains to you, please let me finish."

"Baxter—"

"I'm filming Hot Cakes here. At least for the next week or two. Then I'll pack up and be gone."

"Back to New York?"

He shook his head. "Sugarberry is just our first stop."

Her mouth dropped open, then snapped shut. "You're taking your big city dessert show and . . . what, exactly?"

"Going to another small town, where I will bake again. For the same people you've come here to bake for. I want to teach them how to expand their imaginations in the kitchen, and I hope to learn from them as well. The difference is, I don't know how to make even one season out of that. You plan to make a whole life out of it." He crossed the room. "So show me how you're doing it."

"So now you want me as . . . what, some kind of mentor? Is that why you're really here? You have this big idea for a new season, but you don't know how to pull it off?"

"No, I pitched the entire idea so I'd have an excuse

to come to Sugarberry, to work with you again, see you again."

She snorted. "You did no such thing. One show, maybe—and I'm not saying I really buy that, yet—but a whole season? Seriously?"

"Seriously."

She held his gaze a moment longer, then her expression shifted to one of bewilderment. "You really mean that? And they went for it?"

He flashed a short, dry grin. "I can be a good pitch man when I really want something. Present company notwithstanding." He stepped closer. "And you've always been a mentor to me. Does that really surprise you?"

"What does that even mean?"

"It means I learned from you just as you learned from me. You pushed me, you provoked me. I was a better chef because of you, trying to impress you."

"Impress *me*? Baxter, you impress the world. Without even trying. I seriously doubt I had anything to do with that."

"But you did. You absolutely did." Heedless of buttercream frosting and every last cautionary rule he'd made for himself, he framed her face with his hands, thinking if she couldn't hear his sincerity, maybe she'd feel it. "Show me your world, Leilani, your new world. I loved having you in mine. I marveled constantly, over how you just walked into the only world I've known my whole life, and turned it into something completely different from anything I've ever known or understood. You know, maybe I shouldn't be at all surprised that you're still doing the unexpected, heading down a path I would never have predicted for you. You've always marched to your own drummer, I guess, and while I might not know all of you, Leilani, I do know that every part of you I've come to know so far has captivated me. I'm certain this will be no different."

She stared at him, her face expressionless. Except that her eyes didn't look so lost anymore. More like . . . barricaded. That it was a barricade against him broke his heart a little. Okay, maybe more than a little. But she was still talking to him. He was still in the room.

"If I confuse you, that can't even hold a candle to how much you—this—is confusing me. I don't know what to think anymore. Am I some kind of strange muse to you, then?" Lani drifted off, shook her head. "Nothing about this is normal. You're not even close to normal. I want normal. I just . . . want . . . normal."

He smiled then, fully, for the first time since entering the kitchen. "Ask anyone, from here to New York, to D.C., and I'm certain to Brussels and everywhere else you've ever been . . . and I bet they would all agree that the very last thing you are is normal. From your talent, to your point of view, to the way you approach . . . everything. Including your life here. I hate to be the one to tell you, Leilani. This"—he motioned with his head to the room around her—"is not normal. Not for you."

She searched his face, and he wanted—badly—to know what she thought she was finding there.

"I don't want this," she said, her voice barely above a whisper.

He knew she wasn't referring to her shop—but to him. And everything he'd brought with him. "I am sorry. I honestly didn't mean to bring you trouble, or heartache. But I'm here. The show is here. I can't undo what's been done. So, why not just do it with me? Jump in, go for it, and we'll find a way to make it work for you, and not against you. I know your concerns and I'm not discounting them. But trust me, okay? Trust me to do my part, and to do whatever I can to make sure good things come of this."

"And when the show is over? Poof?"

"Poof?"

"You said you're going on to the next town. For the record, I can't believe you're doing a whole season set in small towns. I can't even imagine you outside the city for more than five minutes without getting twitchy and breaking out in hives. You're like . . . umbilically attached to the energy of the city. In fact, I'd started to think that maybe the city gets its energy precisely from people like you. You feed the vibe as well as feed off the vibe. It wasn't like that for me. The city just fed off me, sucked everything out of me; then I had to find a way to recharge—only I couldn't because I was always there. So, I can't teach you how to appreciate this, what I have here. You either get it, you either need it, or you don't."

"I think I understand a small part of that."

She gave him a look that clearly said she thought he was full of it.

"I mean it. When I got back to my hotel late last night, I thought the peace and the quiet would drive me mad, but instead I slept like a babe. I truly felt better rested this morning than I have in ages." When she offered no response to that, he said, "I don't know what happens next. All I know is that this show will happen. Please, be part of it. Team up with me. I'll make certain it's a smart business decision if nothing else."

"You know, I think I just realized something."

"What is that?"

She pulled his hands from her cheeks, held them briefly, then let them go. "You're like the city. Vibrant and engaging, but ultimately draining. You want and you want and you take and you take, and you think you're giving back, because you're a nice guy, and you make sure others benefit from your wants. And you are a very nice, good guy. But you're not hearing me. I don't want what you have to give. Not the show, not the business, not any of it. You think you're helping me, but all you're doing with this whole thing, while fulfilling your needs, is draining me.

"Don't you get it?" she implored him, not angry so much anymore, as . . . weary. "*I* don't care if you understand why I'm here, and I don't care about making you understand. *I*"—she jabbed a finger toward herself—"don't need you to understand. I also don't want or need you to boost my business. I truly and very sincerely want my shop to be successful, but I want to do it all on my own. I think that's a big part of the attraction for me. Finding out what I'm made of, if I can do it. But what now? You come down here and team up with me, indelibly linking my life here to my past, to you, and to your success, and then you take off again. I'll never know what part of any future success I have is me, and what part is the notoriety and celebrity of you." She framed her hands above her head in the shape of a sign. "Chef Hot Cakes baked here!" She dropped her hands back by her sides. "Where do I go to recharge then?"

Baxter took a giant step back. In every possible way, he'd seriously, very, very seriously, miscalculated. "I'm . . . I wish there was more that I could say to convey how sorry I am." He was never more sincere, and never, not ever, feeling himself to be so completely and utterly inadequate. "I never meant this. I . . . didn't think. Well, I thought, but I thought that you—that we—that—" He finally stopped the stammering, knowing he wasn't helping either one of them. "You're right. I didn't think about you, consider you. Not in the way I should have." He looked away, then let out a deep sigh as he raked a hand through his hair, heedless of the buttercream he likely dragged through it as well. "I'm just—I'll stop production." He straightened and looked directly at her. "I'll figure it out, absorb the cost if I have to. We'll take the show to the next town, or—it doesn't matter. I shouldn't have done this."

"No, you shouldn't have. But, you know what, the town already knows you're here. And, much as I wish you could, now that I think about it, I don't think you can undo this, Baxter, even if you wanted to."

"I'm telling you, I'll do whatever—"

"No. I don't think we have a choice, either of us. You have to do the show."

"But—"

"You have people counting on you, too. Mostly I'm changing my mind because I just realized that the island will rise up as one and lynch me if you don't. If they even suspect I'm the reason you bailed out, my life here is done. Certainly my business will be." She turned her back to him, bracing her hands on the table for a moment, then picked up her pastry bag. "You have to do it now. You really can't change things back."

She'd been dancing and singing. Before. Looking at the tense set to her shoulders, it seemed like a lifetime ago.

"And since you're going to do this, you'll do the show here," she said, matter-of-fact now. "Because that's what everyone is expecting. They're excited about it, and, frankly, where else would you set up? The closest grocery store with a professional kitchen is across the causeway, our only church doesn't have a kitchen, and one of the things the fall festival was raising money for was to add a small banquet facility to our senior center."

"Didn't you say you had some kind of big dinner here? Before the festival? Where did they prep for that?"

"Potluck. Or 'covered dish' as they call it here."

"Where is that?"

"You mean *what* is that. We set up tents and put up tables and everyone brings a dish. Potluck means you get whatever people bring. No, we'll do it here. And don't worry, I'll smile for the camera and we'll do what we have to do to please the people of this island, because they're the ones I care about. I'll do whatever you need to get your damn show done, because, as far as the rest of the world knows, that's what you came here for. And that's what you owe the people who count on you." She walked over to the counter where the stereo sat. "But that's all I'm going to do. I'll figure out what comes after, and how to handle it, but I'll do that on my own. I don't want your help with that, so don't even think about butting in.

"Now, if you don't mind, I have to complete some of the most kick-ass cupcakes you'll never have the pleasure of tasting and I'd like to get back to it. Please, lock the door behind you." She cranked on the music. And went back to work. Without ever once looking at him.

Chapter 7

"Chef? There's someone here to see you. He's, um . . . not a customer. I don't think."

Lani glanced up at the kitchen clock. Five minutes to closing. "Well, at least he used the front door this time," she muttered under her breath. More loudly, she said, "Thanks, Dre. I'll be out in a minute." *Or ten.*

Neither Baxter nor any of his crew had made an appearance, to her knowledge, anywhere on Sugarberry since she'd kicked him out of her kitchen the morning before. She'd known it was merely a matter of time, and that the time would be short. Though she was thankful for the day and a half to regroup and catch up after the festival, she still wasn't ready for Round Four. No matter what kind of pep talk she'd given herself, she'd let him get to her every time their paths had crossed. And he'd gotten to her quite directly each time. As in hands-on directly. Maybe she could see if Dre would stay after work. They closed early on Mondays, at six, but there was still plenty to do, and she could use the extra pair of hands.

Lani immediately rejected that idea. Had she really

grown so pathetic that she was going to coerce her college student employee to run interference for her personal life? Not that Dre wasn't fully capable of handling the job. At the tender age of twenty, Lani's very capable new kitchen assistant and counter help had the kind of frank aplomb of someone twice her age. Okay, so perhaps *aplomb* wasn't exactly the right word to use, but Dre was nothing if not frank. Sometimes too much so, but her rough edges were more than made up for by her dedicated work ethic and burning desire to learn.

"Wait! You can't go back th—" Dre burst into the kitchen, right behind a short, stout guy, with a somewhat scraggly red beard and black rimmed glasses. "Sorry, Chef, he just—"

"That's okay, Dre. Go start closing up. I'll handle this."

Dre glared at the man before going back to the front of the shop. With her plum-colored flat top, overly kohled eyes, and twin eyebrow piercings, that glare would normally be enough to at least give a person pause. Especially when you combined it with the Tim Burton version of the Willy Wonka apron she was wearing.

Nerdy-glasses-guy didn't even blink. Well, he did blink—a lot in fact—but he didn't seem to be really aware of the ruckus he was causing, or of Dre and her glare.

He stuck out his hand in Lani's general direction, but his attention was focused on sizing up her kitchen. "Hello, I'm Bernard."

Of course you are, Lani thought. She took his hand, which was warm and a little damp, and gave it a quick shake before he wandered off and forgot he'd stuck it out there.

The contact seemed to startle him into looking at her. He smiled, though it was more of a squint really, that just happened to be accompanied by a brief flash of teeth; then he went back to sizing up the joint. "I'm here to do advance prep for the show setup tonight. Production sent me."

"Right." Lani should have realized that her guest wasn't Baxter even before the abrupt kitchen invasion. If Baxter himself had walked into the front of the shop, Dre wouldn't have called back as she did. Her young assistant might want the world to think she was far too cool to be starstruck. But Lani knew the one thing Dre considered worthy of her respect was a great chef. Dre knew the life story of every chef who had ever made a mark on the history of cooking, and a good many others who were known mostly only to industry insiders. She was on scholarship at a small art institute across the causeway, but in addition to her incredible skills as an artist, she was a dedicated foodie and chef groupie.

Lani had met Dre when she had popped up at the shop, ostensibly to offer her graphic art skills, gratis, as part of a class project to generate a shop logo that could be used as store signage, but also on T-shirts, coffee mugs, and any other marketing items Lani might have in mind. Intrigued by the offer and by the person, but uncertain if Dre's rather dark personal stylings would translate to something as whimsical as a cupcakery logo, Lani had asked to see samples of Dre's work.

That Dre was a supremely talented young artist was clear at a glance, but it was the focus of her art that had captivated Lani. Not surprising, Dre's work was entrenched in the fantasy realm. But rather than the postapocalyptic–Mad Maxian type work Lani might have expected, she was transported to richly colored Utopian gardens filled with brightly winged fantasy creatures, and intricately detailed fairy worlds so richly imagined, Lani felt that she could step right into them. All she needed was a yellow brick road.

She had agreed to work with Dre that same day. What had begun as a school project collaboration had developed into something completely different when Dre had sampled one of Lani's new cupcake creations, and proceeded to comment, specifically and one hundred percent correctly, on every single ingredient Lani had used. She also offered her own opinions on why the various flavors and elements worked so well together.

Lani had then discovered Dre hadn't found the cupcakery by accident. She had specifically chosen it because she had followed Baxter's amazing career arc, and, in tandem with that, had followed Lani's career as executive chef at Gateau. Lani had been amazed by the revelation . . . and more than a little flattered.

Of course, as a full-time student, Dre hadn't been looking for a paying job, nor was she targeting a career in the culinary world. Her foodie passion was a hobby, not a future goal. And Lani hadn't figured she needed to hire help until closer to the holidays.

While they were discussing the logo in the shop kitchen, where Lani was working steadily away, Dre had just sort of jumped in and helped while they brainstormed, and when the front of the shop suddenly got busy, Dre stepped up to the counter to let customers know Lani would be right out. She ended up answering questions and ringing up sales . . . and generally being the bright, amazing, and indispensible person she was. By the end of that day, Cakes By The Cup had its first official employee.

An employee who insisted on following the indus-try standard and using the respectful title of Chef whenever she addressed her new boss, despite Lani's request for her to be more informal. It was a cupcake shop, after all, not . . . well, Gateau. Although, if Lani were to be completely honest, she kind of liked hear-ing the respectful form of address again. It had been disconcerting to discover there were bits and pieces of her old life she still missed.

Smiling, she shook her head, and then the rest of what Bernard had said began to sink in. "Tonight?"

He'd been pacing the perimeter of the kitchen, but turned back. "You're closing now, correct? Baxter told us we could get in, but not until you close. You might want to rethink having us drag all our gear in through the front. You really don't want us tracking up your shop. We'll have to do a lighting install out there, but Baxter said to set up in here. Filming starts in the morn-ing, so we're already behind schedule." He glanced at her, looking as if he wanted to shake his head in dis-gust.

For what? Keeping him and his crew out of her place of business during business hours? How dare he. "Morning? As in, tomorrow morning? But I have—" She broke off when Bernard started frowning. Clearly he was not the person she should be having this par-ticular conversation with. "I need to make a quick call. Before you do . . . anything."

He lifted a clipboard and some other technological device that looked like a Geiger counter. Or some-thing. "Just making notes," he explained. "Gotta take measurements, look at your electrical panel. See what kind of generators we're going to need so we don't blow all your circuits."

Oh, you're already blowing my circuits, she wanted to tell him.

Especially when he added, "Trucks will roll about an hour from now."

"Of course they will. An hour." Serious anxiety began to set in just as Dre came through the swinging door from the front of the shop.

"Locked up, register done." She lifted the corner of the heavy blue bank bag she was cradling on top of the nightly checklist clipboard. "Should I . . . ?" She glanced at Bernard, who was currently captivated by the fuse box, then nodded quickly toward the office and mouthed the word *safe*.

Lani nodded.

"Do you need me to stay?"

"No, I'm fine, I—" She was already fishing for her phone when she realized she didn't have Baxter's number. Nor did she know where in Savannah he was staying. "Dammit."

"Are you sure?" Dre asked again.

Lani opened her mouth to reassure her assistant she didn't need watching over, then glanced up and realized Dre wasn't so much worried about Lani being stuck in the shop after hours with Bernard. She was angling to be involved in the production setup . . . and, Lani imagined, maybe get a gander at Chef Hot Cakes himself. Unlike every other female on Sugarberry, Dre hadn't peppered her with a million questions about Baxter and what it had been like to work with the reigning McDreamy of the kitchen. But Lani was sure that was only because Dre already knew more about Baxter than anybody.

"I—well, Alva is going to be dropping by to get her cupcakes shortly."

"Marathon poker championship night. Right. I took a bet with a guy in my illustrations class on whether or not the police would be involved. Then we realized that was pretty much a given. So we narrowed it down to before midnight, or after." Dre took on a considering look. "What time did you say she was picking these up?"

"Very funny. You should just call Alva and ask her what the over-under is. I'm sure she's already taking bets."

"Good point."

Lani gave Dre a quick list of instructions on how to remove the liners and glaze the bottoms of the cupcakes, then package them upside down in the specially lined boxes she'd already prepared. "Glaze them all, then the best three dozen are for Alva. She'll be by before seven."

Dre was already washing her hands. "Are we going to add this one to the menu? Looks intense."

Lani and Alva had decided on molten upside-down cakes. If there were laws on the amount of chocolate one cupcake could have, molten cakes would break every one of them. The cake was her take on devil's food, the filling was a melted, gooey blend of dark and Dutched chocolates with a spicy kick thrown in, and the glaze was a thick, glossy chocolate ganache. Alva had declared them heavenly.

She'd shown up bright and early the previous morning for their consultation, decked out in her church finery best. Yet somehow that hadn't stopped her from donning her My Little Pony apron, which she'd hung on a peg next to one of Dre's—as if she worked there—then had lent a helping hand with Lani's morning preopening prep as they'd discussed which secret weapon cakes to make for the poker tournament. Lani had initially groaned inwardly, thinking she'd created something of a problem by letting Alva help her with her therapy roulade the other night, but before she could deliver her politely worded explanation about boundaries, Alva was halfway through piping frosting—perfectly—on the first rack of cupcakes. So Lani had kept her mouth shut and let the woman work. By the time they'd discussed all of Lani's various weapon cake ideas, Alva had proven herself to be quite the helpful little assistant. So much so that Lani had offered a discount on the molten cakes as a way to thank her.

Always the cagey one, Alva had pretended to consider the offer, but in the end, had refused, explaining that she'd enjoyed both of their impromptu baking sessions and didn't want Lani to think she was angling for preferential treatment if she ever happened to drop by and help out again. Lani reduced her charge for the order anyway, because it was the right thing to do, and told Alva they'd work out the details of any future orders as they came along. She'd been in such a good mood after Alva took off, she'd cranked up the stereo and bopped her way into the extensive morning catch-up prep.

Which was when Baxter had shown up. She hadn't felt much like bopping since.

"They weigh like half a pound apiece," Dre said, carefully removing the paper liners. "Maybe I should change my bet to whether or not the oldsters will be able to do justice to these bad boys."

Lani glanced at Bernard, then back to Dre. "You haven't met our oldsters. I don't know if I'm putting them on the menu here. A lot of prep, and they won't save well for day olds. We'll see how they go over tonight. Excuse me for a moment."

"Yes, Chef."

Lani smiled to herself, then crossed over to where Bernard was busy checking out the fuse box.

"We'll need to bring in our own grid anyway, so not to worry," he told her.

"Worry about what?"

He squint-smiled at her. "About production shooting your electric bill into the stratosphere."

"Ah." *Seriously?* Now her electric bill was going up? She hadn't really thought through any of that part. She'd been too hung up on how she was going to handle working side by side with Baxter again. In front of television cameras, no less. She should have been thinking about her business and what else this might cost her, besides her sanity. After all, that's what she'd told him she was focused on, right? Maybe it was time to get her head in gear and her mind strictly on business. And away from how he made her feel every time he got within three feet of her. She was really going to have to do something about that. Her hormones took a happy leap, just thinking about being near him again. *Dammit.*

She pulled out her phone and was about to ask Bernard for contact information, when the back door to the kitchen opened and her dad walked in.

"Evening, Dre." He nodded at Lani's assistant, then looked at Lani with a questioning lift of the eyebrows as he glanced beyond her to Bernard.

"Evening, Chief," Dre said, never breaking focus on the task at hand.

Lani saw her father get the same little smile she got when Dre addressed her, and noticed he didn't correct her on the title. He was the sheriff, not the police chief. Dre was originally from Boston, so the sheriff concept was something she apparently didn't directly connect with. Or maybe she just looked at Lani's dad and saw D.C. cop. Compared to the rest of the guys in the Sugarberry sheriff's department, he clearly still was.

She also noticed her dad give Dre a second glance—a quick onceover that took in the Wonka apron, purple hair, pale skin, and fairy neck tat, all in under two seconds—then give his head the smallest of shakes as he continued on into the room.

Lani smiled to herself as she rounded the worktable and walked over to meet him. "What brings you over after hours? I hope you're not angling for a handout. These are all for Alva's ladies. You'll have to crash the poker tournament later, confiscate them or something."

"They almost look worth the hassle, but that's not why I'm here."

"Oh?"

"I'm here in an official capacity, to meet with your Mr. Dunne."

"He's not *my* anything."

"We got a request for a series of permits from his production crew. I need to go over some information before we can get them issued. Where is he?"

"Not here." *Yet, apparently.*

"Chef Dunne is coming? Tonight?" Dre stopped her precision glazing to look over at the two of them. "Sorry. I didn't mean to eavesdrop. I was just—"

"It's okay, Dre. Hang around, you'll get an introduction."

Dre nodded and tried hard not to look as if she'd just won the lottery and double the presents on Christmas morning combined, but Lani couldn't recall her assistant ever looking quite so . . . twinkly. Or anything resembling twinkly. Lani should be amused.

After all, Baxter could elicit the twinkly from the most hardened of hearts. Why it irked her, she had no idea. Other than wanting to explain to Dre that her twinkle-inducing Chef Hot Cakes was about to turn their lives into a three ring circus. "I'm becoming a crank. And it's all his fault."

"I beg your pardon?" her dad asked.

"What? Oh, nothing. I don't know when he'll show up. Mostly because I don't know anything about the schedule. He hasn't bothered to share that with me."

Her father frowned and Lani immediately saw the stubborn glint in his eyes and could have kicked herself. She knew better than to speak her mind around her father, especially where Baxter was concerned.

"You want me to hold up the permits? Give you time to make all this go away? For that matter, you want me to make this all go away, because—"

"Dad, no. I'm sorry, I didn't mean to make you worry. I already agreed to all this and everyone on Sugarberry is excited. I'm just a little annoyed, that's all." She gave him a look. "No needless delays, okay? The sooner we start shooting, the faster we can be done."

"How long is this going to last?"

"I really don't know. We haven't discussed—" She broke off when the back door opened yet again . . . and Alva strolled in, all smiles.

Lani took a deep breath, trying to quash the latest little adrenaline spike, which occurred each time the back door opened.

"Look at all my lovely little cakes." Alva beamed at the glossy rows of upside-down cupcakes. She glanced at Lani with a twinkle of her own, but it was of a decidedly different nature. She clasped her hands in

front of her chest. "I'm feeling luckier by the moment."

"I'll have the rest of these boxed up in just a few
minutes," Dre told her.

"Not to worry. I'm early. I'll help!"

Before Lani could intercede, Alva had spryly all but
skipped over to the apron rack, whisked on her Little
Pony getup, and was back by Dre's side in a flash.

Lani just shook her head. "What have I done?"

"Beg pardon?" her dad asked again.

Lani looked away from the visually jarring Dre-Alva
duo to her father. "Maybe you should go talk to
Bernard over there. I think he's in charge of lighting
and equipment and whatever other setup is going to
happen in here. He might be able to answer some of
the questions you have about the permits."

Her dad nodded, then glanced over at the two
women currently boxing up molten cakes and once
again shook his head slightly. He strolled over to
where Bernard was taking some kind of test reading
of . . . something.

Lani started to follow him, wanting to find out just
how much equipment they were moving into her
kitchen, thinking it was already feeling more than a
little crowded, when the back door opened yet again.

And, in walked . . . "Charlotte?"

"Surprise!" She waved and stepped fully inside.

"What?" Lani scurried around the tables and met
an also scurrying Charlotte in the middle of the
crowded kitchen, each catching the other in a tight
hug, that might also have included a little simultane-
ous jumping up and down. "How?" Lani asked, still
thinking she had to be seeing things.

"Well, you did invite me. Multiple times."

"I know, but how did you manage to get away? Your schedule was—"

"Kitchen fire."

Lani leaned back and held Charlotte by the arms. "Oh no! Is everyone okay?"

Charlotte nodded. "Happened when we were closed, thank goodness. Everyone is fine, but it will be at least two weeks before we're back up to speed, maybe longer if the health department doesn't clear us."

Lani glanced past Charlotte to the still open back door. "Did Franco—?"

"No. You know him, always has his hands in ten different projects in twice as many kitchens. He doesn't leave the city."

"Neither do you," Lani said with a laugh.

"You need me. I'm here." Charlotte looked around at the handful of others standing around them. "Although, you suddenly seem to have a lot of people."

"I was just thinking the same thing. But you're the best addition ever. Come on, I want to introduce you." Lani slid her arm through Charlotte's and squeezed it, still processing the fact that her closest friend and ally was really and truly there. "Are you staying the whole two weeks? Because you've got a room at my place, though I'm afraid you're on your own for board. I never seem to get to the grocery. Of course, if you're up for a bitch-and-bake night, then we can live on flour and buttercream."

"We've made that work before." Charlotte made a cursory nod toward the others, who were openly watching them. Except for Bernard, who was busy doing . . . Bernard things. She lowered her voice and tilted her head toward Lani's. "But I'm thinking you might be a bit busy for Bake Night."

"We're never too busy for Bake Night."

Charlotte smiled. "This is true."

"In fact, I have a feeling I'll be needing a heavy therapy schedule."

She sketched a short bow. "I'm here to serve. And bake."

Lani squeezed her arm again. "I can't believe you're actually here."

"Neither can I." Char then turned her attention to everyone else and smiled, a bit like one would at the locals while still trying to decipher whether they were friendlies or not. "Hello. I'm Charlotte Bhandari. I went to culinary school with Leilani."

Lani finally snapped out of glee mode and stepped into the middle of everyone. "Charlotte is one of the premiere pastry chefs in New York City. She's executive pastry chef for the Mondrake. Charlotte, this is Dre, my new assistant. And Alva—"

"Her senior assistant," Alva said, with a kindly smile, but a gleaming twinkle that Lani noted she should probably pay attention to more often.

"And you've met my dad," Lani added, as her father left Bernard doing his thing and came over to where they all stood.

"It's good to see you again, Charlotte. It's been far too long."

It had been since Lani's mother's funeral, to be exact, but of course, neither of them mentioned that.

"Agreed," she said. "Lani tells me you're doing well. I'm very happy to hear that, Mr. Trusdale. Excuse me, Sheriff Trusdale."

"Leyland is fine."

"Only if I want my mother giving me the evil eye," Charlotte replied, with a smile. "And trust me, none of us want that."

Lani's father smiled and nodded. "So noted." He

turned to his daughter. "You have your hands full here, and I think I have the preliminaries of what I needed from Bernie there, so I'll be heading out. Tell Mr. Dunne I'll need to speak to him or Rosemary at some point."

Lani frowned. "Rosemary?"

"His producer," Charlotte and Lani's father answered at the same time.

"I spoke with her earlier," he said.

"I only know because one of my co-workers is dating her assistant." *Brenton,* Charlotte mouthed in an aside to Lani.

"Right." Lani smiled brightly at her father and spoke before any follow-up questions could be asked. "Okay, so no worries. I'll pass the word."

"Pleasure to see you again, Sheriff," Charlotte said, neatly ending any further discussion and earning an arm squeeze of thanks from Lani.

He nodded, but didn't waste time exiting the room. "I'll lock up the front again, no need to follow me out," he called as the kitchen door swung shut behind him.

"Is Brenton here?" Lani asked Charlotte.

She shook her head. "Franco would have packed himself in my luggage to get down here if that were the case."

"Oh, sure, sure. He'd leave New York for a *man,* but not for me."

"Duh." Which, from Charlotte, had them both laughing. "Brenton is on postproduction of the season starting to air this week, so he's still in the city. Franco promised to give us an immediate heads-up if he hears anything we should know."

"We're all done here," Dre said, pulling Lani's attention back to the more immediate project of the moment.

She turned to find that Alva and Dre were sealing up the final box of molten cakes.

Charlotte stepped over to the table and examined them more closely, but without picking one up. "They look sinful." She glanced at Lani. "Will you share?"

"Do you play poker?" Alva asked her.

Charlotte smiled. "I'm afraid not. But if you have a mahjongg team, I'm your girl."

Alva's smile turned decidedly more speculative. "I'll keep that in mind."

"Dre, can you help Alva get the boxes out to her car?"

"Sure thing." Dre glanced between Lani and Charlotte. "Should I take off then?"

"Uh . . ." Lani looked at Charlotte, then over to Bernard. "I'm not really sure what all is going to happen next in terms of setting up for filming, but I know I'm definitely going to need you. Can you e-mail me your class schedule for the next two weeks? Then I'll send you dates and times I'd really like your help and we'll hammer it out from there. Sound good?"

"That works."

"And I promise you'll get the introduction."

Dre's smile was usually more of a sardonic quirk of the lips, but she actually flashed teeth. "That works, too." She had an actual spring in her step as she went to help Alva.

Charlotte leaned in to Lani. "Hot Cakes crush?" she murmured under her breath.

"Oh yeah," Lani murmured back.

"Happens to the best of them." Charlotte sighed, then added a sideways glance at Lani and a sly smile.

"And to think I offered you a bed."

"I know," Charlotte said, entirely unrepentant. "Good thing for me I make a most excellent bake therapist. And I don't charge extra for after-hours calls. I even bring my own chocolate."

"You didn't."

"Oh, I believe I did."

"From Frustat's? On Seventh?"

Charlotte nodded.

Lani hugged her again. She might have squealed a little.

Alva popped her head back inside. "Pleasure to meet you, Miss Charlotte. Lani May, you and your friend are welcome to drop in anytime over at Laura Jo's tonight." Her smile took on a decided twinkle. "Feel free to bring any other pastry chefs you might know along as well."

"Thank you, Alva. I think I'm going to be tied up here a good part of tonight, but I appreciate the invite. You'll have to let me know how the cupcakes go over."

"Oh, you'll hear all about it," she assured them. "It's going to be the lead in my first column."

Lani's eyes widened. "You finally won Dwight over?" Then they narrowed. "Wait, you didn't tell him you had an exclusive with Baxter did you? Because you know I can't promise—"

"My dear, I've already taken care of that on my own. Chef Dunne is a gentleman who keeps his word. Our dinner is scheduled later this week."

Really? Lani wanted to ask about a dozen follow-up questions to that, but since she'd told Baxter she'd do his show but to stay out of the rest of her life, it was hardly any of her business what else he did while he was on the island. "That's . . . great!" She almost managed to sound sincere. "I'm glad you worked it out. I'm surprised you're not leading with the interview as your first column."

"Have to strike while the iron is hot, dear. His schedule ties him up for the next couple nights and tonight's poker action promises to strike a lot of hot iron, if you know what I mean." Alva's smile widened, and that twinkly gleam took on a decidedly wicked light. "Molten hot, I believe."

"This is true." Lani was amused, even though she knew she shouldn't encourage Shark Betty in any way.

"You just wait until tomorrow's edition comes out! They'll still be talking about it by the following edition, which is when I'll spring my Chef Hot Cakes article on 'em."

"That should keep things interesting."

"Oh, I should think you'll be doing enough of that all by yourself, dear." Alva wiggled her eyebrows. Before Lani could even react to that, Alva popped out the back door, closing it behind her with a final click.

"I see what you mean," Charlotte said, staring at the closed back door.

"It's one of those things you have to experience to understand."

"Absolutely," Charlotte agreed. "You do realize she's going to write about you and Baxter in this column of hers, don't you? Do you think that's why she's suddenly become your happy helper?"

"I wouldn't put it past her, except on both occasions she was all about the whole poker tournament scandal. But it might have occurred to her since then."

"What are you going to do about it?"

"Nothing."

Charlotte shifted a surprised gaze to Lani. "Really?"

"First of all, you've met her. Do you really think

I could stop her? Besides, she's actually been really helpful."

Charlotte considered that and nodded. "There's that whole 'keep your enemies closer' thing."

"She's not my enemy." Lani smiled. "But you have a point."

"Miss Trusdale?"

Charlotte and Lani both whirled around at the sound of Bernard's voice. Lani had completely forgotten he was still there. "Yes?"

"I just got a call from Baxter. He's stuck in a production meeting with our producer and director. We're not going to set up until tomorrow."

"I'm open for business tomorrow."

"Right." Bernard looked distinctly uncomfortable for the first time. "About that—"

"Bernard—" Lani started, her tone a clear warning.

He immediately got twice as blinky and held up his clipboard like a shield.

She felt like she'd kicked a puppy. A near-sighted puppy. She sighed. "Okay, okay. But I need to talk to Baxter. Sooner than later."

Bernard seemed to breathe a small sigh of relief. "Good. He asked if he could drop by your home after they wind things up." At her raised brow, he talked faster. "To go over the production schedule, and . . . anything else you need to know. I'm sure that's what he's doing right now, getting all the answers and information so he can brief you on—"

"It's fine, Bernard." Lani decided there wasn't any pleasure to be had in picking on the messenger. Besides, if Baxter had any ulterior motive in meeting on her home turf—and duh, of course he did—little did he know she had her own secret weapon cake tonight.

She slid her arm more tightly through Charlotte's and smiled. "Tell him that's fine."

An hour later Lani and Charlotte had cleaned up and closed the kitchen and Lani was giving her best friend a tour of the front of the shop. Charlotte was the first person from her former life, well, other than Baxter, to get a glimpse of her new one. Of all the people from the big city chapter of her life, Baxter included, Charlotte was the only one whose opinion truly mattered.

Turning slowly, she took in the glistening vintage glass-and-chrome display cabinets that ran in an L-shaped pattern along one side wall, then wrapped around to extend the width of the shop. Her turn finally stopped at the pale blue wood shelves lining the wall behind the register. Each one was filled with an eclectic mix of antique baking implements and vintage cookbooks, all interspersed with whimsical figurines and collectibles relating in some way to the various aprons Lani wore. "You know, I wouldn't have pictured this for you. Not for New York you." Charlotte turned and looked at Lani. "But somehow . . . with you standing there, beaming with pride like the mother of a newborn she thinks is an adorable little angel . . . you know, this really suits you."

Lani beamed, every bit as proud as that fictional mother. "Thank you. That means more than you could possibly know."

Charlotte smiled. "Oh, I know. You don't owe me an I-told-you-so for the honesty."

"Deal." Lani grinned. "Does it make you think differently about wanting your own place?"

"Not in the least."

They laughed at that. During all the times Lani had waxed rhapsodic about running her own place, Charlotte had listened, but shuddered at the thought on a personal level. She claimed she wasn't cut out for management, not even if she was the big boss. Especially if she was the big boss. Considering how bossy she usually was, the idea was a constant source of amusement to Lani.

"I want to be able to leave work at work."

"I do that here," Lani said, which was sort of true. She did live, breathe and literally eat her shop a good part of the time, but mostly that was her own enthusiasm, along with a healthy dose of anxiety about wanting to see it succeed.

"The key word being *here*," Charlotte said. "The shop suits you, but, I have to say, I still can't figure out the allure of the location. Personally or professionally."

"Maybe it's precisely because here is where I can have a life."

Charlotte looked at her as if she couldn't fathom what kind of life one would have there that would be worth living, but both were smiling. It was why she loved Charlotte best. They didn't have to see eye to eye or agree on everything to still be each other's best support.

"I'm really glad you're here," Lani told her.

Charlotte's smile widened. "Location and god-forsaken drive notwithstanding, I am, too."

Lani flipped the lights off and they headed to the back, switching off lights as they went. "I can't believe you drove down here. I didn't even know you had a driver's license."

Charlotte slid her a glance. "Who says that I do?"

Lani's mouth dropped open, but Charlotte just laughed. "I grew up in New Delhi, remember? Your American roads are mere child's play to me."

Lani laughed. "Still, I can't imagine you behind the wheel. And definitely not for that many hours straight." They exited out the back door of the shop, laughing as Lani shut, then locked, the door behind them. She turned and plowed directly into Charlotte's back. They grabbed the porch handrail at the same time as Lani whispered, "Holy Mother of—"

She gawked at the three mammoth white trailers parked behind her shop, filling up not only her parking area, but that of the entire block of shops. Her mouth snapped shut as she spied Baxter, hopping down from the steps leading out of the middle trailer.

He offered her his most endearing smile. "I can explain."

Chapter 8

Baxter crossed the narrow space left between the
trailer steps and the rear entrance to Leilani's
shop. Only then did he realize who had exited the
shop with her. "Charlotte?"

"Chef," she replied politely, but otherwise showing
no emotion.

Lani hid her wry smile, but not quickly enough.
Chef was a title of position and respect. Normally.

Baxter nodded. "Chef Bhandari," he responded
with a smile.

"Play nice," Lani warned them both.

Baxter's smile grew. He actually liked and respected
Charlotte. And he understood where the cool response was coming from. He could only imagine the
earful Charlotte must have been getting about him
from her friend. She was simply showing solidarity. He
envied them the strong personal bond.

So it surprised him when she turned to Lani and
said, "It's been a long drive, long day. I'll head to your
place and leave you two to discuss . . . things."

She'd left her natural habitat to come all the way

down to the wilds of Georgia to support her best friend . . . but wasn't averse to said friend fraternizing with the enemy. Interesting. Unless, of course, there was something new he didn't know about in the "discuss things" column.

Doubly wary, he started to speak, but Lani spoke first.

"Let me take you over, get you settled in," Lani said to Charlotte, not sparing him a glance. "You've had a long day and I'm certain whatever Baxter needs to discuss with me regarding his super-secret production schedule can be shifted to accommodate my far less important one."

Ah. Apparently Bernard left something to be desired as his point man while Baxter had been delayed by his meeting with Rosemary.

"That's okay. Why don't you two go ahead and talk it out now? I plan on face planting on the nearest soft surface." Charlotte pulled out her phone. "I plugged your shop and home into my map app. It'll get me there. Key?"

Lani just looked at her.

Charlotte frowned. "You're not serious."

"Not exactly a hotbed of crime here on the island. And my father is the sheriff."

"You have a point."

Lani smiled. "Good, because it's the only one I've got. But, honestly, let me go get you settled in. The place is a bit of a disaster."

"I'm not company-company, you know. I all but lived at your New York studio. It couldn't be worse than that." She paused when Lani just arched a brow. "No."

Leilani lifted a shoulder and smiled a bit sheepishly. "I mostly live here."

"I'm sure it will be fine," Charlotte said. "I'll . . . make do."

Baxter stepped in. "Why don't I follow you over? You can get Charlotte settled, then we can head out, grab a coffee, or dinner if you haven't eaten. We don't have to talk shop in the actual shop."

"Do we really need to talk shop at all tonight? I haven't seen Char since—"

Charlotte put her hand up. "I need sleep. We can play Baker Barbie tomorrow."

"Baker Barbie?" he asked.

"Her term," Charlotte replied. "It's a girl thing." As if that explained everything. And, perhaps it did.

Baxter hadn't missed the look Leilani sent her way, which was more plea than friendly concern. Just as he didn't miss the even look Charlotte gave right back.

Well, well, he thought. Maybe he had more of an ally in Charlotte than he'd thought. Though he was certain it wasn't his welfare she was concerned about, if she was pushing for Leilani to work with him in any capacity on this project, then he was all for it.

"I would love to postpone this," he offered, "but I've just gotten the full production schedule this evening, and we really have to go over everything that's getting set up. It's going to happen very quickly, starting early tomorrow."

"I know," Leilani said. "Bernie warned me."

"Bernie?"

"Your advance guy."

He frowned. "Bernard?"

"Right." Lani turned to Charlotte as Baxter mouthed *Bernie?* "You can follow me over."

A minute later they were all in their cars, motoring several blocks to the ocean side of the island. Leilani slowed before the opening of a narrow, crushed shell drive leading to a small cottage that appeared to back right up to the dunes. With dusk rapidly turning to dark, Baxter couldn't make out all the little details, but her place looked . . . he supposed the word for it was . . . *cozy*.

Charlotte pulled her compact rental into the drive first, then Leilani swung in behind her in her little red SUV, leaving him to idle in front in his rental. He wouldn't have pegged Leilani as the SUV type, or, for that matter, the red car type. Not that he'd ever given it any thought. If he had, he'd have pictured her in a little compact, something practical. Like she was. He supposed the little utility vehicle was practical, especially if she catered any events or made deliveries of any kind, but the red was rather . . . flashy—which didn't seem like her at all.

Not that she was plain, but her work was known for its delicate intricacy and elegance. Her flash, if she had that, was in how inspired her creations were. But the execution was always pure sophistication.

He thought about the decadent little cakes she'd had lining her worktables the morning he'd first walked into her kitchen, and, later, the lavishly topped varieties that filled her shop front cases. Those were overtly sensual, bordering on hedonistic. There was also the offbeat music she played, and the eccentricity of the aprons she wore, the eclectic shop décor in general . . . and he was forced to admit she might have had more of a point than he'd been willing to concede.

He'd known her only as the chef she needed to be to work for him, to work in a place like Gateau. He'd simply assumed the chef was the same person as the woman.

Apparently, he couldn't have been more wrong.

Pulling into the driveway, he watched as Lani and

Charlotte climbed out of their vehicles. Though he was admittedly curious to see the inside of the place, he thought it better to leave them to the settling in.

Leilani had always been a tidy chef in his kitchen, orderly and precise, and her own shop kitchen appeared to be the same. Even taking into consideration the exuberant flavor profiles and interesting apron choices, he had a hard time imagining Leilani being messy. But his interest went beyond her housekeeping style. He was curious about her lifestyle here, outside the professional kitchen. He really did want to understand what might have drawn her to stay in this place, on this island.

He might have been able to fathom a moderate city like Savannah. It would have been a real stretch to imagine her in some suburban retail setting. Anything more rural than that simply defied all understanding. And this? This went beyond rural. Sugarberry was so small and isolated, she might as well have announced she'd decided to relocate to Fiji. At least there she'd have had the tourist trade to tap into. And, he supposed, the beautiful view.

With the car windows down, he could hear the rising night symphony of whistles and warbles, croaking and rustling. There was even something . . . gurgling, nearby. The evening breeze was still quite warm, a bit humid, and he could hear a steady rushing noise he finally identified as the surf, which meant he'd been right about the location. But that's all he heard. It was even quieter, in terms of human noise, than in Savannah. And that had felt like a crypt compared to New York. In the city, the rushing noise was made by the steady stream of tires rolling across pavement and grates, and the whistles at all hours were for taxis, the warbles were sirens, and the gurgling noise was probably made by something he didn't want to examine any more closely in Manhattan than he did here.

It occurred to him they had both chosen to live on an island, and that perhaps the appeal of his was as baffling to an outsider as hers was to him. He thought of her island as being backwoods, whereas his offered sophistication and refinement. Though he'd admit both islands had their uncivilized elements that gurgled in the night, the better choice between the two would seem obvious and clear cut to even the most casual observers.

As the minutes passed and darkness fell, he realized his grip on the steering wheel had relaxed. The tension that had knotted up his shoulders and neck—a result of yet another very long day of strategy meetings and detail chasing—was easing out of him. The gentle evening breeze, and the rhythmic sounds of island night life were gradually enveloping him. It was hard to deny that maybe both islands offered their own unique take on refined living.

Lights went on in the cottage, lending it an undeniably warm glow. He smiled, amused as he recalled his Snow White references where Leilani was concerned. "Of course she lives in a cottage," he murmured. "All she needs now are the dwarves." With all the comings and goings at the shop, which he'd spotted through the trailer blinds as he'd labored through his various meetings with Rosemary and the crew, Leilani did indeed seem to be recruiting her own miniature army.

Well, he had an army, too. Though perhaps not so miniature in size, especially when contrasted with the finite constraints of the size of the island they were invading. Locating production in Savannah had proven too complicated. Even locating over the causeway in the closest town of decent size was a logistical nightmare. Hence the decision to rent more trucks and set up, literally, right in her backyard—along with the backyard of all the other businesses on the block. It had taken a lot of finagling and not a little chunk of the newly expanded show budget to make it all work without wreaking too much havoc on the local industry while he was doing it.

He sincerely hoped the popularity of having a hit television show taping in their town, on their island, would serve to boost and perhaps even expand the island economy. Well, as soon as he was gone and not taking up all the expansion room himself. Even though his show had never tackled anything quite as ambitious as his cross-country trek, his wasn't the first on his network to use a remote location. The bigwigs had files full of facts and figures regarding the positive local economic effects where they'd set their off-site shows. Documentation they used shamelessly on all future off-site locales, with whomever they had to in order to get their production the space, permits, and any other considerations they needed so the show could go on.

He thought about how Leilani was going to take the news of exactly how invasive it was going to be to her island, and her life. It was far more than originally planned and he didn't relish being the one to tell her.

"The passenger door is locked. Baxter?"

Lani's voice had him jerking upright, which was when he realized that he'd put his seat back and closed his eyes.

"Are you okay?"

He turned to find her bent down, peering in at him through the passenger side window.

He blinked away the fog, flashed her a quick smile,

then fought with the door handle for a few more seconds than was suave or smooth, finally conquering the simple piece of machinery and exiting the car so he could swoop around the bonnet and . . . realize he still hadn't unlocked her door. "Drat it all."

"I can get my own door," she said, smiling. "But you will have to unlock it first."

"There is that. You got everything settled with Charlotte, yes?"

"I did. She's nested on the couch with cookie dough ice cream, a big spoon, and an *Iron Chef* marathon. She'll never miss me."

"That actually sounds . . . rather appetizing."

Her smile grew. "It's a short couch, and Charlotte's idea of sleepwear is a bit . . . eclectic. Plus, she doesn't share her ice cream. Or the remote."

"So, she brought her own ice cream?"

"Like I said, she doesn't share."

"I saw the cooler. What else did she bring?"

"Baker Barbie stuff."

Baxter grinned. "Hmm. You might be surprised to discover that girl pastry chef stuff is probably a lot like boy pastry chef stuff."

"Does boy pastry chef stuff include hand dipped, dark chocolate-coated cherries, and a cake pan shaped like a man's?"—she gestured at him in a general southern direction, and lifted one eyebrow

Baxter spluttered a laugh. "Um, chocolate, yes, possibly even the cherries, but my bakeware comes in the generally accepted forms." There was something about the added sparkle in her eyes that had him thinking about her sliding those coated cherries into her mouth, licking away every drop of their juicy sweetness, not to mention her devouring that . . . cake. He very abruptly decided maybe he'd better return to the driver's seat in the car, before there was any chance she'd glance in that general, southern region again. The topography of which was rapidly changing.

"Let me get your door." He was thankful for the growing darkness as he skirted the bonnet once again and climbed back into the car, popping the locks as he did, then leaning across the passenger seat to open her door.

"Thanks," she said, as she climbed in, settled, and pulled on her seat belt.

He closed his door, too, and thought the quiet island night had just gotten a little more . . . intimate.

It was odd. They'd worked for long hours, days on end, physically closer than they were now, seated on either side of a small console. But that had been in the far larger kitchen space at Gateau. This, on the other hand, felt very . . . confined. Between that, the distracting images of plump, chocolate-covered cherries, Leilani's lips, and the sudden lack of air to breathe . . . he found himself having a hard time getting his thoughts in order. And he really needed to be back on his game tonight. He was running out of time, and she'd long since been running out of patience.

"Baxter?" She broke into his scattered thoughts. "Is everything okay?"

He realized he'd been sitting in his seat, hands gripping the wheel, staring out the windshield, but seeing nothing. Except those damn cherries. "Fine, fine. Everything is . . . fine. All buckled in, yes?" He glanced at her as he put the car into DRIVE. Even in the dark, he could see the amused slant to the set of her mouth.

"Yes, I'm all safely strapped in for our wild ride

around the island. Top speed here, even on the relatively straight eastern stretch, is about, oh, thirty-five. Of course, given my connections, I don't think we're in danger of getting any tickets. Unless my dad is in an overprotective mood, which is pretty much always where I'm concerned. Then he might decide to have one of his deputies mess with you a bit because . . . well, because he can."

Baxter frowned. "Would he do that? Bernard said he's been blue chip at working with our production team to get all the permits pushed through."

"This has nothing to do with your television show shooting here. While it might be a headache for him, work-wise, he knows it's good for the island economy and general morale, and that's the kind of goodwill you don't get handed to you everyday. He's willing to put up with the hassle for the reward, though it won't keep him from grumbling about it."

"So, the deputy harassment then would be . . . ?"

"Oh, that would be entirely personal." Her smile widened. "You made his daughter unhappy. So, it's more of a dad thing. It's just that, in my case, my dad happens to be the sheriff."

Baxter smiled, though he wasn't entirely at ease with the scenario she was painting, personally or professionally. "Duly noted."

"So," she said as the moment stretched out, when he continued to smile at her. "Shall we go?"

"Right. Right." He pulled away from the curb, then glanced back at her. "It's just nice to see you smile. You seem more . . . relaxed. And I mean that in a positive way. It's—it's good on you."

"You can thank Charlotte for that."

"I'll do that." He smiled. "You know, I wasn't at all

surprised that her initial greeting earlier was only slightly less frozen than the dessert she's presently enjoying—cookie dough, uncooked, really?"

Lani nodded.

He shook his head. "Anyway, I am surprised she didn't make an effort to thwart this evening's meeting."

"I'm smiling and relaxed because having Charlotte here makes me happy, not because she told me to let my guard down with you."

"Ah."

"And yes, it's good to have someone in my corner, to have the support, but mostly it's just plain good to see her. We talk all the time, but I haven't seen her since I left New York. And I've missed her. A lot. You are right, however, in that she doesn't want to cause friction between us. She knows the show will go on, regardless. And, well, to be perfectly honest, she isn't exactly against anything else going on either."

Baxter slowed the car. "Really?"

Lani smiled. "Really. But just because Charlotte thinks some things are worth a little more effort and damn the consequences, doesn't mean I concur. She's not exactly the go-to person when it comes to relationships, but rather the poster girl for what not to do."

"Charlotte?"

"I'm talking out of school here, but she'd be the first one to say it, anyway. Let's just say she can be . . . impulsive."

"Really," he repeated, with considerably more emphasis.

Lani arched a brow. "Would you like to turn back and see if perhaps she'd be more willing to co-host the program with you?"

"What?" He glanced over at her. One brow was

quite singularly arched, but with a definite amused smile curving her lips. He grinned at that. "No, no, I'm not interested in Charlotte. Not like that. I'm just surprised. She strikes me as being a great deal more . . . restrained."

"She was raised by parents who give new meaning to the phrase *old school*. Quite often, her views are diametrically opposed to theirs. In this case, I would say almost virulently so."

"Ah."

"She also doesn't understand why I decided to stay here and open my own shop. So, there also might be some less-than-fully altruistic advice being given."

"I see," he repeated, still smiling. Anything that made Leilani more receptive to him in any capacity was a welcome thing. "I am sorry."

She sent him a considering look, but there was good humor still clear in her voice. "About?"

"All of this. I know, I've said it before. But I have heard everything you've said to me. I have. I've given it a lot of thought. And you're right, you know. Shooting here does appear rather ridiculous and over the top now, even to me." His smile turned rather self-deprecating. "It seemed like such a good idea at the time." He caught her gaze, held it for a moment, both of them smiling, before turning his attention back to the road. "I should have thought it through better, all the way through."

"I appreciate that you get that." She sounded sincere, and without the irritation that had threaded her words so often up to now. "For my part, I do understand that you didn't mean any harm, that you thought it was a good thing for all. I know you tend to get focused to the point of being somewhat oblivious to other things, but I also have realized you wouldn't be half the chef you are, if you weren't that way. That kind of focus and, at times, blind determination, is what works for you. It's how you thrive."

He glanced quickly at her, the words coming before he could think better of them. "I thought you were what worked for me."

"Oh, Baxter."

He caught her shoulders slumping a little in his peripheral vision as he looked back to the road. "I didn't say that to get the pity vote. But I've thought a lot about all the things you said, and not just the part about what this intrusion does to the life you want for yourself here. You said I don't know you, that I have been infatuated with the woman who worked for me, but not the actual woman herself."

"Infatuated?"

"I explained about that." His smile twitched wider. "I believe I even demonstrated. Perhaps it wasn't as memorable for you as it was for me."

She raised her fingers to touch her lips, seemed to realize what she was doing, and dropped her hand back to her lap. A moment passed. "I didn't forget."

There went that clutch at his heart. He wondered how long it would take before she no longer had that effect on him. He suspected he already knew it would pretty much be never.

"So . . . what are you saying?" she asked. "You realize I'm right, and now that you've been around the not-as-delightfully-sweet part of me, you're not infatuated with the real woman?"

"No," he said without hesitation. "I didn't say that. But it is true that there's a lot of you I don't know, Lei. Certainly not as much as perhaps I should have before I turned countless lives upside down just to pursue the part of you I do know."

"Like I said, your single-minded bullheadedness is what makes you the successful chef you are."

He smiled again, more dryly this time. "Thanks. I think."

"Anytime," she said blithely.

His smile grew. "Honestly though, I would like to think I'm not so impetuous that I just barge into a person's life as if I alone know what's best for all, or use whatever advantage celebrity has given me, and excuse my actions by telling myself I'm helping people in return."

"But you do help them in return. To Sugarberry, to the people who live here, you're a celebrity, sure, but also something of a hero. They're all excited, bordering on delirium, that you chose to come here, that you're taping your show on our little island. I'm surprised there's not talk of a parade, perhaps a tasteful statue in the town square."

"Oh, go on, now," he chided, but was laughing with her.

"Okay, but I'm serious about the rest. The chamber of commerce and all the merchants around the square are thrilled that their revenues will most certainly go up. Or will when the trucks leave and customers can actually park anywhere near their shops," she teased, but waved away his attempted explanation. "I'm truly the only one who wasn't thrilled by this."

He slowed as he looked at her again. "You realize, I'm trying to apologize for being an inconsiderate arse, and you're arguing my side."

She batted her eyelashes at him. "I'm perverse like that. Chalk it up to yet another part of me that, had you known, might have saved countless dollars."

He laughed at that, even as he shook his head. There were so many more facets to her, than he'd previously known. Even the irritation she'd exhibited toward him, and the heartfelt, emotional confessions she'd made on how his choices were going to adversely affect the new life she'd chosen for herself, called to some deeper place inside him. He was finding himself as captivated by each new thing he learned as by what he'd already known. There was a broader range to her, but greater depths as well. The real Leilani—or should he say, complete Leilani—was definitely more challenging than the soothing, perpetually optimistic, intellectually driven woman he'd come to desire, and whose presence in his life he'd so sorely missed.

These new discoveries weren't pushing him away at all. He would miss her more when he left Sugarberry than he had when she'd left Gateau. He wanted to learn every facet, plumb every depth. The more he learned, the more he saw, the more he felt.

"I've done a lot of thinking, too," she said, breaking into his thoughts. "I know I was a bit short with you behind the shop earlier, but I honestly have tried to be on better terms with all this. At that moment, I'd just finished with Bernard crawling all over my kitchen, while Dre and Alva were packing up the secret weapon cakes for tonight's poker Armageddon, my father was stomping around trying to be overprotective, and Charlotte popped up, which is great, but was a complete shock. Then we headed out and smacked right into wall-to-wall trailers I didn't even hear pull in. I want to be a team player. I know that's for the best. I do. But, to do that, I need to feel like I know what's going on, so I can be prepared for what's coming next." She looked at him and her smile was sincere. "I'm a little blindsided-out, that's all."

"I understand that," he said, every bit as sincere.

"I'm sorry about Bernard, and not having a full brief for you sooner. That was my plan, but we were just figuring out the scheduling ourselves and it proved to be more complex than we'd thought. If I hadn't gotten tied up in that string of production meetings, I'd have been there to explain everything before Bernard ever stepped through the door."

"I appreciate that. I have been listening to everyone on the island wax rhapsodic about the big event since the word got out last week. Plus, Charlotte hasn't been shy about giving me her opinion on how you mean well and surely didn't intend all this fallout for me, which you've said as well. I guess I've always known that. It's just taken some . . . adjustment. If you'd keep me in the loop more, and no more surprises, that's all I ask."

A quick glance showed there wasn't anyone on the single lane road behind him. Baxter braked the car to a full stop so he could turn and look directly at her. "Lei, I realize nothing else has changed for you, or will, in the aftermath of hurricane Hot Cakes. I appreciate that you're being so generous. It's far more than I'd hoped for. Or deserve."

Her smile turned wry. "I know."

He smiled back. "I do plan on keeping you 'in the loop' as you say. You know, as much as I like the sweet, even-keel-at-all-costs you, I must say, this perverse side is growing on me."

"Good," she replied, then smiled fully, which made her eyes twinkle a bit devilishly by the dashboard light. "Remember you said that."

He grinned. "I'm sure you'll remind me. And Charlotte isn't wrong, you know."

"Charlotte? About what?"

"I am a well-meaning bloke. One who has hopefully

learned something from all this and will do better the next time he's tempted by an impulsive idea."

She laughed at that. Outright.

"I'd be insulted"—he smiled ruefully—"but I suppose I earned that."

She patted his arm. "Well, at least you're charismatic with your impulsivity."

"Don't forget well-meaning."

"Right. Which is why I'm just as sure you'll continue to get away with it."

Still smiling, he covered her hand before she could pull it away. "Except with you."

She glanced at his hand covering hers. "Someone has to keep you humble." She lifted her gaze to his.

"I'm very thankful for all I have. I've worked hard for it, but I know it's been a blessing."

"Humble *and* earnest," she teased. "So . . . what happens next?"

"Are we talking about the show, or—"

She slid her hand free, but her smile remained. "Yes, the show."

He rather liked talking about each other, but he knew that to continue further was treading back into dangerous territory, made ever so clear by how just touching her hand had set his entire body to hoping again. Some parts more than others. "Right," he said, determined to stay on the professional path from that point onward. "We're going to set up production, which will take most of tomorrow, then we'll need a day to test lighting, sound, while we go through and choose all the recipes, test them out, make sure we have the necessary product, then block out how each episode will progress. I imagine we'll probably shoot the first episode on Thursday, or get it started anyway. There will be a learning curve across the board with that one, then things should progress more smoothly with the other episodes."

"How many others?"

"The plan is for five, if you approve, which would be a week's worth. Rosemary thinks that will give the viewers a real taste, so to speak, of each town we visit. I'll have enough shows to really get into the local dessert cuisine, or explore whatever specialty or theme I'm delving into in that particular area, as well as bring something new and different to the town."

"And the trucks in the back lot? In everyone's back lot? They stay the entire time, or do they just unload stuff, then move out?"

"They stay for the duration. Your fellow business owners were all notified as part of the permit process. Apparently there weren't any hang-ups there."

"That's good," she said, but he could see reality beginning to ease back into her body language, and he could hear the tension creeping back into her voice.

"What are all those trucks for?" she asked.

"Production mostly, but also makeup and wardrobe, and one is a full utility support kitchen."

"A kitchen?"

He nodded. "We have to do a lot of advance prep for each show, along with a lot of prep as filming is going on. We need a secondary kitchen to handle that as we're going to be filming in the only other kitchen we have."

"Which has more than one of pretty much everything, you know."

He nodded. "Oh, I know. Down to how many cooling racks you have and what sizes they are. Bernard is very thorough."

She smiled at that. "Good old Bernard."

"With all the cameras, lights, crew, etcetera, a lot of

the functional workspace other than the part where we'll be cooking and demonstrating, won't really be accessible. It's easier to have a satellite kitchen."

Lani nodded thoughtfully. "How many people are traveling with this—"

"Circus?"

She matched his smile. "I didn't say that. But since you did . . . how many performers are we talking about, Ringmaster?"

"Enough to make you feel like there should be three rings involved, but, in truth, we'll be running at about sixty percent our normal staff, so everyone will be putting in extra time."

"For how long?"

"We have the permits for thirty days, but the schedule right now is designed to wrap things up in ten to twelve days. It can and usually does take a good part of a single day to film each twenty-two minute program, then there's all the planning and prep, postproduction, and, invariably, delays due to this snafu or that. It's our first time coordinating everything this way, so we've got flextime scheduled in for that. My network has other shows that have gone on location, though those have been isolated instances and not an entire series. We've consulted with their teams to get an idea of what we're in for, what we're going to need, and will hopefully avoid some of the pitfalls they experienced."

"So . . . a few weeks here, then you pack up and go to the next town, right?"

He met her gaze, nodded.

She held his a moment longer, then glanced toward the passenger side window. "So, are we going to get coffee? I thought you promised me coffee."

"Leilani—"

She looked back at him. "What you said before,

about not knowing me . . . You know that a few weeks isn't going to change that, right? Even if it did, there's not much we could do about it anyway. You're leaving."

"Yes, I know."

"Okay. I just . . . you say you've come to terms with it, but I do know you. You don't just give up. I don't want you to think that because I'm being a good team player, and I might even laugh and enjoy myself while we're together . . . that it means I'm rethinking what I said before. I'm not. And I won't."

"I know. That's what I started to say earlier." He shifted his gaze forward, put his hands back on the wheel, and put his foot on the gas. It was easier to talk if he wasn't looking at her. Wanting to touch her. "Yes, it's true I thought I'd come riding in on my white steed, storm the castle, and hie off with the lovely maiden."

He heard what sounded like a snort, but didn't risk looking at her.

"Like I said, I didn't think it through much beyond that. What, was I just going to keep you like an abducted wench, and drag you cross-country with my band of merry pastry chefs?"

"Well, Bernard would make a good Friar Tuck."

He did glance at her then, but the shadows had grown too deep to see her eyes clearly.

"Go on," she said, her tone more sober.

He liked it better when they were both laughing. "Even if I did come sweep you off your feet . . . then what? When we're done marauding the countryside, leaving satisfied, chocolate-and-powdered-sugar covered smiles in our wake . . . the truth is, I have no castle to take you back to. Just a sound stage, an office, and a brownstone in the Village I barely sleep in." He wound through the narrow island roads, not really paying attention to where he was going, then found himself back out on the loop road again. "I guess what I'm saying is that I'm a man who is fortunate to have gotten everything he could have ever dreamed of wanting and so much more . . . yet has nothing to give you. Nothing you'd want, anyway."

She kept quiet, and he drove on in silence for several minutes. "I should have thought it through," he finally said. "All the way through. And I didn't." He looked over at her, and let the car slow again. "I get it now. I'm sorry it took a circus and a merry band of chefs for me to figure it out . . . but I have. I well and truly have. It's not about giving up, it's conceding I should have never entered the field of play to begin with."

Chapter 9

Those were the exact words she'd hoped to hear from him, but had never honestly expected him to say. But now he had. And, what's more, he truly seemed sincere about it. He'd listened. And he'd agreed with her.

In all possible ways, it was a far better outcome to this disaster-in-the-making than she could have hoped for since first reading the write-up of his impending arrival in the island paper.

So why wasn't she happier about it? Or, at least, relieved?

Yes, she could be perverse at times, but not so perverse that she'd want a man pining after her, chasing after her, when she'd made it perfectly clear she didn't want to be caught. No, she wasn't that perverse.

Was she?

A light throb began in her temples. It was just so . . . complicated.

Intellectually, she was relieved. She could relax now, let her guard down a little and not be so damn vigilant around him. She could be herself, and not worry that her actions would lead him to believe she was doing anything other than being a good sport and making the best of the situation.

But, emotionally . . . emotionally was a much different story. After all, he was still the one man she'd wanted. For a very long time. In every possible way. In fact, though she'd dated other men, and had even fancied herself in love for a brief time when she'd studied overseas . . . Baxter Dunne was the first and only man she'd truly fallen for. Fallen for in the ways that mattered, ways that went beyond the butterflies and pheromones. They'd had a natural rapport right from the start that had made communication easy, and at times, was even unspoken. Despite their differences in demeanor and approach, they shared a connection of the mind as well as the spirit, and it bonded them in the way of true friends. She respected him, she liked him . . . and yes, there were all those lovely butterflies and pheromones to keep things buzzing along on other, more visceral levels.

It wasn't until he came to the island that she knew for certain she hadn't just had a crush, or started to fall for him. She had fallen. All the way. She loved him. Or had loved him. Past tense, right? Or maybe it was a different kind of love.

She'd decided, hadn't she, back in New York, that he wasn't the one. Couldn't be the one. For so many reasons, big and small, not the least of which was that he hadn't even realized she existed as anything other than a pastry chef.

Then she'd come to the island, and started down a new path, opening a new chapter in her life filled with new experiences, new people, new hopes, and new dreams. It had been the right time to move on, get over her silly crush. It had just been proximity, she'd told herself. Even if time and distance didn't seem to be working in and of themselves for her to get over him, surely she wasn't so pathetic as to pine over feelings so completely unrequited, was she?

No, she was certainly not. She'd missed him, yes, and had pined—somewhat pathetically for a time— but she'd gotten past that, too. Through many late night bake sessions, some with Charlotte via phone, some alone, she'd come to terms with what would never be, and had finally, mercifully, moved on. She'd pushed herself to hope there would be another special someone, who would fit into this new life of hers. Someday. She wanted that. She was healthy, whole, and looking forward to what came next. She had accepted that whoever the person might be, it wasn't going to be Baxter Dunne. Would never be Baxter Dunne.

It had been impossibly cruel for him to show up when she'd finally gotten over him.

How could she be anything but incredibly relieved that, after dangling the dream she'd finally given up on right in front of her, sparking back to life all the feelings she'd finally boxed away, that he, too, had come to realize what she had already come to understand? They had no future. Not together.

She hadn't been secretly hoping he'd change her mind, show her there could be a way, some way, that it would work. Be that white knight on the charger, after all. No, of course not. She wasn't that ridiculous.

It meant they were both on the same page now. Win-win. All good.

Yea, them.

So, why was it, sitting next to him in the car, driving through the quiet island streets, with nightfall all around them . . . relief was not at all what she was feeling?

"I, um—" She had to clear her throat from the

tightness that seemed to have formed there. "Thank you. For saying all of that. For telling me. I . . . appreciate it. All of it." *Except for the part where it feels like my heart is shattering into a million pieces.* She wanted to look at him, but she just . . . couldn't. She looked down at her hands in her lap instead and realized she'd twisted her fingers together in a tense knot. She forced herself to straighten them, and tried to get a grip on the silly surge of emotions that was swamping her as she smoothed the fabric of her pants over her thighs. It was just fatigue talking. It had been an incredible couple days for her, a veritable roller coaster of emotions. A little sleep, a little bitch-and-bake with Charlotte—oh, thank God, she'd come—and Lani knew she'd be good as new. It had always worked before.

She straightened in her seat, and somehow managed to find a light tone. "So, with that all cleared up, why don't we go find that cup of coffee and discuss the production schedule. I'm assuming you'll have some kind of contract I'm going to need to sign, for the use of my shop, and, I guess, for the use of me, too."

She could feel him looking at her, but what he said was, "Right, yes, of course. You're going to be well compensated for our shutting your shop down, and for your own contributions. I think you'll approve of what we've drawn up, but if you want to have your lawyer look it over—"

"I'm mostly concerned with my shop being protected from any damage that might occur, with all the lighting and camera equipment. I'll want it in writing that you'll fix or replace whatever needs fixing or replacing and that when you're done, it will look exactly like it did when you started."

"Don't worry," he reassured her, "we'll take the best care. And you'll be there, so you'll see how it's all done, and how it will all be put back to rights."

That was the trick, she decided. Just keep her mind completely focused on business, on the production details, on tackling the project at hand, and her role in it, whatever the hell that was going to be. God, she didn't even want to think about that, about being on camera. With Baxter.

Well, she'd just do whatever they told her to do, stand where they told her to stand, say what they wanted her to say, bake what they wanted her to bake, then go home, hide in her cottage, and marathon bake with Charlotte until she had to be back on set. That would be the routine. Every day. For the next two weeks. She could do that. She had to do that.

Maybe she should move her pantry stock from her shop kitchen to her home. She was going to need those supplies for the nightly therapy sessions. Let Baxter's crew buy their own damn product.

She was pulled from her thoughts when he reached between them to the backseat, and came back with a big green thermos. She hadn't even realized they'd parked.

He used the thermos to point through the windshield at the sign posted by the side of the road. "Says there's a picnic area over there. Full moon tonight, so the lighting should be okay."

She looked blankly at the sign, then at him, trying to corral her thoughts back on track. "You want to go for a walk?"

He wiggled the thermos. "You remember Carlo, from Gateau?"

She lifted her eyebrows. "You mean the Carlo you selfishly stole from Gateau where I really, really needed him, to be a prep chef on your cute little cooking show, where surely someone else could have done the same job. That Carlo?"

He smiled at her mutinous scowl. "My restaurant, my show. I just . . . reassigned him. You were much nicer about it at the time."

"You signed my paychecks back then. You don't now. Carlo stealer."

He just laughed.

She looked at the thermos and understanding dawned. She shivered in anticipation as she nodded toward the thermos. "Is that . . . Carlo's coffee? Carlo is here? On Sugarberry? With his coffee?" She clasped her hands hopefully under her chin. "Really?"

Baxter smiled, and nodded, and Lani sighed in abject appreciation.

"I was going to bribe my way into your cottage with it, so we could talk about the show schedule. But, it occurred to me that anywhere we sit and talk in town would probably come with a lot of interruptions, and certainly very little privacy. I saw the sign there, and thought this might provide a good alternative." He glanced toward the path leading away from the road, into the dunes. "Unless it's not wise to go back there in the dark."

She laughed at that, and he looked back at her, pretending to be affronted. "I bring coffee from the gods and you mock my well-founded city boy fears?"

"Well-founded how? Did a cat run across your path while you were walking in Central Park once or something? In fact, I can't even imagine you walking in Central Park, much less anywhere truly uncivilized."

"I've heard plenty of unfortunate wildlife encounter stories, and I'm more than willing to learn from others' mistakes. And I would stroll Central Park, if I had the time." When she rolled her eyes, he smiled. "Okay, so maybe I wouldn't. But that's only because it's never been part of my regimen."

"Right." She popped open her door. "Come on, city boy. I'll protect you from the beach beasties."

He climbed out his side and came around the back of the car, holding her door open as she untangled herself from the forgotten seat belt. He closed the door behind her and she offered to carry the thermos. "Unless you want me to carry a big stick instead, to beat away the sand snakes."

"Quite amusing." He motioned for her to lead the way. "Ladies first."

"How gallant." She was smiling as she struck off down the path ahead of him. He was just so . . . British. And ridiculously charismatic. Honestly, Hugh Grant could take charm lessons from Baxter Dunne.

"I'm assuming if there was truly anything to be concerned about, you'd have eighty-sixed this entire idea." He jogged a few steps to catch up with her. "It goes without saying if you see anything that alarms you, I'll carry you all the way back to the car."

"And knightly, too."

"Aye, well . . . go with your strength, I always say."

Lani was laughing as they made their way down the trail path, which was paved for the most part, though the sand regularly blew over and buried long sections of it. The park rangers would shovel it clear periodically, to keep it from getting permanently socked in. The moon was rising and the stars were beginning to light up for their nightly show. It was a lovely, unseasonably warm night, even with the ocean breeze.

She felt the tension in her muscles ease, and the throb in her temples subside as the sound of the surf grew stronger. It was hard to be tense at the beach. It was too elemental, so rhythmic and soothing in its eternal ebb and flow. She started to think maybe that's what she should do. Just go with the ebb and flow of . . . well, all of it. The stress about the show, the worry about being hurt. Just let it roll off her shoulders like the tide going out, tackle the show as it came along, and simply enjoy his company along the way. Maybe that would be her new mantra for the duration of his stay. Sure, it was torture being around him, but only if she constantly put it in the "life is so unfair" perspective. The fact was, she was going to be around him whether it was unfair or not, whether she liked it or not.

So . . . why not allow herself to like it?

"I don't believe I've ever seen so many stars in my entire life. Collectively, I mean," he said. "I'm fairly certain, in fact, that I wasn't aware there even *were* that many stars in existence. The sky is literally choked with them."

Lani paused. Smiling to herself, she turned back to find him standing in the center of the path, face tipped heavenward like a young boy—a very tall, broad-shouldered boy—in awe as he took it all in. He was endearing and sexy as hell standing there, a bit of Cary Grant dash to go along with the Hugh Grant charm.

"It's always like that, you know," she said. "Every time you see the stars out here, you think maybe your memory was playing tricks and you exaggerated how many of them there were."

"It's positively awe-inspiring. Rather puts things in the grander perspective, doesn't it?"

She came to stand next to him. "I was thinking the same thing about the surf. No matter what happens in the world, the waves will always keep rolling in, for all eternity."

She followed his gaze upward, and marveled along with him. It truly was a spectacular sight. "You wanted to know my reasons for coming here, staying here. This is part of it. I can't imagine ever getting tired of it."

"Yes." There was a touch of reverence in his tone that she completely identified with.

When she shifted her gaze forward again . . . it was to find him looking at her.

There was a moment, and then another, when their gazes remained locked, the rumble of the surf providing the only soundtrack.

He broke the moment first, looking down the path in front of them, lifting the thermos in his hand. "Is that a picnic pavilion ahead?"

Maybe it was the thrumming in her ears, but his voice sounded a bit gruff. She decided it wasn't wise to think about that. Or how badly she'd wanted, in that expanded moment of silence between them, for him to kiss her again. So much so, she ached with it. "Ah, yes." She forced the image, the idea, from her head, looking to where he was pointing. "That's the place."

He walked a step ahead of her, leading the way, brushing the sand from the bench seat when they arrived under the open-sided, wood-beamed pavilion. Moving around to the other side, he took a seat for himself—putting the wide planked wood table neatly between them.

He popped the lid off the thermos to reveal another smaller cup under it. He filled both, and she reached for the smaller one.

She took a savoring sip, then groaned in bliss. "How is it better than I remember, when what I remember is nectar of the gods?"

"I know," Baxter agreed, after taking his own first sip. "If he wasn't such a good pastry chef, I'd hire him as my own personal barista and have him follow me around all day and produce this on demand."

"You know, the perks of celebrity are starting to look better to me all the time," she said, enjoying the heady scent as it filled the air.

He grinned, his teeth flashing white in the moonlight. "I won't deny, there are a few. Although I haven't let it go so far to my head that I've taken to hiring personal personnel, if you know what I mean. Well, that's not entirely true. I do retain a maid service for my home. Since I'm never in residence, I suspect I'm the easiest client they have."

"I'm ashamed to admit I've thought about it." She laughed. "They'd probably charge me extra. Things tend to lie where dropped for far longer than I promise myself they will when I drop them."

"You keep saying you're a bit of a sloth, but knowing your work methods, I find that hard to believe."

"You ran a tight ship."

"I'm motivated to never let the health department cite a single violation."

"I'm pretty sure they make some of them up, just out of spite."

"I'm not doubting you're wrong. Which is why I take great personal pleasure thwarting even the most overactive imaginations amongst them."

She laughed, and took another sip. "And here I thought you were just a Felix."

"Felix?"

"Unger. From *The Odd Couple*? Broadway play

turned into iconic movie starring Jack Lemmon and Walter Matthau, then a television show in the seventies? Still in reruns, I'm sure."

"Sorry. Can't say as I followed the cinema or telly growing up. Not that there was one, at any rate, even if I had."

"No television? The horror," she teased, then saw that his brief smile didn't quite reach his eyes. "I was just kidding. Lots of kids grow up without television. Stunted emotionally and lacking all social reference, I'm sure, but nonetheless, I hear that it occurs all the time, and those poor, poor, deprived children do survive. Somehow." She mock shuddered and finally drew a smile from him.

"I take it your experience was somewhat different, then." His eyes warmed as the conversation shifted to her.

"My mother called me square-eyes because I spent so much time parked in front of it. In my defense, I was doing my homework at the same time." She smiled when he merely lifted his eyebrows in question. "Okay, most of the time." She propped her elbows on the table and cradled the warm plastic cup between her palms. "So, you probably had a childhood filled with culture and art and music and all things insufferably British, which I'm certain you cling to, mainly to make us Americans feel like the inadequate, uncultured heathens we are for deigning to vacate the royal soil and start up our own gig across the pond."

He laughed outright at that. "Nothing so grand, I assure you. But had I known about or even considered the potential global ramifications, I'd have worked extra hard to add at least one or two of those things to my regimen."

She was grinning as she finished her last sip. Baxter

took the cup from her before she could refill it herself. His fingers brushed hers, briefly, casually, but tell
that to her suddenly skittish pulse rate. You'd have
thought he'd run his palms straight down her naked
body, given the way her nipples had gone instantly
hard and the more sensitive muscles of her inner
thighs had twitched and quivered.

She took the refilled cup back, and managed to get
that shivery-all-over sensation when they came into
contact again. For a whole fraction of a second. That
did not bode well for her newly voted in relax-and-
enjoy-the-ride edict. And the on-camera kitchen
time she was about to spend with him was looking especially dicey.

Yeah, she'd have to work on that. And fast.

"So, no television, no museums and art," she said,
striving to get back to the conversation. She did fine
with conversation. Just . . . no more touching. Or staring deeply into each other's eyes. No more of that.
"You know, come to think of it, there's never been
much press about your childhood. I'm not asking
about it, it's none of my business, but when someone
gets the kind of media attention you have through
your show, I'm surprised there's not more out there
on you."

He smiled over his cup. "What, have you been
Googling me?"

"No," she retorted, rolling her eyes, "but during
the time I worked with you, I was aware of the content
on Gateau's website, and—don't let this go to your
head—I read the bio stuff on your network's website
after *Hot Cakes* started. It's sort of thin. Just this long
list of your accomplishments and awards, blah blah
blah." She grinned when he raised his eyebrows.
"There's nothing fun and dishy."

"There's not much of interest to report, I'm afraid. I spent most of my time accumulating the accolades on that list, I suppose. The only thing dishy in my world is the food I put on the dishies."

"Ha ha. I'm teasing, you know. That list is something to be ridiculously proud of. We all wish we had such a list."

"I didn't work for the accolades. Or, only as much as they helped me to keep working."

"So . . . what is the story of you? Siblings? Parents? What was your hometown? Did you grow up in London proper?"

"I thought you weren't going to ask."

She gave him a patented unrepentant-Charlotte-shrug. "You don't have to answer."

He held her gaze, and, it was only because she knew him as well as she did, enough to read even the most subtle of nuances in his facial expressions—first rule of any kitchen, always learn to read the head chef as accurately and thoroughly as possible, because not all of them communicate well—that she realized he wasn't as comfortable as he'd been a moment ago. "Never mind," she said quickly. "I was only teasing. It really is none of my—"

"London," he said, easily enough. "East end. No siblings. I'd ask the same of you, but I already know you grew up in your nation's capital city, as an only child."

"Yes, well, you had the advantage of reading my employment documentation when I was first hired to work with you."

He smiled. "Maybe I just paid attention. Or maybe I Googled you."

She laughed at that. "Right, because I'm such a rock star."

"You've been interviewed plenty of times, Ms. James Beard Nominee. Your list is growing. And, okay . . . maybe I might have glanced at your employment forms. Once I tasted your ancho chile and cherry dark chocolate soufflé cake, with that incredible dulce de leche"—he drifted off, closed his eyes for a moment as he savored the memory—"you weren't going to work for anybody else. Not if I had anything to say about it." He opened his eyes, and grinned at her. "And I did."

"Yes, well, it's a good thing you skipped over that part in my background check about liking sharp things a little too much."

"I must have missed that part."

"In fifth grade home economics class, I gave Caroline Haxfield a haircut she'll never forget."

He chuckled. "You have a long—what do you call it?—rap sheet, do you?"

"Oh, yes, I was a delinquent of the first order."

"I find that rather hard to believe."

"Just ask Caroline Haxfield. I bet she'd still beg to differ."

"Just what did Miss Haxfield do to earn her new coiff?"

"She said I cheated on my homework, that there was no way I could have made my strudel by myself. It was Great-grandmother Harper's recipe, and it was complicated, but I made it with my own two hands. I'd done it dozens of times, right in Grandma Winnie's kitchen in Savannah. I could have made it blindfolded. I was all ready to explain every step to the teacher during final tasting. But before she got to mine—and this was for our final grade in cooking—Caroline 'accidentally' knocked it on the floor and destroyed it. So, I got a failing grade. I'd never had anything less than an A in a class in my life."

"Well, I can understand the umbrage. Let's hope you weren't likewise blindfolded when you relieved Miss Haxfield of her ponytail."

"Yes, well, that too I could have done with my eyes clo—wait, how did you know I chopped off her ponytail?"

"Maybe I did read your file."

"Okay, that was not in my file. I mean, it happened, but my dad assured me that even though Caroline's mother called the police on me after Caroline got home that afternoon, no police report was ever filed. I'd already been sent home from school early, which if you knew me—the kid who'd never missed a single day of school—that was punishment enough. It ruined my perfect attendance record. I was ten, for God's sake. I just had to give her all of my saved allowance so she could go get her hair professionally styled. And I know they didn't normally go to Alexandre's. She only went there so I'd have to give her every last penny."

"Was it worth it?"

Lani could swear his eyes were twinkling. And maybe they were. "Every last snip and dime."

"Well done, then."

"So . . . how did you know?"

He grinned. "Good guess."

"Ah." She eyed him consideringly, still not entirely sure.

"So, your grandmother was from Savannah?"

"My mom's mother, yes. Grandma Winnie. And her mother, Great-grandmother Harper, lived here on Sugarberry. It's where my grandmother grew up and where my mom spent most of her summers growing up. Harpers are very well respected here. Everyone loved my grandma Winnie and my mom. And my mom has always loved the island."

"Is that why your parents relocated here?"

"My dad was up for retirement right around the time I decided to head to Europe to study, and my mom was all done with him putting himself in danger every day. She was homesick for the South, and when she heard through an old friend that the sheriff's position here was opening up, she pushed my dad pretty hard to go after it. She knew he wasn't ready to stop working, she just wanted him out of the city. It's a testament to how well loved the Harpers are that he got the job, given he's otherwise an outsider. I know I owe a large debt to all my Sugarberry Harper forebears, and to my dad, too, for the goodwill that's been extended to me by the locals here."

"I can't imagine you wouldn't have earned it anyway."

She smiled. "Thanks, that's very kind of you, but I'm grateful for the hand up, nonetheless. All I have to do now is live up to it. And that's no small thing, so it does motivate me." She lifted her cup in salute. "Of course now, with my being responsible for bringing you here—even though I haven't taken any credit—my future status is probably sealed."

Instead of accepting her toast, his expression turned more serious. "You know, I can't help thinking about what you said, about wanting to know you'd made it on your own here, and not on the back of my show, or celebrity, or any of that rubbish. You've decided to be a good sport, and I appreciate it, deeply, but I still feel sorry that I've interceded where you—"

"Baxter, it's okay. No," she said, when he started to

argue. "I mean it. Charlotte said something to me on the phone the other night that made me think about it. Things happen in life we can't control. Like my mom passing too young, and my dad almost following along right behind her. I don't know what that might have done to me, or my projected goals and dreams. Just like I don't know what my life would have been like here if my mother and her family hadn't been so beloved. I'm accepting the benefit I get from that, and am grateful for it. So why is this any different?"

"That's family. That's your bloodline, your heritage. It is different."

"Maybe. But, you understand what I'm saying, right?"

He nodded. "Doesn't make me less sorry for it, though."

"What's done is done. I know I was hard on you when you showed up. Though there's a lot of me you don't know, or haven't seen, I'm not generally like that. And I didn't like feeling that way. If something unexpected happens that I don't like, well, that stinks, but I usually try to find a way to deal with it, and maybe take something positive from it. Like with my mom passing. Instead of feeling sorry for myself, or for my dad, for what we lost, we tried to celebrate who she was, and led with that example, so all the good cheer and warmth she spread around her everywhere she went wouldn't be forgotten. She was this bright shining star in our lives, in everyone's lives that she touched. I really wish you could have met her."

"You talked about her often enough I felt as if I had. I was heartbroken for you when she passed away. You were so devastated and, from hearing all your stories, and occasionally hearing you talk with her on the phone . . . the love you shared, the bond, was self-evident. It was a tragedy and I hate that it happened to you."

"Thank you," she said sincerely. "You were very supportive, though I honestly don't remember a whole lot about the time immediately after I heard. But . . . I did, and do, appreciate how good you were in letting me go and do what needed to be done."

"You didn't stay here, then. Afterward. Your father was alone, with her gone. Did you think about it then? Consider moving down?"

"Not specifically. I was in such a different place in my career then, finishing my first year working for you at Gateau, and the nomination had just happened. My father, well, he was absolutely gutted by losing her. We both were. I think being here helped, because everyone felt the same acute sense of loss, so it was . . . comforting. Very comforting. And healing. But no way would he have let me stay down here. In fact, he pushed me to go back before I thought I was ready. We Trusdales, we don't wallow. We pick ourselves up, find something positive to focus on, and work toward making the one we lost proud of us as we move on." She could still hear those words, spoken almost verbatim by her father more than once, echoing through her mind. "I also think he couldn't stand it that I was watching him grieve. He wanted to be strong for me, and be that person who moved on, head up, eyes forward. So, he pushed, and I eventually went. It probably was for the best. It did make both of us move forward, and follow her example."

"You were always so good-natured, even-keeled, and optimistic, but I knew there was steel there. The way you handled the kitchen, the chaos. I was sad for you . . . but I never once worried you wouldn't find your way through it. I worried that you might feel you had to stay with your father out of family obligation, and that I might lose you that way . . . but I knew grief wouldn't cripple you, or make you walk away from what you'd begun."

"Thank you." She was touched by his sincerity. "Ironic then, isn't it . . . that two years later, I chose to do just that."

He shook his head. "I thought so, at the time, yes. I mean, I understood completely. You'd just gotten past dealing with the sudden death of one parent, only to risk losing the other so soon afterward. With the continued health concerns and your father being your only family, it made sense that you came down here. I'll admit, I was surprised—gobsmacked, really—when you announced you were staying for good. But, your reasons for doing so . . . I understood family sometimes trumps everything else."

She tilted her head, studying him. Her vision had long since adjusted to the moonlight, and she could see his features very well, but with the deepening darkness, she could no longer make out the nuances of his expression. She could hear them, though. "But you wouldn't have, would you? Relocated, I mean, like I did. Change paths."

"I can't answer that."

"Because you've never been put in that position?"

"Because I was never in the position where that could have happened to me."

She frowned, confused for a moment, then realized what he was saying. "Oh. I'm sorry. I can't imagine losing both parents as a child."

"I never knew them, so it's okay."

"Truly an orphan then? You weren't adopted?"

He smiled briefly. "Don't get all Oliver Twist on me. Obviously, I made out fine."

"That you did." She was thinking about what he'd revealed, and she'd bet his life had been a whole lot more Oliver Twist than Little Orphan Annie. But it was the kind of thing she could imagine forging him into the chef he'd become.

She noticed him shift in his seat and he stretched his feet out, bumping hers. "Sorry," he said, pulling them back. "Trying to sift the sand out of my socks."

She finished her coffee and slid the cup back to him. "Come on."

He took the cup. "Are we leaving?"

"Just the picnic table."

He lifted his eyebrows in question.

"Well, if you're going to have sand between your toes, I was thinking you should experience it the right way."

"There's a right way?"

She laughed. "C'mon." She nodded her head. "This way."

"The water is that way."

"Which is good, because that's where the beach is."

"Oh." He sounded less than enthusiastic. "Bloody fantastic."

Chapter 10

"Okay," Baxter said, after they'd trekked about fifty yards down the beach. "You might have a point." Once they'd gone over the remaining dunes and through the rough sea grasses and washed up flotsam and jetsam, they'd ended up on sugar soft sand. A lot of which was in his shoes and, he was fairly certain, probably always would be. At the moment, his shoes and socks were fifty yards back up the beach behind them. The farther they walked, the more he forgot about them, and the sand currently in them.

They were barefoot, pant legs rolled up, as they made their way down the narrow strip of sand. The water was a bit chilly, but the sand was still somewhat warm, or at least not cold.

"For me," Leilani said, "if you're going to hear the surf, and look at the stars, you should feel soft sand beneath your toes. By now it would normally be too chilly for this, but with all the heat we're still having, this is one of the nice benefits of an Indian summer."

"Well, I don't see myself parking on a blanket

under the blistering sun and risking sand in other in-teresting places, but the strolling, the surf, and the stars? Not a bad way to end the day at all."

They smiled at each other, and he was careful to keep from bumping into her, or wandering into her path, which, with the unevenness of the sand and oc-casional encroaching waves, was easy to do. But he couldn't seem to keep from watching her as they walked. Well, he was walking. She was marching rather steadily down the shoreline.

He smiled to himself, thinking she wasn't quite as relaxed as she thought she was . . . but in contrast to the constant chaotic dash that had been her life in New York, he supposed this could be considered a leisurely stroll.

"The company isn't so bad, either," he said as the si-lence between them stretched comfortably.

She sent a sidelong smile his way, but kept up her steady pace—perhaps picking it up a bit. It occurred to him that maybe her inability to relax wasn't so much an indicator of the impact of her life in the city . . . but her company of the moment. Since climb-ing into the car earlier, she'd shown a completely dif-ferent attitude than she had since he'd first stepped into her kitchen. He'd been relieved, happily so, for them to regain their even footing, despite being quite unhappy that all he'd be leaving Sugarberry with was a week's worth of programming. And, perhaps, after this evening, some very special memories.

He wished that felt like enough. It would take con-siderably more than a simple stroll on the beach to feel anywhere near close to enough. And longer still before he was at peace with the idea of walking away when the show was done filming.

He considered and immediately tossed the idea of

putting a moratorium on interacting with Lani in any capacity not directly work related. She was making an effort to be a sport about the chaos he'd brought back to her life. Likely it wasn't coming as easily as their banter and laughter made it seem. The least he could do was make a similar effort.

So, the stroll continued.

"I'd have thought you'd be a city girl, too," he said. "When did you learn to appreciate the sand and surf?"

"Nanny—my great-grandmother Harper—passed on when I was fairly young. I think I was six. When we'd come down to Savannah to visit Grandma Winnie, we'd usually make the trek to Sugarberry and spend some time with her. There was no causeway then. You had to take a ferry over. I think I have more specific memories of the ferry rides than any real memories of the island itself. I do remember Nanny's kitchen here."

"Is the house still here?"

Lani nodded. "Harper House has been in the family through four generations. Five, with me, I guess. Nanny's husband, Roy, grew up here. He passed long before I was born, but I've seen pictures. There aren't too many from back in that day, but the ones that did get preserved are pretty fascinating. The town wasn't much more than a fishing lodge and a combination general store and post office back then."

"So, Harper House isn't your cottage then—"

"No, my father lives there. Nanny left it to Grandma Winnie, who used to rent it out. Then she left it to my mom, who continued with the leasing, until she and dad decided to come back down. They did a major overhaul on the place before they moved in. It's really wonderful."

He smiled. "I can see it's a place of good memories."

"Oh, definitely. I remember Nanny teaching me to make cobbler in her great kitchen, which my mom updated but kept otherwise intact. It's a grand old Southern-style kitchen, big butcher block island, huge oven, glass front cabinets on top and maple underneath. Mom resurfaced the counters, but kept the butcher block. That's where we made cobbler and I learned to can my own peaches. Well, I was too young to actually do the cutting and canning, but I sat on a stool and watched. And I got to help whip the topping for the cobbler."

"So you come by your baking skills honestly," he said.

Fond memories softened her moonlit smile and Baxter felt the ache bloom inside his chest again. He'd long ago come to terms with his past, but listening to her stories, seeing the affection and joy she had reminiscing, it made him wonder how it would feel to have a connection like that, reaching back through the generations.

"I like to think so," she said. "My mom was a wonderful cook in her own right. My father, on the other hand . . . well, he's good with the grill and he can make a mean pot of chili, but beyond that, grilled cheese, canned soup, and scrambled eggs pretty much round out his skill set where pots and pans are concerned."

Baxter smiled, trying to imagine a kitchen filled with warmth and laughter. The kitchens of his youth had been filled with yelling, swearing and chaos, though that had still been family to him. "I think it's nice, family stories and traditions passed down through the generations."

"Do you know anything about your background at all?"

"No. That's all right, though. There's not much to tell. I was given up as an infant."

"Did you ever look? At the records, I mean?"

He shook his head. "If they'd wanted me, they'd have come for me. They didn't, so I don't see the point."

"Since you've become a celebrity, no one has come crawling out of the woodwork, hoping to cash in?"

"That won't happen."

Lani smiled, but her expression said she wouldn't be so sure of that. "Well, if it hasn't by now, you're probably right. So, where did you grow up?"

"I spent my first half dozen years in a church-run orphanage, then, when I wasn't adopted, I was sent to live in a home for boys in the east end."

"How long were you there?"

He shot her a quick grin. "I wasn't there at all when I could help it."

"Ah." She matched his smile. "So, this isn't going to be a story about how you were taken into the bosom of the boys' home head cook, who became like a surrogate mother to you, teaching you everything she knew from the old country, and inspiring your journey to culinary greatness?"

"Um, no," he said, on a surprised chuckle. "Old country? Really?"

"I'm a pastry chef, not a novelist. I was picturing someone like a Helga or a Brunhilda."

"The cook at Peckham's was named Harry. His food was inedible. When he was sober enough to cook it and remember to feed us at all, that is. I regularly stole my supper from the dust bins and garbage cans behind kitchens all over London from the time I was eight. By the time I turned ten, I figured out it was better if I actually got a job working in the kitchen. Then I got food I didn't have to steal, and a chance to sit somewhere warm and dry while I ate it."

"Okay, now you're making that up. That's Oliver Twist."

He shrugged, smiled. "I'm not that good a story-teller."

Her smile drooped. "Baxter, that's . . . that's horrible."

"Which answers the question of why you don't see that stuff in my bios anywhere."

"Actually, the gossip rags would eat that up with a spoon. I'm stunned they haven't put it out there."

"They won't, because I've never put it out there. No one from those days remembers me. No one will connect my childhood to me."

"I can't believe that. You're a pretty memorable guy, and as a child, I can only imagine the incorrigible charm factor worked twice as well in your favor."

"I was definitely incorrigible, aye, but there was very little charming about me in those days. I didn't learn the value of a well-placed wink and a grin until I was a little older and started noticing the waitresses."

Leilani rolled her eyes, but she'd slowed down her steady beach march. She kept glancing over at him as they continued walking. "You don't want to hear it, but I am sorry."

"For? You don't get to pick your childhood. I'm not deeply scarred by it or anything. It was what it was, and it led me to the path that would become my passion. So, I can hardly complain about how I got there now, can I? Seems rather ungracious, don't you think?"

"I honestly don't know what to think. But . . . I'm glad you've put it in such a healthy perspective."

"We Dunnes—well, this Dunne, anyway—doesn't believe much in wallowing, either. I took the positive, and ran with it."

She nodded, and smiled. "Well, that I definitely understand." She glanced over at him. "Pretty amazing, though. A lot of kids would have crumbled under the weight of the situation."

"You do what you have to do. I wasn't special. It was just survival and dumb luck. I can only take credit for not being stupid and throwing away the one chance I had."

"Did you know from the first kitchen you wanted to be a chef?"

"My first goal was just to eat, but once I got going, I decided I wanted to go from scraping and washing dishes to being a line cook. Maybe, if I was really, really lucky, I'd become a sous chef one day. My dreams were focused, but small. And so was I. You know what kitchens are like. The ones I grew up in make any kitchen you've been in look like the Disneyland version of a chaotic kitchen. I didn't have the physical presence as a ten, or even twelve-year-old lad, to take any kind of stand. I learned, growing up as I did, that it was better to keep your mouth shut if you wanted to stay fed."

"When did that change?" She motioned to him, head to toe. "Small of stature you're definitely not. Quiet and shy are hard to fathom as well."

"I was never shy, simply careful. Seen and not heard was the better path. I was gaining height more rapidly by twelve, thirteen, but still scrawny and a little uncoordinated. Gangly, all arms and legs. No more than eight stone. It was around fourteen, I think, when I started filling out. Summer before I turned sixteen I grew four full inches in less than five months."

"Ouch."

"Indeed."

"I'm still trying to picture you in a fast kitchen as a ten-year-old. I can't imagine having any child in a kitchen like that!"

"I was never really a child, luv. By ten and three, I'd seen more than most do well into manhood. I just needed my body to catch up to what was inside my head."

"And when it did?"

"I figured out that trying to be the toughest guy in a back alley kitchen didn't make much sense." He smiled. "Even Caroline Haxfield would have lost more than her ponytail in those places."

Lani gaped, then grinned. "That is so . . . wrong. Funny, but wrong. So, what was your strategy, then?"

His smile grew. "Well, I'd also figured out about that whole wink and a smile thing right around then. My height gave me a bit more advantage outside the kitchen than it did inside."

"Ah."

He chuckled. "Oh, ah, indeed."

She elbowed him for that, as they walked, but she was laughing, too.

"I also figured out that in order to make sous chef, I had to find a kitchen where they actually used one."

She laughed. "So, where did you end up?"

"Well, I made friends with a certain, um . . . lady who was from a decidedly different part of London than I had ever been in."

Lani wiggled her eyebrows. "How . . . salacious. Are we talking a Mrs. Robinson sort of deal?"

He raised his hand, like an oath-taker. "I don't kiss and tell. But she did help me work on getting rid of my EastEnder accent, polish me up a bit."

"She was your Henry Higgins then."

"She was an angel. To me, anyway." Baxter smiled. "And a Henry, too. All rolled into one amazing package."

"What happened to her?"

"I lost the glow of my youth, as it were, and she moved on to other . . . friends."

"Ah," was all Leilani said, but her tone was kindly, and compassionate. "I'm sorry. Was that hard? It must have been."

He lifted a shoulder. "It was simply what happened next. She was and will always be someone very special to me."

"Have you seen her? Since . . . you know? I can imagine she'd be pretty proud of you. At least I hope that's the kind of person she was."

"I've never met another person like her, that's the truth. I tried to look her up, years later, but never was able to track her down. I wouldn't be surprised if she wasn't around to be tracked. She tackled life with passion, and was always rather fearless. At least that's how I remember it."

"What did you do, after you parted ways?"

"I'd discovered the joys of chocolate by then, and making sweet things, delectable things. Her father had been a candy maker and she definitely had a taste for sweets. I'd made it my mission to see to, um, all her needs . . . so, I poured some of my burgeoning energies into developing my baking skills, but it quickly became my passion in earnest. I'd already switched from kitchens to pastry shops before we parted, learning as fast as I could. I stayed on that path. I knew that was where I was meant to be. I lived, ate, breathed, slept, and dreamed pastry." He smiled, thinking perhaps he had at least one affectionate family memory after all. "And, at core, I have Emily to thank for that."

They walked for another several yards in silence, then Leilani elbowed him again.

He glanced down at her. "What was that for?"

"Nothing. Just—" She looked up at him, and the moonlight caught and highlighted the structure of her face, lending a sparkle to her eyes. "You're a very gallant man. And a kind one. I don't think anyone can teach that part."

"I—thank you." He was caught off guard, by the sentiment, and the affection for him that colored it.

He stopped then. She took another step before she realized it, and turned back. "Baxter?"

"My real name is . . . well, I don't rightly know that, I suppose. But the one I was given by the sisters was Charlie Hingle."

She walked back to him, but there was no hint of amusement on her face, no teasing smile, just honest curiosity. "When did you change it?"

"When? Well, I lied about it long before I made it legal."

"Why? Were you teased about it for some reason? It seems rather . . . normal to me."

He lifted a shoulder, a hint of self-deprecation coloring his smile, and his response. "Maybe it wasn't gallant enough."

She smiled at that. "Is that really why?"

"No. I . . . I don't know why I lied the first time. I guess . . . well, I guess when I found that first kitchen, when they let me come inside, I felt like . . . I don't know. Like I was my own person. Like it didn't matter where I came from, or who I came from. I could be anyone I wanted to be."

"You just wanted the right to define yourself, to choose who you were going to be," she said.

"That was exactly it."

"So, where did you come up with the name? Had you been thinking about it?"

He shook his head. "They'd ask my name and I'd tell them the first thing that popped into my head. Nobody cared, but they had to call me something if they wanted me to work. It only mattered to me. I'm sure more than a few others working in those same kitchens weren't using their real names. It wasn't a particularly—shall we say—well-heeled part of town. Nobody poked into your business too closely."

"So, when did it become Baxter Dunne?"

"Around the time I was working to lose my accent, posh myself up a bit."

She smiled more widely then. "So, did you come up with it? Or did 'enry 'iggins?"

He smiled at that. "It was mine. Cobbled together from ones I'd used over the years."

"When did you make it legal?"

"When I got my first real job, with an honest paycheck. Before, it had always been cash under the table, sometimes food, or a place to sleep. But when I had to fill out actual forms, I paused over the name. I couldn't write in the real one. It had never felt real. It wasn't me. So I put down Baxter Dunne, then when I got paid, I went and made it legal."

"A little backward, perhaps. And weren't you still underage? That didn't cause problems?"

He shrugged. "It all got worked out."

She smiled. "Well, I can see how that whole thing might be a little complicated to include in your celebrity bio, but I'm still surprised no one ever ferreted it out."

Again, he lifted a shoulder. "There's no one to know. Except me. And now, you. I've never told another living soul."

"Why? It's nothing to be ashamed of."

"No, and I'm not. But it's mine, not for public consumption."

"What do you tell interviewers when they ask about your childhood?"

"Just that I grew up hard and worked kitchens my whole life. It's the truth. They don't need the details."

She nodded, then looked up into his face. "Why tell me?"

"Because we've been talking about me not knowing all there is to know about you. And you were sharing about your family, telling me about yourself. I guess I wanted you to know that it went both ways. You didn't know me, either. And . . . I wanted you to."

She paused for a moment, then nodded. "Fair enough."

"Does it matter? Now that you know?"

"In what way do you mean?"

"Does it change anything?"

"I appreciate you telling me, sharing that with me. You know you can trust me with it. I won't tell anyone. Not even Charlotte."

"That's not what I mean. Does it change what you think of me?"

"Of course not," she said, without hesitation. "Why would it? I mean, it helps me to understand more about you, but, if anything, it just makes you more"— she paused—"it just makes you more. That's all."

He lifted his hands, wanting to cup her moonlit face, wanting—needing, perhaps—to make contact in a more tactile way. He was feeling more connected to her in that moment than he'd ever been, and he wanted to . . . engage all his senses. Sight . . . smell . . . sound. Touch.

Taste.

"Leilani . . ."

She looked up into his eyes, searching for what, he wasn't quite sure.

"Coming here, getting to know you . . . it just makes you more, too. Do you understand?"

"Baxter"—she took a small step back—"you conceded, remember? You said you knew, agreed even, that we can't—"

"That's all I'm saying, Lei. That's . . . all I'm saying." He curled his fingers into his palms, and dropped his hands back to his sides.

She looked down at the sand between their bare feet. "We should be getting back. It's late." When she looked up, she was smiling, but whatever it was he'd been seeing in her eyes, almost from the moment she'd gotten into the car—that extra little sparkle— was gone.

"Right. Right." *Too late.* He didn't regret telling her. Didn't regret anything he'd said. But he did regret the loss of that spark.

He turned and gestured for her to lead the way. As he watched her trudge quietly back down the beach, lost in her own thoughts, he found his drifting as well.

He had always gone after what he wanted. *Always.* He believed if he worked hard enough, he could achieve any goal. It had been no small thing for him to admit that, where Leilani was concerned, he couldn't get what he wanted. For once, no amount of hard work was going to achieve that particular goal. In the end, Leilani also deserved to have what she wanted, to achieve the goals she was working toward. And he didn't fit into that picture. Nor could he make his goals dovetail with hers.

He knew exactly what he wanted. All the parts of Leilani Trusdale—the parts he knew, the parts he'd yet to discover. He didn't need to know another thing about her to know the absolute truth, the utter certainty of that want.

But he had nothing to offer her that she wanted. She didn't want his life.

The question now was . . . what kind of life was he going to have, going forward without her?

Chapter 11

Leilani punched her fist into the dough. "You should see it, Char." She punched again. "My poor, adorable, cute little shop *thwump* it's overrun, with cables, cameras, racks of lights, and *thwump* and strangers. Tromping all over it. Putting their hands—their stranger hands—all over my stuff." She shuddered. Then punched the dough again.

Charlotte gently elbowed her out of the way. "Killing our bread isn't going to change that."

"I know, but it might keep me from kneading that guy who keeps pawing through my aprons."

Charlotte looked up. "Why on earth is anyone pawing through your aprons?"

"The producer, Rosemary? Privately I call her Rosemary's Baby if that gives you any clue. She's five-foot-nothing, somewhere between the age of sixty and infinity, steel gray hair cut into a short, razor edge bob, steelier gray eyes, and thin lips that are always pursed. You know what I mean? She scares me. Anyway, she got wind of the fact that I wear some of my collectibles to work and she thought it would make a cute story angle for the show. But apparently I can't be trusted to pick out my own aprons." Lani folded her arms. "My shop is overrun with cables and wires, I have pawing strangers, and I've been reduced to a cute angle." She air-quoted the last part with yeasty fingers. "Remind me again why I signed on for this?"

"Community goodwill?" Charlotte pasted on a fake smile.

"Right. I'd rather run for Miss Kiwanis and wear a bikini made of palm fronds. That's goodwill."

"That's . . . just wrong. Come on, knead some dough, we'll bake, it will smell good, we'll eat too much, and trash men." Charlotte patted Lani on the shoulder. "You'll feel all better by morning."

"I have to go back there in the morning. Very early in the morning."

"You're used to early mornings."

"Yes, when it's just me, a very big cup of coffee, three hundred cupcakes that need me, and the theme from *Hawaii 5-0* keeping us all company. That is an early morning I can live with."

Charlotte grabbed Lani's fist before she could punch the dough again. "Wine. We need wine. Let me finish up here while you pour us each a glass."

"You can have a glass. I'm getting a straw."

"Whatever keeps you from committing harvest bread homicide works for me."

Lani wedged herself around behind Charlotte and got two glasses down, then pulled out a dusty wine bottle from the cupboard.

"So," Charlotte asked, "how many glasses of wine is it going to take before you spill the beans on your date last night?"

"It wasn't a date." Lani yanked out the cork with a

bit more force than absolutely necessary. "It was a business meeting."

"I found your sandy shoes on the front porch and rolled up jeans in the laundry this morning. Sand in those, too." She gave a quick wiggle of the eyebrows as Lani handed her a glass. "I like how you islanders do business."

"It wasn't like that. And what are you doing in my laundry?"

"Hey, I woke up, you'd come and gone, and I'd already caught up on *Iron Chef*. I made cinnamon rolls, then needed something to occupy me until Tyler Florence. Ultimate cheesecakes today. Tyler. And cheesecake." Charlotte took a moment, hand to chest, sighed. "It's the closest I've been to multiple orgasms since February. Your pantry is organized now, too. By the way, what is up with the fifty pound bags of flour?"

"I stole them from myself. I knew we'd bake and I figured I was giving Baxter my whole shop, so his crew could buy their own damn flour." Lani sipped, sighed, and shuddered with great pleasure as the bittersweet bite of grape slid past her tongue and down her throat. "Maybe if I just take the rest of this bottle with me tomorrow, I'll make it through."

Charlotte slid the bread into the oven, picked her wineglass up again, and leaned back against the counter as she sipped. "So . . . is this really about the shop invasion?"

"This?"

Charlotte widened her eyes. "I'm not in New York on speakerphone, I'm standing right in front of you. With two perfectly functioning eyes in my head."

"This"—Lani lifted her glass, then downed the last sip—"is about the shop invasion. And it might also have a tiny little bit to do with the date."

"I thought you said it wasn't a date."

"It wasn't." She poured another glass, but just swirled the wine around in the glass without taking another sip. Finally she looked up at Charlotte. "But I wanted it to be." She let out a deep, shuddering sigh. "I *really* wanted it to be. There was a moment, toward the end, that I thought—" She shook her head.

"Thought what?"

"I thought he was going to kiss me again."

Charlotte's face lit up. "And?"

"And I ended the evening right there, before . . . before we both lost our resolve."

Charlotte's excited expression fell. "Why?"

"*Why?* Charlotte, we'd agreed there was no future in it. And we were right."

"So why the moonlit stroll on the sand? Seems to be tempting fate, doesn't it?"

"I don't know. He'd never gotten sand between his toes and we were laughing and . . . it just sort of made sense at the time. But we kept it civil, friendly. For the first time since he came down here I was enjoying being with him. So, I thought—stupidly thought—maybe I could just go with the flow. Accept the fact that the show was going to happen, accept the fact that doing the show meant spending more time with Baxter. Accept that he's going to leave in a few weeks when it's all over no matter what . . . and put my big girl pastry chef panties on and just try to enjoy the time I get."

Charlotte studied her with a considering eye. "How is that working out for you?"

"We haven't even started filming yet and already I'm a bread murderer, that's how." Just like that, her eyes welled up and her mouth went all wobbly. "And I love bread."

"Oh, dear." Charlotte put her wine down and pulled Lani into a tight hug.

"This is so stupid," Lani whispered. "I'm so stupid. Why can't I just deal with it?"

Charlotte untangled their arms, steadied Lani's wineglass in her hand, then looked her straight in the eye. "Because you love him, you idiot."

Lani sniffled and nodded. "I know. I sort of figured that out last night."

Charlotte picked up her glass again. "About time."

Lani squinted one eye at her best friend. "Hey."

Charlotte shrugged, completely unrepentant. "All this time, I was supportive. Like a good friend, I didn't say anything. I let you find your own way to the truth. But anyone with eyes to look and ears to listen could see this." She nudged Lani's glass up and Lani obediently took a small sip.

"When you left for good, I thought, well, no point in saying it now. You've ended it. You'll move on and so will he. Then I find out he's moving his entire show to your island, and I thought, she'd better not screw this up."

Lani's mouth fell open, then snapped shut. "Screw this up?"

Charlotte nodded, her chin set.

"Is that why you're here? To make sure I don't screw things up?" Lani's eyes narrowed. "Was there really a kitchen fire?"

"Yes."

"Really?" Lani prodded.

Charlotte suddenly studied the wine in her glass. "It was a small grease fire. And we do have to wait for HD to clear us. Should take maybe a day, three at most. I got someone to cover the rest for me. Franco can manage." Stronger now that she'd made her little admission, she finished with another defiant lift of the shoulder. "Clearly, you needed me."

"Well, I'm not going to lie and say I'm not thrilled, relieved, and ecstatic that you're here." Lani took another sip, enjoyed it all the way down, then looked at Charlotte. "So . . . how am I screwing this up?"

"By not giving him a chance. You want him, you love him, but didn't think he'd even noticed you that way. Now he comes here and tells you he can't forget you and wants you in his life. He kisses you, lays claim to you, right there in the front of your shop, for the world to see, and what do you do?" Charlotte was working up a good head of steam, and she downed the rest of her wine and smacked her glass on the counter with enough force that Lani was surprised the stemware didn't snap in half. "You reject him! Of course I had to come."

"What choice do I have?" Lani demanded. "He's leaving in two weeks. My life is here."

"And this is the life you would choose over a life with the man you love? I know your father is here, but you say he's disappointed in your choices, too. You can still have your own shop, Lan. It doesn't have to be here."

"I know. With a few more evenings like the last one, I probably would have started to reconsider. But, Char, it's not that simple. Yes, he wants me, but he doesn't have a life to offer me, even if I was willing to try. He said as much last night. He told me that he hadn't really thought it through, but now he has. He said he shouldn't have come down here. That it would never have worked."

Charlotte was all geared up to deliver some other strident piece of commentary, but that made her pause.

She opened her mouth, then paused again. "Oh," she said finally, then grabbed her glass and filled it again as she pondered this new piece of information. "You said he almost kissed you."

"I said I thought he wanted to. For a moment. Maybe it was wishful thinking. But it doesn't matter."

"What, exactly, did he say?" Charlotte took a sip of wine, then pointed her glass at Lani. "Leave nothing out."

Lani took a fortifying sip of her own. "He said that he is going to be on the road filming this show for the next few months, but that even when he goes home again, he really doesn't have a home life. His work is his life. He knows how much running my own place means to me. He still has Gateau. Even with everything else he has going on, he doesn't want to give that up. He, of all people, understands that proprietary sense of pride and accomplishment. Granted, our goals with our respective shops are worlds apart, and he has others running his place now, but it's still his, and the desire is the same. Just like his schedule is crazy and demanding, mine would be too, running my own shop, especially just starting out. Even if I was willing to move north, start over, what kind of life would we have? He's running one direction, I'm running another; we'd be lucky if we passed each other in the hallway occasionally."

"It would probably be a much bigger hallway. And a better home kitchen," Charlotte offered, though with little real enthusiasm.

Lani sighed. "I know. In a fully renovated brownstone. In the Village."

Charlotte shifted so she was leaning her back on the counter, too, elbow to elbow with Lani. They both sipped.

"You'd have to live with a boy, though," Charlotte said. "All the time."

"Yeah," Lani agreed. "With all his boy stuff lying around everywhere."

"And boy smells."

They both wrinkled their noses.

"But, there would be regular boy sex," Lani said.

Charlotte sighed. "That is true."

"I'm pretty sure it would be really great boy sex."

"Almost makes it worth the smelly parts."

"Doesn't it?" Lani finished off the second glass, then turned her head to look at her best friend. "I'm pretty sure Baxter has sweet parts," she whispered, then snickered.

Charlotte did, too. Then both of them were giggling uncontrollably.

"We might have had a little too much wine," Lani said.

Charlotte held up two fingers. "Just two glasses."

Lani held up her glass. "Really big glasses. Really quick."

The oven timer went off, making them leap away from the counter with a squeal, which sent them into another peal of snickering laughter.

"We, on the other hand," Charlotte said as she pulled out the perfectly risen, perfectly browned loaf of savory harvest bread. "We only have good smells."

"Delicious smells," Lani agreed, breathing in deeply.

"Heavenly harvest smells," Charlotte agreed. "But I think perhaps we should switch to tea while we enjoy a slice. I'll brew, you get the herb butter." She looked at the oven clock. "Bobby Flay comes on in ten minutes."

"Bobby Flay," Lani said with reverence. "I wonder if he's smelly."

"I don't know." Charlotte snorted. "But I'd smell Bobby Flay firsthand and let you know."

That sent them off all over again.

"I'll get the plates," Lani said, hiccupping for air. "Last one to the couch is a smelly boy!"

Their mad dash was abruptly cut short when the front doorbell rang.

"I think you have company," Charlotte said.

"I didn't even know I had a doorbell," Lani said. "I'll get it. You finish the tea."

"Careful," Charlotte called out. "It might be a smelly boy."

Lani snickered, and thought they really should have more wine with all future bitch-and-bakes. "Welcome to Bake Club," she announced as she flung the door open. She knew she was punchy from fatigue and half looped from the wine, but she just didn't give a damn. "No smelly boys allowed."

"Oh. Dear."

Lani had been looking up, half expecting it to be Baxter. Not because he was due to drop by, but because he always seemed to choose the most inopportune times to show up. She dropped her gaze lower, then lower still. "Alva?"

"Why yes, dear. Have I caught you at a bad time? Oh my, something smells heavenly."

Somehow Lani was backing up and inviting her in before she quite knew what was happening.

"Well, hello again," Alva said to Charlotte. "I'm sorry, dear, but I've forgotten your name."

"I'm Charlotte. Can I get you a glass of wine?"

Lani made a neck-cutting motion behind Alva's back, but Charlotte was already turning away to get another piece of stemware from the cupboard.

"What have you made that smells so wonderful?"

"Harvest bread, with savory butter," offered Charlotte, who'd suddenly become the hostess with the mostest. "We were just about to cut ourselves a slice or two. Would you care for a piece?" She turned away from the cupboard and picked up her own wineglass.

Bobby Flay, Lani mouthed to Charlotte when she caught her eye, but Charlotte merely waved her glass and smiled. Apparently when Charlotte felt good, everybody was going to feel good.

"Oh, my, well, if it's no imposition." Alva's eyes were on full-Alva-twinkle. "I'd love to give it a try."

Even sober, Lani had to admit it was hard to resist Alva on full-twinkle. "I'll get another plate."

"And a glass, too, dear," Alva added sweetly. "I'd love a sip of wine. If there's any left."

Lani's eyes narrowed behind Alva's back, but Charlotte swiftly moved in, slicing the bread and handing the plates to Alva to put around the small dinette table.

When they were all settled, sipping and snacking, Alva said, "This is delicious. Any chance I can beg the recipe? I haven't baked bread in ages, but this is such a perfect thing for when the weather cools."

"Which will be soon, I hope," Lani added, pushing her wineglass away. She'd stick with the solid carbs for a while.

"Well, Miss Lani May, dear, I was out for a drive—bit of insomnia, don't you know—and saw your lights on. I thought I'd just say thank you for those wonderfully addictive little cakes you made for the tournament last night."

"You're very welcome. I assume they went over well?"

"Between the lava flow of chocolate and the fountain of sangria, it was a rather . . . lively evening."

Lani couldn't help smiling. "So, did Beryl regain her title?"

"Yes, though it didn't exactly happen as planned. She more or less earned it back by default."

"Did some of the other players . . . overindulge?" Lani asked.

"Yes, but it was the fight that broke out, resulting in the local constabulary being called in, that ended the tournament rather prematurely for a few of the players."

Lani blamed her inability to contain her snicker on the wine. "Um, did that happen before or after midnight?"

"Oh, that was well after," Alva said. "Why do you ask?"

"No reason." Lani hoped Dre had taken the right line on the bet. "I didn't hear anything about it from my father, but he wouldn't have been on duty that late and I've been in the shop all day, out of touch. I hope it all worked itself out okay."

Alva's smile was quite self-satisfied. "Let's just say that my first column will start off my new career with a bang."

Charlotte hid her snicker by taking another quick nibble of bread. The whistle on the tea kettle went off just then and she scooted her chair back. "Let me get that. Tea?"

"Oh, I'm fine with my wine, dear," Alva said.

"I'll take a cup," Lani said.

"I went by the shop first," Alva continued, after Charlotte stepped into the kitchen and made the shrill whistling stop. "I thought perhaps you'd be having another late night bake session." She sighed somewhat wistfully. "I've really enjoyed our little impromptu sessions."

That earned Lani a quick arched brow from Charlotte as she stepped back in carrying a tray with the teapot, cups, and saucers.

Lani lifted one shoulder in a half shrug as if to say *I didn't plan it* but Alva went on, saving her from further explanation.

"I hardly recognized the place. Trucks everywhere, people all over." Alva set her glass down and clasped her hands as she leaned forward a bit in her seat. "Is it as exciting as it looks?"

Charlotte looked pointedly at Lani as she poured the tea, but her tone was sugary sweet. Like corn syrup. "Yes, Lan, tell us how exciting it is."

"It's a bit overwhelming to me right now," Lani told her. "A lot to learn. It was mostly a day of logistics, getting everything set up so the shoot goes as smoothly as possible."

"The shoot," Alva echoed. "Sounds so glamorous. You must be excited about being on camera. Just imagine, your shop will be famous! All that, and you get to cook with Chef Hot C—er, Chef Dunne." Her smile went twinkly again. "We're having dinner, you know. A late dinner."

"Yes, I heard," Lani said. "Thursday."

"We changed it to Friday, something about the shooting schedule changing."

Lani hoped that meant production would wrap up at a decent hour that day. She'd already been warned to expect some very long days, ten to twelve hours being more the norm than the exception. She couldn't really complain—though she likely would at least whine a little to Charlotte—as the compensation package they'd offered in trade for essentially shutting her shop down for several weeks, was pretty ... well, sweet.

In fact, she'd had to look at that page of the contract twice to make sure her eyes weren't playing tricks on her. She didn't know how much money they thought she'd normally have netted over that period of time, but their offer had been more than a little generous. Add in the commercial exposure of having her little shop on television and whatever new revenue that would send in her direction, there was no way the ordeal could be considered as anything but a big check in the win column.

That was if she didn't count the chunk of her heart Baxter would be carting off with him.

"Have you decided on a dinner menu?" Lani asked Alva, hoping to advance the conversation past the show talk.

Before Alva could respond, however, the doorbell chimed. Again. Lani glanced at the clock. It was after eleven.

Alva clasped her hands together. "Gee, I wonder who that might be?" It was clear who she was hoping it would be.

"I can get it," Charlotte offered, but Lani was already on her feet.

"That's okay. Alva, why don't you tell Charlotte your dinner menu for Baxter. She's a pretty good regular chef, too. I'm sure she'd love to give you some guidance."

Charlotte shot her a leveling look, but Lani merely smiled. Her smile faded as she turned toward the door leading out of the kitchen. She really wasn't ready for more Baxter, even with the addition of the guest panel currently parked in her kitchen. "Hello?" she said, leaving the door shut. It was, after all, late at night. Though the door wasn't locked, she wanted him to at least acknowledge the hour.

"Chef? It's Dre."

"Dre?" Lani repeated, then tugged open the door to find her young employee standing on her cottage porch. Apron in hand. Concerned, she said, "Is everything okay?"

"Yeah. I mean, yes, Chef. Fine. I'm sorry to be coming so late, but I went by the shop first and it was locked up tight and dark."

"Well, it is a little on the late side."

"I know, but it said recipe testing on the show schedule and Bernard had said how the first few days they'd almost be there around the clock, so I figured that's where I was supposed to go."

"Go for what?"

Dre's expression shifted, and she looked worried. "For recipe testing. When I faxed my class schedule to you, you said to show up whenever possible. I got done with my lab about an hour ago. I knew it was late, but from the schedule, I figured testing would be going on till the wee hours, so I thought I'd come help out. When the shop was closed down, I thought I'd at least swing by here. I—I wasn't sure where else to go. There are cars here and the lights are on so . . . I thought maybe I misunderstood and we are testing stuff here."

Charlotte's rental and Alva's car, along with her own, were parked in the drive in front of the house. With the house ablaze with light, Lani supposed it did look like something was going on. "I honestly have no idea what you're talking about, but since you're here, why don't you come on in?"

A burst of chatter came from the kitchen just then, and an embarrassed Dre shifted her weight, but didn't step inside. "No, that's okay. I shouldn't have stopped by so late. Sorry I interrupted, I must have read the chart wrong."

Lani frowned. "What chart?"

Dre frowned right back at her. "Bernard sent out charts detailing the production schedule for the rest of the week. I assumed you gave him my e-mail, but—Listen, no problem. I have an early class tomorrow anyway. I can be back over the bridge by seven tomorrow night. I'll—I'll see you then."

She backed up a step, but Lani said, "Wait. When did you get this chart?"

"About four this afternoon. Don't—didn't you get one?"

Lani supposed she should have been embarrassed, looking like an idiot in front of her only employee, but the annoyance she was feeling at that moment outweighed everything else. "Obviously there was a glitch somewhere, but no, I didn't. You don't happen to have a copy, do you?"

"No, it's on my computer. Wait—my mail comes through on my phone. I can probably access it from there and forward it to you."

"That would be great. Come on in. Charlotte and Alva are in the kitchen. We're sampling harvest bread."

"It smells amazing."

Lani smiled. "Tastes even better."

Dre hedged for another second, then went ahead and stepped inside. "Thanks."

"Absolutely. The more the merrier."

"I really am sorry for barging in, Chef."

"It's after eleven and you're not on the clock. You can call me Lani."

Dre looked at her. "That's probably not going to happen."

"Why?"

"Because you're the chef, Chef." As if that explained it. With Dre, it probably did.

Lani shook her head and smiled. "Suit yourself."

They stepped into the kitchen to find Charlotte and Alva behind the counter, mixers whirring and things being measured.

"I leave for five minutes—"

Charlotte lifted an unapologetic shoulder. She was getting very good at that, Lani noted.

Alva twinkled. "She's showing me how to make individual serving cheesecakes in a muffin pan, like little cheesecake cupcakes! If they come out right, it'll be just the thing for my dessert menu Friday. We can top some with blueberries, some with raspberries, and some with strawberries. Isn't that just delightful?"

"Delightful," Lani echoed.

Alva looked past Lani. "Well hello, Dre dear. Care to give us a hand? We need someone to crush the graham crackers, then cut the butter into them and I'm afraid my wrists aren't what they used to be."

Dre shook out her apron and had it tied on in a flash. "Excellent."

"Small crumb." Alva handed Dre the package of graham crackers and a pastry blender. "Well, my word. What—or who—is that?" She was staring at Dre's apron.

"Captain Jack Sparrow," Dre said, as if unable to comprehend that anyone wouldn't recognize the image. When Alva merely kept staring, she added, "Johnny Depp?"

Alva finally tore her gaze away and went back to blending. "I like pirates." It was all she said, but there was an added gleam to the twinkle.

"Me, too." Dre took the butter from Charlotte. "Okay if I use the table, Chef?"

"Sure." Charlotte and Lani answered at the same time.

Dre smiled her dry half smile, said, "Thanks," and got down to business.

"Something happened to my life when I wasn't looking," Lani said to Charlotte.

"Yes. You got one," she said, not looking up from the handwritten recipe she was staring at.

"You're one to talk," Lani muttered, but went to the refrigerator and got out the cream cheese. If she couldn't shame them, she might as well join them.

When she looked up again, Charlotte caught her eye and sent a nod Dre's way with a lift of an eyebrow.

"She said tonight was recipe test. According to Bernard's chart."

"What chart?"

"Exactly," Lani said.

"Why wouldn't they send you the chart?"

"I have no idea. Bernard might be a little imperious about his job description, but the man misses nothing, so I can't imagine it was an oversight. He's like a human spreadsheet."

"So . . . are we—or were you—supposed to be testing the recipes for the first show or something?"

"I have no idea. If I was, obviously I didn't make the meeting. And no one apparently missed me." Lani stripped the wrappers from the cream cheese, then Charlotte chopped the soft blocks into smaller pieces. "We didn't wrap up tonight until after six, and no one said a word, so maybe Dre just has her dates or times mixed up."

"Still, Dre has a chart," Charlotte said.

"Right," Lani said.

"So?"

Lani looked at her. "So, what?"

"Aren't you going to call? Find out what's going on?"

"Call Bernard? At midnight? Um, gosh. No."

"Not Bernard."

Lani's eyebrows lifted. "Baxter? You must be kidding. It's torture enough having to be around him all day and that's with a dozen other people crammed into the room, all talking at the same time. I don't have any desire for there to be only two of us in any room at any time, or me doing any of the talking, unless it's directed at a camera."

"You should call him. It's a good excuse."

"I don't *need* an excuse to talk to him."

"Good." Charlotte smiled. "So, what are you waiting for?"

"Pigs sprouting wings? I thought you'd come to the dark side with me on this and agreed. I must resist temptation."

"You said he has sweet parts. Sounds pretty tempting to me."

"I can be strong."

"Let him be strong. Manly with sweet parts. Honestly, Lan, you're an idiot to hold out. Life is unpredictable. You could suffer a tragic mixer accident, and then where would you be?"

"The hell with tea. I think we need more wine."

"Who has sweet parts?" Alva wanted to know.

Charlotte just looked at Lani with a raised brow.

"Is Chef Dunne coming to our party?" Alva asked, with a hopeful smile.

Lani glanced over and noticed that Dre was paying special attention, too. "No. We're not having a party, we're just having an impromptu, um—"

"Bitch and bake," Charlotte finished.

"A bitching what?" Alva asked.

"Leilani and I used to get together after hours when we both lived in New York and let off steam by baking. And bitching. About whatever was bugging us."

"You know," Alva said, "I was telling our Miss Lani May the other night how therapeutic it was to help her with her sponge roll."

"Passion fruit roulade," Lani said to Charlotte.

"Right," Alva said, "the fruit roll. Anyway, I so enjoyed it. Then we had another chance to work on those cupcakes last Sunday morning. I can't recall when I've enjoyed myself more. Until this evening." With glee, she cranked the mixer on high and went back to doing . . . whatever it was she was doing.

Dre merely nodded and went back to grinding cracker crumbs.

Lani looked at Charlotte. "Don't even think about shrugging that shoulder. I'm not calling him. So, deal with it. If there's a chart, I can get one from Bernard in the morning."

"So," Alva announced, as she flipped the mixer back off again. "If we're having a bitching bake, then it's probably okay to tell you the poker tournament was almost a complete bust. Laura Jo's sangria was a lot more potent than any of us recalled it being the last time she made it. Add in those devilishly decadent volcano cupcakes and, well, things got a little out of hand. When Dee Dee flat out told Laura Jo that she thought Felipe was too good for her, and that it didn't matter if she died her hair orange and stripped naked, well, Laura Jo didn't take too well to that. I'm not sure exactly when the sheriff's department arrived. That handsome Deputy Maxwell was the first one on the scene and let me tell you, no one minded being frisked by that one. We were lining up."

"Twelve forty-five," Dre said offhandedly. Everyone

looked at her. "It was twelve forty-five. I won twenty-five bucks."

"Good for you, dear." Alva nodded with approval. "Dee Dee should have taken that bet. It would have helped with her bail money."

Charlotte might have snickered under her breath.

Lani elbowed her in the side, but was having a hard time keeping her grin to herself. *When did this happen?* Lani wondered, standing in her tiny, crowded kitchen in the middle of the night. But, the truth was . . . she didn't mind really. *In fact,* she thought, with a smile to herself, *it's kind of nice.*

"Welcome to Cupcake Club," she murmured under her breath.

Chapter 12

"Leilani, move your hand, you're blocking—"

"Right. Sorry." Lani shifted her hand so the overhead camera could clearly capture the contents of the mixing bowl, then belatedly realized she'd yet again spoken out loud in response to the instruction that had come through her earpiece and the director was once again calling to cut. "I'm sorry." She smiled despite her frustration with herself. It was one o'clock in the afternoon and they weren't even halfway through taping the first episode. And they'd started at six that morning. "I don't know why I can't get this."

"It's okay," Baxter said genially. "It's not a natural way to work, so it takes time. Don't ask Rosemary how many times it took me during the first month of shoots we did, because she'll tell you, in great detail."

He'd been like that all day. Endlessly patient, good-spirited, consistently supportive.

Lani smiled briefly, grateful for the backup, but perversely wishing he'd get at least a little put out with her. Was it too much to ask for him to be human? Or at least not so damn perfectly . . . perfect? Surely it would be easier if she could be irritated at him and therefore make herself believe that her screwups were all his fault.

It was impossible enough to remember everything she had to remember—where to look, where not to put her hands, how to handle things so the camera could see them, don't forget to explain the steps and the smells, tastes, textures, and, oh right, by the way, be naturally charming and ad lib all of her dialogue banter with Baxter. Hadn't they heard of cue cards?

On top of all that, he was standing right beside her and had been for going on their eighth hour now, being positively charming and gracious and sexy as all hell. And he smelled so good. The words *sweet parts* kept running through her mind.

Try as she might, she couldn't find the center of the storm. She'd always been able to block out the insanity by focusing on the next step, then the next one. Chop, chop, chop, mix, mix, mix, bake, bake, bake. The rituals of measuring, blending, sifting, rolling were as soothing to her mind as a full body massage would be to her body. She could always depend on the confidence and comfort she found in the rhythm of it all, as if she was simply another piece of equipment, doing its job, producing the next product. As long as she kept on task, it didn't matter what was going on around her.

The problem was, she couldn't just focus on her own little world of creation. Her own little world was being filmed, so she had to find a way to invite the whole freaking universe into her quiet, focused place. And be bright, cheerful, and casually charming while she did so.

They'd spent the entire previous day blocking everything out, and teaching her where to stand, what to do, what not to do, where to look, what to say, what not to say. Clearly, one day of training had not been enough. At the moment, she wasn't sure a master class on the subject would help.

"Let's go again," Rosemary called out. "Overheads only. Then sides, then we'll do steps."

Good, Lani thought. Overheads meant she didn't have to talk, just let them film from above. All she had to do was keep her hands in the right places so as not to block anything. Surely she could manage that. She'd learned there would be multiple takes of the same exact section of the recipe they were demonstrating, from different angles, along with additional film of the discussion and explanation, as well as the dreaded casual banter, which would all be spliced together afterward to produce the seamless episodes she'd taken entirely for granted when watching cooking shows on television.

Lani thought about the late night hours when she'd unwind with her television chef pals, whom she'd never met. Those she was certain would be her very best friends if they ever did. She'd relax as she enjoyed the lovely soothing background music, and Giada in her kitchen, cooking so happily, and so competently. All by her sweet, charming, relaxed little self. In her serene, beautiful kitchen.

Yeah. Turned out it wasn't like that.

Of course, Lani had known that. Intellectually. But the reality went so far beyond what she'd imagined went into the making of a single episode. Just the time spent choosing which recipes were going to be recreated, then breaking down exactly how to show the pastries being assembled in as entertaining and understandable ways as possible. Plus the testing, the tasting, the prep work, the camera angles required and how her hands—which felt enormous to her now—were always, always blocking every shot. How did Giada, Bobby, and the Contessa do it? *How?*

Baxter . . . well, she knew how he did it. Effortlessly was how he did it. Which was why she smiled at his attempt to make her feel less of a dork, but didn't buy it for a second. To look at him, a person would never know he didn't cook on the hastily assembled set every day of his life, and that he hadn't been doing it all in front of the camera for decades, rather than just a few years. The camera loved him, the crew loved him, Rosemary—despite being pretty scary with her barking orders and charging about—Lani could tell, adored him. Privately she thought it was probably more because Rosemary looked at him and saw dollar signs cha-chinging in her head, but whatever the motivation was, he was the golden child in this arena every bit as much as he had been in the kitchens they'd worked in together.

She, on the other hand, felt a lot like the ridiculous, clumsy sidekick. She glanced down, took a calming breath. Yeah. Wearing her Roald Dahl *Charlie & the Chocolate Factory* apron for inspiration seemed a bit laughable. Definitely a bit of a reach. She'd even make the Oompa Loompas cringe at her performance thus far.

"Rosie, let's get this section in the can, then break," Baxter said. "We can do the sides and the final reveal after we get something to eat, yes?"

Lani glanced at Rosemary, who nodded, albeit seemingly reluctantly. Lani still could not fathom anyone calling the director-producer Rosie.

"Gus," Rosemary directed the cameraman, "from the top left. Lani, left hand on the counter, use your right to tilt the beaters up from the mixing stand, then take out the bowl so the overhead can get the shot. Baxter talks. Then you both use the ice cream scoops to fill the cups, and into the oven with the trays."

"We've got it," Baxter said, and looked at Lani, who nodded and smiled gamely.

Sure thing, she thought. *Right. Piece of cake. Ha.*

Rosemary clapped her hands. "Okay, quiet please. And? Go."

To everyone's pleasant surprise—and great relief, she was sure—Lani managed to get through it in a single take. A short cheer went up from the crew as lunch was announced. Given the remote location, they'd hired on Laura Jo to cater during the shoot. Tents had been set up across the street in the park and within minutes, Lani's kitchen and shop were deserted. Except for Baxter. She turned to follow the guys out, not so much hungry as mentally exhausted. All she wanted was to find a place to sit and do nothing more complicated than contemplate her navel for the next half hour.

"Leilani, wait." Baxter untied and took off his *Some Like It Hot* movie poster apron.

Dre had shown up yesterday afternoon near the end of the actual recipe testing time—Lani had found both the original and the updated schedule on her office fax the next morning—to bring Baxter a few aprons to wear during filming. She and some of her graphics classmates had custom designed the aprons for him, making them longer to accommodate his above-average height.

He'd gotten a kick out of them, as had Rosemary, so they'd gotten the go ahead. Dre had been so thrilled she'd straightened from her typically slouched frame, to practically skipping when she'd headed out again.

Lani smiled briefly at the memory as she slipped

the neck loop of her own apron over her head, then groaned a bit at the tight muscles in the base of her neck. She was used to standing, hunched over a work-table, for very long hours, but it had been a while since she'd been so tense while she did so. And the last thing to help reverse that was alone time with Baxter. "Can I catch you la—oh. My."

Baxter had stepped up behind her and put his warm, wide palms on the upper part of her shoulders and started massaging the muscles at the base of her neck with his thumbs.

She should politely slip out from under his touch, but all she could do was groan in abject appreciation as he skillfully worked out each and every kink and knot. "All that time we worked together, you never once offered up these mad massage skills of yours," she said, feeling the tension release all the way down her spine, even through the backs of her legs. A few more minutes and she'd be like wobbly gelatin.

"Well, luv." He cupped her shoulders and turned her around to face him, waiting until she looked up into his face. "I thought it best to keep my hands only on the pastry dough." He smiled, and worked his fingertips gently into her shoulders, which kept the tingles going, but for an entirely different reason.

"Baxter—"

"I've thought a lot about our walk on the beach the other night."

Alarm bells went off and she stiffened all over again. "Nothing has changed."

His hands tightened on her shoulders, more to steady her than anything. He rubbed his thumbs along the curve of her muscles and it felt so good she was helpless to shrug them off, even knowing she should.

"The past few days, in the test kitchen and on set with you," he started, "have been—"

"Nothing has changed," she reiterated. "Chef."

His fingers went slack, but only for a moment. Then he gave her shoulders a quick squeeze, and let her go.

She wished she didn't feel so damn bereft when he did, but the fact that had been her gut response only proved it was the right way to go. She was more vulnerable than she cared to be, but she couldn't seem to do much about that. The best thing to do was keep him at a distance as much as she could. Physically, and emotionally.

"You conceded," she reminded him. "We both did. For a good reason."

"We?"

She held his gaze for another moment, then let out a soft sigh. *Crap.* The last thing she wanted was for him to regain any hope regarding a future with her. He'd said it himself. He had no life to offer her, even if she wanted it—which she didn't. In reality. In her dreams? Maybe there it was different. Every night, in fact. Very different. But in reality, they had no future to offer each other.

"Lei?"

Still, no matter how big and strong and capable he was, he had feelings, too, and it wasn't fair to let him hang out there, thinking he was suffering alone. She took a breath, and just put it out there, once and for all. "Once you realized there was no future to be had between us, you've been kicking yourself about bringing the show here, about being shortsighted, not thinking this through, just setting your sights and full speed ahead, damn the torpedoes."

"I think you have that last part backward," he said with a bit of a smile.

"I just—and this doesn't change anything—but it's only fair you know that it's not just you making the . . . adjustment."

"Adjustment," he repeated. He did not make it a question, but his expression was one of confusion.

"To not being able to act any further. On your . . . attraction."

His smile winked briefly back to life. "You're saying you have to make the same . . . adjustment?"

"Nothing changes, remember?"

"Right, right. So . . . when did you first realize you needed to make this . . . adjustment?"

She held his gaze, and thought hard on how to respond. She could just tell him it was since he'd arrived on the island and made his intentions clear. She'd responded to that last kiss he'd laid on her, he knew that. They both knew that. She should just tell him that. At least he wouldn't think he'd been completely crazy to want what he wanted. She opened her mouth, and what came out was, "Do you remember when you told me you took the offer to do your own television show as a way to put some distance between you and your feelings for me?"

"Yes. That's the truth, Leilani. It's been a wild ride, and has changed things for me in ways I never would have expected, most of them good. I don't regret the decision, but it wasn't a move I made to reach for something; it was a move away from what I couldn't reach for."

"Well," she said, determined to hold his gaze, "deciding to stay in Sugarberry was a move away for me, too."

His smile slipped. "What?"

Her smile wobbled a little. "You weren't the only one in the Gateau kitchen who had to work on keeping things professional."

He took her shoulders again. "Why didn't you—"

She covered his hands and pulled them away, but he just took her hands in his and held on. "You didn't do anything because you were my boss. And I didn't do anything . . . because you were my boss."

"I didn't know, Lei. How did I not know?"

"How did *I* not know? Maybe we both knew, on some level, at least subconsciously, we were tuned in. The other reason I didn't do anything was because I honestly didn't think the feelings would be reciprocated. At all. I felt foolish, like a schoolgirl with some kind of crush on her teacher. It was so silly. Then there was all the supposition that we were involved, and all those nasty ugly things the staff were saying about me. It was so ironic that I was so hurt and disgusted they didn't have any respect for me, for my talents. And yet, the whole time I knew, given a chance, or any encouragement, maybe I would have been that girl, maybe—"

"No," Baxter stated, almost defiantly. He pulled their joined hands up between them and tugged her a bit closer, his gaze so intent on hers, she couldn't look anywhere else. "You earned your spot through skill and hard work, and would have no matter what. I do know that about you. They were jealous. Of your talent, of our rapport, I don't know, I don't care. But no one—no one—can say you weren't worthy of and capable of handling every bit of the responsibility I handed to you."

"I know that. I do. And yet, I wonder now, if I'd

have been able to resist . . . or even stay on, working for you, with you, had I—had we—"

"Doesn't matter. You didn't. We didn't."

"Right. I know." She finally broke the hold his gaze had on her, though her hands were still clasped tightly within his own.

"Why are you telling me this?" he asked. "Why now?"

"You're trying so hard to make this experience easier on me, stepping in with Rosemary, the crew—"

"You're new. It's not easy. Everyone knows that, no one expects—"

"Oh, I'm sure they'd expect me not to be such a total dork. But I appreciate what you're doing. Calling lunch when it was getting to be too much for me."

He tried a smile, urging her to do the same. "We do eat, you know."

"On your set, when it's just you, would you have taken a break right then," she challenged him, "or finished getting that recipe done on camera?"

"It doesn't matter," Baxter told her. "It all gets done. We eat at some point. Who cares when?"

"I'm just saying, I see how hard you're trying, and I know it's because you feel badly for forcing this on me. I wanted you to know that I'm not ungrateful, for one. As I said on the beach, I do realize this is going to make a difference for my shop. That it's a good thing. It is. I wanted to tell you that, so you wouldn't feel you'd just come barging into my world. It didn't seem fair to leave you thinking you'd forced yourself on me, too, and so I just—it was only right for me to—" She stopped when he grinned. "What? Why are you looking at me like that?"

"The lady doth protest, quite a lot, in fact, and talks a wee bit faster when realizing she's cornered herself."

"I'm not cornered. I'm setting us both free. Don't you get it?"

He tugged her closer, until her elbows bumped his torso and he could let her hands go, but keep them trapped between them while he reached for her face. "I don't want to be free of you. Don't *you* get it? You're telling me you feel something, too. Do you want to be free of me, Lei? Honestly? Do you?"

Before she could answer him—and heaven help her, what she might have said—he bent his head down and kissed her.

It wasn't awkward like the first time, or staking a claim like the second one. It was just a kiss. His kiss. He wasn't in a hurry, or surprised, or acting out of frustration. He was just . . . kissing her. Easily, earnestly, and quite thoroughly.

She could tell herself had her hands not been trapped against his chest, she'd have pushed him away. She'd have made it clear, once and for all, they simply couldn't indulge themselves. It was senseless torture.

But she couldn't. And so, she didn't. She let him kiss her, let all the sensations he brought with his kiss course through her freshly relaxed body. His mouth was warm, strong, and he tasted sweet and spicy, partly from the ginger-laced cupcakes they'd been baking and testing, and partly because she knew that's just how he tasted. Under his continued exploration, she relaxed further, opened her mouth to him, took him in . . . and sighed as he filled her so perfectly. She groaned softly, or maybe it was him, as he took the kiss deeper, and it slowly turned more ardent. She realized she'd dug her nails into his shirt, pressing her knuckles into him as she clutched the linen in her fists in her urgent need to get closer to him.

"Wow," she gasped against the skin of his jaw as he left her mouth to kiss the corners of her lips, then her cheek, her temple, and dropped his head down to nuzzle at the tender side of her neck. It was the sweetest seduction and a primal rush, all at the same time. She rose up on her toes, wanting more heat, more contact, more . . . Baxter.

"How can this not be the right thing, Leilani," he whispered gruffly against the sensitive skin below her ear. "Tell me, and I'll step away. I won't—we won't do this again. But it's bloody brilliant, it's perfect, you're—"

"Oh. My."

They sprang away from each other as if they'd just put their bare hands on a sizzling hot cake pan.

Leilani covered her mouth with her hand, as if she could hide the evidence of what they'd been doing, of what she was feeling, of . . . She turned to find Alva standing just inside the swinging kitchen door, carrying two large paper plates loaded down with Laura Jo's golden fried chicken, steaming mashed potatoes and gravy, corn on the cob, and oversized buttermilk biscuits. It smelled heavenly and, to add to the turmoil in Lani's head, her stomach chose that minute to growl. She dropped her hand from her mouth to her stomach. "Ah . . . Alva, hello."

"I thought the two of you might be hungry." Alva smiled as if she hadn't just walked in on the two of them about a half second away from tearing their clothes off. She slid the plates onto the nearest clean work surface. "I see I was right," she added with a little wink. "Rosemary asked me to bring out the trays of cupcakes from the recipe test last night, for the crew. I can't believe they have any room left . . . my goodness, the spread Laura Jo put out there. They fell on it like a pack of starved hound dogs." Alva looked between the two of them, who just stood there, blinking back at her. "The ginger-marscapone cupcakes?"

"Right." Lani finally snapped out of her Baxter-induced stupor. "They're in the display cases up front. We ran out of room back here this morning, so Dre put them there."

"Do you need any assistance?" Baxter asked, finally finding his own voice.

It sounded more than a little rough to Lani's ears, setting off her overly sensitized little pleasure receptors all over again.

"It's just one big tray. I think I can take care of it," Alva responded, moving back toward the swinging door that led to the front of the shop. *"Bon appétit."* She shifted her gaze between the two of them, not even glancing at the plates of food. With a last gleaming twinkle, she ducked out.

Lani could feel the steam rising from the plates of food; the mingled scents were making her mouth water. Or maybe that was Baxter. Between the taste of him, the smell of the food, the remembered feel of his hands on her she was on sensory overload. And she was suddenly ravenous. "We should eat." She stared at the food, but didn't move. "That's what we need to do. Eat, recharge, refocus."

"Right. Just . . . right." Baxter still sounded distracted. He wasn't looking at the food. Or the door where Alva had exited. He was looking at her. "Lei-lani—"

She jerked her gaze to his. "Don't. Don't tell me we should just go for it anyway, or take what we can get. If I thought that was something I was capable of, I'd have already—"

"Actually, I was going to suggest you might want to

follow Alva out there, and . . ." He waved his hand in a vague circular motion.

"Stop her from talking?" Lani snorted. "Really?"

"Right. You have a point."

"She's either already sharing her eyewitness account with all and sundry one picnic table at a time, or we're going to be the new lead item in her first column. Or both."

The desire for her was still there, in his eyes, and she wondered what it was he saw in her own. But there was regret in his, too. "I am sorry this is going to cause you additional grief."

"I think that ship has sailed already. The speculation has already been rife, and I'm fairly certain our favorite little octogenarian out there is a goodly part of the gust of wind that's filling those sails." Lani smiled resignedly. "It's going to be whatever it's going to be. I knew there would be no stopping that, and for all my concerns about it, to be honest, it hasn't really been all that bad. Most of the folks here seem tickled by the idea. It's all been rather harmless and kind of charming, actually. It's nothing like it was back in New York, probably because the people here have no stake in whether we are or aren't. They're just naturally nosy." Her smile softened. "I'd like to think they just want what's best, and if the story is juicy, all the better." She wiggled her eyebrows. "Well, Chef, I think we just gave them the juice they were hoping for."

Baxter's smile deepened at that, and she was happy to see the cloud of regret clear away. "You're right, I suppose, to just ride the wave in. Or wind gust, as it may be." He reached out and tucked a stray lock of hair behind her ear. She reached up as well, surprised it had come loose, what with all the bobby pins and other torturous devices the show's hairstylist had poked in there. Her hand brushed his, and she started to pull away, but he curled his fingers around hers and pulled her hand to his chest.

"Now you're just begging for trouble," she said, trying to sustain the light humor they seemed to have found in the situation.

"Worried Alva might pop back in, or—"

"I was thinking about Alva, or worse, my father." She laughed when Baxter blanched. "But, I'd be lying if I didn't say the *or* part plays a role, too." At his look of surprise, she said, "What, you don't think this— you—tempts me, too?"

He shook his head, not in a way that said he didn't believe her, but in a way that said he was having a hard time taking it all in. She knew exactly how that felt.

"It's just . . . you're different," he said at length. "Now. Or maybe it only seems that way to me, because now I know that you—well, now I know. And, I'll admit, it's making my whole conceding the field decision far more of a challenge."

Hearing him say that made her stomach knot . . . and her pulse pound. *Danger, danger,* her little voice whispered. Like she didn't already know that.

"Well," she said, trying to keep her tone steady, on track, "one thing you do know about me is that I can always create that calm space in the center of the storm. I need to do that, so I can stay focused, and productive. Here, today . . . that's been a real challenge for me. The television part of this is a lot more overwhelming than I thought it would be." She smiled wryly. "In case it's escaped your notice, I'm definitely not a natural on camera. In fact, the whole thing has me a little freaked out. Since this is going to air on network television, there is added pressure. I know I have to get a grip and not make a fool of myself."

"You're doing fine. It's a big learning curve."

"Well, I definitely haven't felt like I'm doing anywhere close to fine. I need to find a way to shut out the distractions and focus. It's been hard, really hard, actually, trying to balance my decision to push you away, while simultaneously having to work side by side, on camera no less."

"But?" He smiled when she gave him a disbelieving look. "I heard a distinct *but* there at the end."

"But," she said, with exaggerated emphasis, "at the same time . . . you're the one thing I do know, the one constant I have in this madness. I can't find my calm center in this particular storm, but you already have. So, it's like—you're the one thing I feel I can rely on, and trust to guide me through it all."

"Good, because I am."

"Which makes all the rest, ultimately, that much harder. Now we've done this. And we got caught, and . . . well"—she lifted her shoulders—"I don't know how I'm going to pull it all together. Alva's out there having a field day, Rosemary is somewhere pulling her hair out because I'm going to end up costing her a fortune trying to get this show taped, and I have to find a way to put all that aside and somehow make it work." She looked into Baxter's beautiful brown eyes, and if a person could physically feel their heart crack, hers definitely developed another fracture or two. It wouldn't shatter completely until he left. It was just a matter of how tiny the pieces were going to be. "So, the one thing I need, the only thing that's going to work, is to be able to trust you."

"Of course you can. Always."

"What I mean is, I need to know, with absolute certainty, when we're on set, when I'm really trying to get the five million things I have to be remembering at all times, and to not—repeat not—respond out loud to those little voices in my headset . . . I need to know I can count on you to guide me and be here for me. There's no way I can begin to do that if I think we're going to be doing any more of—"

"This?" He rubbed the pad of his thumb over her fingers, which he'd curled inside his wide palm.

"Yeah," she said, her voice barely above a whisper. She needed him to agree to help them both stay on track. When he looked at her the way he was right at that moment, touched her like that . . . she didn't think she had the strength to resist it. To resist him. "I am being as honest as I can be with you." She held his gaze, and, letting everything else fall away, bared her soul to him. She had no choice. He had to understand this. "If you push . . . I don't know that I can resist. But I do know that I should. We should. It would be easy now—too easy—to just give in. The whole town will be all but shoving us together."

"I don't need the town to give me a nudge in that direction."

"I'm just saying, the pressure to give in will be coming at us from all directions, not just from the two of us. But, no matter what, the outcome won't change. You'll go. I'll stay. So . . . I know this probably isn't fair, but I need to know I can count on you to be here for me, so we can get the shows taped. But I also need to trust that you won't do any more of . . . this." She covered his hand, which was brushing against her cheek, and slowly lowered it.

"You know I'm here for you," he said.

"And . . . the rest? Can I count on you there, too?"

"If it's just up to me, then you have my word."

"What does that mean?"

"It means I won't push you, or nudge you, or do anything to overtly tempt you. But if you're the one to do the pushing, for whatever reason, whatever the provocation, then . . . all bets are off."

"But—"

"Because I can't resist you any more than you say you can resist me. Fair's fair, luv."

"You do agree with me, though, that we shouldn't? That it's pointless to torture ourselves like that?"

He lifted his hands up beside his head, palms forward, as if in surrender. "I'll respect your request, Leilani. Unless you say otherwise, it's hands off. And lips. And mouth. And tongue."

She swallowed, hard. He'd never been so . . . explicit.

A slow grin slid across his face, lighting his eyes with a very different, decidedly wicked glow. For the first time, she could honestly believe he'd come from the rough part of town. There was something elemental in the way he was looking at her, like a man willing to brawl, to fight with his bare hands, if that's what it took to get what he wanted. It made her skin prickle with awareness . . . and her muscles shudder with need.

And her heart ache with want.

"But you should know, Lei, that kissing you, feeling you kissing me back . . . didn't feel much like torture." He stepped in, and lowered his mouth until his lips were almost, but not quite touching hers. A mere breath of air separated their bodies.

Her breath caught in her throat as his warm, spicy-sweet breath fanned her lips . . . lips he'd so recently taken with his own. She quivered when he framed his hands, palms in, then moved them slowly down the outline of her body without ever once touching her. She was trembling by the time he finished.

"And this," he whispered gruffly, "is never going to go away, whether we will it to or not."

Chapter 13

"I don't know what you said to her during the break, but my God, Baxter, the afternoon tape is . . ." Rosemary trailed off, reached forward to the editing panel and punched a button to pause the replay, rewound it, then hit PLAY again. "Damn," she murmured, then fanned herself as she watched the segment play out. For the third time.

Baxter stood behind the seated Rosemary, silent as he watched the replay. *Damn, indeed.* Bloody damning hell, actually.

He and Lani were doing and saying all the right things, the same things they'd been saying for the camera all morning long. But there was a kind of . . . unspoken energy between them now. Smoldering energy. The kind where, any second, you expected one of them to just say the hell with it, clear the counter off with one arm, and get on with an entirely different sort of cooking. The kind usually reserved for pay cable.

Baxter understood it. Hell, he'd lived it for the last

torturous ten and a half hours—which, he supposed, was his just desserts, given he'd provoked the whole mood in the first place.

Understanding the source, and cursing himself for pushing them there, didn't change the fact that he couldn't stop looking at Lani like she was dessert on a stick. His own personal, delectably private parfait, simply waiting to be devoured, one sinful layer at a time.

He swallowed a groan, and shifted again as he stood, thankful for the long apron still tied around his waist. He glanced down at the movie poster art that had been skillfully airbrushed onto his custom apron, thanks to Lani's interesting assistant, Dre. He had thought the eclectic collection clever and a fitting contribution to the tone the show was trying to strike, being set in a cupcakery, and featuring its whimsical owner.

Whimsical she might be, Baxter thought, *but when it comes to smoldering sensuality, even Marilyn Monroe in her movie star prime doesn't hold a candle to little Miss Snow White.* He'd been attracted to her drive, her focus, her steady demeanor and steadier hand. She'd been steel wrapped in sunshine, a dependable beacon of light he could rely on and trust in his always loud, rushed, chaotic world.

Now he looked at her, with the warm, buttery, bakery sweet scents filling the air, accented with rich, dark, chocolate undertones . . . and all he could think about was adding the taste of her to the mix. He wanted to have her, inhale her, lick, taste, suckle, savor and devour every last inch of her. Like a man craving his next fix and willing to crawl over hot coals to get it.

Oh . . . she could make him crawl. At that moment, she could make him howl at the moon.

"Excuse me," he said, clearing the sudden grit from his throat. "I need to step outside a moment. I'll be right back."

"Go home." Rosemary absently waved him off as she continued to work through the tape. "We're good." She was smiling, he noted, which was rare indeed, but the fierce quality to it had him hastening his steps to the back door. Quite frightening, actually. Rosemary. Happy. A new concept, for certain.

He couldn't think about that right now. He had to get some air, clear his head . . . and find a way to calm his body right the bloody hell down.

Of course, as soon as he stepped off the final metal step to the crushed shell lot, it occurred to him there wasn't really anywhere for him to go. If he skirted out the back alley, he'd be in the town square proper or on one of the main side streets leading from it. Experience had told him even at that late hour, he wouldn't get far before being stopped by a happy, well-meaning local, eager to chat him up a bit. He'd normally be fine with that, but at the moment, he needed to be alone with his thoughts. And his raging hard-on.

He changed direction, thinking he'd hide out in the prep kitchen for a bit, which should be empty. There was a light on inside, but that didn't surprise him. With all the buzzing in and out that had been going on, whoever had left last probably hadn't known they were last out. He gave a quick glance around, but the rest of the crew had apparently retired to their rooms in town, most having been booked into the handful of bed and breakfasts that operated on the island. With the summer season recently over, the owners were happy for the business. There had been talk of getting him a tour bus type deal, where he could make his home away from home at each location, but that had struck him as being rather a bit too rock star-ish. He'd just bunk locally like the rest.

But, only three nights in, his presence was already proving to be a bit more of a distraction than any of them had anticipated. The citizens of Sugarberry meant well, but their idea of extending hospitality didn't seem to have any defined boundaries. He didn't mind the cards left at the desk, or the fresh flowers or baskets of fruit delivered to his room. Or the freshly baked pies, cookies, or casseroles, either. They were all very sweet and he was quite flattered. He did draw the line, however, at being served breakfast. In bed. Unannounced. Though he was sure Alva's friend Dee Dee had meant well.

Come the next town, he'd have a tour bus. And be grateful for it.

Next town, he thought, as he shrugged out of the apron, hopped the trailer stairs and ducked quickly inside before anyone spied him and thwarted his get-away. He didn't want to think about the next town. About leaving Sugarberry. Or, more to the point, leaving Leilani in Sugarberry.

He slapped the door shut behind him, only to hear a short squeal of surprise.

"Holy crap, you scared the daylights out of me!"

Baxter spun around . . . and found the subject of his thoughts parked at a worktable at the far end of the trailer, with a half-paper-peeled cupcake in her hands.

"I'd think you'd be sick to death of those right at the moment." He nodded at the gingerbread cupcake while trying to slow his own adrenaline-accelerated heartbeat. This morning alone they'd had to do at least a dozen takes with her tasting a bite of cupcake and exclaiming for the cameras about all of its delectably delicious qualities. And that had been one of four different varieties they'd filmed for the first episode.

"I'm a pastry chef. There is no such thing as being sick of cake. Why do you think I became one?" She was clearly aiming for amused, but her tone was weary, and she wasn't looking at him. Her attention was focused exclusively on the cupcake, which she went back to freeing from its paper cup. Once that was discarded, she slowly licked the frosting off the top, closing her eyes as she did so, and keeping them closed as she devoured the cake in three deeply appreciative bites, if her groan of satisfaction was anything to go by. There was nothing sensual about her actions. It had been more like an act of desperation, by a person seeking some kind of . . . salvation.

"Are you all right?" He frowned in concern. When they'd called it a wrap for the day—or night, as the case had been—he'd gone directly into the production trailer with Rosemary to look at the tape footage, and Leilani had been excused to go home. The afternoon and evening had gone well—amazingly well, by production standards, anyway—but the day in its entirety had still run quite long. They'd broken for dinner late, with one last segment still left to be taped. They'd ended the shoot right around midnight and it was going on one in the morning. "I thought you went home an hour ago. Why are you still here?"

She licked the mascarpone frosting from the corner of her mouth, then finally opened her eyes and looked at him. "Because there are people in my house. Baking. I don't want to bake anything else today. Eating things that have already been baked? That I can do. But baking new things?" She shuddered. "No. Can't make me."

"Surely Charlotte would understand that you need to sleep."

"It's not just Charlotte."

Baxter's eyebrows lifted a bit. "It's not? Has someone else come down from New York to provide moral support?"

She shook her head. "Long story. I have somehow managed to form a . . . well, a club. Of sorts."

"A . . . club?"

"A cupcake therapy club. People show up. We bake. We vent. We eat. It used to just be Charlotte and me, but apparently it's catching on."

Baxter walked to the end of the trailer, quietly pulled up a stool, and sat catty-corner to her. "How many people?"

"At the moment, Alva, Dre, Charlotte. And me, of course."

"Dre works for you."

"I know."

"Can't you send her home?"

"Why bother? I kind of don't want to. I mean, most of the time, it's been . . . well, good. Really good, actually. We laugh, we talk. We're all very different, different backgrounds, different generations." She took a short breath, and straightened a little on her stool, started fiddling with the empty cupcake wrapper. "It's kind of interesting, really. Dre is twenty, Charlotte and I are thirty and thirty-one, Alva is five decades older. Charlotte was raised in a different culture, and I'm—" She laughed, but it was more tired than happy. "I don't know what I am. But it's comforting, in a way." She shrugged. "I can't explain it, and I don't want to really. But tonight . . . I don't want group therapy. I just want to crawl into my bed and not talk or think about anything."

"It was a really long day. It will get better. I promise."

She looked at him again. "About . . . anything," she repeated.

He realized she wasn't talking about the show. Or not just the show. "Oh," he said more quietly. "Yes. Right." He wished then he had a paper wrapper of his own to fidget with. Anything to give his hands . . . and the direction of his gaze, someplace to focus. Other than on Leilani.

"Why are you still here?" she asked at length.

"I was in production. Watching the tape."

She nodded, but then looked down again. And very pointedly didn't ask him what he'd thought. Given what both he and Rosemary had so clearly seen, it wasn't something he was eager to share, either. For once, he didn't push.

"Did you need something from the kitchen?" she asked.

"What?" he said, realizing his thoughts were still on the tape replay. Making him shift on his stool again.

She motioned to the kitchen setup. "Did you need something?"

"Oh. You mean, why am I *here*."

"Right."

"I—I'm hiding. I guess."

Leilani's expression went from weary to concerned. "From Rosemary? Is the tape that awful? I *knew* it." She said the last part more under her breath. *"Dammit."*

"Um, no. Rosemary is quite happy, actually."

Leilani lifted her head, her one arched brow making it quite clear what she thought about the plausibility of that statement. "Really." She didn't make it a question.

"No, I'm being quite sincere. She was smiling when I left."

Lani made a face at that. "Rosemary can smile?" She rubbed her arms. "I'm afraid. Very afraid."

Baxter smiled for the first time since entering the trailer. "Not an unwise reaction, really. But that's not why I'm hiding. Though the lingering images of it might well give me nightmares later."

He thought he spied the slightest hint of a smile threaten to surface.

"I promise, I won't out your location. I'd just as soon stay hidden myself."

"Were you planning to spend the night here?"

"I hadn't thought it through that far. Actually, I was thinking I'd sneak back into my shop once everyone cleared out."

"And do . . . what?"

"Sleep. My building has a second floor. The person who owned the place before me used the open floor space above as a sort of loft office-slash-bedroom. There's a full bath up there, and the wiring for a small kitchenette. I gave some real thought to living up there, but I know myself and I already eat, sleep, and breathe my work. If I literally lived where I worked . . . well, it wouldn't be healthy. I need to step away at some point. Actually, it's when I'm away from the shop that I get most of my new recipe ideas."

"I'm the same."

She looked surprised. "I thought you didn't spend much time at home."

"I don't," he said. "But I don't spend all of it at the studio, either. And when I'm not there, doing what-ever else it is that demands my attention, I find that's when I get the most inspiration. I think it has to do with being around outside stimuli. Of any kind."

"I'll agree with that. To be honest, I've spent more time in my cottage on a daily basis since Charlotte got here than I have at any time since I leased the place."

"Leased?"

She nodded. "I was sinking almost everything I had into my shop. It didn't make sense to tie myself to a mortgage, too. Plus . . . well, there's Harper House to consider."

"It will be yours someday?"

"Yes. Hopefully not for a lot of years of somedays, but tying myself into a long term mortgage on the cottage, when I knew at some point I'd have to sell it, wasn't a potential hassle I wanted to take on."

He nodded in understanding. "I only bought the brownstone because I needed an investment." He chuckled at that. "Hard to believe a boy from Spitalfields would ever be worried about having to invest money."

"Spitalfields? You're making that up."

His chuckle turned to a full laugh. "I promise you, I'm not. Wonderful marketplace there now."

"Lit'l Charlie 'ingle from Spitalfields, all grown up," she said, in a rather delightful attempt at a Cockney accent. Her smile was warm, and the light in her eyes when she looked at him was one of affection and respect. "You've really done well for yourself, Baxter."

He'd thought he'd kick himself later, for telling her. But he realized, she was, in truth, the only person he knew whom he could have shared that part of himself with. He was glad he had. "The same with you," he replied.

"I thought you didn't respect my opening up a cupcake bakery."

"I never said that."

She laughed then. "You didn't have to. You should

have seen your face when you stepped into my kitchen that first morning. Your expression said it all." She lifted her hand, waving off any need to explain. "That's okay. My father doesn't get it, either. Or Charlotte, for that matter. You all think I'm wasting my talents here."

"You're right. When I heard what you were doing with yourself, even when I first got here, I did think that."

She didn't look surprised, or insulted, which he appreciated, because his reaction was an insult, one which he felt ashamed of now.

She tilted her head slightly and said, "That implies you've since changed your mind?"

"It's humbling to realize I'd become such a food snob. As you say, a bloke from Old Spi'alfields makin' good of 'imself hardly has any room to point fingers now, does he? And yet, I absolutely passed judgment on your choice to do this, rather than—"

"Make the same choices you did?" she finished for him. "You were working to elevate yourself so you could escape poverty and make a better life. That's not only okay, its laudable, in every sense. But I wasn't escaping anything, or trying to elevate my way out of something. I was merely trying to learn, to grow, to find out what I had inside me in terms of creating amazing, delicious desserts, and become the very best I could be. Nothing so noble as your cause."

"Nothing noble about survival. That's all it was, pure and simple."

"But being a pastry chef is not a means to an end, it's your true passion. How lucky you are that you found something you felt so passionately about it could also be the solution you needed to get out and move up."

"What about you, then? What drove you to Belgium and Paris? Then on to New York? What were your goals?"

"To be the best chef I could be. To learn everything I could about my craft, about baking, pastries, chocolate, all of it. I wanted a global perspective, and, when I came back, I thought the best place for me to continue my education was New York." She smiled. "And it absolutely was."

He sketched a bowing motion, but said, "I learned from you as well."

She laughed. "I'm flattered you think so, but you had so much to offer, knew so much, had the most interesting take on things. It was like my brain exploded with new ideas, just being around you."

His smile softened. "Again, I can say the same. You think very differently, creatively, than I do. My work is more rustic, and yours more refined, yet grounded in much the same sensibilities. You made me think differently, too."

He thought her cheeks might have pinkened a little. "I—well." She grinned a little self-consciously, which sent his heart teetering quite dangerously. "Thank you."

"You're quite welcome."

Her smile turned a bit sardonic then, prompting him to add, "What?"

"Oh, it's nothing, just . . ." She twirled the cupcake paper in her fingers. "Ironic, isn't it, that you're the more rustic-trained pastry chef, and I'm supposedly the elegant, refined one, yet, I'm the one who ultimately finds happiness and fulfillment in the rudimentary little cupcake."

"There is nothing remotely rudimentary about your little cakes," he said quite sincerely.

"Well," she said, unable to keep a bit of smugness

from sliding into her smile. "Thank you for saying that. Very much."

She'd earned that bit of nose-rubbing, he'd give her that. "You're quite welcome. It's the truth. I'll be honest and admit that I truly couldn't understand how someone with your natural talents and thirst for creating would be fulfilled, much less inspired, by what I thought of as such a constricting, elemental product. I was certain you'd become creatively stunted and feel stifled, even trapped after a while. I mean, I suppose at any point you could have broadened your shop concept and become a full bakery or patisserie, but—"

She was shaking her head. "No, cupcakes represented happiness and joy to me. I think they're symbolic of that to everyone."

"Don't you feel all desserts are that?"

"No, not at all. I think they represent all sorts of things, and, certainly they're all meant to be enjoyed . . . but none so much as the happy little cupcake. And that's what I wanted to do. Spread the joy."

"But your work in New York was doing exactly that."

"In a very different way, maybe. I know people liked and respected my work, but it was more about wowing with construction and details, than it was about the flavor profiles and the actual food itself. I'm quite certain more than half my desserts routinely sat unfinished on plates, not because they didn't taste good, but because the consumer was more concerned about maintaining the perfect size zero, or not appearing to be a glutton, or thought it was awesome to be eating a Gateau creation more than they were actually indulging themselves in the experience of the food itself. But I can tell you this . . . no one eats half a cupcake." She ended on a laugh.

He smiled, too. "You have a point."

"Don't get me wrong, I was inspired by you, by Gateau, by the city, and by impressing our very important and demanding clientele. I am an overachiever by nature, so the greater the demand, the more challenging the criteria, the better it was for me. It was a real test of what I could do, of where I could go with what I knew, how far I could grow, reach, become."

"And you were doing all those things. Wondrously so."

"Thank you. I mean that. Your opinion matters, and not just because you're a world class chef."

"But?" He smiled again. "I can always hear them."

She smiled back. "But," she repeated, "I was also always stressed out, always worried, always cramming my brain with everything I could think of, to make sure I never ran out of new ideas, which was the main thing that drove me. Topping myself. When I took on the executive chef role at Gateau, I was proud I'd achieved that, and so soon in my career. It was what I wanted, right? I was climbing the ladder, challenging myself every day to become a better chef. It was my dream come true. How else could I measure success? If you're successful doing something you love, that has to bring with it fulfillment and happiness. Right?"

"It's the logical conclusion."

"It was hard. Running Gateau. So hard. I thought I would thrive, but it was really scary, shouldering that much pressure. I hoped it would get easier as time went on, that I'd learn to handle it better. Enjoy it more. I thought it was about the staff, all the negative gossip, and a lot of other things, and surely, once that smoothed out and I proved myself—both to them and to me—it would feel more rewarding. After all, again, my dream was coming true."

"And then your father got ill."

She nodded, and he could see the stark fear flash across her face. They'd talked about family before, and he'd thought about her upbringing, in such a strong, matriarchal family, with a father who also loved her deeply. Though he'd empathized with her need to rush to her father's side, he'd never been in a position to feel that same urgency, that same fear. The kind that grips your core, shakes it numb.

But, watching her now, listening to her talk so passionately, so certainly, he realized he envied her courage. Courage to deal with losing someone she loved so dearly, courage in confronting the terror of possibly losing her only remaining family, then making choices—fearless choices—on what she knew had to be done, what was the right thing to do. To hear her tell it, her father had been no proponent of her move south, or her business launch. But she'd done it anyway. It boggled Baxter and inspired a great deal of respect from him.

It was in that moment he also came to the realization there was one person who, if her life were in sudden jeopardy, could inspire in him the courage to make those same tough choices, face the same terrifying consequences. That person was Leilani.

The thought of forever losing her . . .

"When I came down to take care of him, it was my first trip out of the city for any length of time since I'd become a chef," she went on, mercifully pulling him from his thoughts.

His heart, however, didn't recover so quickly.

"I thought the slower pace would make me crazy, and that I'd be worrying the whole time that things were completely falling apart back in New York. Between my father's heart attack and walking away from our insane schedule at Gateau, I thought I'd be a stressed out, anxiety ridden disaster."

"But—" They said it in unison, and both of them laughed.

"But," Lani repeated, "once the doctors assured me Dad was expected to make a full recovery, I was able to focus on helping him get his strength back and make sure he followed doctors' orders. I was still worried, but not in a panic that I was going to lose him. It wasn't until I'd been here a few days I realized that while I did worry, of course, whether business was being handled properly back in the city, I wasn't anxiety ridden about it. To be honest, by the end of the second week, I was starting to feel guilty, because the predominant feeling I had at the time was relief. I wasn't under so much pressure anymore. I baked and baked at Harper House and I enjoyed every second of it, because no one cared, no one was looking over my shoulder, or tapping their toes impatiently waiting for me to finish, or worse, pointing fingers and whispering snidely behind my back."

"Leilani—"

"No, I'm not blaming you. I just didn't realize how miserable I was. After all, I was living my dream. Sure, I was tired, stressed out, but that's the life I signed on for. I could hardly complain about that. Look at the opportunities I was getting. Look at the people who were sampling my work, my food. I was stressed because I cared, and it was just the price of success."

"I didn't realize you were so unhappy."

"That's just it. Neither did I. If you'd asked me, I'd have told you I was the luckiest pastry chef in the world. Because I was."

"You always seemed so calm, so focused, so centered."

She smiled then. "Nothing noble about survival, you said. And you're right. And that's what it was. It took stepping out of that life, stepping away from it, to really understand. Last spring, I made the desserts, or some of them, for the big Easter dinner we have on the island. I got to sit and watch folks eat and enjoy my food. Many of them came up to me and told me how much they loved this cake or that pie and asked for the recipe. They shared stories of my mom's cooking, and those who were old enough even had stories of Nanny's dishes. By then, I'd already been kind of dreading going back to New York. And was having a hard time facing it. I felt guilty for not being more thankful for what I had. I felt ungracious, and part of me wondered if those first inklings of an idea to open my own place weren't really just a cop-out, or an escape, an excuse not to go back to Gateau."

"What made the final decision? It doesn't seem like you had all that much support, at least not from those who knew you best."

"My father said it was because he didn't want me fawning all over him, making him feel like an invalid, but it wasn't until recently I realized just how much it bothered him that I didn't go back to my big career in the city. And Charlotte . . . she supported my decision to be happy; she just didn't get it. I hadn't actually told anyone what I was thinking about. I spent a lot of time playing with recipes in the Harper House kitchen while my dad was convalescing. He was used to me baking all the time and thought I was just keeping my skills sharp while away from the city."

"Instead, you were . . . working on your new menu?"

"That's eventually where it took me, yes. Those were the kinds of things I could never introduce at

Gateau, but I could imagine every one of them making the people in Sugarberry happy."

A twinkle of excitement lit her eyes in a way he'd never once seen. He'd seen her quiet pride in her work when they'd been at Gateau, but this was entirely different.

"I'd been giving it thought, kind of toying with the idea, talking myself into daring to really give it a chance . . . and then I spied the shop space for rent on the square. It had been a bakery before, but it had sat empty for over nine years. Gutted. No equipment. But all the wiring was there, the setup, the structure. It just needed a new face and new equipment. And a lot of tender loving care. But I think I knew. Maybe not that exact day, but when I called the agent to take a look at the place, I knew then I was really going to do it. If it was at all feasible, I was going to stay and open my own place."

"How?" he asked, sincerely wanting to know.

"You mean how did I know? Finding the shop seemed like a huge, giant sign, especially given where my thoughts had been taking me. But how I knew for sure was when I stood inside that shop, and looked around . . . and I could see it. Easily. Clearly. All of it. Right down to the figurines on the shelves. And I was excited, terrified—still am—and challenged. I wanted to do it, try it. It just felt right. More right than any step I'd ever taken. I did grapple with the guilt, the worry, the wondering . . . but I never doubted that it was a challenge I wanted to take on. Once I'd allowed myself to think about actually doing it—"

"You were happy."

She nodded, beaming. "Some would say it was actually delirium from all the stress of my dad's heart attack and my career, and questioning my sanity. I did, too. But, wow. I stood in that gutted out, horribly ugly little space, and . . . it was just . . . it was mine."

"Did you ever think of getting your own place in New York? Was that ever a goal?"

"Not really. If I'd thought about it, I'd have assumed it would have to be a place like Gateau. Otherwise, why bother, right? Cute and homey would just be a gimmick in the city, if anyone really got it at all. I saw what it took to actually own and run a shop like that in the city. I wanted to cook, to create. Not manage. Being executive chef was as far up the management chain as I wanted to go. On really tough days I fantasized about becoming a private chef, or starting a catering business, but those were the dreams of the overtired and overstressed. At least that's what I told myself."

"And now? Any regrets?"

She shook her head. "I miss Charlotte and Franco." Her smile softened, and grew a little poignant. "And you. But you know what my dilemma was where you were concerned, and I knew that if my friendship with Charlotte could sustain itself while I was overseas learning, it would surely survive my moving to Georgia."

"I've seen you with the people here. And I know you're happy. I can see a joy in you that I didn't see in New York. You were proud of your work, but that pride didn't include the kind of lively, full-bodied delight I see you living and breathing all the time here."

"I am happy here, Baxter. You're very right about that. I never lived here growing up, but the ties to my family feel so strong. I feel connected to my mother, and enjoy seeing how people admire and respect my father. Instead of just being good at what I do for the sake of proving I'm talented, it feels like I'm sharing my talent—my gift, if you want to call it that—with folks who'll truly appreciate it. They don't have the first clue what goes into it, or that it's something I studied long and hard to learn, not just something I do, or picked up, like they can knit, or build tree houses, or chop wood. And I don't care. It's so much easier to experiment, to think, to create, to . . . well, to just play. The end results are recipes I'm ridiculously proud of. It doesn't matter that my customers have no idea of the complexity that goes into my cupcakes. I enjoy that challenge. I get it, so that's all that matters. It doesn't matter that my cupcakes won't ever grace the plate of a formal state dinner, but instead be the featured dessert at the Kiwanis Club cookout. In fact, that's turned out to be a hell of a lot more rewarding, and a lot more fun." Her animated expression sobered a little, but the light of excitement didn't diminish in the least. If anything, it grew stronger. "That's why I know I won't leave here. It wouldn't be the same somewhere else. I'm meant to be here. But, more important, I want to be here."

"I know that," he said. "I honestly do. It's obvious, like I said, just looking at you. Beyond that, I've tasted your work now, and it's nothing short of inspirational. What you can do inside a fluted paper cup is unbelievable. You've made a convert of me. You haven't walked away from your talent at all, but embraced it and pushed it in an entirely new direction. In fact, you've already done what I was attempting to do with this season of the show. Take elegant, fussy, elaborate desserts and find a way to combine them with the more local, the more rustic and rudimentary, so they'll work for anyone. Rosemary hasn't stopped raving since we did the recipe read through and narrowed down the choices. You saved me because I honestly hadn't a clue how I was going to pull off the theme."

"Don't you think your show already does that? Bringing elegant desserts to the masses? I mean, your viewers are those very same people."

"Not really. I mean, yes, they are, but that's not why they watch. I explain technique and the recipes are available to them online, and I have to keep things somewhat simplified in order to be able to demonstrate them within the time constraints of an episode. But I think viewers tune in not because they think they're going to really make my desserts, but just to see them, be wowed by them a little, and—"

"Drool over your handsome face and hot British accent."

He felt his face warm a bit. "I'm thankful they tune in, whatever the impetus."

"And humble, too," she teased.

Their gazes met and held, as did their smiles. "I do understand why you're here, Leilani," he said at length. "Truly. You've found your home."

She nodded, but with a bit of sadness, maybe resignation. He really, really didn't want to think about that.

She pushed her stool back rather abruptly, and stood. "I should be heading home. Early start tomorrow."

"Right. Quite." He stood as well.

"They have you over at Frank and Barbara's place, right? At least, I heard—"

He nodded. "Yes, yes. I couldn't commute from Savannah and I'd put the kibosh on the tour bus idea, but I'm rethinking that."

She grinned widely. "Tour bus. You're a rock star. You totally should go for that."

"Thanks," he said dryly. "Precisely why I passed on it. But for privacy's sake, I'm reconsidering."

"I can understand that, actually," she said with a light laugh.

"Are you going back to the cottage?"

She nodded. "I think so. I'm so tired I don't think any number of people who might be in my kitchen at the moment could deter me from a good, solid face-plant."

"Face-plant," he repeated. "Very descriptive."

"And true." She laughed. "Hey. You know, I have a bed up in the loft above the shop. I stayed there often when I was cramming to get everything built and installed. You'd have to share the space with a bunch of storage shelves, but the linens are clean and it's comfortable. And private."

He had to admit, it sounded pretty much perfect at the moment, but in the end, he shook his head. The last thing he needed was to wrap himself in Leilani's sheets. "I don't want the Hughes's to think I'm not grateful for their hospitality."

"I doubt they'd care one way or the other; they're a pretty sweet old couple. But suit yourself. You have a key to the shop anyway for production, so you could let yourself in up there if you change your mind. Same lock. Separate entry outside, and up the back stairs."

He nodded. "I saw those. Thank you." He moved to the trailer door and opened it for her.

She waited for him to go through first, but realized he was holding it for her. "Oh, thank you."

Stepping through it meant brushing close to him to get by, and though it had only been the two of them in the trailer for the past half hour or so, it wasn't until that moment that the proximity felt truly intimate.

He wanted—badly—to block her there, trap her in

the doorway, and . . . he didn't know what he'd do next. He just wanted to keep her right there, her body next to his, for one more moment in time.

Their gazes caught and held, and she paused, making his breath catch in his chest. But then she stepped through, and down the steps.

"Good night." She lifted her hand in a short wave, before trotting over to her little SUV.

"Night." He lifted his hand in an automatic return wave. "Sweet dreams," he added, more to himself, as he watched her taillights while she drove off the lot. "Dammit," he muttered, and slapped the door shut behind him, before trotting down the stairs himself. Couldn't have her, couldn't get her out of his bloody mind. There was no future for them, none. He knew that. Just in case he'd tried to talk himself into believing otherwise, listening to her in there had been all the proof anyone would ever need that this was where she belonged. To make it more frustrating, he was happy for her, seeing how truly content she was. He wanted that for her, though it would have been a lot easier if he could have found some fault in it, yes?

But no. No, this was where she belonged and he wanted what was best for her. He wished what was best for her didn't also leave him feeling as if his heart was being ripped from his chest, and stomped on until lifeless. As if he was being forced to give up the one thing he'd ever cared about more than his work. Work was his life. It was what defined him. What fed his soul. What made him happy. So there was no reconciliation. No way to combine their dreams.

He didn't want to leave her. And yet, he couldn't take her with him.

"Bloody goddamn hell."

"Baxter?"

Rosemary. "Yes," he called out. "Right over here."

"Oh good, you haven't left. I'd like to talk over tomorrow's schedule with you, make a few changes based on this afternoon's tape."

"Certainly," he said, with a deep sigh of relief. If work was what he had, then work was what he'd do.

Chapter 14

Lani pulled up in front of the cottage and sighed when she spied the lights on, then noticed that only Charlotte's little rental sat parked out front.

"Thank God," she murmured as she pulled in behind it. Charlotte had come by a few times during the day to watch the first round of taping, but there had been no time to talk. She'd seen enough to know Lani would likely be exhausted and wouldn't be surprised by her wanting to head straight to bed—which was just as well. She wasn't in the mood for a bitch and bake session. That would mean talking about Baxter. But she was too tired to talk about him.

It had been such a challenging day on so many levels. No recipe was therapeutic enough to allow her to think clearly at the moment. She just needed to go to sleep and not think at all. Rest. Restore.

"Right, so you can get up and do it all over again first thing in the morning," she muttered. "Without any time to think at all." She could only hope she woke up with sudden clarity about the situation with Baxter.

That entire morning had been brutal, trying to figure out how to handle herself on the set and handle her rioting hormones where Baxter was concerned, all at the same time. Then had come the lunch break— which had given her libido a whole new raft of things to fantasize about. If Alva hadn't come in when she had, Lani couldn't rightly say where that kiss would have gone. The rest of the day on the set had been pure torture. The only saving grace being she was so hyperaware of every breath Baxter took, she couldn't worry about all the other demands being made of her at the same time.

She was basically on autopilot, worrying that Rosemary would have a fit because she was coming off like a zombie. Either the producer had more or less given up on her putting in a good performance, or she was so desperate to get the day over with, she'd told Lani whatever it was she thought Lani needed to hear. It had seemed as if Rosemary was pretty happy with how the rest of the day went. Maybe Baxter had had a talk with her or something. Lani wasn't sure—and didn't much care. It was over. She prayed she didn't come off looking like a complete spaz, but at the moment, she didn't even care much about that. All she cared about was bed. Sleep.

Tomorrow she'd deal with another day in the trenches. Tomorrow, she'd deal with her rioting emotions about Baxter. Tomorrow, she'd get a grip.

She stepped up onto the porch . . . and that was when she saw the sock. A white sports sock that wasn't hers was draped over the front doorknob. "What in the . . ." She picked it up, thinking the only time she'd ever seen a sock on a doorknob was in the movies when— "Oh. *Oh!*" She shook her head. *Nah. That can't be it. Who would Charlotte be entertaining?*

Then Lani heard what sounded like a squeal, and she instinctively glanced through the gauzy drapes covering the front picture window—and immediately slammed her eyes shut and spun so her back was to the front door. "Well," she said, gripping the sock against her chest. "That certainly answers that question."

She blindly stepped down from the porch and went back to her car. Once safely inside, she stared at her house. And tried like hell not to picture what the current occupants were doing inside it. On her fold-out couch. "Thank goodness the house is set back off the street." She looked at the sock in her hand and wondered if she shouldn't put it back on the doorknob. Would Alva or Dre know the signal? Normally, she wouldn't be worried about having anyone drop by so late. Charlotte had texted her that they'd already come by earlier, and baked. Clearly they were gone. But the way her life had been lately, it wouldn't be completely out of the question for them to come back.

Well, Lani wasn't going back up on that porch, so she could only hope that Charlotte had locked the door. Lani squeezed the sock to toss it on the passenger seat so she could start the car, but felt something crinkle inside it. She pulled out a rolled up piece of notepaper, which she recognized as being from the Strawberry Shortcake grocery list pad she never used, but kept magneted to the side of her fridge. Her mother had given it to her when she'd gotten her first apartment, and Lani had moved it to each successive fridge in each apartment she'd leased. Just in case. And because it made her smile whenever she looked at it.

She unrolled it to find a hastily scrawled note from Charlotte.

Yes, I'm the worst houseguest ever. But it's been TEN months, Lan. Turns out Carlo makes more than good coffee.

There was a smiley face after that. And lots of exclamation points. Which was so un-Charlotte-like, Lani had to laugh. The note ended with

Hope you can stay over the shop. I'll make it up to you! Promise! TEN MONTHS! The drought, it is over!

Lani smiled, and folded the note back up. Just because she was stupid enough to turn away the only man she'd ever wanted didn't mean her best friend had to turn down an opportunity. So . . . Carlo. "Huh." She shook her head. She didn't see it. Except, well, for the part she *had* seen. Now that the shock had worn off, she had to admit . . . "Go, Charlotte."

Her smile faded before she was even halfway to town as weariness settled in bone deep. She was going to crawl upstairs, crawl into bed, and let tomorrow take care of tomorrow. A night spent not tossing and turning and overthinking everything would be a blessing.

She parked behind the kitchen trailer and shimmied between it and the production trailer, then climbed the narrow, wobbly set of metal stairs leading to the second story door. There was entry from inside the shop, but she didn't want to look at the cameras, cables, and lights littering her kitchen. In fact, she wanted to block everything out of her mind completely. She let herself in the back way, having to push a bit to make the warped wood door open. The dampness from the sea air made doors and wood flooring a challenge to keep properly fitted, but she thought it added to the charm of the place. Most of the time.

She worked the door shut again, then leaned against it for a moment, and oriented her vision to the shadowy open space. The wood floor, covered with linoleum, had buckled here and there from the damp air. A few area rugs helped to cover the worst of it, and take a bit of the chill off during the cooler months. Lani kicked her shoes off and curled her toes into the rug she was standing on, then took a moment to stretch them again, and let the soles of her sore feet relax fully into the pile.

The entire left side of the loft space was used for storage of nonfood items like packaging, shop bags, storage containers, and extra kitchen equipment. The other half contained the old double bed frame that had been left there by the former tenant, to which she'd added mattress, box spring, and linens from one of the guest room beds at Harper House. A small bedside nightstand with a lamp, an aging rolltop desk with a banker lamp on top, and an old television with rabbit ear antennas were also left behind. The TV actually picked up the local networks surprisingly well.

The bathroom was in the far corner. Originally she'd thought about taking a long, hot shower, but she just wanted to go straight to bed. The moonlight coming in from the two front dormer windows provided enough light. She shuffled straight over to the side of the bed and peeled her clothes off, letting them fall in a heap at her feet. When she felt a light breeze on her skin, she absently realized the overhead paddle fan was moving. And the front windows were cracked open. She must have left them that way after she'd hauled up her last order of shop bags, and done a quick inventory of stock. Even though the entire building was wired with heat and air conditioning, the steamy temperatures during the day made the upstairs pretty muggy.

At the moment, she was thankful it felt freshly aired out. As she flipped back the covers she made a mental note to remember to turn the fan off and close the windows before going back downstairs to the shop. With a sigh of appreciation, she slid between the cool sheets and reached up to plump the pillow . . . right at the same exact moment her toes came into direct contact with very warm, very naked flesh.

She squealed and shot upright and would have flown out of bed, but she got tangled in the chenille cover, trying to preserve modesty and get away from whoever the hell was in her—

"Whoa, whoa, slow down there, luv. It's just me."

A large, wide hand closed around her upper arm, keeping her from flailing herself right to the floor.

She twisted around, clutching the white, fuzzy-nubbed bedspread to her chest, while spluttering her hair from her mouth. "Baxter?"

"In the, um . . . flesh."

She was too discombobulated from tangled hair, twisted blankets, and a serious punch of heart-pounding adrenaline to be able to see him clearly, but she couldn't mistake the amusement in his voice. "What on earth are you doing in my—"

"I believe I was invited. So to speak. I ended up okaying some edit work with Rosemary after you left, then opted to just climb up here and sleep. I didn't know you planned on joining me, or I'd have left a light on."

"I'm glad you're finding this amusing. You scared me half to death."

"Perhaps I should be the one asking why you're here. I thought you headed home."

"I did. But Charlotte was already there. With company."

"Ah, more of those marauding all-night bakers?"

"Oh, no." She tried to get her heart under control. "Just one baker."

Maybe he heard something in her voice, or maybe he was just a good guesser. When he said, "Oh," he clearly understood that the baker in question wasn't Alva or her shop assistant.

"Oh, indeed."

"Is your friend in the habit of bringing home stray . . . bakers?"

"She's impulsive, as I believe I mentioned, but this would be a first, even for her. She did leave a note."

"Decent of her."

Finally Lani managed to scrape the last of the tangled mess of hair from her face and make him out in the moonlit darkness. Perhaps it would have been better if she hadn't. He was lying half on his side, half on his back, one hand behind his head, the sheets draped somewhere between his chest and a dangerously low spot below his navel. She'd thought about him many times, in a variety of settings, but she'd never once imagined he'd look that damn good in her bed.

"Yes," she finally said, knowing she should look away, but not exactly managing it. "I—I'll just be—can you like, roll over or something, so I can get my clothes back on?"

"I'm hardly going to kick you out of your own bed, luv."

"Yes, well, I appreciate that, but you were already deep asleep, and so it seems to be smarter for me to just—"

"I have another bed."

"And I can go to Harper House."

"And explain to your father why both of your beds are taken at the moment?"

She sighed, and might have even sworn under her breath. "You have a point." She couldn't seem to get her heart rate back to normal, her thoughts were a rioting jumble, and she wanted everything to slow down for five blasted seconds so she could think straight.

"There's a perfectly good bed right here. And you're already in it. Might as well stay."

"You know that's not—we can't—"

He reached out then and traced his fingers up the side of her bare arm. She shuddered in pleasure at the sizzle that single touch sent skittering over her skin.

He slipped his fingers around her upper arm, and tugged ever so gently. "Come here, Lei."

She sighed, and her willpower wavered dangerously. Oh, who was she kidding, her willpower deserted her completely. "It's going to make things so much harder," she said, as she let him pull her toward him.

She could see his grin in the moonlight. "Luv, I don't believe it could be any harder than it is already."

She shouldn't have laughed at that. But she did. And that's what did in any last chance she had of reclaiming control of the situation, or at least control of herself.

It was one thing to get swept away in a moment of passion, but laughter—especially shared laughter—had a way of grounding the moment, making it a conscious choice, not something mindlessly swept aside to be dealt with in the morning. And still, she wasn't choosing to move away.

"You're beautiful in the moonlight." He eased her

down next to him. The chenille was bunched up between them, so they weren't skin to skin . . . quite yet. He rolled more to his side as he tucked her close, then skimmed the backs of his knuckles across her cheeks as his gaze roamed over her face, her neck, her bare shoulders.

Her breath caught in her chest and she couldn't seem to form words. She was too busy reveling in the reality that she was in the exact place she'd dreamed of being, for so long. It was light years better than anything she'd ever fantasized it would be. His hands were big, but gentle. His words soothed, but there was an edge to his voice that incited as well. And he was bigger somehow, more imposing, more densely muscled than she'd imagined him to be. She'd thought of him as the tall, lanky golden boy, all sunny good looks and breezy charisma.

But, looking up at him from where she was, tucked in the shelter of his body, she could see the street in him. She'd had a hard time imagining that such a good-natured charmer could have been forged from the rough and tumble life he'd described. But she believed it now. There was a hard edge to his jaw, and the muscles in his shoulders bunched tightly as he skimmed his fingers into her hair. He exuded heat, and she swore she could feel the thudding beat of his heart, even with the bedspread bunched between them.

"What are you thinking?" He brought his fingertips back to her cheeks, then ran them along her bottom lip.

She moaned softly at the contact, and recalled, quite vividly, the way he'd leaped the counter and taken her in that claiming, branding kiss. Yes, there was a lot more rough and tumble to Baxter Dunne than she'd ever imagined. And now all that rough and tumble was sprawled naked in her bed, focusing a formidable level of attention on her.

"You've nothing to be afraid of, luv," he said, as if reading her mind. And maybe he had. Or maybe there was something of what she was feeling in her eyes.

She felt like she was tucked up against a jungle cat, muscles coiled and bunched . . . just waiting, tail flicking, all languid and relaxed to the casual eye, all poised for just the right moment to pounce. She tried to speak, but her throat had gone desert dry. She didn't know what to say to him.

He leaned down then, and she held her breath as her pulse rate tripled, waiting, spellbound, mesmerized . . . in almost excruciating anticipation for what he was going to do next.

He didn't kiss her. He nuzzled the side of her neck as the palm of his hand lightly skimmed her bare shoulder. Her hips already wanted to arch up—violently so—and it was only the wound bedspread between them that kept them from doing it.

"I'll leave you alone," he whispered roughly, against her soft skin. "If that's what you really want."

"You—" The word came out on a strangled croak. She tried again. "You promised. Not to push."

She heard him chuckle against her shoulder, where he was presently pressing the hottest, sweetest kisses she'd ever received. "I promised I wouldn't start it," he murmured. "You climbed into my bed, luv. Naked, I might add."

"Not on purpose." She intended the tone to be heated, but instead it came out like a plea.

He lifted his head. His hair was tousled and impossibly sexy, and his grin lent the whole look a wicked air. "Well, whatever the cause, the result has us here.

Together. With no schedule demanding our attention, no eyes prying . . . and nowhere to be until morning."

She held his gaze, and tried—hard—to reclaim a single shred of common sense, a sliver of the rationale she needed so neither of them would make such a colossal mistake. "If we give in now, it's going to be so much more painful when you go. At least for me."

His smile faded, but as her eyes had adjusted to the moonlight, she could see the desire in his eyes, along with a wealth of emotion she shied away from labeling. It looked an awful lot like what her heart was feeling at the moment.

"Whether we give in or not, walking away from you will be the hardest thing I've ever had to do."

She swallowed, not sure what to say to that, or how it made her feel. Other than more conflicted.

"Less pain, more pain," he said gruffly. "I don't know that there's a real measure for it any longer, Lei. Or that it matters what we do or don't do."

Her heart clutched at his earnestly spoken words. Being held in his arms, his warm touch on her skin, made the thought of his leaving all the more wrenching. "I wish there was a way," she whispered back.

"They say love conquers all, but I think reality can crush even the most devoutly dedicated." Baxter propped himself up higher on his elbow so he could look more fully into her eyes. "Even if you were willing to move back to the city, and I turned my world upside down so we'd have more time together . . . at the end of it, after what you've found here, you'd be miserable back in New York. We both know that. Eventually you'd either resent me for it, or simply drown in the chaotic, stress-filled frenzy of it all."

"I wouldn't resent you," she said. "I make my own

decisions. But you're right. I don't want to go back to that kind of life again. I'd feel suffocated and cut off from what I really need. Just as I know your goals are different from mine, and you can't do what you do on some dinky island off the coast of Georgia." She untangled one hand from the bedspread to reach up and brush the tousled strands from his forehead. "I know that."

He smiled down at her, and there was that sizzling combination in his expression, of gentle charmer and back alley survivor. She'd never again see him any other way. The impossibility of it all broke her heart just a little bit more.

Turning his head, he kissed her palm, his warm lips on her sensitive skin making her tremble. He traced lazy circles along her collar bone with his fingertips. "Do we take what small stretch of time the fates will give us, revel in that, and be thankful for the rich memories left behind? Or do I get up, get dressed, and leave you to sleep here alone . . . and do my damndest—for the next two weeks while we work together— not to picture you as you are right at this moment, knowing I'll never truly have you."

"Baxter," she said, and it was a plea, pure and simple. A plea for which thing, she couldn't have said. There was nothing simple about the situation. The need, and the want, however, were both pure. Blindingly so.

He leaned down, and she held her breath, thinking if he would just kiss her, she wouldn't have to decide. She could slide right over the edge into the escape of complete and utter sexual need.

But instead of brushing her lips with his, he leaned farther and brushed them past the soft swell of her ear lobe. "Perhaps the answer is to be found by asking yourself which you would regret more. I know what my answer would be."

She shifted until he lifted his head enough to look into her eyes. "I honestly wish I knew, Baxter. I don't know which will be the greater torture while you're still here. Working next to you like I did all afternoon and evening, with us knowing exactly what we want, but knowing we'll never take it. Or taking it, then having to work next to you knowing exactly what it was like."

He smiled again. "Maybe it will be bloody awful and we'll wonder what all the worry and fuss was about."

She gave him a sardonic look. "Then maybe you weren't having the same kiss I was having in the kitchen earlier."

He leaned in and whispered right next to the corner of her mouth. "Oh, I was having the same kiss, luv."

She could feel his heat, smell the lingering scent of ginger that had been steamed into them all afternoon.

"I should tell you this, though." He brushed his lips against the corner of her mouth, then lightly along her jaw, making her moan softly, and shift her body under the bedspread, seeking something, anything, that would assuage the ache building up inside of her.

"What?" she said, quite breathless, as he trailed his almost-but-not-quite kisses to the tender spot just beneath her ear.

"If we decide to take . . . it won't be just for tonight."

Her hips jerked at that, and there was nothing she could do about it. The very idea of having him, like this—repeatedly—was all she could do to lie still. "Baxter—"

"No. No more rules. No more boundaries. No more

restrictions. If we're going to take what time we do have, then I'm going to be quite greedy." He nipped at her ear lobe. "Voraciously, relentlessly, unrepentantly so."

"But . . . there's Charlotte." Lani squirmed, wanting so badly for him to stop torturing her and just take her, for God's sake. She couldn't be still if her life depended on it. "And . . . and the Hugheses."

"And there's this bed, and us. And a whole island to explore, and beyond, if the time presents itself. I don't just want you naked, Lei. Well, that's not true. I will always want you naked. But no boundaries means just that. This isn't only about sex. I'll want your time, your attention, your laughter, your thoughts." He tipped her face to his. "If we're to have this time, then I'll want all of you in it."

The idyllic picture he was painting was that of her deepest desires. And she realized then that the stolen kisses, the burning need to have him naked, joined, thrusting hip-to-hip, wasn't the driving force behind the feelings that were growing by leaps and bounds. They continued to grow, despite her attempts to steer clear of physical contact. It was the walks on the beach, sharing stories of their childhoods, sitting across the worktable from him after a very long, very trying day, and realizing that just having him there to talk to was pretty much the best thing ever.

She was going to be spending time with him, falling more deeply in love with him, whether she walked away that night, or not. And dammit, if she was going to feel all those things anyway, and have her heart ripped out after anyway . . . then she wanted to feel this, too.

More terrified, and more exhilarated than she'd ever been before, she deliberately reached up and slid her hand along the back of his neck, burying her fingers, as she'd so often longed to do, in the thick, slightly shaggy waves that curled along his hairline. "Agreed then. No rules," she whispered, pulling his head slowly down. "No restrictions." A hot thrill coursed through her as she saw desire punch his pupils dark and wide. She lifted her head, and nipped his chin. "No boundaries."

Then she tugged his mouth to hers, and for the first time—the first gloriously unrestrained, thoroughly uninhibited time—*she* kissed *him*.

Chapter 15

Baxter didn't think there could be a torture more brutal than the cat and mouse game they'd been playing since his arrival on the island.

He'd been wrong.

So very, very wrong.

With Leilani as the aggressor, kissing her was a completely different experience. His body, already close to the edge of control with nothing more than a bedspread between them, was pushed to limits he didn't know he had. And she was just kissing him.

Her hands were in his hair, nails raking his scalp. She was lifting up from the bed, pressing against him, as she took the kiss deeper, then deeper still, until he thought he'd embarrass himself in a way he hadn't even as an untried lad with his first roll.

Moving on pure instinct, he pulled her beneath him and drew her hands down, pinning them on the bed next to her head. "Leilani," he panted against her lips, "I'm—" He broke off and slid his mouth from hers, needing to find some semblance of sanity.

He kept her hands pinned, but her hips were still

moving beneath his, begging him to rip, tear, shred, or do whatever was necessary to remove the goddamn bedspread from between their heated bodies. He wanted to glory in the feel of her skin . . . all of it on all of his. Oh, sweet Mary, but he was never going to survive this.

"I've thought about this," he said, as he nipped and licked his way along her shoulders, making her moan and writhe beneath him. "I've thought about every glorious detail. How I'd disrobe you, how I'd look at you in the moonlight, the sunlight, candlelight, or no light at all. I'd come to know your body so well, that by touch alone I could rightly imagine every last dip and curve." He leaned in, pressed heated kisses to the side of her neck, making her gasp. "But oh, I'd want to see you. Watch you. Like right now, the way you respond to me, to my touch." He drew his tongue along the soft line of her jaw, not sure who was being tortured more by the little whimpers she made as he did so.

"Baxter," she breathed.

"You drive me mad, Lei." He bit her ear lobe with a little more edge than maybe he'd meant, making her body jerk, but the accompanying moan was one of pure pleasure. "I want to take, and take, and take, to drown in you. I want to sip, to suckle. I want to run my tongue into every nook." He pressed her wrists to the bed, meaning for her to keep them there, then slid his hands to her shoulders as he moved his body lower on top of hers . . . and took the bedspread with him.

"Peeling the linen from you is like unwrapping the richest, creamiest chocolate. And I know you will taste even sweeter, more decadent, more intoxicating." To punctuate his words, he dropped kisses along her collar bone, then slid the twisted edge of the bedspread lower still, until he came close to the crests of her breasts. "Are they taut for me, Leilani?" he whispered roughly. "Are they waiting for my tongue, for my mouth to cover them, to lick them, suck them, make them wet, make them plump?"

"Yes," she said, the word seemingly wrenched from her, as her hips tried to thrash beneath his weight.

He tugged the coverlet slowly down so the fabric dragged softly across the two tightly budded tips. She moaned, twisting beneath him.

"So perfectly tight, perfectly rosy, like the most exquisite toppings. I need to taste you." He circled one nipple with the tip of his tongue, making it damp, then skimmed over it with his fingertips as he had with the bedspread, while he paid attention to the other with his mouth.

Lani was jerking beneath him, moaning loudly, and only because he kept all of his focus on attending to those two, perfect pleasure points, in the same way he could focus exclusively on the most intricate detail of a single dessert creation and tune everything else out, was he able to keep from coming right then. His body, his needs, were a distant second to fulfilling hers.

"Baxter . . ." His name was a growl on her lips, and she reached for his shoulders, digging her fingertips in. "Please."

"Not yet, luv." He pushed her hands back to the mattress. "So much more to see. So much more to taste."

Her responding groan of pleasure was long and low, her hips moving in a steady rhythm, as he smiled against her skin . . . and moved lower still. "I love baring your warm skin to the cool air, love baring you to me." He licked his fingertip then reached up and traced it over her nipples again. "Look at them glistening in the moonlight."

Gasping, she pushed her head back into the mattress, arching her neck and shoulders, filling his palm with the soft roundness of her breast. He was tempted, so very tempted, to slide up . . . slide in. Instead he continued his lazy path downward.

"I want you, Leilani. I'm so hard it hurts. But your scent entices me, lures me." He drew the sheet farther down, past her navel, along the soft swell of her stomach. "I want to taste, to savor. Here." He kissed his way to the tender flesh high inside her inner thigh. "And here." He traced a similar path to the other side. "But I want to feast . . . here." He drew his tongue along the center of her, and groaned at the sweet taste of her.

Lani's hips started to pump harder, and he could feel a fine quivering begin along her skin. She rocked and keened, and when he plunged his tongue deeply into her, she cried out, reached down and buried her fingers in his hair. Guiding him, urging him, demanding him, release broke over her in wracking, wrenching waves.

"Baxter, please . . . please." Her hips slowed, but her body continued to gather and jerk as the aftershocks kept twitching through her. "Now," she demanded. "I'm—I'm safe, protected, we don't need—" She broke off as he kissed his way back up the center of her torso while she continued to writhe beneath him.

The way she responded to him, making herself vulnerable to him, moved him in unpredictable ways. He shifted so he was directly on top of her and pressed himself between her thighs, which she parted, wrapping them around his hips, digging her heels into his lower back as she lifted for him, and took him in.

Take her, he did, sliding all the way in, groaning as she gripped him fully, so tightly, so wetly, so perfectly, it was the fulfillment of every fantasy he'd ever had. Even though his heart was drumming inside his chest, and his body was priming itself for a ferocious release, climaxing wasn't the only thing dominating his thoughts. He met her every hip thrust, echoed every groan, every growl, as they worked their frenzied way to completion, together.

He could feel her climb again as she rolled her hips beneath him, and reality continued to eclipse fantasy. "Come with me, yes," he said, claiming her mouth even as she was nodding in agreement.

He pulled her into his arms and moved more deeply, as she instinctively shifted to take him more tightly inside her. They moved with a rhythm that was as old as man's creation, and uniquely and utterly their own. What stunned him, rocked him, as he raced straight to the edge of control, what ultimately drove him over the edge, taking her right along with him, was the deep, fiercely protective way he felt about her, cradled beneath him.

She was a strong, equal partner, proving herself a match for him in every possible way. But that wasn't what was responsible for his heart being tugged, nor the way his conscience was being tugged even harder. He wanted her, all of her, in as primal a way as a man could want a woman. At the same time, he wanted to protect her, make sure no harm ever came to her. She was in his care. That's what it came down to.

She was in his care.

Every part of her mattered to him. He knew he would lay down his life before he ever let anyone or anything be a threat to her.

To that end, as the shudders pulsating through their bodies gradually subsided, and their breathing struggled back to some semblance of normalcy, he kept her close, nestled in his arms. Rolling his weight from her, he took her with him, and tucked her against him, even as she was wrapping herself around him in much the same way. His heart tripped. The idea that they each were instinctively reaching to protect the other, nurture the other, moved him far more profoundly than the most powerful climax ever could. How mutually satisfying it was to give that, and to so naturally and honestly be given it in return.

Maybe that's what an equal partnership truly was. Putting the other first, the feelings of fierce loyalty, and the need to protect, defend. It wasn't just a man watching over his weaker, more vulnerable woman. Watch any lioness protecting her cubs and you get a glimpse of a woman's innate strength and ability. He wanted to be protector, and . . . to be protected, too. His heart, his emotional well-being, if not his physical self. He wanted to know she was there, would always be there, loyal to that desire, to him, as he would be, in all ways, to her.

She slipped one arm around his waist and snuggled closer, opening her hand and pressing her palm against his chest. Directly over his heart.

He closed his eyes, and pressed a kiss to the top of her head. He knew he wouldn't share with her any thoughts or feelings presently rioting through his body, his head, his heart. He didn't want to think about the inevitable, which was the future they would spend apart. It was far too brutal to contemplate in that moment. He didn't think it fair to burden her with the true depth of his emotions.

He had no regrets, however, about having gotten to this place, to this new awareness, and hoped she didn't either. A part of him thought it might be the better part of valor to get up, and go, leaving what they'd just shared as a singular, crystalline memory that he—and hopefully she—would forever have to savor. But even as he thought it, he knew the prospect of being with her again, whether in bed, walking on the beach, sharing a late night conversation, or smiling, side by side, at the camera, would be too tempting—too good, too . . . much—to pass up.

He wanted it all. And unless she put a stop to it, he would take whatever was there for them, for as long as their time together allowed.

His next lucid thought came at some unknown point later in the night, when he stirred—literally—as he came to awareness, realizing she had slipped on top of him, and was presently re-creating their original scenario . . . only with her in the leading role. She was sliding the sheet down his body . . . and following the trail with her tongue. And with very clever fingers.

He groaned as he came awake—fully awake—and had to fight the urge to roll her to her back and take her. He wondered if it had been as frustrating . . . and intensely pleasurable, when he'd performed the same torturous journey on her.

"I love your scent," she murmured, inciting him further, "your taste."

Then he was the one growling and arching his hips when she took him into her mouth, her hands, until he could no longer contain himself.

"Lei, come here." He reached blindly for her.

"Let me finish," she said, but he sat up and pulled her to his lap, thrusting into her even as she straddled him.

"I want to be buried deep inside you when I—" And that's as far as he got before the words were nipped off by the rampant surging of his body.

She held on, rocking with him as he roared into

her, her arms around his neck, her teeth nipping at his ear lobes, which only served to intensify his pulsating response.

"I swear I'm seeing more stars than I did on the beach," he managed, struggling to get his heart to slow, and air back into his lungs.

He rolled her to her back, making her laugh as they continued to gasp for breath. "You're a danger," he panted. "A menace."

"Yes," she agreed quite readily. "I should be locked up. Held somewhere private, by someone who would keep a close eye on me." She nipped his other ear, then punctuated her words with kisses. "A very . . . close . . . eye."

They were laughing then, quite helplessly, until the need to breathe quieted them, and their playful nips turned into softer, more languorous kisses. He rolled them to their sides again, and they curled easily into the same position they'd nestled into before. Somewhere along the way, the sleepy, languid kissing turned into a slow, steady seduction. He couldn't have said who was the seducer, and he didn't much care.

The difference wasn't in intensity; despite their earlier activity he was just as ready, just as wanting. With that edge of urgency removed, there was a softness, an easiness, a feeling that they had all the time in the world to simply sip, and take, talk, and kiss. He'd half thought they'd fall asleep at some point in the midst of it, either while she was dropping little kisses on his chest while he toyed with her hair, or while he traced his fingertips along her thigh, her arm, the contours of her chin and cheeks.

Instead, they came together quietly, gently, easily. As their need built, perhaps they were more intently focused than before. They shared long gazes, longer kisses, and when he slid slowly inside her, and she arched in a slow stretch of her back to meet him, he felt his heart slide up and over any remaining obstacle there might have been between them.

Afterward, she kissed him, smiling into his eyes, then curled up against him, under the protective wing of his arm, and fell instantly to sleep.

He was bone weary from the day, and wrung completely out by their lovemaking, yet he stayed awake far longer into the night. Holding her, stroking her hair, feeling her heart beat against his he wondered how in bloody hell he would ever find the strength to walk away from her.

She was in his care. She was his.

It really was as simple, as elemental, as that.

Chapter 16

Falling asleep with him, so sweetly at ease, so supremely contented, had been sublime. So it stood to reason that waking up in the light of day together would be, at best, a cold douse of reality. Exactly what she'd need to put their night ... their whole, fantastic, amazing, ridiculously perfect night, into its proper, once-in-a-lifetime-be-thankful-you-experienced-it perspective.

But no, Lani thought, snuggling under the weight of his arm draped over her waist, reveling in the way his cheek was nestled against the top of her head. She was still deeply, happily, merrily ensconced in fantasyland.

"It's time." His raspy voice was far too sexy for first thing in the morning.

She started to shift, so she could look at the little plug-in clock on the nightstand, but his arm became an instant steel band. "No wriggling."

"I wasn't wriggling, I was trying to see the—" She tried to lean, but he held on. "Can't—breathe," she said, and would have laughed, if she could draw in enough air. "I thought girls were the clingy ones."

"One more wriggle and I'll give new meaning to clingy." He shifted his hips just enough so she could feel the very hard length of him pressing against the back of her thighs.

"Oh," she said with a surprised laugh.

"Quite," he replied, sounding sleepily amused.

Lani wriggled.

An instant later she was on her back with a very aroused man on top of her. "I believe you were warned, yes?"

"Quite," she replied. *That was a pretty decent impression of his accent,* she thought. "I'm just not sure why. Morning . . . uh, clinging is good."

"Unless you're the one who has to tell Rosemary why both of her principals are late."

Lani froze as laughter and teasing gave way to sheer panic. "It's not that late, is it? The sun isn't up. Call time for hair and makeup isn't until seven."

"It's raining."

She stopped, listened, and heard the soft pitter-patter. "I can't believe I didn't hear that and you did."

He pushed the hair from her face and smiled. "I've been awake longer than you."

"So, you're telling me we had time for . . . clinging? And you didn't wake me up?"

"It was quite the internal struggle. Well"—he pressed himself a bit further between her thighs—"partly external."

"Greatly external if you ask me." She sighed, wanting badly to shift just a little, so he could do again what he'd done so well, so thoroughly, last night. Several times, in fact. "You had to debate it?"

"I wasn't aware of your morning, um, clinging proclivities. You'd had a long day yesterday, followed by a short, rather strenuous night—"

She grinned, she simply couldn't help it. When he continued to wait and look at her, she said, "Go on." And kept grinning.

"We're facing a new day of interminable length, and so I was debating the relative merits of letting you get some extra, much needed rest, or . . . starting the morning off with a, well, bang. As it were."

"So . . . what time is it?"

"Time to shower and get dressed. Which we'll have to do separately—"

"It's a decent sized shower, and I'm all for water conservation."

He pushed forward a little. She groaned a lot. "Right. We'd run out of hot water, as well." She wriggled just a little. "Are you sure we can't just stop talking and—"

"Rosemary."

Lani blanched. "Okay, that was just mean."

"Had to be done, luv. My willpower is about on par with yours at the moment." He leaned down and kissed her.

It was easy, comfortable . . . and perfect. All of it had been that way, natural and compatible, as if they'd been together a very long time, rather than just one night. Of course, they'd been friends first, or co-workers who greatly respected and liked one another. The real friendship had begun on Sugarberry. But it all added up, along with the sizable zing of sexual attraction, to form something she'd never known before. It felt deep and strong, and very real to her, in a way that promised durability and longevity.

"How do you want to handle this?" he asked, breaking into her musings.

"Handle what? You can shower first." She grinned and wriggled her toes. "I'll force myself to stay snuggled here in this nice, warm bed."

He smiled. "I meant how do you want to handle things when we leave here and reenter the world. I guess we should have talked about it last night. I'm sure some of the crew, if not most of them, are already downstairs. Maybe I should have gone to the B&B at some point last night, or—"

"I thought this was no boundaries, no rules?"

"Between us, yes. I didn't think—wasn't sure— you'd want to announce it to the world."

"I'm pretty sure when Alva walked into the kitchen yesterday any hope of keeping this secret flew out the window."

"I meant the world beyond Sugarberry."

Lani's smile faltered. "Oh. Right." It was one thing for the citizens of Sugarberry to happily prod the two of them into what, to their eyes, would seem to be the beginning of a happy, burgeoning relationship. Quite another for word to spread beyond the island shores to the regular news outlets. It would, of course, if they chose to be open about everything. If the only news that leaked out was that an eighty-plus islander had spied them in a lip-lock, it would be rumor and innuendo, especially if they didn't address it. Or get caught again. "I guess I didn't think about that. I don't want to do anything to put you in a difficult situation."

"Me?" he said, clearly confused. "I was talking about you."

She laughed. "You know, I don't care anymore what anyone says. I don't have to live in that world, and I think I've changed a lot in terms of how I think about all that, since you've come here. Charlotte pointed out to me that I had always filtered my feelings about that time through the person I was while I worked there. I'm a very different person here, living a completely different life. So . . . I can let that go. It can't really touch me here. On the island, I only have to deal with the locals, and there isn't a mean spirit amongst them. No matter how excited they get over the proposition of us getting together, once you're gone, the buzz will eventually die down and they'll see it's back to business and life as usual."

Lani tried hard, very hard, to stay casual and detached about that last part. "You're the one who will be out promoting the new season of your show, and filming on location. The media might hound you about it."

He framed her face with his hands and brushed aside the loose strands of hair clinging to her cheeks with his thumbs. "I honestly don't care about all that. I never have. I can handle whatever they throw at me. I just don't want them hurting you."

"You want us to sneak around, then?" She wiggled her eyebrows. "Do we get to use code words?"

"I'm actually being serious, Lei. I don't know what kind of fallout this might bring on either of us, but at the end of it, it's you I don't want hurt."

"You know"—she reached up to push his tousled hair from his forehead, still feeling too warm and afterglowy to be willing to spoil it with whatever came next—"I just don't think I really am going to care. No matter what."

"But—"

She pressed a finger on his mouth, then pushed at his bottom lip, and felt him twitch hard against her thighs. Her body moved instinctively toward him. "So much has changed. Everything has changed. I don't want to care about all that. I just want to care about"—

she lifted her hips—"this. And you. I don't want to spend the next week and a half worrying about what the rest of the world might think, or say, or do. If you don't think it's going to adversely affect your show in any way, and Rosemary's not going to have a coronary or anything, then let's just be ourselves and do whatever we feel like doing. Wherever, and in front of whomever, I don't care."

He looked into her eyes. "I believe you really mean that."

"I do mean that. Every word." She tugged his face down closer to hers. "Baxter, you mean more to me, being together for what time we have means more than anything they can throw my way. You've already proven you're not going to be cavalier about it. You're trying to be thoughtful and you obviously have my best interests at heart. I feel the same. We'll handle things as they come. It's too hard to second guess what's going to happen, anyway. Maybe no one will really care."

He snorted. "You, of all people, know differently. And that was before I was on the telly five days a week."

"So what? You're linked with actual famous people all the time. All you have to do is drape an arm on a shoulder at this benefit or that wine and food festival, and you're instantly married, having twins, or already breaking up." She cupped his cheek with her palm. "You'll go on to the next town, and the story will shift to someone there. Or something else. Or someone else will make a new headline and you'll be yesterday's news for a while. What we do will go away, because you're going away. And I'm staying here."

She saw something flicker in his eyes then, and it was too close—far too close—to that emotional edge she'd been purposely dancing away from all morning.

"Lei—"

"I don't want to waste any more time talking about it, okay?" she said quickly. "I think Rosemary's already on a full head of steam, so if she's going to blow, then I think we might as well make it worth the misery she'll be raining down on us later because of it." With that, Lani hooked her ankle over his and, only because she caught him unaware, was able to roll him to his back, sliding right on top of him . . . pinning his hands for a change.

He didn't fight her. In fact, he grinned. "You're going to have your way with me then, is that it?"

"You're not the only one who can play marauding pastry chef."

His grin turned into a groan of deep appreciation. "You can maraud me anytime."

Lani couldn't respond. She was too busy reveling in just how amazing they felt, joined. She'd thought maybe it was the delirium of the first time that had her thinking rosy thoughts. Well, and the second time. And the third.

"How is it even better this time? How?" she panted, moving on top of him.

She squealed an instant later when she found herself neatly on her back once again. He pushed deeper, and growled a little. "Am I hurtin' you?"

"No. Don't stop," she panted, then growled a little herself as he thrust into her, again and again. She knew now, when he was fully beyond controlling himself, bits and pieces of his childhood accent resurfaced. For whatever reason, that was just hot as all hell to her. It was earthy, primal.

"Oh," she said, then, *"Oh!"* when he pulled her thighs up higher along his waist, tilting her so she was just at the right angle to—

"How do you—*do* that?" she managed. That was it as the crescendo of sensation washed up and over, taking her on a hard, fast ride in to shore.

He held on while she jerked against him, then pinned her back to the bed and thrust deep, one last time, as he shuddered his way there himself.

He was big, tall, and heavy. She would miss the sheer, breathless weight of him, pressing on top of every part of her.

"Shower," he said, still trying to find his breath. He rolled to his side, relieving her of his weight, but taking her with him as he did, keeping her nestled against him.

He'd done the same each of the other times. It was the thing she'd already decided she liked best. Well, one of the things. But being intimately joined was one thing when their minds were mostly on stimulation and want and release. Afterward, staying wrapped up in each other, was an entirely different kind of intimacy.

"I wish we didn't have to go anywhere," she murmured, leaning up to kiss the base of his throat, then along the curve of his shoulder. "Rainy days should be spent in bed."

"I couldn't agree more." He let out a deep sigh.

"I know, don't say it." She tucked her feet on the backs of his calves. "From now on, we'll just refer to her as 'She who will not be named.' "

He was chuckling as he kissed her forehead. "As long as you don't ever let her hear you say it."

Lani laughed, but grew more serious as she asked, "Will we—will you want to sleep here again tonight?"

He tilted her chin up so he could look into her eyes. "You're uncertain?"

"No, I mean, I assume we want to be together, but—oh, wait. You have dinner with Alva tonight."

"I do." He kissed Lani on the curve of her cheek, then her temple, then dropped a hard fast one on her mouth. "If you want, you can go grill Charlotte about her date, do bake therapy as needed depending on how today goes, then I can either come by and get you after dinner is over—which would give me a nice excuse to not let it go on too long—or you can meet me back here if you'd like. Whatever is most comfortable for you. But"—he kissed her again, groaned, then stole one last one, before rolling away from her and getting straight off the bed—"we're never going to get to this evening if we don't get to work. I'll shower first—"

"I have some fresh clothes up here, but don't you need to go back to your room and change?"

He stopped just before ducking into the bathroom, which gave her a quite delightful view of his lanky, sinewy, beautifully naked frame in the morning light. She was never going to get tired of that view, and, in fact, made a mental note to come up with many reasons why he should stroll around naked. Often.

"Right. Maybe I should duck out now, shower there." Baxter walked over to where he'd left his clothes on the chair paired with the rolltop desk. "Meet you in makeup? Or in the kitchen?" he said as he shrugged on his shirt and pulled on his trousers.

Lani stretched languorously, and couldn't quite seem to wipe the grin from her face. "You don't get any sick days? My shop happens to be closed for business right now, so I find myself available to play hooky."

"It's so very, very tempting, luv." He stopped right in the middle of pulling on his socks when she let the sheet slide off her body. "Now who's being mean?"

It wasn't playing fair, she knew that, but she couldn't get past how he looked at her, couldn't really wrap her head around the fact that it was actually happening, and he truly wanted her, desired her, in all the same ways she'd wanted and desired him. "I'm not just hallucinating this, am I?"

He crossed to the bed, leaned down, and kissed her. "No," he said, rather roughly, when he finally lifted his head. "But it is a rather perfect dream, isn't it?"

She was still in bed when he let himself out. She knew she should be getting dressed and bracing herself for the day. But she was still too overwhelmed by the night before. She needed to think about it, let it sink in, figure out how she was going to handle the veritable tidal wave of emotions just one night spent with him had already ignited inside her.

She wanted to bake. Badly.

And not on camera, thankyouverymuch.

Yet, that was her only option at the moment. She reminded herself it was only because she was going to be baking on camera with Baxter that she'd had the night she'd just experienced.

She rubbed her hands over her face, and took a deep, bracing breath . . . then still lay there and stared at the ceiling. "Yes, it is the perfect dream."

The idea that she was going to have a week or so more of that dream with Baxter, in and out of bed, was pretty much the best thing she could possibly anticipate. Better than the best thing.

But the day after the last day with Baxter? She couldn't imagine that. And she definitely wasn't anticipating it.

She dragged herself upright and slid her feet to the floor beside the bed. "What in the hell have you gotten yourself into, Lan?" she muttered.

* * *

Forty-five minutes later, she was freshly showered, dressed, and disconnecting from a quick call to Charlotte. They'd shared only enough to let the other know the night before had pretty much been life-changing for each of them. Charlotte wasn't so much surprised by Lani's part, as she was by the fact that Lani had taken the leap. Lani, on the other hand, had no idea what to make of the Charlotte-Carlo pairing. As far as she knew Carlo had never been on Charlotte's radar. Their paths had crossed numerous times at Gateau, because Charlotte had been a frequent visitor, but otherwise . . . Lani shook her head. It was too much to think about. For all she knew, it was just Charlotte waxing rhapsodic due to the end of the long drought. Although that wasn't the usual morning-after reaction. Usually, those were more along the lines of "what was I thinking? Was I really that desperate?"

Carlo, in addition to making godlike nectar coffee, was a really good guy. But not Charlotte's typical choice. She specialized in the emotionally unavailable and relationship challenged. Lani had her own theories about why that was, which she'd shared with Charlotte in many a morning-after bake session. But this had been different. Or maybe the rose-colored glasses were Lani's.

Too much to think about, not enough time to run home and bake it off. Lani jogged down the back outside stairs, thankful the rain had stopped, wondering if anyone had seen Baxter leave earlier, wondering what, if anything, she was going to face. She'd been one hundred percent honest when she'd told Baxter she didn't care what people said. She didn't. In the end, it didn't matter to her, nor would it affect her choices.

But that truth was about the big picture. Living it from minute to minute, she realized, was going to be entirely different.

Rather than duck into the shop to see where the crew was in terms of pre-show prep, she opted to head straight to wardrobe and makeup. She knew by heart the recipes being featured in the show they were taping, and she could smell delicious scents wafting through the warm morning air, coming from the direction of the prep kitchen trailer. Maybe that would be her first stop instead. If she couldn't bake her way into therapy, maybe she could eat her way there.

She climbed the stairs, pausing long enough to take a short, steadying breath and make sure her expression was sunny and normal, as if her entire life hadn't changed last night. "Here goes nothing," she murmured, and opened the trailer door, coming to a dead stop when she saw who was in the prep kitchen. "Charlotte?"

Charlotte looked up, ice cream scoop in hand, from where she'd been filling paper liners with cupcake batter. She smiled. "Hello, Lan."

"Weren't we just on the phone?"

Charlotte nodded.

"You said you were baking."

Charlotte waved the empty ice cream scoop. "I was. Am. By the way, these strudel cakes are going to be incredible. Where did you get the idea to create miniature apple strudel in a cup?"

"Thanks. I adapted one of my great-grandmother's recipes. You didn't mention you were here, on set. Baking. How—?"

Charlotte shifted to the side and Lani saw that Carlo was standing behind her. He lifted his hand in a half wave, and smiled.

"Hey, Carlo." Lani's gaze shifted between the two of them. "So—"

"You're short one prep chef this morning," Charlotte explained. "He had to fly home—family emergency—so when Carlo got the call about it, I offered to come in and help."

"That's great," Lani said, and meant it, now that she was past the initial surprise. "Thanks."

"My pleasure." Charlotte kept glancing at Carlo, whose grin was almost as sappy and goofy as hers.

Lani thought she'd seen every expression Charlotte was capable of making, but this was new. She looked . . . happy. And not in that end-of-drought-yea-me giddy kind of way, but truly happy. For that matter, Lani noted, so did Carlo, who, other than pausing to wave hello to her, hadn't taken his eyes off Charlotte. The way they were looking at each other was a lot like the way Lani had looked at—she broke that thought off with a silent gasp, stopping just short of lifting her hand to feel her own face.

But she'd seen her own face in the bathroom mirror, just minutes ago. She had, indeed, looked . . . exactly like Charlotte. There was pretty much a hundred percent chance she and Baxter were going to be looking at each other in the same way Charlotte and Carlo were looking at each other.

Only she and Baxter were going to be on camera.

Being taped.

For all posterity.

"Dammit," she whispered.

"Lan?"

"I—uh, just remembered, I forgot something. Just keep on . . . doing what you're doing. And thank you," she said, knowing she sounded like a stuttering fool.

She hadn't thought things through. She'd been in a post-drought haze. "I mean it."

She ducked back through the door and closed it behind her before she heard Charlotte's reply. They'd catch up later. Apparently there was a great deal of that left to do. She still couldn't get over that look. "Could it happen like that? Just like that?"

"Could what happen like that, luv?"

She looked up to see Baxter crossing the crowded lot toward the makeup trailer. He changed directions.

"Oh, um, nothing. I just—Charlotte is helping out." She made a vague motion over her shoulder to the trailer behind her. "Carlo asked her. You're short a—"

"Prep chef, I know. I just got off the phone with Rosemary. Johnny's father has been battling Hodgkins a long time," he said, referring to one of the crew chefs Lani had met and gotten to know over the past few days, "but he's taken a turn for the worse, so we sent him home."

"I'm really sorry to hear that."

"So it's good that Charlotte could help; we were worrying we'd get backed up." He glanced at the trailer behind Lani, then back at Lani. "I guess things went well between Carlo and Charlotte, then, yes?"

Lani nodded. "Very well, it appears."

Baxter closed the remaining distance and looked into her face. "Is that not a good thing?"

"What? No. I mean, yes, it's a good thing." Lani finally snapped out of the distracted mental loop she'd been in since she'd realized—"We're going to be on tape today."

"We are." Now he frowned. "Is that a problem?" He stepped up on the bottom riser. "Did something happen after I left?" He reached up and touched her cheek in a light caress. "Did you have a change of heart?"

No, Lani thought, *I just realized that my heart is going to be taped for all posterity.* She didn't care that the rest of the world was going to see her sappy, happy, giddy-in-love expression. She cared that she was going to see it. Forever.

She was always going to have a handy reminder of exactly how she felt. Today. She knew if she ever saw so much as one of their episodes, she wouldn't even need a copy of it. Watching herself with Baxter—if they looked at each other the way Charlotte and Carlo had been just now—would be forever emblazoned in her memory.

It was one thing to be living it, feeling it, in the moment of it, when she could only see one side of it. His face, his smile, his looks of desire . . . for her. She didn't see her own reactions, her own giddy smiles, and really hear her silly, infatuated laughter. She wouldn't have that mental imagery to call up, on demand.

Except, now she would. It was like knowing, after the divorce, there was wedding footage of a happier time, sitting innocently on the shelf.

"Leilani?"

She looked at him, and though he'd asked the question calmly enough, gently enough, there was genuine concern, and not a little trepidation in his clear brown gaze. "No, of course I haven't," she said, feeling sorry for making him worry, even for a second. "I'm fine."

"Are you sure? You rather look like you've seen a ghost."

I have, she thought. *The ghost of us.*

"Why, there you are!"

They turned to find Alva bustling across the lot, decked out in a trim periwinkle jacket and skirt, with matching hat and handbag, no less.

"Miss Alva," Baxter said, smiling easily, but he'd rested his hand on Lani's arm, was squeezing it as if to reassure her.

If Lani's heart wasn't already completely compromised by him, it would have been in that moment.

"I'm headed over the causeway to market," Alva was saying.

"Don't go to any trouble for me, Miss Alva."

"I know you must eat all fancy every night, living in the city, so—"

"I've been thoroughly enjoying my meals here, trust me." He patted his stomach, which Lani could vouch wasn't sporting an extra ounce anywhere.

So unfair.

"Probably too much," he added with a grin.

"Well, I just wanted to show you that we know fancy cooking in the South, too. I think you'll be pleasantly surprised by the menu this evening." She looked past Baxter and seemed to notice Lani for the first time. "Where are my manners? Why hello, Miss Lani May, I didn't see you there."

Lani smiled, nodded, and held her breath, hoping there wasn't an invitation forthcoming to dinner. She already knew that come the end of the day, she was going to hole up somewhere, with only her own thoughts for company. She was already almost desperately looking forward to. It appeared more than likely Charlotte would head off somewhere with Carlo, or would once Lani gave her blessing. With Baxter dining at Alva's, Lani was guaranteed at least a little time completely to herself.

She didn't want to have to come up with a polite

way to decline, but was saved the trouble when Alva turned her attention immediately and fully right back to Baxter.

Lani's smile relaxed and became more natural as she realized Alva wasn't dressed up for market. She'd dressed in hopes of flagging down her Friday night date. She looked quite snazzy, actually. If Lani wasn't mistaken, she'd even penciled her brows and opted for a bit deeper shade of her trademark rose lipstick.

"I hope you don't mind if I excuse myself," Lani said a moment later, as the two continued to chat. "I am supposed to be in hair and makeup." She started to make her way past Baxter, but he blocked her path, though he kept his gaze on Alva. "I'm sorry, Miss Alva, but I need to talk with Lani, before she heads in."

"That's okay," Lani said, "I'm—"

Baxter looked up at Lani. "No, I do need to talk to you. Something else." He turned back to Alva, who Lani noted was watching the byplay between them quite closely. Baxter reached out his hand and took Alva's in a brief squeeze, which made her already expertly powdered cheeks pink up a bit more. "I'll see you this evening."

"Seven sharp," Alva said. "Unlike you city folk, I put stock in punctuality. My menu is precisely timed."

"I won't be a second late," he assured her, grinning broadly.

Alva beamed, full twinkle, then patted her hair, tucked her purse under her arm, and waved them good-bye.

They waved back; then Baxter turned and surprised a squeal out of Lani by framing her hips with his hands and swinging her off the steps.

"What are you doing—?"

"I have a proposition."

She stopped, closed her mouth, and lifted her brows. "Really?"

He nodded, and there was a mischievous twinkle in his eyes that rivaled Alva's.

"Did you rethink my idea about playing hooky?"

"First, are you sure everything is okay?"

"What? Oh, that. Yes. Seeing Charlotte in the prep kitchen just kind of . . . threw me." That was true enough.

Baxter tilted his head slightly. "Are you sure that's all? You seem quite distracted. Did something else happen between Charlotte and Carlo? Should I talk to him, do you need me to—"

"No, no, not at all. They look like they're practically setting up house together already. They're fine. I'm happy about that, trust me. Carlo's a good guy." She waved her hand, wishing she could wave away all the rest of her cluttered thoughts and emotions so easily. In the meantime, until she could unclutter them, life was going to keep happening. Most especially the part of her life with Baxter in it. One thing she did know was that she didn't want to miss any of it.

He held her gaze for another gauging moment.

"What proposition? I believe I tried doing that upstairs, and basically had to strong arm you into it." She smiled. "Or was that a strong leg?"

He smiled back and relaxed again. "That might be a subject worthy of discussion. One we could have Sunday. On our flight to LAX."

"Sunday isn't going to be any diff—what did you just say? L.A.? California?"

"Last I checked, that's where they're keeping it, yes."

His smile widened and he took her hands in his.

"Remember last weekend, I had to go to New York, to do promo for the new season? Well, we already had a few more things slated for this weekend—"

"I didn't know that. You're going to leave for the weekend?"

He nodded. "I didn't purposely not tell you. I think we've been focused on getting the taping up and running, and I just didn't think to mention it. And, before we—" His gaze shifted to the stairs leading up to the second floor of her shop, then back to her. "I guess I didn't think it was going to be of any real importance to you, beyond the fact that you'd get a break in the production schedule."

"But—" they said together, and laughed.

"But," he repeated, "now being gone for two whole days isn't as acceptable, at least for me, as it was before. I wanted to talk with Rosemary before saying any—"

Her brows climbed. "You told Rosemary? About . . . ?"

He chuckled. "I don't think there was much need to spell it out."

"What do you mean? How could she—?"

"Well, I didn't mention it last night because I was . . . otherwise distracted." He flashed a quick grin, which sparked all kinds of thoughts about those exact distractions, which, in turn, did all kinds of unwise things to her libido. He must have seen something in her eyes, because his grip on her hands tightened and his eyes darkened slightly as he started to pull her closer.

She pulled back. "We're going to be on camera shortly you know."

"Yes." He let her ease back, but nothing changed about the look in his eyes, and Lani thought it was going to be a very long day on the set. A long day of trying very, very hard not to look like she wanted to clear the table and have him on it instead of whatever they were baking.

"And, well," he continued, "that's the thing, really. You see, we were on camera yesterday, too."

"I know, but now—"

"Lei, we were already a bit . . . obvious about our feelings, even before last night."

"What are you talking about?"

"The tape from the latter part of the day, the part that was shot after our little . . . talk in the kitchen, at lunch. Let me just say Rosemary was fanning herself while she was watching."

Lani's mouth dropped open.

"I watched it, too. And . . . well, I was thankful I was still wearing my apron. And standing a foot behind her at the time."

"Baxter!"

He grinned, clearly not at all disturbed. "It wasn't just the ovens generating some heat, that's all I'm trying to convey."

"I got that." She felt her cheeks flaming up. "And I'm not sure how I feel about it."

"Well, if you're worried about how Rosemary feels about it, don't be. She's thrilled."

"First smiling, now thrilled. Are you trying to scare me?"

His grin deepened. "No, I'm trying to reassure you."

"It's not working," she said, but she was fighting a smile, too. Apparently she could stop worrying about how she was going to look on camera, as it was already too late for that. "So, you asked her about taking me to L.A. with you?"

"I don't have to ask permission for that, but I wasn't sure if they wanted you here for any of the exterior and island shots they'll be taping while I'm gone. They want to get the local color to set the scene for the show location. I'll have to do some spots, too, but I can do that when I get back."

"Oh, right." Bernard had mentioned something about that when he'd tried to go over the entire schedule with her, but she hadn't been willing to think about more than one day—one hour even—at a time, so most had gone in one ear and out the other. "And?"

"And that worked out fine. The part they need you for they can do when they shoot my intros."

"How long is the trip?"

"We're flying out early Sunday, back on the red-eye Monday night. We'll get back here before dawn Tuesday. We aren't scheduled to tape until one in the afternoon that day. Will you come with me? The schedule will be a bit frantic, but we'll have some time on the flight out and back. I know Charlotte is here, but—"

"If there's no prep cooking to be done while you're gone, and Carlo has the same time off, I'm thinking Charlotte will find something to occupy her time."

Baxter grinned. "Good. Then you'll come."

"Are you sure? I mean, my running around with you will definitely get noticed, won't it? I know I said I didn't mind that, and I don't, but if we spark media attention right off, the paparazzi could show up here before we're done taping."

He did pause then. "No, I don't want to do that to everyone here."

"Well, to be honest, Alva would be in heaven, and who knows, maybe everyone else would enjoy their fifteen minutes, too. I do know my father wouldn't be too thrilled, but—"

"We'll be discreet while traveling to and fro. We don't need to be a public pair." He smiled. "We were purely professionals for years. We know how to do that." He tugged her closer. "I just want you with me. I want your company, Lei, your smile, your laugh."

"I'd like that." She didn't want to lose two full days of their time together, either.

"Brilliant," he said, his gaze on hers. "Oh, there's one more thing. Tomorrow night we're having a viewing party at your little pub."

"Stewies?"

"I believe that's the name I heard, yes. We're screening the premiere of the new season. It actually airs Sunday night on the network, but I'll be in L.A., so we're having the party tomorrow night instead. The whole crew will be there, and whoever else is in the tavern at the time."

"Word gets out and everyone on Sugarberry will try to squeeze in."

"Possibly, but I hope you'll come. I know we'll be putting in a long day first, and you'll want some time with Charlotte before we take off, so—"

"I'll make it all work. I'd like to be there." She smiled up at him. "And, thank you."

"You're welcome. For?"

"Understanding. Letting me work my way through this in whatever way feels right at the moment. I know I'm sending out confusing signals, but that's because it's confusing to me. This part of it, the public part. I'll get the hang of it. But, just know, it's not about you."

"I was hoping as much."

The door to the makeup trailer opened and Andrea, the dresser, stuck her head out. "Come on, you two. Rosemary's yellin' in my ear. We need to get you into makeup and aprons."

"Be right there," Baxter called out; then to Lani, he said, "Whatever you need today, while we're filming, just let me know, yes? We're still just us, and we're good in the kitchen together. We always have been. Let go of the rest. I've got this. And I've got you. Do you trust me?"

She nodded. "I absolutely do." She could hear the hint of emotion roughening her voice. "Come on, before I get mushy."

He wiggled his eyebrows. "Do you promise to get mushy later?"

She elbowed him, and he laughed as he guided her to the makeup and wardrobe trailer with a hand on the small of her back.

Just think about today, she told herself. *Just today.*

Maybe if she repeated that often enough, she'd be able to look at him and not think about what it was going to be like when she didn't have him. When he left for good. And she didn't leave with him.

Chapter 17

"I think that's good," Charlotte said as she rolled out the dough on Lani's kitchen counter. "Cross-country trip. Long flight. Very good."

"But . . . traveling together. All the way to the West Coast and back. I don't know, Char. Maybe I should have said no. If I stayed here by myself for two days, it would give me a chance to put all this in better perspective. Find some balance to the wild feelings I'm having."

Charlotte smiled, looking off into space for a moment. "Wild feelings aren't so bad."

Lani worked the pastry blender a little harder. "For you, sure. You and Carlo will both be heading back to live in the same city."

"After he goes on the road with Baxter for two months." Charlotte sighed. "Two months."

Lani glanced at her friend. "You know, my panic attacks aside, I meant what I said before. I'm so happy for you. And Carlo. I don't know how it happened, but I'm glad it did."

"Me, too." Charlotte smiled sweetly sincere. "I wasn't even looking, or thinking about that. Well, I was thinking about sex. I always think about sex. But I came here for you, not sex."

"For which I am grateful. Both parts."

"I stopped by Laura Jo's after I saw you on set yesterday, to pick up something to take back to your place for dinner—you really have nothing here to eat that isn't made of flour, butter, and sugar—and Carlo was doing the same. We started talking and"—she shrugged, and went back to rolling dough—"things just happened. I have no idea why I didn't look at him that way before. It's the only way I can look at him now."

"You didn't look at guys like Carlo at all before, that's why. You looked through them to the guy standing behind, the one who wouldn't stick around."

"I know you're right. Maybe it took coming here, being out of that environment, seeing things out of context, for me to even think about it. If our paths had crossed at some grocer in the city, I know we wouldn't have struck up a conversation. I don't operate that way when I'm running errands or working. I just . . . I wouldn't have stopped and noticed him. Much less talked to him."

"What matters is that you have now."

"Yes." Charlotte had that private smile, the one Lani recognized, because she'd had one of her own of late.

A few minutes later, after they'd retreated to their own thoughts for a bit, Charlotte said, "Do you really think, when you're done taping, that you're going to be able to just let him walk away?"

Lani paused in the middle of blending the brown

sugar and butter. "I don't have a choice." She wanted to rub at the tight pinch in her chest, but she went back to grinding instead.

"You always have a choice."

"We've already been over this," Lani said, a bit wearily. She and Charlotte had talked it through already once this evening, and Lani had already thought it through a thousand times before that.

"I know. I just . . . think there should be a way."

"A long distance relationship isn't going to work," Lani said. "For either one of us. We're too much to settle for that."

"So, you'll take your too much-ness and settle for nothing?" Charlotte rolled with a bit more vigor than was absolutely required. "That makes no sense to me. None at all." Her accent grew sharper the more she rolled the dough.

"I'm just trying to be realistic. It's a fairy tale right now, while we're here. But my moving back to New York isn't going to work for me. Is he just going to give up his entire career and move to Georgia? And do . . . what? I mean, Charlotte, trust me, I want there to be a solution. I'm looking forward to every day I'll have with him and simultaneously dreading every minute that goes by, knowing it puts me one minute closer to the end. That's what I meant about letting him go to L.A. by himself. I don't want to lose that time, but maybe it would be smarter to pace ourselves a little. Maybe both of us will cool off a bit, regain a little perspective."

Charlotte's snort told her all she needed to know about her opinion on the matter. "I just say that what you do isn't all of who you are. A large part, yes, but not all. There is more to life, more to happiness. I know, coming from me, that sounds ludicrous. But I'm thinking differently today. Very differently."

"I know," Lani said quietly.

"I just think that when you find something special like this, you make compromises, you find a way. Maybe you'll find that you won't mind living in the city again, if it means having Baxter in your life."

"Trying to start up my own place there? Char, I'd have to look out in the boroughs for a place. I don't have the start-up capital for a place in the city. Not to mention what I have tied up here. I just opened, for God's sake. Even if I could open up a place right smack in the middle of town, the prospect of doing that there doesn't excite me, not even a little bit."

Charlotte looked up. "What about going back to Gateau? You don't want to run a shop in the city, fine. I understand that. It wouldn't be anything like what you're doing here. So, maybe you do something different altogether. Maybe not Gateau, either. Be a private chef. Cater."

"I don't think it would work," Lani said, giving voice to the same conclusion she'd already come to privately. "Not in the long run. Being a pastry chef might not be all I am, but it's a big part of it. And, now, so is having my own place. My own small, off the beaten path place. I don't know if I can convert back to city pace. And city clients."

"Of course you could," Charlotte said. "But you don't want to. You want what you already have. I'm just asking, do you want that more than you want Baxter?"

Lani was saved from answering that question by a short knock on her front door. It was early enough that it could be anybody. Except that Baxter was din-

ing with Alva, and Charlotte had opted to therapy
bake with her, then meet up with Carlo when Lani
went to meet Baxter. And Dre actually had a date herself that night—with a guy who was just a friend, she'd
made sure to stipulate. They were attending a signing
by a comic book artist in Savannah. "I don't know who
that is," Lani murmured as she rinsed her hands and
wiped them on her apron. "Coming," she called out,
as the rapping repeated.

She opened the door. "Dad? Is everything okay?"

"Of course. Can't I drop by and see my baby girl?"

"Of course you can, it's just . . . you never come
here."

"Because your shop is close to the station house
and you're always there."

"Right." She stepped hastily back. "Come in. Charlotte and I are baking tarts for the viewing party tomorrow night."

"Good, fine."

Lani smiled to herself as she stepped back to let
him into the house. "You can be our taste tester."

"Don't think I'll be here that long," he said. "Just
stopped by to check in. Make sure things are going
okay."

"That's . . . good." Lani frowned briefly. Something
was up, she just wasn't sure what. Yet. "I'm fine. Filming today went a lot better than yesterday. I guess you
heard about the viewing party tomorrow."

"I've heard. Also heard you were going to Los An-
geles. With Chef Dunne."

Ah. So that's what this is about. "I'm thinking about it.
Sounded like fun."

Her dad shifted his weight on his feet, and didn't
meet her gaze directly, but was clearly determined

despite being obviously uncomfortable. "So, about Dunne . . ."

He let that trail off, and Lani knew exactly what he was hoping for. That she'd spell out exactly what was going on between them, so he wouldn't have to come out and ask. "Dad, if you're asking if we've started to see each other, outside of working on the show, then yes. We have."

He did meet her gaze then. "And you're going off to L.A. with him."

"For two days, yes. Probably. Dad, I am a grown woman. You do know that I—"

"Of course I do," he said gruffly. "But I also know . . ." He trailed off, then sighed deeply, and seemed to re-group. He held her gaze directly. "I know how you felt about him, LeiLei. And I just . . . I don't want you hurt. Does he know? He's not just thinking you're . . . available?"

Lani didn't know whether to laugh, or cry. Instead, she impulsively hugged him. After a second of sur-prise, he hugged her back. Tightly. She didn't realize how much she'd needed that, until right at that mo-ment. She squeezed back, then let him go. "You don't have anything to worry about, Dad. He cares about me as much as I care about him." She blinked away the threat of tears. "He's taking very good care of me. You'd approve. Okay?"

"Okay." He looked down at the floor again. "So . . . does this mean that when this hoopla is over, you'll be going back to New York?"

"Oh." Lani realized he'd been worried about a lot more than just who his daughter might be sleeping with. "Dad, I—no. I don't think so, no."

He looked at her again. "You don't think so."

She sighed, not sure if he was happy about the prospect of her staying, or dismayed that she wasn't going to go back to the career she'd had in the city. "No, Dad," she said quietly. "I don't." That was all she was willing to say. All he probably wanted to hear. Whether he liked it or was disappointed wasn't going to change her answer, so there was no point in prodding.

"Okay then," he said, after an awkward moment or two of silence. "I'll, uh, let you get back to your baking then. I'll see you at the shindig tomorrow."

"Oh, good, you'll be there." She was grateful for the change of subject.

"We'll want increased presence, in case things get out of hand. Not usual to have all this attention and activity. People do stupid things."

"True." She tipped up on her toes and bussed him on the cheek. "Thanks, Dad."

His cheeks turned a bit ruddy. "I don't know for what. You can take care of yourself."

Lani smiled, and followed him to the front door. "I can, but I like knowing you're looking out for me, all the same."

He nodded, and then he was gone.

Lani closed the door, and pressed her forehead against it.

"He loves you," Charlotte said.

Lani straightened and turned to find Charlotte standing in the hall that led to the kitchen. "I know. I just . . . hate thinking he's disappointed I'm not having a big career in the city, and I hate thinking he's worried I'm going to get my heart broken. It's lose-lose at the moment."

"He's a grown man; he can handle himself," Charlotte said, echoing what Lani had just told her father.

"I know. But I feel like he's been through enough. He shouldn't have to worry about me."

"He's your father. That's his job. Come on, we need to get the tart crusts crimped."

Lani followed her into the kitchen, thankful for the task at hand. "You know, a week ago, everything was fine and dandy in my world. How did that all change so fast?"

The changes seemed to come faster from that point onward. Friday night with Baxter was every bit as wonderful as the previous night. Charlotte had gone off to stay with Carlo, with clear instructions to Lani not to wait up for her. But Lani had opted to meet Baxter over the shop after his dinner with Alva, which he'd recounted in delightful and colorful detail as they'd sipped wine . . . and each other. She wasn't ready to have him in her home, in her bed. She wasn't sure she'd ever be ready for that. Memories were one thing, and taped cooking shows, yet another. But she wasn't sure she wanted to compound all of that by creating memories in the place where she lived. It was enough that they were spending twelve hours a day in her shop kitchen.

To that end, Saturday's taping had gone quickly and, even by Lani's standards, pretty damn well. Rather than an awkward obstacle, it seemed her relationship with Baxter had relaxed her in front of the cameras. They laughed easily, the banter between them came quite naturally, and she didn't feel so self-conscious.

She'd decided she simply wasn't going to think about what he'd said, about their chemistry or the sexual tension, or whatever it was he claimed they had together on tape. Rosemary was more chipper than Lani thought was humanly possible, and that outweighed everything else. Including the notion that her love affair was being permanently recorded. She'd decided to give herself permission not to think about that either, and had made excuses both times she'd been invited into the production trailer to look at footage.

Baxter had immediately keyed in to her discomfort, but hadn't pressed her to talk about it, which she appreciated. She didn't want him to take her lack of attendance as a personal insult, but he hadn't seemed to. In fact, he'd run interference with Rosemary and gotten her out of the other requests to view tape.

They'd taken their relationship fully public at the viewing party. As Lani had predicted, Stewies had been packed past capacity almost from the start, which had made her father and his deputies a bit irritated as they'd had to turn folks away. In the end, the party had just extended outside, into the street. Baxter had gone out and shaken hands and talked to everyone, then Bernard had saved the day by hooking up a big monitor screen outside Stewies, so the outdoor partiers could watch the show, too. They'd already closed off the part of the square in front of the restaurant to traffic, so it turned into a block party.

The crowd had been boisterous, but all in good spirits, and when the credits had rolled at the end, they'd all clapped. When Baxter had pulled Lani into his arms and kissed her soundly, the applause had turned to cheers.

And she hadn't minded at all. In fact, she'd loved every minute of it.

If only everything could have stayed just like that.

* * *

Two days later they were in Baxter's rental car, bleary eyed and sleep deprived from the long flight from the West Coast. "I can't believe we aren't home yet," Lani murmured, her head resting on Baxter's shoulder as he drove, her eyes blessedly closed.

"Right," Baxter agreed, sounding just as raspy and fatigued as she did.

He'd given a string of radio show interviews, taped segments for two local talk shows, then, to her surprise, had done a taped bit that was going to air on the *Late, Late Show with Jimmy Kimmel*. She'd been well aware of his celebrity status, but hadn't experienced it firsthand, not the way she had the past two days. Viewing-party kiss notwithstanding, they'd stuck to their plan to appear in public as professionals, but rather than leaving her behind at the hotel, Baxter had taken her with him everywhere, and introduced her as, well, exactly who she was. The chef who used to run his place in New York, and whose new little cupcake shop in Georgia was going to be featured in the premiere of the next season of *Hot Cakes*.

It had been great promotion for her, and had explained, for the most part, why she was traveling with him, though she wasn't sure they'd really fooled anybody. She supposed it remained to be seen if anyone popped up once they were back on Sugarberry, but, so far, there didn't seem to be any press trailing them back home.

Home.

It was funny, Lani mused, as the lulling motion of the taxi and Baxter's big, warm body threatened to pull her into a light doze, but in a short time, Sugarberry really, truly had become home. Not her parents' home, or her ancestral home, but *her* home. Where her shop was, her little cottage, and the people who

would sincerely welcome her back . . . and whom she'd
sincerely missed while she was gone.

She'd felt that way about her home in D.C., where
she'd grown up. But, she realized, she'd never felt
that way about her dinky little place in New York. And
she'd been so proud, when she'd finally earned
enough to be able to rent a place in the city. It hadn't
felt like home, so much as the place where she was
making her mark, building her career. It was just
where she was supposed to be, a sign of her growth
and success as a chef.

That was why, when she thought about going back,
it didn't connect with her anymore. She had nothing
left to do there, to prove there. She'd done what she'd
gone there to do. It had never been home.

The next thing she knew, Baxter was nudging her
awake. "We've arrived, luv." He shifted her upright
and kissed her on the temple while she cleared the
cobwebs and oriented herself.

"Right," she said. "Good."

Baxter smiled and took her hand and squeezed it
as he parked behind the production trailer. He slid
out, then guided her out after him. "I'll get the bags."
He paused then. "I should have asked—thought. Did
you want to be dropped at the cottage? I was just
thinking of our room over the shop and—"

She shook her head. *Our room.* She smiled. Not
home, but something that was just theirs. At the moment, she'd take that. "No, no. This is fine. I'll have
Charlotte bring my car over later. She can grab a ride
back with Carlo, though I haven't talked to her since
yesterday, so she might have plans." She shrugged it
off. "We'll work it out." She pushed her hair back and
took a breath of the sweet, humid, Georgia air. It had
been so much drier out west, she hadn't realized how

used to the warmer, moister air she'd gotten. "Did you want to go to the B&B?" she asked, as the thought belatedly occurred to her.

Baxter had moved a few things over to their upstairs room, but hadn't officially moved out of the bed and breakfast, partly for appearance's sake, as they hadn't really gone public until the night before they'd left for L.A. But mostly because he didn't want the Hugheses to suffer the loss of revenue.

"No, no. I'll be fine. I'll go back over later, after we're done taping today."

It was very early, with the sun just casting the first bit of a glow on the horizon. With production not slated to start until one in the afternoon, the lot was deserted and all the trailers were closed up and dark, as had been all of the town square when they'd driven through it.

Baxter turned back to Lani. "Shall we go upstairs, try to get at least a bit of rest?"

"If the offer comes with a steamy, hot shower, you have a deal." She wriggled a little in the light sweater she had on. "I want to wash the plane off me."

"I understand the feeling. Come on then, off you go." He let her lead the way up the stairs, while he shouldered their carry-on bags up behind her.

She unlocked the door and turned on the overhead fan and the light, then crossed the room to crack open the dormer window so the air could circulate a bit. She'd have to remember to close it again before they went down to work, so it wouldn't get too hot when the sun came up. She heard Baxter put their bags down, but before she could turn back, he'd come up behind her and slid his arms around her waist.

She sighed and leaned back against him. "I'm glad I went, but I'm glad I'm back."

He kissed the side of her neck. "Thank you for coming with me."

"Thank you for taking me. It was fun. I liked getting to see that side of you. It was pretty intense and crazy, but you were so great the whole time. So patient, and always a friendly word for everyone."

"Everyone was working just as hard as I was."

"Well, I was proud of you, and happy to be with you." She shifted enough to look up at him over her shoulder. "Do you think any reporters from the excursion will trail us back here?"

"I don't honestly know. I'm not sure we exactly fooled anyone."

"I thought the same thing."

"But it would be nice if they'd respect our privacy, at least until we're done filming."

"Yes, it would." But she knew better than to assume that. She sighed again, and leaned back against him.

He tightened his hold on her, as if feeling the same things.

"I can't believe it's already Tuesday," she said a few moments later.

"I know." His voice was a bit gruff. He turned her around in his arms, then framed her face with his wide palms, tipping it up to his as he pushed her hair back. "I don't know how we're going to do it, Lei."

She didn't have to ask what he meant. "I don't, either," she whispered, her throat suddenly tight.

He kissed her then, and though it started gentle and sweet, when she threw her arms around his neck, the exchange shifted instantly into something hungry and demanding.

He backed her toward the bed, lips locked, as they each began to peel off their clothes. But before she bumped up against the bed, he scooped her up in his arms.

"Baxter, what are you—"

"I believe the lady requested a steamy shower. You're providing the shower, so it's only fair I provide the steam."

Her laughter quickly turned to gasps of pleasure when he let her feet slide to the tiled bathroom floor, and did just that. Partly by tugging the knob for the shower and setting it to hot . . . and partly by slowly undressing her the rest of the way, as the room filled with steam. Only when she was completely naked, and he'd kissed his way back up the entire length of her torso, ending with a sweet nip to the side of her neck, did he pick her up and step them both into the walk-in shower.

"Baxter—wait, you're not all the way undressed—"

"I will be. Come here."

Water cascaded over them as he pulled her up against him, then walked her back until her skin met the tiles. She gasped. They were still cooler than her skin, despite the steam swirling around them.

His shirt was open, his belt unbuckled, and his trousers unbuttoned. His feet were bare, but that's as far as he'd gotten. He slid her up the wall. "Wrap your legs around me, Lei," he said, then took her mouth again. He was demanding, insistent, and something about him, standing in the shower, half dressed, with her naked and wrapped around him just made it all the more arousing for her. As if he was so desperate for her, so hungry for her, he couldn't wait to have her.

She dug her fingers into his shoulders and arched away from the tiled wall as he slid his mouth down the side of her neck. He pushed her higher still, and ran his tongue over one nipple, then the other. She jerked against him, grunting as pleasure shot straight down through her core, making her ache to feel him there.

She sank her fingers into his wet hair and held his mouth where she wanted it, then let go as he allowed her to slowly slide down the wall, licking his way up, under her jaw, and back to her mouth. She shoved his shirt off his shoulders as he shoved his tongue into her mouth.

She took it, suckled it, held on, then gave hers to him in return. She unlocked her legs from around his waist, and though her knees were wobbly and felt about as sturdy as pulled taffy, she shoved at the waist-band of his pants.

Kissing the side of her neck, palming her breast with one hand, he managed to help her strip off the rest of his clothes.

She started to pull him back to her, but he spun her around.

The move surprised her, but she was so deeply entrenched in her need to have him inside her, fully, hard, and fast, that the primal feel of the position only served to intensify every nerve ending, every twitch, every flicker of pleasure.

She braced her hands on the tiles as his hands spanned her hips and guided her back onto him. She groaned, a deep, guttural sound, as he slowly pushed himself into her. She shifted her hips up so she could take him in even deeper, and it was his turn to growl.

The shower was small enough that he could brace his back on the opposite wall, and slide down a bit, bending his knees so she was almost straddling him backwards, but the angle was perfect and she whimpered as he began to move inside her. Every stroke set off a whole new wave of sparks, the friction exquisite as he reached places inside her that their previous positions hadn't allowed.

She used the wall as leverage, pushing back as he thrust into her, panting as she started the climb toward what she knew was going to be the most shattering climax she'd ever experienced.

As if sensing it, maybe feeling her tighten around him, he shifted up slightly so he could slide one hand around her as he held her hip steady with the other. He slid wet, slippery fingers up to toy with her nipples, making her cry out with the sharp tug of pleasure that was wrenched from her.

Then he slid his hand slowly down, over her stomach.

"Oh, *oh,*" she gasped. "I don't know if I can—" The very idea of him rubbing his fingers over her when she was already so stimulated she could barely stay balanced upright made her start to shake.

"You can," he said. And proved himself right.

She climaxed the instant he touched her. Wracking, wrenching waves of pleasure shook her so hard, she saw all those stars he'd been talking about.

She'd barely gotten past the crest of it, was still shaking hard from the wave upon wave of sensations gripping her, when he pushed her forward and she instinctively pressed her palms hard and flat against the tile . . . and pushed right back.

He shouted as he thrust hard into her, and came, in deep, shuddering jerks, every bit as strong as the climax that had just rocked her.

They were both panting, she was almost whimpering, and then he was sliding out, turning her into his arms, moving her into the far corner, shielding her from the spray of the shower with his body as he tucked her tightly against him. They struggled to stand without shaking, to breathe, and she clung to him even as he held on to her. Neither of them spoke. He had his cheek pressed to the top of her head, she had hers pressed to his still thundering heart.

How long they stood there, she lost all track. But, at some point, he reached behind him and turned off the shower. He kissed her softly, so at odds with the ferocity of how he'd just taken her, it made her heart squeeze tightly in her chest. She'd taken him every bit as voraciously, and felt every bit as tender toward him.

He grabbed towels and dried her off, then wrapped another one around his waist after giving his hair a quick rub. Scooping her up in his arms, he carried her to bed.

They gasped at the coolness of the sheets on their still damp and heated skin, but he quickly pulled her to him and they curled into their place, their space. She remembered he kissed her temple and she kissed the spot over his heart . . . then, mercifully, sleep claimed her before her thoughts of their time being almost over did instead.

And, in her dreams, they lived happily ever after.

Chapter 18

Baxter gave up on the candles, then adjusted the plates and flatware laid out on the linen table-cloth for at least the fiftieth time since he'd placed them there. How had it gotten to be their last night?

They'd finished the final taping the night before, and had enjoyed a Laura Jo–catered wrap-party, with all the cupcakes they'd made that day as their celebration cake. He had eaten little to nothing all day, and still had no appetite. It wasn't because of the feast the night before, or the long hours he and Rosemary had spent going over all the tape, getting the rest of the location shots done, and making certain they weren't missing anything before they packed up and left Sugarberry behind.

He was due to head back to New York on an early flight in the morning for another weekend of promotional stops; then he'd meet up with the crew in Texas on Monday. They'd really tightened up and streamlined the setup and production that went with the taping through the course of their stay, so they hoped to be taping by Tuesday afternoon, Wednesday morning at the latest. The team would already have gone through the recipe selection and testing process by the time he arrived, with him teleconferencing throughout. He would spend a little time with the bakery owner, who, in the case of the Texas stop, was actually a mother-daughter team. They had some very interesting takes on infusing Tex-Mex flavors into their desserts and baked goods. That would be the theme of the Texas show. Hopefully he'd quickly establish a good rapport with them.

From there, he'd be heading north, first to Missouri, then to Minnesota, then on out west to the coast of Oregon, followed by a trek back south again, to Arizona. Their tour would end with two stops in the east. One in Maine, the other in Amish country, in Lancaster, Pennsylvania, then it was back to New York.

All of that would be happening without Leilani.

"Hey, there," she called out. He looked up to see her coming down the path between the dunes.

For their last dinner, they'd decided to eat under the stars, at the little picnic table pavilion where they'd spent that first long evening together, walking the beach, and letting down their guards.

She was smiling as she ducked into the pavilion.

"It's too windy for candles," he said inanely. He was afraid if he said even one thing he was really thinking, it would all come out in a rush of emotional need and want. He'd promised himself he wouldn't do that. Wouldn't burden her. It was enough that he knew how he felt. And he was pretty damn sure she felt the same way. It would have to be enough.

"It all looks so beautiful," she said of the nice china he'd borrowed from Alva, along with the silver.

"Thank you. I kept the plates covered. Sand. Would you like some wine?"

"I'd love some." She slid onto the bench opposite the spot where he was standing. He poured them each a glass, then took his seat.

They were smiling, ostensibly relaxed . . . but what it felt like was the first truly awkward moment they'd ever shared.

"Lei—"

"Bax—"

Both spoke at the same time, both broke off. "You, please," he said, as much to be a gentleman as to buy himself some much needed time to gather his wits.

"No, nothing, just . . . this is nice. I'm glad you thought of it."

They'd already decided they weren't going to spend that night together. He had to leave at four in the morning and drive all the way to Atlanta to catch his flight out. They knew they wouldn't get any rest and it all seemed too wrenching a thing to do, parting in the wee hours after yet another sleepless night.

The previous night had been like that. They'd spent it together, but any imagined long talks into the wee hours, summing up their thoughts and feelings, and finding a way to part that seemed more kind and less brutal, hadn't been realized. They'd made frenzied love to one another, then clung together in silence, then done it all over again, and repeated the cycle until they were finally forced to leave the room to go down to work.

Neither of them had spoken of it, but when he'd suggested a last dinner on the beach, and said he thought it might be best for him to retire to the Hughes's B&B later so he could pack . . . she'd looked relieved.

And though that had hurt, he understood. He'd felt almost hollow, and it had taken every last scrap of his considerable will to remain focused on the requirements of work. It was all going to happen whether he thought about it or not, so he chose not to waste precious moments on the inevitable.

"What's on the menu?" she asked brightly. Maybe overly bright.

"Oh, right, sorry." He lifted off the cloches. "I thought we'd stick with traditional foods."

"Mmm, I know that scent. That's Laura Jo's fried chicken."

"It is. And Alva's potato salad. One of my chefs contributed the rolls. I tossed the salad."

"And two cheesecake cupcakes," she said, as he uncovered the small basket to the side. "Perfect."

"I also have lemonade or tea."

"The wine is fine." She made a big business of picking up her chicken leg, fiddling with the skin. "It all looks so good. I don't know where to begin."

"Neither do I," he said, but he wasn't looking at his plate of food.

She felt his gaze, and put her chicken down, meeting his gaze with her own. "I know. Me, either."

"Are you starving?" he asked.

She shook her head. "It all really looks wonderful, and smells amazing. And I don't know that I could eat a single bite."

He nodded, then covered the food up once more. He stood and held out his hand. "Walk the beach with me?" The sun was just starting its descent to the west, so the distant horizon over the water to the east was still golden from the sun.

"Sure."

They crossed the dunes and climbed past the high tide flotsam and jetsam, then kicked off their shoes and rolled up their pant legs. He took her hand, and they started down the beach.

"How do we do this?" she said.

He knew she wasn't talking about their walk. "I don't know. I guess time will simply do it for us."

"I'm not ready for it to be over," she admitted.

"I don't know that I'd ever choose for it to be." He stopped and turned, pulling her around in front of him, and taking her other hand in his as well. "Does it have to be, Lei?"

"Baxter—"

"I'm not asking you to come to New York with me, but . . . does it have to come to a complete and utter end? Why not at least allow ourselves the chance to see what might happen if we keep communicating?"

"Because we can communicate all we want, but all that's going to do is make us yearn for something we can't have and delay the inevitable. I don't want us to get irritated and frustrated by the limitations we'd surely face trying to continue anything long distance. I don't want this to end with us upset or angry with each other. We're good now. And this . . . this has been the best ten days I've ever experienced." She tried a brief smile. "Taping the show notwithstanding."

He tried a brief smile, too, only it was close to impossible to sustain. The moment was too bittersweet, and his trademark charm and good humor seemed to have abandoned him. Much as she was about to do. Only he was guilty of the same. "I've grown used to talking to you, sharing the day, laughing over the mistakes made, and all the brilliant moments."

"We've been spending the days together working," she reminded him. "So there's been a lot to talk about."

"I don't know that that will change, Lei. When I'm on the road, there will be stories, moments good and bad, highs and lows. I know I'll want to share them, make you laugh as I describe them. Make you still be part of them, part of my life. Part of me. I don't think that will change when the tour is over, either. I'll want to know what's going on here." A smile did come. "Find out what kind of uproar Alva's latest column has created."

Her inaugural column had indeed featured the two of them, and Alva crowing about how she'd been the first to know, and the first to entertain their celebrity chef in her home. She'd also given the lowdown on the poker tournament, which had stirred up a bigger hornet's nest, resulting in yet another night in the local lockup for both Dee Dee and Laura Jo. No sangria or volcano cakes had been involved that time, to his knowledge, but some bloke named Felipe had factored in somehow.

If that weren't enough, two photographers and a tabloid reporter had shown up the day after they'd returned from L.A., wanting to dig dirt on Baxter and his former employee. The town had risen up and barricaded the two of them behind the joined forces of their collective silence on the topic, and Sheriff Trusdale had all but run the three guys off the island. But not before Alva had gotten her scoop, of course.

Lani shook her head, smiling briefly. "It's probably best you don't know."

"You may have a point. But enquiring minds will still want to know. Or this enquiring mind will."

She looked up at him, the wind whipping strands of her hair about her face. She framed the side of her forehead with one hand to block the slanting rays of the setting sun and keep the hair from her eyes. "I'm going to miss our talks, too. Although I might wish to be spared Rosemary's latest tirade, I will miss the rest of the crew. I've gotten to know them all, and heard about their families back home and . . . well, it will be weird not having them around. My shop is going to feel so quiet when all the equipment is gone and it's just me and my cupcakes."

"I'd have thought you'd be relieved to get back to that very peace and quiet."

"I am. I will miss everyone, but I do miss having my haven to go to, my oasis. Do you feel that way about your kitchen set? After all, you're the only one who cooks there. Or Gateau's kitchens?"

He nodded. "Maybe not in the way you feel about your shop, but yes, I miss creating for myself, and not the camera."

"Do you ever cook or bake in your own kitchen? In your brownstone?"

He shook his head. "No. If I was going to spend time alone, it was usually at Gateau, after hours. I think that is the place that feels most like home to me."

"I feel that way about my kitchen here. Although, I have to say, having Charlotte here, and Alva, Dre . . . all of us cooking at the cottage has changed my feelings about it. It definitely feels more like a home to me now, too."

"That's good," he said. "I envy you that. Finding your place, your home."

"You don't feel that way about New York? I thought you were like one with the vibe and energy of the city."

"I was. Am. I suppose. There is an energy there I can't imagine living without, not fully. But, I have to admit, having spent time here, where things aren't so rushed, where there isn't such a sense of urgency all of the time, has actually been kind of nice. It's . . . settled me, I think. I've learned the value, anyway, of taking a true time-out, of removing myself entirely from the chaos. I'm happier. More content."

"Good." There was sincerity in her voice. "I'm glad we're both taking something from this that's bigger, maybe, than just having gotten to spend time together."

"That's just it, Lei. I can't separate the happiness, the contentedness of my time here, and my time with you. It's all intertwined."

"You have beaches in New York. You could get a place in the Hamptons."

"I don't know if it would bring the same peace, the same balance, to be there alone."

"Maybe you won't always be alone."

"Don't say that."

"Why? Maybe that's something else we'll take from this, the knowledge of how good connecting feels, to be part of something bigger than just ourselves, or our work accomplishments."

"Is that how you feel? You want to go searching for this same connection? With someone else?"

"No." She reached out and cupped his cheek with her hand, letting the wind whip her hair freely again. But she kept her gaze on his. "I couldn't hope to ever find this. I don't think anyone is that lucky, twice. I'm still feeling blessed that I found it once."

He covered her hand when she'd have taken it away. "Then don't throw it away."

Something fierce and strong and . . . possessive flashed in her eyes, and his heart immediately took wing, but then she looked down, and pulled her hand from his. "If there was a way I thought we could keep this, being together, you know I would." She looked up. "But we can't keep it like this. Because it's going to end tomorrow. Then everything changes, whether we want it to or not."

He looked away then, too, and struggled to re-group. "I'm sorry. I shouldn't badger you. I know it's not just you making this choice. I'm just stubborn, as you know, and I hate giving up."

"We're not giving up. We've taken everything we could, and we need to find a way to be happy for what we have had."

"I am, Leilani. Don't think I regret this. I don't, not a single second."

"Good. Then that's where we start." She turned, and started down the beach again.

He watched her walk a few steps, then closed his eyes, and asked himself how he was going to deal with it when every time he opened his eyes after today, he was never going to find her within his sight.

Or lying next to him, sleeping. Smiling down at him as she woke him up in the best way a woman could stir a man from sleep. Tugging him into the shower. Pouting when they had to leave to go to work. Smiling again as she tried to talk him into five more minutes in bed.

Rolling her eyes as she screwed up the twentieth take on the simplest part of the recipe. Dancing in the kitchen when she thought no one was looking. Cooking with Charlotte and laughing over things only they understood.

"I don't know how to do that," he said to himself. "I can't start, because that means letting you go."

She couldn't have heard him, she was too far down the beach. But she stopped walking then, and realized he was still standing where she'd left him.

Turning back, she waited a few seconds, then walked back toward him. She stopped in front of him, and looked up into his face, but didn't say anything.

He reached out, tucked a windblown strand of hair behind her ear. And the words were just there. "I love you, Leilani."

Her expression crumpled for the briefest of seconds, then smoothed, though her bottom lip quivered slightly. "I love you, too, Charlie Hingle Baxter Dunne."

He reached for her, but she quickly jerked back a step. "Don't," she said, and he heard the raw emotion in her voice. "And don't make me be the bad guy. It's not fair. This is unfair enough already, for us both."

"You're right. It's not fair." He knew, in that moment, exactly what it felt like to lose something so vital, so precious, that he didn't think he'd survive without it. It was heart-shattering, and blindingly, viciously cruel. He thought the pain of it might drive him straight to his knees. "So, I'll do it, then. But know this, Lei. You're in my care. You're in my heart. And no matter what the world brings us, you always will be."

Then he turned and walked away.

Chapter 19

Leilani picked up the filled pastry bag and aimed it at the first row of cupcakes. The stereo was blasting out the theme to *Mission Impossible*. She made a face as the opening riff crescendoed into the staccato beat of the refrain. It was an impossible mission, apparently, because she wasn't feeling the least bit better knowing she had two hundred cupcakes to fill or pipe frosting onto before opening that day. "No salvation cakes for you."

So what else was new?

She felt her phone vibrate in her pocket. Only one person would be calling her this early in the morning. She put down the pastry bag, clicked the MUTE button on the stereo remote, then put the phone on speaker.

"Morning, Charlotte."

"So?" was all she said. A single word, but loaded with anticipation.

Lani knew exactly what she was referring to. "I told you yesterday, it's not going to happen. He's not going to call."

"Damn him," Charlotte swore. "I know they got

back in the city from the Lancaster taping yesterday. Well, I know Baxter did. Carlo gets back tomorrow. He went to visit his mother first. I thought for certain—"

"You thought. But I knew. We don't talk, Char. We text. We e-mail. But we never talk. We're . . . pen pals. Friends."

Charlotte's response to that was language so blue even Lani was shocked.

"Did you just say—"

"Damn straight I did. It was one thing, when he was on the road, for you two to play at this silly game—"

"It's not a silly game." *Okay, so it was definitely a game,* Lani conceded, *but there was nothing silly about it.* It was all her fault. She'd said no communication, but then she'd gone and caved first. She'd made it three whole days. Then she'd texted him. Just to make sure he'd landed in Texas okay. Or that's what she told herself. And to thank him, for being strong enough for both of them to walk away, end it right, so they could be okay with it. Move on. He'd texted her back that he was fine and that it was good to hear from her.

And that's how it had started. They'd sent notes, all anecdotal, about what was going on. Never anything personal, never anything emotional. Just . . . two people, two friends . . . staying in touch. She'd e-mailed him a scanned copy of one of Alva's more . . . incendiary articles, and he'd responded with an attached file of his appearance doing the Top Ten List on Letterman. She'd sent him the front page photo of Laura Jo and Felipe's engagement announcement. And he'd texted her with photos of some of the strangest regional desserts she'd ever seen . . . along with photos of every "Biggest Ball of Yarn" and "Worlds Largest

Prairie Dog" type things he'd discovered as he criss-crossed the country in his decked out tour bus.

A friendship. A good one. She was proud of herself for how mature they were being about the whole thing—which is what she said to Charlotte. "We're being grown-ups about this. Taking the good from what we had here, the part we can keep."

"Then why is it that two mature grown-ups can't talk on the phone?"

Lani didn't answer that, because anything she said was going to be as lame out loud as it sounded in her head. They'd never come out and said phone calls were verboten. They just . . . never called.

As long as it was just words on a screen, or photos—not one of which included either of them, except for his Top Ten appearance—she could handle being friends. It beat losing him forever. Thankfully there hadn't been any tape of show footage sent to her, or she knew she'd have watched it in an ongoing loop. Every day. And night. This way, she could just smile at his texts, feel connected to him, and . . . not think about the rest.

"Except you don't sleep well, you're not eating right, you don't seem to be enjoying your life."

"I do, too, enjoy my life. I love my life. That's the one thing that hasn't changed, and thank God for that."

"In the way you cling to it like a teddy bear for security, yes, you love it. But I don't know if the love affair is so healthy anymore."

Lani fell silent, and Charlotte did, too. Finally, Lani gave voice to the thing that had been eating away at her for nine long weeks. "I miss him, Char. I miss him so much I can barely stand it. It's like I'm not breathing now. Not deeply and fully. It's like I can only take shallow breaths, so I can hold it all together, and not fall completely apart." She blew out a shaky breath. "There. I said it."

"Good. What are you going to do about it?"

Lani didn't bother pretending she hadn't been giving it plenty of thought. It was all she thought about. "I-I don't know. Exactly. I don't want to give up the shop, but I don't want to be pen pals with him. I don't think I can handle it much longer. So, I either have to cut that off . . ."

"Or?"

She took a breath, then just blurted it out. "Or . . . start the process of closing the shop and moving back to New York. I don't want to run a place there, but I am thinking maybe of catering. I know that will be a slow start, but I can't leave here immediately, so I'll have time to book in advance and hopefully hit the ground running." She held her breath, waiting for the squeals of happiness and joy that were surely to follow her capitulation. After all, that meant she was also going back to Charlotte.

Instead, her announcement was met with total, deafening silence.

"Did you hear what I said?"

"I did. And you sounded quite miserable about it. Like a woman walking to the gallows." Her accent was becoming more pronounced as the conversation continued and Lani knew she was far more upset than she was letting on.

And, the bitch of it was . . . Charlotte was right. Lani wasn't remotely enthusiastic about the idea. But it was all she had. "Well, what the hell do you want me to do then?"

"Selfishly, I was hoping to hear those exact words . . .

but with actual enthusiasm. How can I be happy about saying I told you so if I think you're miserable?"

Lani smiled at that, even though she was still upset. "Well, you're right, I'm not super excited about it, but I keep telling myself that being with Baxter will make it all doable. Who knows, I hated being on set, on camera, and he made that fun. Maybe he'll make me feel enthusiastic about catering. Or being a private chef. I don't know. I don't care what I do. Whatever ends up working. As long as we're together."

"What about Sugarberry? I don't mean the shop, I mean—"

"I know what you mean." Lani sighed and slumped a little against the worktable. "I don't know, Char. I just know I'm miserable here without him, so I at least want to—need to—try to be away from here with him. I don't know what else to do." She jumped when a knock came at the back door. "Oh God, not now."

"What?" Charlotte asked.

"Knock at the door. This early, it has to be Alva. Since she started doing her column, she got Dwight to give her her own desk at the paper. I think she's in there before sunrise every day. She even has an old-fashioned newspaper visor, only it's lavender."

"Hasn't she been baking with you a few nights a week, after hours? How does a woman her age operate on no sleep?"

"I don't know, but if she can find a way to bottle it, she'll die a very wealthy woman. And I'll be the first to buy stock. I'll call you back." She disconnected and slipped the phone into her pocket.

"It was unlocked. I hope you don't mind."

Lani spun around so fast she had to grip the worktable to keep from sliding straight to the floor. "Baxter?"

He smiled, but it didn't quite reach his eyes. "Who

else barges into your kitchen before daybreak? Bad 'abit, I know."

Her heart was beating so fast, it seemed to interfere with her ability to process what her eyes were seeing. But, even so, she'd heard the slip of the accent. "Is something wrong? Did something happen? Is someone hurt? Are you okay?"

The smile took on a semblance of his trademark grin then. "No, no, luv, no worries on that. We're all fine. Everyone's fine." He fidgeted, shifting his weight. "That's no' entirely true. I'm no' fine. No' fine atall."

"Baxter—"

"I know we agreed. No future, no way. And I appreciate, more than you know, your willingness to keep the lines of communication open. That's been the only thing that's kept me sane, I think. But it's—I don't know if I can—"

"I don't know if I can, either," she said, finishing for him. "It's been my lifeline, too. But I think . . . I think it's strangling my heart, Baxter. I don't think I can just be friends with you." Her voice cracked on the last part.

"I know," he said. "It's the same for me."

In that moment, Lani knew what her choice was. She loved Sugarberry, she loved her father, she loved her shop, and all of her customers. But she loved Baxter more. How was it she hadn't already figured out what, in that moment, seemed so very, very simple?

"Well, I've been thinking," she began, in case he was there to tell her it was over and done and no more texting, no more e-mailing. Though, he could have just stopped writing back. Couldn't he? She tried to keep her heart from beating straight out of her chest, but she couldn't keep the tremor from her voice. "In fact, I was just telling Charlotte. I—I'm thinking I want to come back to New York. Cater. Maybe private chef. I don't know. It will take time to get out from under this, see if I can break my lease, I don't know. But—"

"You don't really want to come back, do you?" he asked.

She didn't think she'd ever heard him sound so dead serious. For once, she couldn't read his every emotion on his face, either. In fact, he was more or less expressionless at the moment. "What I want . . ." She took a breath, and just put it out there. "What I want is you. And you're in New York. I'll always love Sugarberry, but my father is here, so I have an excuse to come down and visit, holidays and whatnot."

"You said you told Charlotte. Have you told him?"

"My father? No, not yet."

"Good."

Her heart fell. "Oh."

Baxter crossed the room, and she would have scrambled away from his touch if she'd anticipated the sudden move. It was hard enough just looking at him while he turned her offer down. Touching him would be nothing short of painful.

"Good, because I'm in a bit of a dilemma, and I was 'opin' you could help me out."

"What are you talking about?"

"We finished taping the next season."

"I know," she said, confused. "We've been texting about it. Nonstop."

"Right, right. Well, I've had an offer come my way, and I'm very excited about it, but it will mean expanding the time between seasons—which we've been discussing anyway. We started doing two seasons a year because it was a good way to launch, and build momentum, but the show's been established pretty well. We've discussed making the season longer by a few episodes, and only doing one stretch a year—which will give me time for this other project."

"Which is?"

"I've been asked to do a series of cookbooks. One geared to my viewers, home cooks, with recipes they can try in their own kitchens. And another geared toward teaching home cooks how to be chefs, but in layman's terms. There's also talk of doing one based on the road tour stops, but the publisher wants to see how the first two work out."

"That's—that's amazing," she said, surprised, but thrilled for him. "They're going to do great. It's a perfect fit for you."

"I thought so, too. Thing is . . . I need a kitchen."

"You have several."

"A private kitchen. One where I can test recipes and work on what I'm going to include in the books, how I'm going to convey them in writing, so anyone can do them. I have six months to get started on them, maybe complete one, before I'll have to stop and break to tape the next season."

"Six months," she repeated, as her heart tripped all over the place. "So . . . what are you saying, Baxter?"

He was standing quite close, but he put his hands, those beautiful big warm hands she'd never thought she'd feel again, on her cheeks. "I'm saying I want to use your kitchen. At the cottage, or I could install one upstairs. I don't care where, but I need space, and peace and quiet, and I need you. By my side."

"To help with the cookbooks?"

"To help me breathe," he said. "Lei, I can't catch

my breath anymore. I feel like I'm paddlin' water and about to drown anyway. I need you in my life. It was bad the first time you left New York, but now . . . I can't breathe."

"I-I just said the same thing. To Charlotte."

For the first time, his eyes lit up, and his grin appeared. "You'll let me back into your life!"

"Baxter, you never really left it."

He scooped her up and spun her around.

"But wait, wait," she said, laughing, wanting to leap right over the moon with him. "I'm—I don't understand it all. Are you just going to be here for six months? Because—"

"No. I have six months clear from the studio. Then I'll have to tape, which will take about three months."

"So, you'll go back to New York, then."

He shook his head. "We've rented this beautiful place. In Savannah. Or we will be. They're in talks with the owners right now. It's a plantation with the most amazing kitchens, and we'll film *Hot Cakes* from there."

"The whole crew is moving to Georgia?" She blinked, unable to really believe that.

"No, no. Some of them will relocate. It'll be their choice."

"Carlo?" she asked, thinking it would be cruel for her to get Baxter only for Charlotte to lose Carlo.

"That's up to him, but I don't anticipate he will, no. He will always have a place at Gateau if he wants it."

"Good, good, so"—she could hardly think straight— "so . . . when?"

"Is two weeks too soon? We have postproduction and I still have promotion to do. I'll have to do that in the future, too, by the way, so I'll be gone some of the time, especially when a new season starts, but maybe by then you can get someone to run the shop here so you can come along, and—"

She grabbed his face and kissed him. Then she jumped up and wrapped her legs around his waist and kissed him again.

He held on tight. "Is that a yes?" he said, breathless himself as he spun her around.

"Yes! Yes, yes, yes. I can't believe this is happening. I can't believe this solution just fell into place."

"I might have nudged it a bit."

She looked at him. "The cookbooks? Your idea?"

He shrugged. "I might have suggested them as an idea, to my agent, who might have shopped the idea around a bit while I was on the road."

"You're bloody brilliant." She made him laugh with her accent. "Wait, you're willing to uproot—aren't you going to miss New York? What about Gateau?"

"Gateau stays mine. It will always be mine, as long as it remains in business. But it has been running without me for some time now. I can keep track from here as easily as I can anywhere. The brownstone will go on the market. I won't miss it. And I'll be back there often enough, for meetings, for marketing, and for Gateau when needed."

"But that's not the same as living in the city, the energy, the vibe—"

"You're my energy. I've learned in the past few months that I can live without the city. As I've shared with you, the trip around this country has opened my eyes to so many things, things I've never experienced, never even knew existed. And yes," he added dryly, "some I wish I still didn't."

He let her feet slide to the floor, then pulled her into his arms. "But one thing I did see that really made an impression on me was how much every single shop owner I worked with valued their home, their family, their community, above all else. And it was because of that foundation that they thrived."

"But you've thrived, too, Baxter."

"Commercially, yes. But in here"—he pulled her hand to his chest, placed it over his heart—"I haven't. I know what you have here. I've seen it. I've lived it. Even in the brief time I was here, I was coming to care about people here. I missed them."

"Your crew is like family."

He shook his head. "I care a great deal about the people who work for me. But, other than a handful, very few stay working for me for long. Not because they don't want to, but it's a very transient business. You know that from your time in the city. Hopefully some of those who have been with me since the start of the show, and some even from before, at Gateau, who followed me to the show, will be willing to come down here. I have to think that maybe they'll find it a more rewarding place to raise their families, or start one. I don't know." He caressed her face. "All I know is that my family, my foundation, is you. And I want to build on that. I want to see what we can do together. I already know I don't do well without you. I love you, Leilani."

"I love you, too." Tears pricked at the corners of her eyes, but they were happy tears. The happiest. "I can't believe this. I get the cupcakes, and I get the guy."

Epilogue

"Franco, just—no. You can't put those in the front of my shop. Those are so completely . . . inappropriate."

"But I found the pans in your very own kitchen, *ma chérie.*"

"He did," Alva offered. "At the last bitchy bake."

"Charlotte—" Lani started.

Charlotte lifted her hands. "I do not control him. I am not his keeper."

"They were your cake pans," Lani reminded her.

"I think we ought to put them in the front case," Alva said. "Shake things up a bit. Only, you can't use that white frosting," she told Franco. "Shouldn't it be pink? You know . . . fleshy-colored?"

Lani thought she was going to swallow her tongue. "Okay, you know, I don't mind having Cupcake Club at the shop, since we've kind of outgrown the cottage kitchen, but I'm making a new rule. What is made in Cupcake Club—"

"Stays in Cupcake Club," they all recited together, but not all sounded equally enthusiastic about it.

"All" on that particular evening consisted of Charlotte, Franco, Alva, Dre, and the latest addition to their club, Riley Brown. Former food stylist for a Chicago based foodie magazine whom Lani had caught rearranging her displays a few weeks before. She wasn't exactly sure how that had led to Riley joining Cupcake Club, but she'd long since given up trying to control her life.

It had been ten months since Baxter had made her the happiest woman on earth, a favor she did her absolute best to return every single day. Carlo had opted to follow Baxter, which had led to Charlotte following Carlo. They were living together in Savannah, where Charlotte was the one who'd started a catering business, a very successful one at that. And now that it was blistering hot, Charlotte was actually a happy camper. The suffocating heat and humidity reminded her of the better parts of her childhood in New Delhi that she'd kind of forgotten—which surprised Lani, even as she was grateful for it.

Production assistant Brenton had also followed Baxter south, bringing his committed partner Franco with him. Franco, unlike Charlotte, hated the heat and humidity with every fiber of his very big and very swarthy being, and told everyone and anyone who would listen to him complain about it. But he was head over heels in love with his partner, so they made it work— and traveled back to New York whenever possible. Franco was also Charlotte's business partner.

Collectively they were turning Lani's life into a chaotic scramble all over again, but in the best of all possible ways. Her shop was flourishing. The *Hot Cakes* season featuring Cakes By The Cup had aired and she was definitely reaping the benefits. Baxter had just finished his first cookbook, after breaking to film season four. It had taken longer than he'd anticipated, but everyone was excited about the result. He was presently in New York to discuss layout and cover art and choose photos from the bazillions that had been taken during the testing phase.

Lani had recently talked with him about maybe using Riley to style the food for his next book. As she was already in Sugarberry, it seemed easier than having someone come in from Atlanta or New York every time they wanted to shoot another batch. Lani had looked up Riley's former work, and it was amazing. She just wasn't sure if Riley would do it. She wasn't sure yet what Riley's story was, but she knew it would come out eventually. Cupcake Club would worm it out of her at some point.

"What do you think, Mademoiselle Alva?" Franco's French accent was always set on THICK whenever he baked with Alva. She simply adored him and didn't quite understand about the whole fake accent thing—which made it all the more amusing.

"A bit pinker, dear." She glanced at him. "Or browner, maybe?" She frowned, then shrugged. "It's been a while."

"Some things you don't forget," Franco shot back with a wink.

Alva smiled privately; a little twinkle came out. "Pinker then," was all she said.

"What on earth are those?"

Baxter! Lani spun around, then dashed across the kitchen and jumped into his arms.

He caught her tight and kissed her soundly. "I missed you, my luv."

"You've been gone two whole days," Charlotte commented.

"You kiss Carlo like that at the end of every day, " Franco commented.

Charlotte just smiled a private smile, much like the one Alva had given.

"I think it's refreshing," Alva said. "If you're young, and in love, there's no reason to hide it. Welcome home."

"Thank you," Baxter said. "It's good to be home."

Home, Lani thought, knowing it was the full and utter truth. "I thought you weren't due back until late tonight."

"Got an early flight, thought I'd surprise you. Say, those really are—"

Lani steered him away from the worktable. "What happens in Cupcake Club—"

"Stays in Cupcake Club!" Everyone else in the room raised a spatula, pastry bag, whisk, or cupcake in solidarity.

"It's true," Lani told him. "And you really don't want to know, anyway."

"Maybe I do. But right at the moment—" He scooped her up in his arms. "Can you all make do without your fearless leader for a few hours?"

Another salute of raised pastry bags and hand mixers was his answer.

"Brilliant."

Lani started to put down her pastry bag on the nearest surface she could still reach, but Baxter stopped her. "No, bring that with you." He wiggled his eyebrows.

Her cheeks went flame red, but the rest of the room cheered.

"And what happens at the Dunne house, stays at the Dunne house," Lani warned.

"But you will tell us, dear, how that frosting turns out, won't you?" Alva asked.

"Now, now. We never pipe and tell," Baxter said. "And Franco? Definitely go darker pink."

Lani was still laughing as Baxter carried her out the back door.

Want to bring home some of the sweetness of Cakes By The Cup? Try Donna Kauffman's original recipe for *Gingerbread Cupcakes*.

2 cups all-purpose flour
1½ teaspoons baking powder
1 teaspoon baking soda
1 tablespoon ground ginger
2 teaspoons ground cinnamon
¼ teaspoon ground cloves
⅛ teaspoon nutmeg
Pinch of salt—as little as possible, up to ¼ teaspoon (to taste)
½ cup (1 stick) unsalted butter, melted
¾ cup brown sugar
2 large eggs
½ cup molasses (unsulfured)
1 cup water

1. Preheat oven to 350 degrees F. Line a muffin pan with 12 paper liners.
2. Sift together the flour, baking powder, baking soda, ginger, cinnamon, cloves, nutmeg, and salt in a separate bowl and set aside. (*Note:* I'm not as keen on salt beyond the barest flavor enhancement, so I use closer to ⅛ teaspoon, but others have liked it with a bit more. So add salt to taste, up to ¼ teaspoon.)
3. To prevent the cake from getting too heavy from overmixing (which, I have learned—possibly the hard way—activates the gluten in the flour, creating cakes that are dense and, well, let's just say not the lightest or most moist; however, as paper weights,

they're fabulous, not to mention, they smell real nice), use this trick I learned from my TV boyfriend, Bobby Flay: rather than using an electric mixer, whisk the dry ingredients (step 2) together by hand. In a separate bowl, whisk together the brown sugar and the melted butter, along with the eggs and molasses, all at the same time until just blended. Do not overwhisk. (Unless, of course, you're short a few sweet-smelling paper weights.)

4. Alternate adding water and the sifted flour and spice mix to the wet ingredients, whisking gently each time, until just blended. The batter should be smooth with a bit of a whipped texture from the eggs being whisked.

5. Divide the batter evenly into the 12 cups. Now, you know I hate doing this kind of math. So I will just tell you that I used an ice cream scoop, the kind with the squeezy handle (technical term alert!) and put a scoop in each cup. Using that method, instead of 12, my batches make about 15. Your batter mileage may vary.

6. Bake 18–20 minutes. Cake should spring back to the touch, or you can use the clean toothpick test. Or both. Just don't burn them. I started checking around 15 minutes, but mine always took closer to 20.

7. Allow to cool in the pans, on wire racks, for 10 minutes, then remove the cupcakes from the pans, and let cool the rest of the way on wire racks before frosting. If you're like me, there might be one or two fewer cupcakes to frost by the time this important step is over. Of course, if you're a purist and dedicated baker, won't you want to do a taste test before diluting the pure gingerbread flavor with creamy rich frosting? See?—that's what I thought!

Cinnamon Mascarpone Frosting

8 ounces mascarpone cheese, at room temperature
½ cup butter, at room temperature
½ teaspoon vanilla extract
1½ cups powdered sugar
¼ cup heavy cream
Cinnamon (ground fresh, if you have a grinder)

I tried many different versions of mascarpone frosting and discovered I really liked the ones that included butter, and the ones that included heavy cream, but couldn't find one that included all of it, so . . . voilà!—my own version. It might be a wee bit on the rich side. But then, isn't that frosting law?

1. Gently mix the cheese, butter, vanilla, and powdered sugar together. Make sure both cheese and butter are soft so you don't have to overblend to make it smooth. If you overblend, the mascarpone can curdle. (Again, I won't reveal exactly how it is I know this, but let's just say, I've heard rumors . . . possibly emanating from my own kitchen.)
2. Whisk the cream until it holds a peak. Don't whisk until you get stiff peaks, as it will make the frosting a bit too frothy and whipped in texture.
3. Stir the whipped cream into the cheese and sugar mixture until just blended. It should be a smooth, thick, creamy frosting. If possible, use immediately. Otherwise, refrigerate, but bring back to room temperature to use later. You may want to stir slightly to regain the creamy texture. Again, don't overstir, as the cheese can still curdle.
4. Grind or sprinkle cinnamon on top of the frosting

as desired. Keep refrigerated when not being devoured.
5. Enjoy!

Red Velvet Cupcakes

2½ cups flour
½ cup unsweetened cocoa powder
1 teaspoon baking soda
½ teaspoon salt
2 cups sugar
1 cup (2 sticks) butter, at room temperature
4 eggs, at room temperature
1 cup sour cream
½ cup buttermilk
1 bottle (1 ounce) red food coloring
2 teaspoons vanilla extract

1. Preheat oven to 350 degrees F. Line 30 muffin cups
   with paper liners. (Super cute paper liners, of course.)
2. In a separate bowl, whisk together the flour, cocoa
   powder, baking soda and salt, then set aside.
3. Use an electric mixer on medium speed to cream
   the butter with the sugar until light and fluffy. This
   takes about 5 minutes (which is like a light year in
   holding-an-electric-mixer-time, so set a timer).
4. Beat in eggs, one at a time, until assimilated. (Yes,
   I'm asking you to *Borg* your eggs.)
5. Mix in sour cream, buttermilk, food color and vanilla. (*Note:* Don't have buttermilk, or tired of getting this huge container for just a cup in a recipe?
   Just add 1 tablespoon white vinegar or lemon juice
   per cup of milk, stir, let sit for 5 minutes, then use
   as directed in recipe. Or get powdered buttermilk

and use according to package directions—that's what I do!)

6. Gradually beat in flour mixture on low speed until just, you know, Borg'd. Do not overbeat (because, as we learned from our TV boyfriend, Bobby Flay, we don't want our gluten activated). Of course, if Bobby Flay wants to activate *my* gluten . . . well . . . that's another story.

7. Spoon batter into 30 paper-lined muffin cups, filling each cup ⅔ full.

8. Bake 20 to 25 minutes or until cupcakes reach clean toothpick doneness.

9. Cool in pans on wire rack 5 minutes. Remove from pans to cool the rest of the way before frosting.

Vanilla Cream Cheese Frosting

1 8-ounce package cream cheese, softened
¼ cup (½ stick) butter, softened
2 tablespoons sour cream
2 teaspoons vanilla
1 16-ounce box confectioners' (10x) sugar (approx. 3½ cups)

1. Cream together the softened cream cheese and butter, the sour cream, and the vanilla until light and fluffy (approximately 3–4 minutes on medium speed).

2. Gradually blend in the powdered sugar until the frosting is smooth.

3. Frost the cupcakes, pour a tall, cold glass of milk . . . and be prepared to have a Cupcake Moment. Just sayin'.

Can't wait to get back to Sugarberry Island and the Cupcake Club? You're in luck! *Sweet Stuff* is available now! Here's a taste to whet your appetite.

Later, she would blame the whole thing on the cupcakes.

Riley glanced through the sparkling window panes of the hand-stained, sliding French panel doors to the extended, multileveled tigerwood deck—complete with stargazer pergola and red cedar soaking tub—straight into a pair of familiar, sober brown eyes. "I know that look," she called out, loud enough so he could hear her through the thermal, double-paned glass. "Don't mock. I can too do this." She turned her attention forward again and stared at the electronic panel of the Jog Master 3000. "I mean, how hard can it be?" A rhetorical question of course. Anyone, probably even the sunbathing mastiff, could figure out how to push a few buttons and—"Ooof!" The belt started moving under her feet. Really fast.

Really, really fast.

"Oh crap!" She grabbed the padded side bars, an instinctive move purely intended to keep from face planting on high-speed rubber, with little actual athleticism involved. Okay, not a drop of it, but if she could keep pace long enough to get her balance, she could relax the death grip of just one of her hands and smack—press, she meant press—the electronic panel of buttons on this very—very—expensive piece of leased equipment. At which point her ill-advised, unfortunate little adventure would end well.

Or at least without the local EMTs being called. Or a lengthy hospital stay. She was way too busy for stitches.

"Yeah," she gasped. "Piece of cake." She managed a smirk at the irony of that particular phrase, but quickly turned to full panic mode as she realized she wasn't exactly gaining ground. Rapidly losing it, in fact, along with what little breath she had. "Crap, crap, crap," she panted in rhythm with her running steps. It had only been a few minutes—three minutes and forty-four seconds, according to the oh-so-helpful digital display—and she was already perspiring. Okay, okay, sweating. She just wasn't sure if it was from the actual exertion, or the abject anxiety that she wasn't going to get out of this latest catastrophe in one piece.

Where were those big, strong Steinway delivery men when you needed them, anyway? Surely they could race right in and save her, in blazingly heroic, stud monkey fashion. She'd let them, too. Just because she prided herself on her total I-Am-Woman independence thing A.J. (After Jeremy) didn't mean she wasn't above a little Rapunzel fantasy now and again.

She'd been awaiting delivery of the elegant baby grand for over an hour. So, technically, it was all their fault. The baby grand in question was the final component, and the pièce de résistance, of this particular staging event. With every other remaining detail attended to, she'd foolishly given in to the urge to run a test check—all right, play—with some of the toys she'd had installed. Once again, she had managed to get herself into a bit of a pickle.

Enough with the food analogies, Riles. Eight minutes, twenty-three seconds. At a dead run. The only way she could have ever pulled that off was if she were being chased by zombies. With machetes. And the world as she knew it would end if she didn't get to the edge of the dark, scary forest in time.

Instead, all she had was her mastiff and his baleful stare. Not exactly adrenaline inducing.

Ten minutes, thirteen seconds. She was well past sweating and deep into red-faced overexertion. She glared back at Brutus, who kept faithful watch, but otherwise appeared unconcerned with his mistress's current distress. "No gravy on your kibble tonight," she called out. Well, in her mind, she called out. She was so winded it was all she could do to think the words. But her expression hopefully conveyed the message to her mutant, one hundred fifty pound mastiff.

He looked completely unmoved by her menacing glare. He knew she was a pushover. She'd taken him in as a rescue, hadn't she?

The sweet sound of the cascading entrance chimes echoed through the room, indicating the delivery men had finally arrived. "Thank God," she wheezed. She didn't even care what they thought of the situation, or how horrible she must look. She'd bribe them with a few of Leilani's decadently delicious Black Forest cupcakes, featuring raspberry truffle filling, and topped with fresh, plump, perfectly rosy raspberries. There were two dozen of them, carefully arranged on the three tier, crystal display dish in the beautifully appointed breakfast nook. That, and maybe throw in a few bottles of imported lager presently chilling in the newly installed, stainless-steel Viking fridge with handy bottom freezer, and surely they wouldn't say anything to Scary Lois about Riley's less-than-professional activities.

Lois Grinkmeyer-Hington-Smythe was easily the most intimidating person Riley had staged showcase houses for thus far, or worked for in any capacity, for that matter. Given her former career as head food stylist for *Foodie,* the number one selling food magazine in the country, that was saying something. Even the most intimidating chef had nothing on Scary Lois, highest performing realtor for Gold Coast properties. Riley couldn't afford to annoy the source of her best bookings.

The chimes cascaded again. *Oh, for God's sake, come in, already!* She tried to shout, but all she could muster was a strangled, guttural grunt. Why weren't they just coming in? Open house meant the house was open!

She could see the headlines now.

Riley Brown Found Dead!
SUGARBERRY ISLAND'S PREMIERE HOUSE STAGER RILEY BROWN FOUND DEAD IN HIGH-SPEED TREADMILL INCIDENT!

DATELINE: BARRIER ISLANDS, GEORGIA—Piano deliverymen and part-time models, Sven and Magnus, claimed they had no knowledge that the front door to the island's newly redesigned, prime lease property was unlocked, and that they could have entered the home and rescued the lovely and talented house stager from escalating terror and certain death.

They did, however, make sure the reporter got their names right and photographed them from their good side.

Meanwhile, poor, dead Riley Brown probably wouldn't even warrant a hunky CSI investigator, who—clearly moved by her still glowing, cherubic face and bountiful blond curls—would posthumously vow to go to the ends of the earth to find out who was responsible for this terrible, terrible tragedy.

Of course, you couldn't exactly arrest a Jog Master 3000.

Right at the point where she knew her sweaty palms couldn't grip the rubber padding one second longer, and her gaze had shifted to Brutus out on the deck, for what could likely be the very last time—someone with a very deep voice carrying the warm caress of a slight Southern accent said, "Beg your pardon. I thought this was the house being leased. My apologies, I—"

Riley jerked her head around to look at the intruder. That was no Sven. Or even a Magnus. He was way—way—better than any Nordic fantasy. Framed by what she knew was a nine-foot archway, he was a rugged six-foot-four at least, with shoulders and jaw to match. Even in his white cotton, button-down shirt, faded jeans, and dark brown sport coat, he looked like he could have delivered a baby grand with his left hand, while simultaneously saving the world with his right. Thick, dark hair framed a tanned face with crinkles at the corners of the most amazing bright blue eyes . . . Wait—she knew that face! How did she know that face?

Her jaw went slack the instant she realized who was standing, live and in the amazingly more-gorgeous-in-person flesh, right there in her Florida room. Well, not *her* Florida room, but . . . that didn't matter. Unfortunately the moment her jaw had gone slack, so had her hands.

She let out a strangled shriek as the rapidly spinning rubber track ejected her from the back end of the machine as if she were a clown out of a circus cannon. Sans the acrobatic skills. Or clean landing.

The good news? The tastefully arranged indoor/outdoor cluster of salt-air tolerant baby cabbage and saw palmettos, cockspur prickly pear and Adam's Needle yucca kept her from being ejected straight through the sparkling clean, thermal double panes she'd spent a full hour on that morning. The bad news? Well, other than the part about saw palmettos and prickly pear not exactly being soft and cushy kinds of foliage? Yeah, that would be lying in a sweaty, red-faced, scratched up heap . . . all while looking up into the breathtaking, turquoise blue eyes of the one and only Quinn Brannigan.

Dazed in more ways than one, Riley found herself thinking that if her life were ever made into a movie of the week, she sure hoped the screenwriter would give her some clever, witty line to say at that exact moment. One that would show her to be adorably spunky and utterly charming . . . despite her bedraggled, pathetic, disastrous appearance.

Alas, she was more a visual person—which was why she was a stylist and a photographer, not a writer. Quinn Brannigan, on the other hand, was a writer. Of the number one with a bullet, *New York Times* bestselling variety. So, of course, he knew exactly what to say. But then, he didn't really need to worry about that, did he?

"I am sorry." The hint of drawl in his voice made

him sound inherently sincere, while the concern etched in every crease of his perfectly gorgeous face underscored the tone. "I don't know how I made such a mistake. I never meant to alarm you like that. Let me help you up, make sure you're all right." He extended a hand.

See? Perfect white knight, perfect amount of sincere contrition, perfect . . . well, everything. She'd always thought him handsome, staring back at her from the glossy book jackets of his many best-sellers. What the photo didn't convey was the magnetism and charisma that packed an even bigger wallop in person. Not to mention his voice. Deep and smooth, with a cadence hinting at warm honey drizzled all over a hot, buttery biscuit. If they could package that voice along with his books, he'd double his already enormous sales.

"You know"—her words came out in more of a post-marathon croak—"you really should read your own books." Then she closed her eyes when his expression shifted to one of confusion. *I said that, right out loud, didn't I?* Another rhetorical question, of course. "On tape," she added lamely, as if that was going to clear matters right up. "You know, audio books." Riley let her head drop farther back into the sharp fronds. "Never mind. I'm shutting up now."

"Give me your hand." He crouched down, so that his handsome face and hot-sex-in-a-summertime-hammock voice were even closer to her. "Are you hurt? Did you hit your head on the glass?"

Given her random commentary, his concern wasn't the least bit surprising. It was an easy out that a lesser woman might have taken. No one had ever accused her, however, of being lesser. Too much, maybe. All right, definitely.

"No," she managed. "Just a few scratches. I'm fine, I just—" She broke off, and with a little sigh and a not-so-little huff of breath, tried to struggle her way out of the forest of serrated-edge foliage by herself. Then just as quickly gave up as the plants seemed to want to suck her in more deeply. She'd lost enough skin already.

She couldn't lose any more of her pride, however. That was all gone. So, she rubbed her dirty, still-sweaty palm on her pant leg, then took the offered hand, steeling her fluttering hormones against the feel of his skin on hers. Not that she was normally so over-wrought about such things, but, at the moment, her defenses were abnormally low. As in, completely missing.

And yep. *Pow.* Right in the libido. Wide palm, warm skin, strong grip. He lifted her overly tall, less-than-lithe form out of the tangle of deadly blades as if she were nothing more cumbersome than a downy little feather. She'd never once been accused of being a feather. Of any kind. She had to admit, it felt rather . . . blissful. So much so, if he'd asked her, she'd have happily agreed to strip naked, have his babies, or anything else he wanted, right there. On the evil Jog Master, even.

Because, oh yeah, that's what he's dying to do, Riles. Take you, take you hard.

Not that it mattered. Even if she had somehow managed to look adorably spunky and utterly charming despite the scratched-up flesh and blotchy red face, she'd sworn off men. Nineteen months, ten days, and dozens of cupcakes ago.

Not that all men were stupid, lying, cheating, ex-fiancé bastards like Jeremy. She knew that. And she hadn't held his actions against the rest of the male members of the human race. Most of the time. But given how thoroughly and completely duped and humiliated she'd been by the one person from that part of the population she'd most trusted with her deepest, truest self, not to mention all of her carefully guarded heart . . . yeah, she wasn't in a mad rush to find out if her judgment in that arena had improved. Hence the switch to baked goods for personal comfort.

Men were complicated. Cupcakes, on the other hand? Not so much.

Books by Bestselling Author
Fern Michaels

___The Jury	0-8217-7878-1	$6.99US/$9.99CAN
___Sweet Revenge	0-8217-7879-X	$6.99US/$9.99CAN
___Lethal Justice	0-8217-7880-3	$6.99US/$9.99CAN
___Free Fall	0-8217-7881-1	$6.99US/$9.99CAN
___Fool Me Once	0-8217-8071-9	$7.99US/$10.99CAN
___Vegas Rich	0-8217-8112-X	$7.99US/$10.99CAN
___Hide and Seek	1-4201-0184-6	$6.99US/$9.99CAN
___Hokus Pokus	1-4201-0185-4	$6.99US/$9.99CAN
___Fast Track	1-4201-0186-2	$6.99US/$9.99CAN
___Collateral Damage	1-4201-0187-0	$6.99US/$9.99CAN
___Final Justice	1-4201-0188-9	$6.99US/$9.99CAN
___Up Close and Personal	0-8217-7956-7	$7.99US/$9.99CAN
___Under the Radar	1-4201-0683-X	$6.99US/$9.99CAN
___Razor Sharp	1-4201-0684-8	$7.99US/$10.99CAN
___Yesterday	1-4201-1494-8	$5.99US/$6.99CAN
___Vanishing Act	1-4201-0685-6	$7.99US/$10.99CAN
___Sara's Song	1-4201-1493-X	$5.99US/$6.99CAN
___Deadly Deals	1-4201-0686-4	$7.99US/$10.99CAN
___Game Over	1-4201-0687-2	$7.99US/$10.99CAN
___Sins of Omission	1-4201-1153-1	$7.99US/$10.99CAN
___Sins of the Flesh	1-4201-1154-X	$7.99US/$10.99CAN
___Cross Roads	1-4201-1192-2	$7.99US/$10.99CAN

Available Wherever Books Are Sold!
Check out our website at www.kensingtonbooks.com

Romantic Suspense from
Lisa Jackson

See How She Dies	0-8217-7605-3	$6.99US/$9.99CAN
Final Scream	0-8217-7712-2	$7.99US/$10.99CAN
Wishes	0-8217-6309-1	$5.99US/$7.99CAN
Whispers	0-8217-7603-7	$6.99US/$9.99CAN
Twice Kissed	0-8217-6038-6	$5.99US/$7.99CAN
Unspoken	0-8217-6402-0	$6.50US/$8.50CAN
If She Only Knew	0-8217-6708-9	$6.50US/$8.50CAN
Hot Blooded	0-8217-6841-7	$6.99US/$9.99CAN
Cold Blooded	0-8217-6934-0	$6.99US/$9.99CAN
The Night Before	0-8217-6936-7	$6.99US/$9.99CAN
The Morning After	0-8217-7295-3	$6.99US/$9.99CAN
Deep Freeze	0-8217-7296-1	$7.99US/$10.99CAN
Fatal Burn	0-8217-7577-4	$7.99US/$10.99CAN
Shiver	0-8217-7578-2	$7.99US/$10.99CAN
Most Likely to Die	0-8217-7576-6	$7.99US/$10.99CAN
Absolute Fear	0-8217-7936-2	$7.99US/$9.49CAN
Almost Dead	0-8217-7579-0	$7.99US/$10.99CAN
Lost Souls	0-8217-7938-9	$7.99US/$10.99CAN
Left to Die	1-4201-0276-1	$7.99US/$10.99CAN
Wicked Game	1-4201-0338-5	$7.99US/$9.99CAN
Malice	0-8217-7940-0	$7.99US/$9.49CAN